Dance With Me

LUANNE RICE

Dance With Me

DOUBLEDAY LARGE PRINT
HOME LIBRARY EDITION

BANTAM BOOKS

This Large Print Edition, prepared especially for Doubleday Large Print Home Library, contains the complete, unabridged text of the original Publisher's Edition.

DANCE WITH ME
A Bantam Book / February 2004

Published by Bantam Dell
A Division of Random House, Inc.
New York, New York

This is a work of fiction. Names, characters, places, and incidents either are the product of the author's imagination or are used fictitiously. Any resemblance to actual persons, living or dead, events, or locales is entirely coincidental.

ISBN: 0-7394-4103-5

Manufactured in the United States of America

This Large Print Book carries the
Seal of Approval of N.A.V.H.

With love to my aunts,
Rose Scully and Janet Lee

Acknowledgments

Profound gratitude to Brother Luke Armour, OCSO.

Loving thanks to Rosemary, Roger, Kate, Molly, and Emily Goettsche.

Maureen, Olivier, and Amelia Onorato: love always.

I am grateful to Jan and Rick Gaunt; Marilyn, Don, John, Danny, Emily, Nick, and Maggie Walsh; Bill, Shelby, Tommy, and Laura Scully; John, Barbara, Bobby, Carolyn, Katherine, and Michael Scully; Bill, Liz, Jeff, and Sandra Keenan.

And many thanks to Barbara and Mary Lou Beaudry; Mary Beth, Brian, and Gary Holland; Howie, Mimi, Elizabeth, and Michael Logee; Lucille Kennedy; and Bobby Kennedy and Mary Keenan.

Beaucoup d'amour to Mia and the BDG!

Thank you to Dr. Rene Horvilleur.

Jim Plumeri is my favorite artist.

William Twigg Crawford: you know.

Leslie, Loulou, and the hummingbirds: where would I be without you?

Dance With Me

PART ONE

The Rule of Thirds

CHAPTER I

You weren't supposed to have favorite children. If there was one thing Margaret Porter knew, it was that nothing could divide a family faster than showing favoritism, even in the most minor circumstances. When the girls were small, she had always made sure to let them take turns riding up front next to her, pushing the shopping cart, picking out the breakfast cereal. So that neither of them could ever say to the other, "You're Mom's favorite."

Now, lying in her bed and waiting for Jane to come home, she watched Sylvie folding the laundry. Her second daughter was thirty-three, unmarried, devoted, and she creased each nightshirt sharply before tucking it into a perfect square. When one tiny mistake was made, one sleeve marginally out of line, the shirt was shaken out and the entire endeavor repeated.

Margaret would have liked some tea, but she didn't want to interrupt. By her silence, she hoped to show Sylvie how much she appreciated her. Nevertheless, she was beset by nervousness. Would Sylvie finish in time to meet her older sister's train? Margaret reclined on her pillows, finding it a bit difficult to lie still. She calmed herself by seeing the scene as a movie. In some eyes, this would be the very picture of mother-daughter contentment: dutiful child, loving parent, clear March light streaming through the big windows.

"Goddamn it," Sylvie mumbled, shaking out the blue Irish linen nightshirt for the third time. "I can't get it right."

"Perhaps you could hang that one," Margaret said. "Instead of folding it. Wouldn't a hanger make all the difference?"

Sylvie gave her a look that could only be described as murderous. It truly made Margaret flinch. Not because she imagined Sylvie genuinely wanting to send her to eternal rest, but because, in spite of her best intentions, Margaret had hurt her feelings.

"Oh, honey, never mind. I didn't mean that," Margaret said.

"It's okay, Mom."

"You're doing such a beautiful job."

"Thank you." Sylvie gave a lovely smile. Margaret lifted her head to see better. It was truly a smile to launch a thousand ships. Sylvie was a radiant beauty, but she kept her light hidden—both the girls did, as if they had become afraid of who would follow it to their doors.

Their fresh-faced beauty was surpassed only by their brainpower. Sylvie had gone to Brown University, with a semester at the Sorbonne. Jane, who had made her mother proud by entering Brown two years before her sister, elected not to graduate. Eschewing academics, she had chosen . . . a career in baking. In New York City.

While Sylvie had stayed in Twin Rivers, Rhode Island. Until recently, she had been the librarian at Twin Rivers High School, where Margaret had been principal. Education was a marvelous field for a woman: It kept the mind rigorous, it offered free summers, and it provided an excellent benefits package. If one wasn't going to marry—and sometimes even if one was—one had to

make sure not to overlook practical matters
like health insurance.

Neither of her girls had married, and although Jane hadn't finished college, Margaret was proud of her independence. In
that way, she supposed that she had been
a good role model. For although she had
been married, she had, for all practical pur-
poses, raised her daughters on her own.

The wall clock ticked loudly, and as the
hour advanced, she could hardly contain
her excitement. Usually time's passage sig-
nified things medical and mundane: time to
take her medication, time for a dressing
change. But right now, it meant time to
meet Jane's train. She gazed across the
room at Sylvie, still working on the laundry.
She cleared her throat.

"What is it, Mom?"

"Isn't it time for you to go?" she asked,
unable to hold back any longer.

"Didn't I tell you?" Sylvie asked, not looking up as she creased a pair of striped pa-
jama bottoms. "Jane's taking a cab."

Margaret's mouth must have dropped
open. She lurched forward, as if to launch
herself out of the bed. She would drive to
the station herself, if she had to.

"What will she think?" Margaret asked. "She'll be hurt, she won't feel welcomed, she'll . . ."

Sylvie gave her a wicked smile. "Just kidding," she said. "I'm going."

Margaret tried to smile back, but she couldn't, quite. She felt rocked inside, as if she'd gone off the tracks. It wasn't easy, being the mother to such sensitive girls. Not picking Jane up at the train—that could cause a resentment that would send her away for the *next* ten years.

"Is the little rock ready?" Margaret asked.

"The what?"

"The wedding cake."

"Mom," Sylvie said, finally ceasing her folding, coming to the edge of the bed. "What are you asking me?"

Margaret smiled, feeling that awful panic. She knew the word she wanted, it was right there, on the tip of her tongue.

"Mom?" Sylvie asked again.

Sixty years ago, when Margaret had been the championship speller in this same small town—as Jane was to be years later and Sylvie after her—Margaret had had moments like this. She would know the word, she could see the proper spelling in her mind's eye, but the order of the letters would be momentarily elusive. But if she just focused, held on, it always came to her.

"Is the . . ." Margaret began again. Something was supposed to be ready. She knew that, and all she had to do was remember what it was. So she could complete her question without Sylvie noticing that she was drifting. She told herself she didn't want to worry her daughter, but deep down it was something worse: she didn't want her daughter to put her into the same home where Margaret had put her mother.

"Is Jane's bedroom ready?" Sylvie asked, helping her out, and Margaret could have grabbed her hand and moaned with relief. Instead, she restrained herself, as if nothing major had just happened. Perhaps Sylvie hadn't even noticed.

"Yes. Is it? I'm sure it is. You're so good, Sylvie. You always take such good care of the house, and me, and—"

"It's ready," Sylvie said calmly, straightening a book on the shelf, lining it up perfectly with the one next to it.

"Sweetheart," Margaret said, taking her hand. She caressed the small hand, thinking of what a porcelain doll Sylvie had been.

She had made heads turn at school, at the beach. And she was still, at thirty-three, a beauty of the first order. Not that Jane wasn't also lovely, but just—not so classically pretty. Just a bit different.

"Individuals," Margaret said out loud. "You're both so special in your own ways."

"Don't get out of bed while I'm gone, okay?" Sylvie asked. "I don't want you to fall."

"Both so pretty, and smart, and talented. I can hardly believe your sister is coming home. To have both my girls under the same roof again."

"Not for very long," Sylvie said impassively, her eyes blank and inscrutable. "Don't get your hopes up, Mom. You know she's very busy."

Margaret smiled. The girls had been so close as children. She had been so happy to have Jane, and then she'd been thrilled when Sylvie had turned out to be a girl and not a boy—to give Jane a sister. There had been some difficult years . . . but now that the girls were older, and the family was going to be together again, everyone would have the chance to get to know each other—in a *new* way.

"This is just marvelous," Margaret said. "I feel like Marmee, in *Little Women*."

"Marmee had four daughters, not two."

"Two are plenty! My girls have more life in them than any four I can think of. Who needs four when I have you and Sylvie?"

"I'm Sylvie, Mom," she said dangerously.

Margaret's stomach thudded. "I know. I said Jane."

"No, you said Sylvie. But never mind. I know what you meant."

"Are you sure? Because I meant to say—"

"I know. You meant to say her name. Bye, Mom. Be home soon. Don't get out of bed."

"I won't. Oh, you take such good care of me!" Margaret said, beaming. She smiled as wide as she could, and made sure to show the light in her eyes. Sylvie had to know how much she was loved and appreciated. No daughter could ever be so generous with her affection and her time. She had sacrificed a lot, taking this leave of absence to stay home with her mother. Margaret had to make sure to show her thanks to Sylvie now—before Jane arrived.

No one could ever accuse Margaret of playing favorites. She had made other mistakes in her life, but not that one. Inside, she thought human nature to be very unfair. Because of course, no matter how hard a person strained against it, one always had a favorite. Presented with two of anything, one couldn't help judging, weighing, determining which—however slightly, however secretly—was dearer to one's heart.

Life's challenge had always been to keep it hidden.

The train was late. Of course.

And not just a little late, but a full forty minutes overdue. Apparently, there was track work in Kingston, and the train wouldn't arrive in Twin Rivers till three-thirty. Sylvie didn't really mind. It gave her a chance to be alone. She got so little time to herself these days. But she couldn't wait to see her sister, and in some ways it did seem symbolic: If anyone could cause an entire railroad to run late, it would be Jane.

She double-checked—with the trackside tote board *and* with the stationmaster. Sylvie was known for her punctuality; she was *never* late. So, with forty minutes to spare, she drove the station wagon out of the parking lot, onto Route 1.

Development had really changed the Twin Rivers landscape. Set between the two rivers, just a few miles from Narragansett Bay, the town had fallen upon hard times fifty years ago, when the old textile mills closed. But then a huge machine works had opened in Crofton, across the river, and support businesses had begun to spill over into Twin Rivers.

All those old farms, with red barns and apple trees and black-and-white cows, were giving way to more Burger Hamlets, Bedding Heavens, and Now-Marts. Views of the Williams River and the canal were increasingly being blocked by new houses and condos and assisted-living facilities.

But the existing orchards were still beautiful. Soon the trees would be in full bloom. Spring in the valley was a sight to behold, and Sylvie was glad Jane would be home to see it. Maybe it would make her want to stay.

Sylvie went past the two malls, the old one in Crofton and the brand-new, more upscale mall in Twin Rivers—Jane hadn't been to that one yet, and Sylvie wondered what she'd make of the fact that Langtry's had come to the region. She drove past Audubon Elementary and Middle School, where she and Jane had both gone.

They had gone to Twin Rivers High School, where Sylvie was still—in spite of the leave she had taken—school librarian. She knew her mother sometimes wondered whether life might have been different if they'd shipped Jane off to Sacred Heart, where the nuns could have straightened her out. But the trouble had occurred after high school.

All things happen for a reason, Sylvie had to believe—even when they made no sense. She knew there had to be order in the world, a method to the universe. She liked to think that good acts brought about happy fortune, and bad acts brought about suffering. The problem was that some people's bad acts brought about good people's suffering.

That was why Sylvie always did the right thing. It was probably what made her a good librarian: She enjoyed order. In the madness of this world, and with all the available texts and documents and information, Sylvie could be counted on to find what was needed, and to put it back when it was done. She liked to help others.

She drove past the high school now. There was the library: six big windows, second floor, just above the front entrance. She could almost smell the books, the library paste. She could nearly feel the quiet, all the energy emitting from all those students as they studied and did their homework. Sighing, she started to drive away. But first, she had to check.

John Dufour's car was there, parked in the assistant principal's spot. He had gotten a new Subaru—it had four-wheel drive. Sylvie knew that aside from Scrabble, he enjoyed skiing and kayaking. She supposed that he would be taking his new car into the wilderness. She hoped that he would be safe. There had been several sightings of black bears this year, near the reservoir north of Providence.

Checking her watch, she saw that it was time to return to the train station. It would take her exactly seven minutes: eight, if she hit the long light at the Steamboat Mall. As she got closer, her stomach flipped. She hadn't let herself think about this much. Sometimes she had thought it would never happen again—that Jane lived in New York now, that she had traded her small-town roots for the big city.

With everything Jane felt about this town, Sylvie could understand her not wanting to come back. In some ways, it was best for everyone that she stay away. But right now their mother was in trouble, and she needed both her girls to help out and decide what should happen next. Sylvie was exhausted, trying to do it alone.

In four and a half minutes, the train would arrive. Sylvie shivered, with anticipation and a weird sort of fear. She could hardly believe this was happening. She hadn't dared to imagine Jane actually coming—she hadn't slept at all last night, expecting the phone to ring, Jane ready with a last-minute excuse for canceling. Not that Sylvie wouldn't, in all sorts of ways, have understood.

But the phone hadn't rung; Jane hadn't canceled. Her big sister was coming home.

And Sylvie wondered how long it would take her to leave again.

†

The train line ran along the shore from New York to Providence, and all the way to

Boston. It passed through cities and villages, fields and marshes. When the eastbound train passed between the river and the bay range, its whistle could be heard all through the Twin Rivers valley.

Dylan Chadwick, working in his Crofton orchard, heard it. Whenever he heard a train, he imagined Amanda and Isabel aboard it. He imagined them getting away, traveling to beautiful, hidden destinations, seeing the world while waiting for him to find them. He remembered that last day, all three of them in the car, speeding through midtown Manhattan toward Penn Station.

They had almost made it. He would have flashed his badge, seen them aboard, watched the train pull out. They would have called him from the Longwood Hotel, when they'd reached Wilmington, Delaware. But they never made it out of New York. They never made it past West Thirty-third Street.

Limping through the orchard, Dylan carried a stepladder, a ten-foot pruning saw, and a light chain saw. His second life, as a farmer, didn't include badges, bad guys, or getting shot. It involved apple variety and rootstock, good planting, site selection, pruning and training, and proper fertility. It involved honeybees.

He'd used his pension, and the money he'd gotten for disability, to buy this land from his father's estate. He had expected to return to the area, the prodigal son, keeping the hundred-acre orchard in the family; he had expected his brother and sister-in-law to be ecstatic. Although their own yard—a gift from the old man during his lifetime— abutted the property, they had barely set foot in the orchard. Their emotions regarding his keeping their father's dream alive had turned out to be complicated.

They invited him to their home for holidays, to their daughter's school for spelling bees and class plays—and that, for Dylan, had turned out to be complicated, in turn. Chloe was Isabel's age. So every play, every concert, every game he saw her in, reminded him of Isabel. He and Chloe had a special bond—it came from the closeness she had had with Isabel. But sometimes seeing her was just too much, and Dylan pulled back, just a little. His brother and sister-in-law saw it all, and they cut him slack.

The train whistle sounded again.

Dylan leaned against the trunk of the old

tree to listen. He could almost see his wife and daughter in their seats, reading books, or maybe playing cards. Would Isabel still like cards? She had loved to play hearts and setback at eleven, the year she had died.

Turning back to his job, Dylan looked for the old tree's first scaffold whorl, then set his ladder, climbed it, and went to work on the light slot—a place where branches were pruned to allow light to reach all lower leaves and fruit.

Late March was prime pruning time—the dormant season, after the last severe freeze and before the start of new growth, time to remove all dead and diseased wood, all dried apples, time to clear the light slots on as many trees as he could get to. Dylan often worked from first light till last—sometimes till just after dark, when the moon was full—trying to bring the orchard back to what it once had been.

The dormant season. When things sleep. Sometimes they slept just until the spring thaw, when the sap started running again; sometimes they slept much longer.

Balancing on the ladder, trying to ignore the way his leg throbbed and was numb at the same time, Dylan reached for his pruning saw. He thought back to when he was a boy, out here with his father: It might have been this very tree.

"Follow the rule of thirds," his father would say. "Remove about a third of the excess limbs each year for three years. It took the tree more than one year to become overgrown. It will take more than one year to correct." The lessons were good, and came between swigs from a jug of hard cider.

It was from his father that Dylan had learned about pruning during the dormant season.

The train whistle had jarred Dylan awake today, this chilly March day with the first hint of springtime sunshine. The sound was distant now, the train probably pulling into the Twin Rivers station. He wondered who would be getting on, who would be getting off. There were probably families reuniting, even now.

Some families. Lucky ones. Others weren't so lucky.

The dormant season.

❧

Jane Porter rode the train, her forehead pressed to the window. The landscape was bone-familiar to her. She knew these rolling hills and open meadows the way she knew her own breath. There were too many new houses, too many trees cut down, but she looked past that to the wild acres, the apple orchards, the gnarled old trees with their branches turning pink for spring.

Leaving New York, she had felt detached about this trip. She didn't like to fly, so she took the subway from her Chelsea apartment to Penn Station, then climbed aboard Amtrak for the pleasant ride along the Connecticut shoreline to central Rhode Island. Part of her hoped that she would just go home, help Sylvie get their mother into the nursing home, and leave as soon as possible. That part of her hoped she'd just take care of business, then leave.

The other part of her, the part that had hung the "Gone Fishing" sign on her bakery door, helped her assistant find a new job, and left a message forwarding her customers to a friendly competitor, knew that wasn't possible.

Didn't the sages say, "You can't go home again"? Jane had grown up in the country, back when Twin Rivers was rural, before the malls and all the new houses, and she had watched the birds build nests. She would climb the trees, to count the eggs, and she would watch the babies hatch, then fledge, and then finally fly away.

"Why don't they come back?" she remembered crying to her mother, inconsolable because the three baby robins that had hatched in May had disappeared by June.

"It's the way of the world," her mother had said, hugging her. "Baby birds learn to fly, and they go off to dig their own earthworms and lay their own eggs. Just like human babies—you'll see."

"I'll never go away," Jane had promised that day.

"You will," her mother had said. "Just the way you're supposed to."

Jane had shaken her head, stubborn about her mother's words the way she was about everything.

"Station stop Twin Rivers," the conductor called through the train. "Twin Rivers, forward end of the car. Watch your step getting off the train, and thank you for riding Amtrak."

Jane stood by her seat, pulling her bag down from the overhead rack. Then, carefully, she reached for the big cake box. Stiff from the ride, she slung her knapsack over one shoulder and began to make her way toward the front of the car. When the conductor offered to help her, she shook her head. She was too independent for that; let him help someone who needed it.

At the train door, she shielded her eyes, looking up and down the platform. A few people were here to meet the train; she saw Sylvie right away. Emotion seized her heart. Her little sister.

Jane hadn't seen Sylvie in two years, and she looked exactly the same: blond, radiant, as gorgeous as a movie star. But of course Sylvie didn't know it, and still dressed like a Depression-era waif in her long floral dress and blue wool coat.

Coming forward, Sylvie waited at the bottom of the train stairs. Jane dropped her knapsack and gently lowered the cake box, then threw both arms around her sister. Sylvie's hair smelled like orange blossoms. She was blushing, and her cheeks were wet. So were Jane's. They both surreptitiously wiped their tears on each other's shoulders, then raised their faces, dry-eyed.

"Your train was late," Sylvie said, making

it sound more like conversation than accusation.

"I know. Sorry."

"Did you have a good trip?"

"Yes, thanks."

"What's this outfit?" Sylvie asked, smiling slightly, plucking Jane's black leather sleeve.

"Um, my jacket?"

"You want to look like one of the kids? Or are you trying to be tough?" Sylvie asked, smiling to take the sting out of her words. It was a Porter family tradition.

Jane smiled back, holding off on her response: "You want to look like Rebecca of Sunnybrook Farm till you're forty?" Instead she picked up her bag and the cake box; Sylvie didn't make a move to take either of them from her. They headed toward the parking lot, and Jane asked, "How's Mom?"

Sylvie's smile evaporated. "Not very good," she said. "She had that fall, and she really gashed her leg. With her diabetes, there's always an increased risk of infection. Plus, the doctor who stitched her up commented about all her bruises."

"Maybe he'll report you to the state."

"That's not funny, Jane!"

"I know, I'm sorry," Jane said quickly, but Sylvie's cheeks and lips were tight with hurt. "I know you take great care of her."

"I gave up my career to do it."

Jane nodded. *No comment,* she thought. Instead, she said, "I was just kidding. It was stupid. Let's not fight."

"We're not even in the car yet," Sylvie said. "It starts the minute you get home."

"I know," Jane said, feeling tension pop between her shoulder blades. "I'm really sorry."

Sylvie nodded. She opened the hatchback, and Jane threw her bag inside but held on to the cake box. They both reached up to close the door, and Jane saw their hands together, side by side: They were the exact same size and shape. Sisters' hands. She wanted to hug Sylvie again, and never let her go. Living in the city, she missed having relatives nearby. She missed having the blood connection of family. More than anything, she missed her sister.

"Be careful with Mom," Sylvie said warningly. "Don't go seeking out the past or anything, okay? She can't take much upset."

"I won't upset her," Jane said.

"Good. Because she can't take it."

"Fine."

"I suppose there's a cake in that box," Sylvie said, casting a glance down at Jane's lap.

"Yes."

"Did you *forget* she's diabetic?"

Jane didn't reply. Her earliest memories included seeing her mother inject herself with insulin. She also remembered her mother having the occasional cookie, piece of pie, slice of cake. Not often, but sometimes. "I wanted to bring her something. It's the only thing I knew to make . . ."

"She's very forgetful—she'd never take her insulin if I didn't give it to her. Her feet are in bad shape. And she wobbles. That's how she got the bruises. She's going downhill, Jane . . ." Sylvie's voice caught.

"We'll figure it out, Syl," Jane said. She looked her sister deep in the eyes. The connection was ancient and didn't really need words. In fact, words got in the way. So soundlessly, without any more speaking, they got into the car. Sylvie adjusted the radio to something classical. Jane tuned it out, turning her face to the window and holding the white cake box on her lap.

She scanned the windows of houses and

cars, the faces of people on the street. She couldn't help herself. Ten minutes in Twin Rivers, and already she was doing something Sylvie wouldn't approve of. Jane wasn't sure exactly where to look, but she was seeking out the past.

If Sylvie would let her borrow the car, she'd drive to Crofton tomorrow.

CHAPTER 2

Margaret sat up in bed, the white wicker tray over her legs, staring down at the most exquisite cake she had ever seen.

"It's too busy to eat," she said, hands held together prayerfully.

"Pretty," Sylvie corrected.

"Yes," Margaret said, staring down at it. The cake looked like a bird's nest. Brown twigs and grasses woven together, spun-sugar sticks protruding from the sides and top—and three blue eggs resting inside. "A robin's nest." She looked up at Jane. "And you carried it all the way from New York?"

Jane nodded. She looked thin. Her skin was pale, almost translucent. Her hair was straight, cut just above her shoulders. It was almost black, the color of the darkest twigs in the bird's nest. Beside her, Sylvie's blond hair gleamed.

"I can't believe you baked it," Margaret said. She poked her finger into the side, truly expecting to find scratchy dry grass, but instead finding soft frosting and cake. She was about to lick it off, when Sylvie attacked her with a tissue.

"Sylvie!"

"Your sugar is high today, Mom," Sylvie said, wiping her finger clean. "Just enjoy the sight of it, okay?"

"Who wants to *look* at a cake?" Margaret asked, hurt and embarrassed, turning her eyes to Jane. "Why did you bother making me a cake at all, if you knew I couldn't eat it?"

"I thought one slice would be okay," Jane said.

A family powwow ensued without words. Glances between the girls, a pleading smile on Margaret's lips, a shrug of Sylvie's shoulders.

"One slice," Sylvie said. "Thin."

Jane did the honors. Using the sterling silver cake server, a filigreed reminder of Margaret's wedding to their father, she expertly sliced off a pamphlet-sized piece onto a plate. Then she cut bigger pieces for herself and her sister, making sure to give Sylvie one of the blue eggs. "Two-day-old cake is good for one thing," Jane said, grinning. "It's much easier to slice."

"Mmm," Margaret said, letting the icing melt on her tongue. "This is delicious."

"It is," Sylvie agreed.

Jane smiled, pleased. The three of them ate in silence. Margaret hadn't had a treat like this in so long.

"I have a question," Margaret began. "Why are there three eggs?"

"I don't know," Jane said. "I guess I was thinking about migrating . . . about flying far away, and then coming home. Like birds."

"Two would make more sense. One for you, one for Sylvie. My baby chicks."

"Chicks," Sylvie said, giving her sister a smile. "Mom's calling us chicks. Remember when she used to call us 'chiclets'?"

"But why *three* eggs?" Margaret asked, something pressing on her mind, teasing a question she wasn't sure why she was asking. "When I have just two daughters."

"One for Jane, one for me, and one for you," Sylvie tried.

"For composition, I guess," Jane said.

"Yes," Sylvie agreed. "It's very artistic."

"Or one for the lost baby," Margaret said.

Jane didn't say anything. She neither raised her eyes nor stopped eating her cake. Margaret watched her thoughtfully collect yellow crumbs with the edge of her fork, lift them to her mouth.

"See what's happened?" Sylvie asked accusingly. "The sugar's too much for her." She took Margaret's clean plate out of her hand and set it down on the bureau with a noisy clatter. Then she went directly to the chest of drawers converted into sickroom use, rummaged inside for the test kit.

"I do feel a bit woozy," Margaret said, glad to be resting on a pile of pillows. They were down-filled, soft as clouds, covered with white eyelet pillowcases. Sylvie knew that Margaret adored white bedding, and she indulged her mother's preference. Margaret sighed, feeling the room spin. She knew it had less to do with the sugar than with the tension she felt between her girls.

"Mom," Jane said, putting down her plate and holding Margaret's hand.

"Excuse me," Sylvie said, bumping her aside to poke Margaret with the Insta-Test lancet.

Margaret closed her eyes. Why had she even asked that question? Where had it come from, anyway? She had two daughters—all she had ever wanted. She had a picture of herself at ten, with Lolly, her beloved baby doll. Her parents had taken her on a picnic to Watch Hill. They had ridden the carousel, played in the waves, had lemon ice. And then a thunderstorm had arisen, and her parents had hustled her into the car so fast, she'd left Lolly lying there, on a bench in the rain.

"I left her behind," Margaret said, trembling.

"Who, Mom?" Jane asked, still holding her hand.

"Lolly. My doll. Can you find her for me?"

"Your lost baby?" Jane asked sadly.

"Stop that," Sylvie said.

"Sure," Jane said. "I'll find her for you."

"She should have a piece of the cake," Margaret said, smiling.

"She certainly should," Jane said.

"Look," Sylvie said, proffering the instant digital test. "Two forty-one. Too high. I'm glad we all had a piece of cake, but now I think it's time to go back on the diet, right?"

"Definitely," Jane said. She squeezed Margaret's hand, then stood up, stretching. Her shirt untucked from her black jeans, showing a strip of her stomach. Margaret reached out to give it a tickle, and Jane smiled.

"I used to do that when you were a baby," Margaret said.

Jane nodded. Their eyes locked, and Margaret had the wild sensation of spinning back through time, to when Jane was first born . . . an infant, a baby doll come to life. Margaret had held her in her arms, every chance she got. She had never wanted to put her down. Looking into Jane's deep blue eyes, Margaret swore she saw all the wisdom of all the women of the ages. No baby had ever had such a clear, cool gaze. And Jane had it now, still. . . .

"You're an old soul," Margaret said.

"I am?"

Margaret nodded. Staring into her elder daughter's eyes, she felt the world turning. Sylvie didn't say anything, but Margaret could feel her watching. Her girls were lovely—smart and successful. But they could be so insecure.

Margaret took the blame. She knew there were ways in which she had shortchanged her children. First of all, by her choice in a husband. Their father had been . . . an inadequate man. A traveling salesman, a handsome charmer, he had come and gone at will. Mostly gone. Early on, Margaret had realized she would have to work to support the family. A Salve Regina graduate, she had gone back to the Sisters and asked for guidance. They had suggested she become a teacher, get her master's degree while working part time, perhaps at a local school.

Margaret had done just that. She had enrolled in the University of Rhode Island's graduate school while working at Audubon Elementary as a substitute teacher. Her mother, thank God, had lived close by, and the girls would spend afternoons at their grandmother's house. What Margaret would have done without her mother, she had no idea. . . .

The girls had had a fine life; that was certain. Their father left for good when Jane was eleven and Sylvie was nine. Margaret knew the scars his leaving had caused—but surely they were no worse than those inflicted by the years of his staying. His drinking, womanizing, disappearing; all the fights between him and Margaret; all the times they had had to comfort their mother while she cried.

Margaret consoled herself by knowing her daughters had received boundless love from Margaret and her mother . . . and they had excelled in school and at everything they did. Jane's sudden wildness had surprised them all.

Now, gazing into Jane's blue eyes, Margaret wondered about the things they had seen. Manhattan seemed a million miles away, such a wild choice for the little girl who had loved birds and nature so. . . .

"Where have you been, my love?" Margaret heard herself asking.

"Living my life," Jane said softly.

Sylvie exhaled.

"But you're home now," Margaret said.

"Yes, I am," Jane said.

That seemed to be all there was to say. No one spoke again. Margaret felt content. She closed her eyes, still tasting the sugar in the corners of her mouth, thinking of

Lolly. She had loved that doll. No one would ever know how much she'd missed her. Oh, how she had cried that first night. . . .

✳

"Can I borrow the car?" Jane asked.

Sylvie stood at the sink, washing the cake plates. She had filled the sink with sudsy water, and she was up to her elbows in it.

"I'm not sure you're on the insurance," Sylvie said.

"The insurance?"

"It's in Mom's name."

"But you get to drive it?"

"Yes, because I live in the same house."

"Well," Jane said, smiling, "I still have a room here. For all the insurance company knows, I could be moving back home. I guess, if we had to, we could say that I live here, too. What happened to your car?"

"I sold it," Sylvie said, handing Jane a plate to dry. "When I went on leave from the library, I knew I had to tighten my belt."

"You loved that car," Jane said. For a Christmas card three years ago, her sister had sent out pictures of herself at the wheel of an old green MGB with the top down, a red Santa's hat on her head.

Sylvie shrugged. "Mom's car is fine. It gets us around. The convertible wasn't practical anyway."

Jane dried the last dish. She had been surprised to know that Sylvie had bought such an amazing vehicle: British, extravagant, unexpected, and impractical. Jane had been so happy to see Sylvie treating herself to such a romantic car, and right now she felt pierced to learn that she had sold it.

"So, do you mind if I borrow the station wagon?" Jane asked again.

Sylvie stacked the plates in the cupboard. Her lips were tight, as if she was trying to think of another reason why Jane shouldn't drive the car. Jane leaned on the counter, waiting.

"No. It's your first night home . . . I thought you might be tired. But go ahead."

Jane palmed the keys and headed for the door. She grabbed her leather jacket from the oak coat tree, slipped it on. Her chest was tight, and she knew Sylvie was

waiting to be asked if she wanted to come
along.

"Where are you going, anyway?" Sylvie
asked. "It's getting dark. . . ."

"Just for a ride. Just to look around," Jane
said, hand on the brass doorknob. If she
turned around, met Sylvie's eyes, she
would have to invite her to come. Her heart
began to pound. She could feel Sylvie wanting to ask something more, or to warn. But
she didn't glance back, and before Sylvie
could say another word, Jane slipped out
the door.

The full moon was rising, a silver disk shining through the tree branches. Dylan was
working late, wanting to get as much done
as he could before the sap started flowing
again. He had spent the day pruning out
dead and diseased limbs, removing
branches crowding out others, cutting
branches growing straight up, others pointing straight down.

Even in the dark, he could look up and
see by the light of the moon that the tree
he'd just finished working on was well

shaped, with no dense clusters of branches anywhere in the canopy.

Restoring an apple orchard was a lot like restoring order to the universe. In that way, it reminded him of the idealism of law enforcement. Shape the wild and overgrown and tangled and dangerous into something resembling goodness. Dylan could actually remember when he had had those ideals. Kind of a cosmic mingling of hope and stupidity.

Folding up his ladder, slinging his saws over his shoulder, he began to walk home. The ground was still hard, and stepping on ruts sent a sharp pain all the way up the back of his bad leg. Sometimes he could actually feel the bullet—fragments of metal still lodged in the femur. He told himself to knock off the complaining and think of Isabel. Didn't that put everything in perspective? His mind was racing, overactive after another day of solitude on the ladder. If he had someone to talk to, would he still have to have these lousy talks with himself?

He thought about stopping by his brother's house. They lived on the same road, just about half a mile apart. They were a close family, and Dylan had always taken his place as older brother seriously. It was past their dinnertime; Eli would probably be finishing up the dishes, Sharon would be helping Chloe with her homework.

And that was the part that made him flinch, made him realize he wasn't in the mood, tonight, for a visit. Seeing Chloe, all excited about her history test or mastery scores or whatever was going on in her life, hearing her practice her violin with that exuberant, breathless, "Uncle Dylan! Listen to this! Mozart!" was sometimes more than Dylan could handle. Tonight, with spring and Isabel in the air, was one of those times.

At the sound of footsteps, Dylan slowed down. He peered around, wondering who was in his orchard. Every fall kids sneaked in to steal apples; in the summer, they sometimes camped out, used it as a sort of Lovers' Lane; in April, when the snow was gone for good, the dirt bikers would roar through, tearing the place up. But it was only March. Still too cold.

The moon rose higher, clearing the crowns of the trees, and Dylan spotted the buck. White-tailed deer and black bears roamed his acres. They ate fruit right off the trees in warm weather, dug through the snow for frozen windfalls all winter. Now, watching the big buck, Dylan held his breath.

Usually they traveled in groups, but the buck was alone. Where was his family? Dylan counted the points on his antlers: ten. He was big and mature. He stood proudly, silhouetted by the moon, staring directly into Dylan's eyes. Two males meeting face to face. Whose territory was it, anyway?

The brush rustled again, and a doe and two young deer emerged. The buck circled protectively back, herding them into cover. Dylan's leg seared, and his shoulder ached from the weight of the saws. He stared after the deer family for a long time, till his vision blurred and he wondered whether he had seen it at all, or whether the moonlight had just played tricks with his eyes.

The moon was hard and white now, sharper as it rose in the clear black sky. His mother had always called the March moon "the Full Crow Moon." She loved it, because the cawing of crows signaled winter's end, and because she had a fondness for crows. A high school biology teacher, she had been a rarity, blending a respect for science with a love of legend.

"Crow language is complex," she taught. "Each caw has a separate meaning, and signifies the birds' deep intelligence. Crows are loyal, and devoted to their families. They honor their ancestors, move freely in the world, work best in a tribe—or council. They are carriers of souls from darkness into light."

Standing still, gazing at the hard Crow Moon, Dylan narrowed his eyes and listened. He heard new tree frogs screeching all around him; in the distance, he heard crows calling. He wanted it to be true, to think that souls were carried . . .

Suddenly he heard a car. His land bordered a country road, with not much going on nearby. Maybe it was Chloe being driven home by her friend Mona's mother or something. Walking toward the clearing, he saw headlights.

The car was moving slowly. He stared through the darkness, catching a glimpse of blue, the shape of a small station wagon. The windows were open; he could hear music playing. Emmylou Harris. He glimpsed a woman at the wheel, dark hair covering her profile, one arm slung out the window, black-leathered elbow sleek in the moonlight.

For one split second, her hair blew back and she seemed to turn her head and see him. He froze, just like the buck. Her eyes locked with his, and then she hit the gas and drove faster. Although he had never seen her before, he thought she looked familiar.

Continuing home through the orchard, he kept picturing her elbow sticking out the window. It was cool and shiny, blue-black, sharp and ready to spring into flight: just like a crow's wing.

✦

Jane found the house.

She hadn't driven past in years, so she'd printed out directions from MapQuest, off the Internet. All she had had to do was type in the last name and the town and state, "Chadwick, Crofton, Rhode Island," and her computer spit out a perfect map, along with driving directions. By hitting another button, she was able to call up an aerial view.

Through the years, on many visits home to Rhode Island, she had looked the name up in the phone book. She had bought a map of the Twin Rivers Valley, located the street on the edge of much green area—apple orchards and a state forest. And she had driven by. That was just before she'd moved to New York. She'd been away for so long— fourteen years—that she had almost forgotten her way to this spot.

MapQuest had been the true pot of gold: an actual aerial photo of the house, so snug at the end of its driveway, located on the very edge of a huge orchard, with streams and ponds and about a million overgrown apple trees. The browser had gotten confused by the name "Chadwick"; there seemed to be several in Crofton, including the science teacher, Mrs. Virginia Chadwick. Also, as well as Eli and Sharon, someone named Dylan, who lived on the same street.

But it was Eli and Sharon's house that Jane sought tonight, as she drove along the deserted road. Her hands trembled on the wheel. The scent of apples filled the air— blossoms about to pop on the branches, silver-pink in the cool moonlight, winter's fallen apples fermenting on the ground. The scent was spicy, hot and alcoholic as hard cider. She felt intoxicated by the sense of returning to a place she never should have been in the first place.

She glanced into the orchard at all those gnarled and beautiful old apple trees, their roots sinking deep into the earth, as if she hoped and prayed that all those trees could ground her.

A man stood looking out at her.

Her heart almost stopped at the sight of him. He was tall, bearded, very slim with broad shoulders; he was weighted down with a ladder and a saw, both glinting in the moonlight. His eyes looked out, unblinking, as if he were the guardian of the orchard.

Jane's mouth was dry, and she felt as if she'd just been caught trespassing. The man's face had been impassive, but she imagined his heart full of the same disapproval she knew Sylvie or her mother would feel.

Pressing on the gas, she sped away, passing a ramshackle, apparently abandoned farm stand. By the time she reached the address, the house she'd visited so often in her mind, viewed so often on MapQuest, her heart was beating so fast, she had to pull over. Her car running, she parked in front of 114 Barn Swallow Way, and stared.

The house was still small and white. It still had dark green shutters. Something new: a briar wreath hanging on the front door. The mailbox was now painted blue, with "The Chadwick Family" in pretty white script. The lights were on downstairs. One window up-stairs was illuminated; it had pink curtains. Jane gazed for a long time; the house looked as if nice people lived there. Her breathing went almost back to normal.

Or as normal as Jane's breath could be; she always felt a hitch, somewhere between her mouth and her heart, as if something had cracked inside and couldn't be fixed. She thought of a clock that had fallen off the shelf, with hands that seemed to move and keep time, but with a rattle—as if an unnec-essary part had broken off and gotten trapped inside.

She felt that little click right now, more pronounced than ever. It hurt to breathe in, and it hurt to breathe out. She knew that something inside her had cracked, a long, long time ago. Humpty Dumpty had always been her least favorite nursery rhyme; she hadn't wanted to believe that things couldn't be put back together.

Things looked very together here.

Jane's presence wouldn't help anyone. She was being selfish—she could hear her mother's voice, asking: "Do you want to be selfish? Do you want to ruin everyone's life?"

No. The answer was no, she didn't. She never had. That's why she had become a baker, to make people's lives sweet and happy. To bake wedding cakes and Thanksgiving pies and cupcakes for children's first days of school and coffee cakes for get-togethers, but especially birthday cakes. Gorgeous, wonderful, dreamy birthday cakes of Amazon rain forests and fairy-tale castles and ocean liners and three eggs in a bird's nest. . . .

Those were Jane's specialty.

Pulling into the driveway, she turned around. She paused for a moment, looking up at the pink curtains. She wondered what kind of birthday cakes they had for Chloe—that was her name.

She took a deep breath, thinking of that man in the apple orchard. She wondered whether he was Eli or Dylan. Either way, she felt comforted by seeing him. She had the feeling he was watching out. . . .

People needed to be watched out for.

Driving slowly down the street, she found herself scanning the moonlit clearing where she had seen him. She would have given him a smile. But he wasn't there. So she drove a little faster, wanting to get to the Now-Mart before it closed.

She wanted to buy a doll for her mother. To take the place of the one she had lost. . . .

CHAPTER 3

Every spring, the wild cats had kittens. It was, in Chloe Chadwick's opinion, one of the best things about living on the edge of an orchard. The cats came out at night to dance in the moonlight; her parents, when she told them, would correct her and say that the cats were just hunting, stalking prey. But Chloe knew her parents were wrong. She would watch the cats out her window and know she was seeing a mad, magical, romantic feline ball.

Over the years, Chloe had coexisted with many of the cats. She couldn't call them her pets—if anything, it was the other way around. The cats had taught her how to climb trees, watch the birds, pounce when hungry, and sit quietly, no matter what was going on around her and what she might be feeling inside.

Just home from school, she filled a large baking pan with dry cat food. The sound attracted many cats, and they darted out from the tall grass, holly bushes, under the car, and behind the barn to swarm around her ankles.

"Hello, everyone," she said, setting the pan down on the ground. The cats meowed loudly, bumping each other out of the way. She watched them intently, hoping they would go for it. Some gobbled hungrily, others slunk away.

"You can't expect cats to quit eating meat just because you have," her mother said, planting pansies in the garden.

"Why can't I?"

"Chloe, cats are carnivores. Lions? Tigers?"

Chloe had recently switched their food, from the regular grocery store variety to something special she'd started buying at the health food co-op. It was expensive, but worth it: vegetarian cat food.

"I have to stand on my principles," she said stubbornly.

"In the meantime, do you want the cats to starve?"

"They won't starve. They're wild orchard cats, Mom. When they're done dancing, they'll hunt."

"And you don't have a problem with them catching mice?" Her mother asked, ignoring the dance comment.

"Hunting is *their* nature, not mine," Chloe said. "What I have a problem with is serving them cat food made from bone meal and pork products. Do you know that pigs are just about as intelligent as dolphins?"

"I know, you've told us," her mother said, patting down the earth.

Chloe stared at her mother. Kneeling by the front walk, she wore a wide-brimmed straw hat with a pretty blue ribbon. She wore green garden clogs and flowered deerskin gloves. She carried her tools in a curved basket—she called it a "panier"—with a handle that looped graciously over her arm. The pansy plants were perfectly evenly spaced, as if she used an imaginary gardening ruler. She liked every-thing to look nice and orderly.

"Pigs spend their whole lives in stalls," Chloe said dangerously, "so cramped, that if their hind legs itch, they can't even turn around to scratch."

"Enough, Chloe."

"What are we having for dinner tonight?"

No answer. Just more digging—making the garden beautiful, which it was. Daffodils, jonquils, scillas blooming everywhere. In a week or so, the apple blossoms and lilacs would burst out.

"Mom?"

"Chicken breasts," her mother said.

"Do you know that most chickens live their entire life—"

"Enough!" her mother said. "You can have a salad and a baked potato. Okay?"

"I have to go to work," Chloe said. "I'll hit the salad bar there."

"I thought you had Tuesdays off."

Were they speaking the same language? Did they sleep under the same roof? Was her mother okay? Chloe had switched days with Marty Ford on Saturday, and she clearly remembered telling her mother. She had heard about older people losing it—getting forgetful, not being able to keep track of things, like their schedules and their shoes. Her mother was fifty-two, older than some of her friends' moms, but still too young for that—right?

"Usually I have today off, but Marty asked me to trade with her," Chloe said slowly. She stared at her mother, looking for signs of a problem. She had always worried that her mother or father would get sick—just stop breathing and disappear. When she was very little, she used to stand by the edge of her parents' bed, watching their chests rise and fall, making sure they were still breathing. Their fights were always behind closed doors, but very intense, and she worried that one of them would drop dead while whispering in that angry, urgent way.

"That's right," her mother said suddenly, glancing up. "You told me. I forgot. Hang on, and I'll give you a ride."

"I'll ride my bike," Chloe offered.

"No, honey," her mother said. "It'll be dark before you come home again, and you know I don't want you riding then."

"Soon I'll have my license."

"Well, we're not going to rush that."

"Yes, we are . . ."

"We'll see. You're barely fifteen—first you'll need a learner's permit." She smiled, reaching up as Chloe gave her a hand, pulled her up from the garden.

"Looks nice," Chloe said, nodding down at the tiny purple pansy plants.

"Thank you," her mother said, brushing the dirt off her gloves.

"Why do you plant them?" Chloe asked. "When we have all the wildflowers? And when all the apple trees are about to bloom? The wild things are so pretty, you don't have to do anything at all. . . ."

"Uncultivated isn't necessarily pretty. The orchard isn't what it used to be," her mother said, frowning over at the tangled trees. "And it doesn't belong to us, anyway. Your uncle's doing his best to bring it back, but that's a losing battle. It's been neglected for too long."

Chloe peered at the trees. She had heard her parents talking, saying that Uncle Dylan refused to let go of the family orchard, of something that should just be allowed to die. They had wanted it bulldozed for expensive new houses. They would have made more money that way.

Chloe's chest hurt, thinking of it; she knew that Uncle Dylan nurturing the orchard back to life had something to do with losing

Aunt Amanda and Isabel. Her heart expanded, taking in the idea of all the gnarled old apple trees, the birds that lived in them, the wild cats that hunted down the rows, the deaths of her aunt and cousin.

Isabel; the closest Chloe had ever come to having a sister. Isabel had lived in New York City, but she had come to Rhode Island on holidays, to see their grandmother, and for a week every summer. Their grandfather had still been alive then; he had owned the orchard, and he had had a lot of people working for him—picking apples, making cider, selling everything at the stand.

When Isabel died, Chloe stopped talking for a month. She felt as if her heart had been pulled out of her; that it was impossible to keep living with such a loss. She would lie on her side, feeling as if her body had been torn in two, as if she was a paper doll. Everyone whispered, and said she was traumatized. She didn't remember much about that time, except for Uncle Dylan sitting on the edge of her bed, holding her hand.

"Your parents love you," he said. "Just like I love Isabel."

Chloe was eleven. She had become like a

baby herself, and she'd gone back to understanding everything in a much different,
more primitive way. Words were beside the
point. She had looked up into his eyes—so
like Isabel's—and reached up to touch his
cheek. His beard felt wiry to her fingertips.

"She's gone," Chloe said, her voice
shaky with the first words she'd said in
weeks.

Uncle Dylan shook his head. "Never. When
you love someone, they're never gone."

"That's not true," Chloe said, starting to
cry, as if she knew much more about loss and
missing someone than he did, having no idea
of how that could be possible. "She is gone,"
she sobbed. "Gone . . ." The word was a
black hole, and it took her back to a wordless
time, and the black hole that had swallowed
her birth mother. "Didn't she love me
enough? Why did she leave?" Oh, Chloe was
getting all her losses mixed up . . .

Uncle Dylan had just held her. Her parents had hovered behind him, and after a
minute, her father had tapped his shoulder,
and her mother had taken Chloe into her
arms. She remembered urgent whispers,
and a feeling of embarrassment, as if she

had somehow hurt her mother's feelings. Of course she sensed that Chloe was connecting to the other disappearing person in her life, Chloe's real mother, the one who had given her away.

Uncle Dylan had never shaved his beard after that. He trimmed it; it was handsome, salt-and-pepper. But he always kept his beard, and Chloe knew why: because Isabel had touched it. Chloe just knew; Uncle Dylan never had to tell her. Isabel had kissed his scratchy face, and Uncle Dylan would never shave again.

That was real love.

Running inside to change into her work smock, Chloe's heart was beating too hard. She washed her face, calming herself as she splashed the clear spring water onto her skin and rubbed the white soap into creamy foam. She looked into her own eyes, staring out from the mirror. She thought if she looked long enough, she could see her real mother's face and ask her *why, how* . . .

She rinsed her face and walked out to the car. It was a new minivan, perfectly clean. Her father washed it every Saturday; her mother used the portable vacuum nearly every other day, to keep it pristine. Her parents' secret behind-closed-door fights were terrible, but their possessions were impeccable. It all seemed related to the fact that her mother preferred straight rows of pansies to the insane snaggle of an overgrown orchard. While Chloe loved the wildness, dreamed of getting lost in it. What was she doing in this family?

Maybe she really was a cat. When she was little, she used to have dreams of being in a fancy blue pram. Of her parents with their hands on the silver handle, pushing her along, stopping to show her off to the neighbors. And of the neighbors' gasps of shock when they saw that Chloe wasn't a little girl, wasn't their daughter at all, but a tiny wild tiger baby, with black and orange stripes and bright green eyes—just like the plush toy she had in her crib.

Now, being driven to her after-school job at the big grocery store in town, she gazed pensively out the window. Her mother tuned the radio to the pretty music station, where every song sounded like an ad for feminine products. Chloe groaned. Her mother smilingly ignored her.

Chloe dug into her pockets. Earlier she had

torn up a sheet of notebook paper into small business-card-sized pieces. While her mother drove, Chloe began to write. One line per piece. Her mother didn't even glance over.

She probably thought Chloe was doing homework.

＊

Across the river, one town away, Jane was baking. She assembled the bowls, pan, butter, flour, and eggs. She had brought her mother downstairs to be with her, in spite of Sylvie's prohibitions.

"You okay, Mom?" Jane asked, measuring flour.

"Oh, I'm fine, honey," Margaret said, looking around. She sat at the table, holding her new doll in the crook of her arm. "It is so good to be sitting in my own kitchen."

"How's your leg?"

Margaret shrugged, smiling bravely. "It's fine. I hope you can get me back upstairs before your sister gets home. She won't let me out of bed."

Jane laughed. "You make it sound as if she's holding you prisoner."

"She is!" Margaret said. "She is so wonderful, and I love her, but my *God*. You'd think I was her six-year-old child instead of her mother. I was the school principal! I'm used to giving the orders."

"I remember you did that very well," Jane said.

Her mother laughed. Jane hadn't meant anything by the comment, and she was glad her mother hadn't taken it that way. But for Jane it hung there, shimmering for a moment between them, until it disappeared like a leaf in an eddy.

"Yes, I was considered to be a strict principal," Margaret said. "I saw so much change at the school. Back when you and Sylvie were little, our biggest discipline problems were kids passing notes in class, talking in the library, fighting in the cafeteria. By the time I left, they had installed metal detectors, to keep out guns and knives. So much victory."

"Violence," Jane corrected gently.

"Now tell me what you're baking," her mother said, seeming not to hear.

"Biscuits," Jane said. "Sugar-free, so you can have them."

"A treat! How wonderful!" her mother

said, squeezing her doll. "Sylvie is so strict with me—sometimes I've thought she's getting me back for all the times I said no to candy bars or cupcakes . . ."

"You know she's not," Jane said.

"I know. She's taking good care of me." Margaret sighed. "And I know that's why you've come home. What did she tell you?"

"That you'd had a fall; and that you're in a lot of pain."

"I cut my leg when I fell, but it's my feet that really hurt," Margaret said, grimacing. "It's the diabetes. They want to try putting magnets in my shoes—can you imagine?"

"Really?"

"It's a type of pain control. Sanctioned by the medical community and, mirabile dictu, the insurance companies! They look like insoles, and you slip them into your shoes, and they magnetically draw the pain from the body."

"How . . . alchemistic!" Jane said, grinning. "It's as if, deep within the high-tech testing lab, there's a secret room with a sorcerer . . ."

"Wearing a tall, pointy blue hat with silver stars," her mother said. "And jars of stardust and sea salt and ancient recipe tomes . . ."

"Sounds like a cooking show," Sylvie said, coming in with an armload of groceries. "What are you talking about?"

"Mom's magnets," Jane said, getting up to help her. "Do they actually work?"

"Well . . ." Sylvie began, unpacking the bags.

"They do!" Margaret said. "Or they will . . . I have to trust that they will. I can't bear the idea of going back to that pain medication. It's so awful—it makes my mind so foggy and makes me forget things. Even after I've stopped taking it, I still get so . . . inquisitive."

"So what, Mom?"

"So unintelligible," she said. She spoke with authority, like the school principal she was, but her eyes betrayed alarm, as if she knew she was saying the wrong thing and hoped her daughters wouldn't notice.

"So forgetful?" Jane supplied.

"Exactly," Margaret said. She kissed her doll, whom she had named Lolly after the one she'd lost. "We all knew what I was talking about."

Seeing her mother hold the baby doll made Jane's stomach drop. What would all those decades of students and parents

think, to see Margaret Porter—their digni-
fied, intellectually demanding school principal mother—playing with a doll? Although
Jane had bought it for her, she somehow
hadn't expected this. . . . Her mother whispered to the doll, as if she were telling her a
secret. Jane shivered. She remembered
whispering to a baby once. She closed her
eyes, knowing her mother had held and
raised two babies, and she had made sure
Jane never had that chance.

"Good Lord," Sylvie exclaimed, unpacking the groceries. She bent to examine the
package of hamburger she held in her hand.

"What's wrong?" Margaret asked.

"Look at this—" Sylvie said, peeling a
piece of white paper from the meat's plastic
wrapping.

"What does it say?" Jane asked.

" 'Cows are beautiful. Do you really want
to eat one?' "

"How odd," Margaret said.

"This is not good," Sylvie said. "I went all
the way to SaveRite in Crofton, just to get
fresh berries, which they didn't even have,
and I wind up buying meat that's been tam-
pered with!"

"Maniacs are everywhere," Margaret said gravely.

"Well, as soon as I check your sugar, I'm going to call the store manager. We are not eating this meat."

Jane watched Sylvie walk over to the counter, to get the test kit. Her posture expressed the dual burdens of being her mother's primary caregiver and encountering insurgent note-leavers. *She really belongs in bed,* she mouthed to Jane; Jane shrugged and mouthed *Sorry* . . . Preparing to prick her mother's finger, Sylvie handed the doll to Jane.

Her mother smiled at Jane. "It's silly, isn't it? Someone my age holding a baby doll? But she does so remind me of the first Lolly . . . and even more, of my two girls. The two happiest days of my life were the days you both were born."

"Hold still, Mom," Sylvie said.

"And here you are now . . . it's such a dream, to have you both home with me," Margaret said. Her blue eyes were light and chalky with cataracts. Her once luxuriant chestnut brown hair was now soft gray. Tears puddled in her eyes, spilling onto wrinkled cheeks. Jane leaned forward. Her mother's cheeks were so soft, like velvet.

Jane and her mother stared at each other, the baby doll between them.

"Sometimes I wasn't sure you'd ever come back again," her mother said.

"You knew I would."

Her mother shook her head. "A Christmas here and there, my retirement party . . . always in and out so quickly. I always wanted you to stay. To have you upstairs, in your old room, with no real plans to leave."

Jane's skin still tingled as she handed the doll back. This was why she had stayed away as much as possible. Because although she loved her mother and knew Sylvie needed help in deciding what to do next, Jane could never, ever forget what her mother had done.

Jane began helping Sylvie put away the remaining groceries.

"Should I make us some tea?" Sylvie asked.

"That would be wonderful," Margaret said.

Jane stood still, holding a package of frozen berries. The cold stung her fingers. Her mother loved her so much; Jane had never doubted that. But no amount of love could make up for what was missing. Years, memories, two lives.

"Jane?"

"If we wait a few minutes, the biscuits will be ready. And I'll thaw the berries . . ."

"Just like shortcake!" her mother said. "Sounds luscious. But there was something else . . . something I was going to say about Jane being home. Now, what was it?"

Her mother tilted her head, torn between thoughts. Jane saw the struggle, just behind her mother's eyes, to hold on to the threads.

"You'll think of it again," Sylvie said, lifting the receiver and reaching for the phone book.

"Who are you calling?" Jane asked.

"The SaveRite manager. This is product tampering," Sylvie said, tapping the scrap of white paper.

"It's someone who likes cows," Jane said. "You don't have to read the note. You can still eat your hamburger."

"Just because *you're* a vegetarian," Sylvie said, dialing the number. "And besides, we don't know whether the meat's been poisoned."

"Safety first," Margaret said.

Jane tried to smile as she looked away. It was so sweet, yet so hard and weird, to be home. Her throat tightened. She felt like an iceberg, drifting from the icy sea into southern waters. She loved these two women more than any other person in the world.

Except the one she had given away.

CHAPTER 4

The manager's office was air-conditioned, as cold as the frozen-food aisle. His name was Mr. Achilles Fontaine, a name that Chloe thought made him sound like the fifth musketeer. He had a swooping way about him that further fit the bill: sallow droopy cheeks, a huge bristly mustache, short gray hair, and a habit of wearing bright, billowy shirts with very full sleeves.

"Look at this, Chloe," he said, spreading the notes and grocery receipts across his desk.

Chloe nodded. Reading upside down, she was able to recognize her own handwriting, and to revisit some of her favorite messages: *This duck was somebody's mother; Moo-Moo, don't eat me!;* and *Vegetables can be found in Aisle One; why not try a delicious, nutritious salad, instead of this slab of dead pig?*

"I am very, very disappointed in you. I liked you very much. I thought you were part of the team."

Chloe nodded sorrowfully, focusing on the top button of his shirt—orange, today. Or, to be more precise, a shade of bright peach. She felt sorry for Mr. Fontaine, because she understood his choice in shirts was a desperate plea to be taken as relevant, the same way certain teachers tried too hard, by wearing cool, funny socks.

"But you weren't part of the team, were you?" he asked.

"Well," she said. "That depends on what team."

"The SaveRite team," he said.

"I guess I wasn't," she said.

"What you did is not to be taken lightly. We can't just treat this as a prank."

"It wasn't a prank," she said.

He looked confused, but he didn't pursue the issue. He reached up to scratch his ear. She stared gravely, thinking of all the imprisoned animals, unable to scratch their itches.

"We had to recall all these items," he

said, showing her the receipts, certain amounts circled in red. "Anyone who received one of your notes has been invited to come in for a complete refund. Do you know how much money that adds up to?"

"No."

"One hundred and forty-nine dollars—so far. How long do you have to work for that much money, Chloe? Do the math."

She didn't reply. She was getting fired— she didn't want to stand here and banter with a man who would never get it.

"You do understand the severity of this, Chloe?"

"Yes, I absolutely do," she said.

"I'm glad to hear that. I can't let you continue working here, but I'll be very happy to think you've learned a lesson that will help you as you go through life. Would you like to tell me what that is?"

Chloe cleared her throat and looked him straight in the eyes. "You're right. This *is* a matter of great severity," she said calmly. "Animal mothers are separated from their babies—have you ever heard a calf crying, Mr. Fontaine? It's so sad . . . and for

what? So people can have cheeseburg-
ers?"

"Chloe," he said, turning pale and slapping both hands down on his desk. "I could
call the police on you, but I won't. Get your
things and leave my store. If I ever see you
back in here, I will call the police."

She nodded, handing him her smock and
gathering her jacket and book bag. His energy was very powerful, filled with anger;
when her father got like this, Chloe had to
get away. Glancing over, she could practically see him shaking. She paused, wanting
to ask him for her paycheck, but she
couldn't bring herself to: He looked as if he
hated her.

Walking through the store, she felt other
kids watching her. Adrian Blocker was stock-
ing the milk shelves; he snickered as she hurried down the aisle. She stopped by the pay
phone at the entrance, to call her mother for a
ride. Jenny West was at the checkout; Mark
Vibbert was her bagger.

"Moo, moo," Mark said as Chloe went
through her pockets for a quarter.

Jenny laughed.

Chloe stared straight at both of them.
She tried to think of something to say, to

make them understand. The longer she stood there, the more she felt like an outcast, and the redder her face got. She couldn't find a quarter, so she decided to walk.

Her mother would just yell at her, anyway.

⁂

Dylan drove his truck north on Lambs Road, checking his rearview mirror to make sure nothing bounced out. He had found a good nursery in Kingston, and he'd loaded up on a few seedlings. White-tailed deer bounded across the road, shadows in the twilight. The road was rutted from a hard winter of frost heaves, and he drove slowly, not wanting to hit a deer or lose his rootstock.

Running the family orchard took up every minute of his time, and that was good. His father had left him a share in the land, along with Elwanger's classic *Growing Apple Trees;* by the time Dylan finished working every day and reading every night, he was too tired to think about Isabel and Amanda.

He was too busy learning how rootstock, soil fertility, and pruning can affect tree size.

That all apple trees sold commercially con-
sist of two parts grafted together to form the
tree; that the "scion"—the top section that
would branch and bear fruit—was grafted
onto a "rootstock," the bottom section,
which determined the relative size of the
tree. Stuff that would have put him to sleep
ten years ago.

Lost in thoughts of cross-pollination, he
nearly passed his niece, trudging up the
road. Slamming on his brakes, he felt the
whole load of seedlings lurch forward.

"Shit," he said. He'd started smoking
again recently, so he ditched the cigarette,
slung his arm across the seat, looked over
his shoulder, and gunned the truck backward.

"Uncle Dylan," Chloe said. Weary under
the weight of her knapsack, she straightened up at the sight of him, eyes wide and
bright, stabbing his heart.

"What are you doing, walking on this road
in the dark? You want to get hit by a car?
Climb in."

She tossed her book bag in with the
trees, stepped up, and looked out the
back window. "Wow, new baby trees!" she
said.

"Yep."

"That is so great," she said. "You're making the orchard beautiful again."

"You think so, Chloe?"

"I do. And it's great for the cats—not to mention the birds, deer . . . even the coyotes and foxes."

"Wildlife have to forage," he said. "I just hope they leave the seedlings alone till they have a chance to grow."

Chloe sighed. "If only everyone had your attitude," she said.

He laughed. He hadn't been known lately—in the family or anywhere else—for having an attitude worth copying. "I don't think your parents agree with you."

"No. They're waiting for you to get tired of the orchard. Then you can all sell out and get rich from the developers. Money," she said, shaking her head.

"What's that about, Chloe Chadwick?" he asked, smiling over at her.

She paused, staring at him, seeming to weigh whether to talk to him or not.

"You'll tell my parents," she said.

"Maybe I will, maybe I won't. Try me."

"I got fired," she said.

"Yeah? What happened?"

"I was standing on my principles—I swear, that's all it was, Uncle Dylan. I was just exercising my right of free speech. Leaving little notes on a few packages of meat at SaveRite. You know, suggesting people try eating salad for a change. Giving the animals a chance. And Mr. Fontaine—took it the wrong way."

"Who is he? The store manager?" Dylan asked.

Chloe nodded miserably.

"Chloe, you're a smart girl. The smartest girl I know. You couldn't have thought he'd be pleased."

"No," she said. "Because he's a jerk and a creep. He wears these idiotic shirts, bright silky things with big sleeves—he looks like someone out of the sixties! And he has a stupid bristly mustache, and he is the most unenlightened person on earth."

Dylan hid a smile. "Because he eats meat or because he wears ugly shirts?"

"For being so intolerant, firing me just like that . . ."

"You can't bite the hand that feeds and expect it to keep feeding."

"Because he hates me," Chloe said. "You should have seen the way he looked at me today, just because I wrote a few notes and he had to give some people back their money. I should hate *him*!"

Dylan listened to his niece, letting her rail, and then fall into deep, static silence. The breeze blew through the cab, and he sensed her staring across the bench seat, waiting for him to say something. He had such a special bond with her, and he was always touched—and a little thrown—by the way she seemed to expect him to be wise. He thought of Isabel: Chloe's age. This could be Isabel, he thought. What would he say to her?

"Hate . . . 'A night devoid of stars . . .' " he said quietly.

"What, Uncle Dylan?" Chloe asked, as if she wasn't sure she'd heard right.

Dylan drove silently. He had a pack of cigarettes in his shirt pocket, and his fingers were itching to reach for one.

"Uncle Dylan?"

He couldn't tell his beloved niece that he'd made the last years of his life a study devoted to hate and how to get rid of it. A big deer stepped into the road, then loped across. Dylan stepped on the brake, and the young trees slid forward in the truck bed. Chloe was fixated on the road ahead. She'd grown up here; Dylan knew he didn't have to tell her what would happen next.

"Here they come," she whispered.

"The whole family," Dylan said as the female followed with her yearling. They stood on the side of the road, eyes glittering, stars in the forest. Dylan stared at the three of them, his heart beating in his throat.

"The whole family," Chloe said, echoing her uncle as she gazed at the eyes in the woods.

Dylan waited until he was sure that all the deer had crossed, that there weren't any stragglers lagging behind, and then he slowly drove along.

❦

Back at home, Chloe went out back to feed the rest of the cats. Uncle Dylan had dropped her off at the door, and her mother had been standing right there, framed in the doorway and lit from behind like some mad, religious figure. Uncle Dylan had just chuckled, looked at Chloe, and said, "You'll be fine. Your mother is a reasonable woman."

"Yeah, sure," Chloe had said. Uncle Dylan didn't know the whole story. The way anger built in her house, slowly, just like a family volcano.

Her mother had just welcomed Chloe with a quizzical expression. Instead of lying, Chloe just went for it, telling the truth about the notes, and Mr. Fontaine calling her into his office, and getting fired.

Her mother had listened, arms folded across her chest, nostrils starting to flare. Then she had called Chloe's father in—from the den, where he was working on the computer, entering the insurance policies he had sold that day—so Chloe had to run through the whole story all over again.

Why did her parents have to look so nice, so innocent, so crushed? They stood there so politely, listening to her with painful little squints in their eyes, as if she was announcing her plans to leave home and join the Shining Path, become a guerrilla. They stared at her, eyes watery and helpless, as if she had let them down in ways too deep to be discussed. The only signs of true anger were her mother's nostril-flares and her father's red face. Also, the deep snap in his voice as he said, "Ace Fontaine is in the Rotary with me."

And the way her mother tightened her lips and said, "You'll have to get another job. You need to save for college, and if you think we're going to give you the extra money to pay for that vegetarian cat food, you're wrong. Life is expensive, Chloe. Protesting doesn't put food on the table."

Chloe had apologized. She had walked away, at first feeling relieved; she hadn't gotten yelled at or grounded. But, then, it always took time to build. As if too powerful to confront all at once, anger did a slow burn in her family. Her parents loved order, and anger threw everything out of whack. Like other messy things, it was officially banned from their house. Unofficially was another story. As Uncle Dylan had said, her mother was a reasonable woman. And her father a reasonable man. At least they tried to be.

She stood in the backyard. Her bare arms were covered with goosebumps in the cool spring breeze. She shook the cat food bag, and the sound brought cats from all over. The night was alive with them. Jumping out of trees, slinking out from under bushes, crying and meowing their hellos. Their eyes sparked in the darkness, and she felt bowled over with love, like the mother of a huge family. She loved the cats so much, she couldn't imagine giving any of them away.

Back when she was younger, Chloe Chadwick used to wish on the stars. On warm evenings, she would go out behind her house, press the tall grass into a nest, and look up into the sky. In her memory, it wasn't quite dark yet, just shimmering with the sun's last glow. One by one, in order of brightness, the stars would appear, connected by a silken web.

Chloe would name them: "Mommy. Daddy. Grandma. Uncle Dylan. Aunt Amanda. Isabel." Every star was a chapter, and together they seemed to tell her family's story. Sometimes she imagined them as golden apples hanging from the spreading branches of a tree. A family tree, up in the sky. There were always two stars far apart from the others: "Chloe" and her real mother. She would squint at them, trying to see her mother's face.

Now she was fifteen and much too old to be staring at the stars. Instead, she stood still until the cats had finished eating. The wind came through the orchard, bringing the scents of apple blossoms and cigarette smoke. It made her sad, because she knew Uncle Dylan had started smoking again.

"A night devoid of stars," she said out loud—for no real reason, except that he had used those words on the way home. What had he meant by them? Chloe couldn't resist: She looked up.

There they were, off to the side, those two lonely stars she used to see. Chloe and her mother. Or maybe they were Uncle Dylan and Isabel. Parents and children who couldn't be together. It didn't really matter, anyway. It was just a story she used to tell herself. Stars were one thing; reality was another. She had spent hours on the Internet looking. And she had taken the bus into Providence, to sign up at the adoption reunion registry—only to be told she had to be twenty-one.

What mattered now were the cats, and getting another job so she could feed them properly. Real life: not the myths and stories of the stars. Off in the distance, she heard the roar of a dirt bike. Sometimes high school kids rode through the orchard. It made Uncle Dylan mad, and she knew it scared the wildlife. Shivering in the night air, Chloe listened till the engine faded. Then she called good night to the cats, and ran back into her house.

CHAPTER 5

The girls gave their mother a bath in the old claw-foot tub upstairs. Clear gray light came through the window, unkind and obvious. Margaret hunched over, embarrassed at having her daughters lift and scrub her, wash her hair. Sylvie had the whole thing down pat: She had the soap, shampoo, and washcloth laid out. She went through the procedure like a surgeon, holding out her hand to Jane, barking, "Conditioner! Rinse!"

"Dears, it's a bit chilly," Margaret said, her arms drawn around her knees. "Could you add more hot water?"

Wordlessly, Sylvie turned on the taps. Jane noticed the tightness around her eyes and mouth. Leaning forward, Jane reached for the container of bubble bath, and squirted it into the stream of water.

"Jane . . ." Sylvie breathed.

"Oh, that's lovely, dear," Margaret said as the foam began to build. She patted the bubbles, scooping them into her hands. Holding them up to the window, she seemed delighted by their iridescence; she looked at her daughters, to make sure they both saw.

"Pretty, Mom," Jane said.

"Let me see your feet," Sylvie said sternly, bending over to examine them for infection.

Margaret wanted to stay in the warm water till the bubbles evaporated, but Sylvie said she needed to get back to bed. The two sisters helped her out of the tub, and Sylvie dried her off with a big white towel. Jane stood ready with her Irish linen nightshirt. Together, they got her into bed.

"Sylvie, she needs . . ." Jane began, as they started down the stairs.

But Sylvie walked faster, rounding the corner, into the kitchen. There, she began making tea. Her blue T-shirt was soaking wet from the bath. Her thin arms were wiry and muscular, from all the lifting. Her golden hair fell to her shoulders, hiding her face.

"I know what she needs," Sylvie said, sounding tired. "We have a pretty good routine."

Jane stared. She wanted to be sensitive. There was a history of meddling under this roof. But Sylvie was her younger sister. These last months—knowing Sylvie had taken a leave from the job she loved, hearing the stress in her voice, and now viewing her daily routine—had made it hard for Jane to hold her tongue.

"You're wonderful to her, Sylvie," Jane said.

Sylvie shrugged, watching the kettle on the stove. The moisture on the sides began to hiss. "She liked the bubble bath," Sylvie said. "She likes having you here."

"You know why I came, right?"

Sylvie looked Jane straight in the eye. Jane swallowed, as if she'd gotten caught by the person who knew her better than anyone else in the world. Seconds ticked by, and Jane felt Sylvie looking straight into her heart.

"I wish I didn't," Sylvie said. "But I do. It has to do with why you keep borrowing the car."

Jane blushed and looked down.

"No, it has to do with Mom. And you. She needs more care than you can give her."

"We're doing fine."

"You're exhausted," Jane said. "I don't know how you lift her yourself, when I'm not here."

"You underestimate me," Sylvie said, flexing her muscles. The kettle whistled, and she turned off the burner.

"Meanwhile, you're giving up your career."

"You should talk! Who's running your bakery?"

"I need a vacation," Jane said quietly. "It's been fifteen years since I've had one . . ."

"Well, anyway. I've just taken a leave of absence. Everyone is very understanding. The whole school loved Mom—she was their principal."

"That rare combination of beloved and feared." Jane smiled. "Just like she was here."

"She had to be both mother and father to us," Sylvie said.

Jane's stomach clenched, hearing those words. Their mother used to remind them of it constantly. Their own father had drifted away a little at a time. A traveling paper salesman, his travels had started getting longer. Jane remembered kneeling by her bedroom window, watching for his car to come down the street. She got so she could recognize the headlights—of all the other cars passing by. She had loved him so much, she felt inside-out when he wasn't home.

"Do you ever wonder where he is?" Jane asked.

"Never," Sylvie said tensely.

"Really?" Jane asked. She watched as Sylvie shook loose tea into the blue teapot and filled it with hot water. Their mother called from upstairs.

"You do?"

"All the time," Jane said softly.

"Then you must be haunted from both directions," Sylvie said.

"What do you mean?"

"I know where you go in the car, Jane," Sylvie said. "You go driving out to the orchards."

Jane stared at the steam rising from the teapot's spout.

The low whistle sounded, unleashing her

private ghosts. They carried her burden of sorrow and guilt, and she had long since stopped trying to push them away.

Her mother called again, and Jane's pulse raced. Being home, hearing her mother's voice rise, with Sylvie's question hanging in the air, made Jane close her eyes and take hold of the counter to keep the room from spinning.

※

Jane had wanted to keep her baby, and her mother had talked her out of it. She understood that her mother's plans had been "for Jane's and the baby's own good." She knew that the child had a good home, so much better than anything Jane could have provided.

To Margaret, it was bad enough that Jane had had to leave school for an entire semester. She had to get on with her life . . . did she have any idea how hard it was to care for a baby?

Her mother had wanted great things for her: She had been a sophomore at Brown, near the top of her class. She'd been on the tennis team, the number two singles player. She had been majoring in English. Her mother had said she had the intellectual rigor to become a college professor, although Jane had wanted to follow in her footsteps and teach high school.

Jane hadn't picked up a tennis racket since that last day. She had never taught anyone at any school—or college. All those young faces: What if one of them turned out to be her daughter, and Jane didn't even know it?

Baking had been such an easier solution. It was solitary. It required precise measurements and focus and concentration. It kept Jane to herself. And her kitchen was far away from here, so Jane wouldn't be tempted to scan every face in the crowd, wondering, always wondering . . . She had always feared bumping into her daughter and not even knowing it.

Jane had signed papers, promising to give up all parental rights. She wasn't supposed to make contact with her daughter, but she had filed her name with the Rhode Island adoption registry and with a national "Find Your Birth Family" Web site, just in case the child ever wanted to find her. Fifteen and a half years had passed.

The truth was, she knew exactly where

her daughter lived. Jane's mother had found the perfect family, the perfect home. A colleague's son, whose wife was unable to conceive. Allowing them to adopt the baby would be helping everyone. A good family, a good home for the child; freedom and a chance for Jane to live her own life.

Jane's identity would be kept secret— completely, one-hundred-percent secret— from everyone. Only Margaret and her colleague, by necessity, would know.

❦

"You're not going to talk to her, are you? Because she's only fifteen. It wouldn't be fair to her, or to her family. The law is clear in Rhode Island—"

"What law?"

"You know. Family Court. The adoption registry . . . I *know* you know about it."

Jane knew. She could practically quote the rules and procedures by heart.

"She has to be twenty-one, Jane," Sylvie said. "Before she can look for you. And you have to let her do it; you can't intrude on her life. She's not even sixteen yet."

Jane looked around the kitchen. Every

inch of it was so familiar. She had come home from the hospital, straight from being born, to this house. And later, straight from giving birth at St. Joseph's, she had come home here.

"Remember looking for Dad?" she asked.

"Jane, stop."

"Remember after he left? How you and I tried to track him down? How we called his company, and pretended to be customers? And how we hitchhiked to Hartford, to intercept him at his sales call?"

"Stop! What are you trying to do?" Sylvie asked. "There's no comparison. We lived with Daddy. She doesn't even know you. She has a perfectly nice family. Her father is a very successful insurance agent. Her mother is active in the Crofton garden club."

"You know them?" Jane said.

"Mom kept track," Sylvie said. "Through Virginia."

Virginia Chadwick, their mother's friend, the science teacher who had set everything in motion.

"What else did she find out?" Jane asked, glancing up at the ceiling, as if she could see into their mother's room.

"Nothing. Virginia had a stroke last year,

and she hasn't been well. Her son takes her out sometimes; we see them at the Educators' Potluck dinners. Mom says it makes her too sad to talk to such a brilliant woman and hear only gibberish. That's how I feel about Mom."

"I know," Jane said, electrified. Could her sister see? Just these few minutes of talking about, or around, her daughter was like high-voltage current. Jane felt herself shimmering.

Sylvie took a deep breath and stuck out her hand. "Truce?" she asked.

"Détente."

"You're right about the stress around here," Sylvie said. "It's hard, seeing Mom go downhill. She's gotten a lot worse since Christmas. That last fall took a lot out of her, and she gets confused so easily. But I don't want her to wind up in a home, Jane. I want to keep her here."

"Even though it's too much for one person?"

"You're here," Sylvie said with a smile.

Jane nodded. "For now," she said.

"How is it, being home?" Sylvie asked. And then, when Jane didn't answer right away, added, "Or I suppose this isn't your home anymore."

Jane looked up at the ceiling again. "Wherever you and Mom are, that's my home," she said, knowing it was the truth. *And Chloe.*

Sylvie looked surprised. She arched her eyebrows, a world of expression in the space just above her eyes.

"What?" Jane asked.

"It's just that, in so many ways, it's seemed as if you couldn't get far enough away from us," Sylvie said.

And Jane just nodded, because she knew that was the truth, too.

On her way out the door for school that morning, Chloe found an envelope stuck in the door. It had her name on it, in Uncle Dylan's handwriting. She saved it, to read on the bus. But then, once she climbed aboard, Teddy Lincoln began going "moo, moo," and Jenny called out that Mr. Fontaine had given everyone a lecture after Chloe had left the store, saying that the police would be called if anyone ever tried such a stunt again, and Chloe just slipped her headphones on and started listening to Michelle Branch.

She'd had a trying day at school. The boy she liked, Gil Albert, seemed to have become surgically attached to Lena Allard over the weekend. Her best friend, Mona Shippen, was out sick. People teased her about the SaveRite incident. During biology class, they watched a movie about monkeys in the Amazon rain forest, and she started to well up when they showed footage of poachers grabbing monkeys out of the trees and sticking them into bamboo cages.

"Monkey lover," Teddy said, seeing her tears.

"Heartless bastard," she said, wiping her face.

During art period, she made Mona a card. She drew a picture of a dense jungle. Peering out of thick green foliage, she drew many yellow eyes. Inside the card, she drew a monkey swinging from one branch to another. She wrote:

"School is a fun jungle. Come back and swing on the branches with me."

Later, she got off the bus two stops early, to deliver it to Mona herself. Mona answered the door in pink flannel pajamas and a flowing purple kimono with an intriguing tomato soup splotch on the lapel. She wore wire-rimmed glasses and had slightly greasy shoulder-length brown hair. Which was interesting, because before she got sick, her hair was down to her elbows.

"What did you do to your hair?" Chloe asked.

"I cut it. I'm bored," Mona said. "You shouldn't come in. I'm contagious."

"What do you have?"

"Legionnaires' disease. Mono. Who the hell knows?"

Chloe flung herself into Mona's arms and took the deepest breaths possible. "God, I hope I catch it," she said. "Then I can hopefully take a turn for the worse and get sent to a sanitarium in Chile."

"I'd love to go to Chile. I plan to name my first daughter Tierra del Fuego."

"What if you have a boy?"

"His name will be Gilbert Albert, after the man you love. Jesus, how could you fall in love with someone with such a dorky name?"

"I don't love him. I hate him."

"That's just because since Friday, he's been 'as one' with Lena. Right?"

"Who told you?"

"I have my spies. Did you bring me something?" Mona said, opening Chloe's book bag. She rummaged through, coughing as she found a Baggie filled with dried apricots and raisins.

"Don't eat those," Chloe said. "I think they've been in there since last fall. I made you this card."

Mona opened it. She looked proudly at the jungle drawing, admiring it as a mother might. Then she opened it and read the message. " 'School is a fun jungle' . . ." she read, giving Chloe a fishy glance. "What are you trying to say?"

"Just trying to get you to come back soon," Chloe said. "I miss you."

"Well, I miss you, too, but lying in a greeting card will never get you anywhere. It reminds me of the card I bought for Rhianna for Mother's Day last year. As you can imagine, the stepmother section is a little thin. And I found this card with a really sweet message, all about how well she fits into the family . . ."

Chloe chuckled. "I remember how much she loved that."

"No kidding. She thinks the family fits into her, not the other way around. Hey—let's start our own line of cards. The Passive-Aggressive line."

"You're spending too much time with your shrink," Chloe said, laughing.

"Yeah, well, you could use one. Leaving anonymous notes at the meat counter, and getting fired for it. Oh! And here's a good one—have you tried forging your parents' signatures lately?"

Chloe's smile vanished.

Coughing and laughing at the same time, Mona pretended to punch her arm. "Come on—that's rich, wouldn't you say? Taking the bus into Providence, to Family *Court,* no less, and slipping them a forged note . . . and when that didn't work, going back with a *hat* on, and with your birthstone ring turned backward so they'd think it was a wedding ring and you were twenty-one and married . . ."

"Okay, okay—stop, Mone."

"*Who* needs the shrink?"

"I know. It was a little crazy."

Mona broke up, coughing again. Chloe,

concerned, patted her on the back. She leaned around the corner, to see if Rhianna was in the kitchen.

"No one's home," Mona said. "She's at the dermatologist. Want to hear something utterly mad?"

Chloe nodded, hoping to get away from the subject of mothers.

"She gets these injections between her eyebrows. Of . . . get this . . . botulism!"

"The poison?"

"Yes! And it paralyzes her face muscles! Just in that little spot, right between the eyes, where the frown lines go. So, no matter how much she frowns, the lines never stick."

"Paralyzes her face? Botulism?" Chloe asked.

Mona nodded, pushing her glasses up her nose and hacking away.

"Botox . . . Botulism—toxin? Should I translate for her? That's the role model I have to look up to. I think my mother would be very sad to know my father had married such a woman," Mona said. Her eyes filled with tears, and Chloe knew they weren't from her cough. The two girls had been friends since childhood. Mona's mother had died when she was six. Chloe and she had gravitated together that year, and the bond had only strengthened since.

"Especially since she was your mother's nurse," Chloe said, taking Mona's hand.

"It's so unfair," Mona said, sniffling. "I feel so crummy, and all I want is my mother."

"Do you remember her?" Chloe asked.

Mona nodded, taking off her glasses. "I see her better with my glasses off. She used to feel my forehead, to tell if I had a fever or not. She'd crack ice into a bowl and let me eat it with a silver spoon. She had curly red hair and a funny space between her two front teeth."

"At least you can see her . . ." Chloe said.

"With my glasses off."

Chloe nodded. She put her hand on Mona's forehead. It felt hot. So she dragged her best friend to the living room sofa and made her lie down. Then she went into the kitchen, opened the freezer, and took a handful of ice cubes from the automatic ice maker. They clinked as she dropped them into a cup, grabbed a spoon, and carried them to Mona.

"Thank you," Mona said, looking up from the pillow. "You'd make a good mother."

Chloe smiled. There was a pen lying on the table. She picked it up, then carefully drew a star on the back of Mona's hand and on the back of her own. Hoisting her book bag, she noticed that Mona hadn't put her glasses back on. As she let herself out the front door, she left her friend lying there with a cup of ice, with blurred eyesight and clear vision of the mother she still loved so much. The whole thing got under Chloe's skin. How could people who supposedly loved you just die? Or, almost worse, just abandon you?

It was the same thing, really.

❧

For the second day in a row, Dylan Chadwick was driving home with a load of seedlings and came upon his niece. Pulling over, he put out his cigarette and gestured for her to get into the truck.

"Did you miss the bus again?" he asked, lowering his window all the way to let the smoke escape.

"No, I got off early. Mona's sick, and I took her a card."

Dylan nodded, not showing any reaction. Mona Shippen. She, Chloe, and Isabel had been inseparable during the summers. He just drove. They didn't have far to go. He glanced over, noticed the hole in the knee of Chloe's jeans, the star she had drawn on the back of her hand. The small details were vivid reminders of Isabel, and he didn't even know why—maybe his daughter wouldn't have worn holey jeans or drawn on her own skin. Or maybe she would.

"I thought you were driving Granny to the school thing tonight," Chloe said.

"That's tomorrow night."

Chloe nodded. "More trees?" she asked, gesturing toward the truck bed.

"Digging all those holes keeps me busy," he said.

"Do you miss solving crimes?" she asked.

"Not a bit," he said. "There are more interesting mysteries to solve here, anyway."

"Yeah? Like what?"

"Like why Empires and Galas are possible cross-pollenizers for Jonagolds. And why the graft union has to be at least two inches above the soil line."

"And why might that be?" Chloe asked in a professorial-sounding voice.

"So the roots don't emerge from the scion."

"The scion," she said. "The father. Even apple trees have parents."

Dylan turned slowly, to look at her. Was she getting started on her adoption again? Eli still couldn't get over being called down to Family Court, to find that Chloe had bought a fake ID online, pretending to be twenty-one, the necessary age for tracking her birth mother.

"You have parents," Dylan said steadily.

"I know," she said, clutching her book bag and scowling. He knew that expression; he had worn it so long, it sometimes seemed frozen on his face. Angst, anguish, fury at the world.

"Then what's wrong?"

"Monkeys are being kidnapped from the jungle, I got fired from my job and can't feed the cats healthy food, I got made fun of at school, my best friend is home sick and has no one to take care of her, I deserve to know my identity, and I hate the world," she said thinly, as if she considered him the enemy, and a dim enemy at that.

"Did you read my note?" he asked.

"Oh!" She slapped her book bag, then

began rummaging through it. "I almost forgot." She reached inside, pulled out the envelope. He watched as she extracted the
paper, squinted at his printing. He remembered writing it last night, long after the
lights in his brother's house were turned off,
when he couldn't sleep.

"Should I read it out loud?" she asked.

"Just the quote," he said.

"Okay," she said, then read, " 'Violence
merely increases hate . . . adding deeper
darkness to a night already devoid of stars.
Darkness cannot drive out darkness: only
light can do that. Hate cannot drive out
hate; only love can do that.' Dr. Martin
Luther King, Jr. Hmm. That's what you
meant last night, when you said 'A night devoid of stars'?"

"Yep."

She looked at him quizzically. "Why'd you
write me this?" she asked.

"Because I thought you needed to know
it."

"But why?"

He drove along in silence. He couldn't tell
her the real reason, or at least the whole real
reason. But he knew she was sensitive, and
he knew she was smart, so he decided to

tell her a little. "Because you remind me of me," he said.

"How?"

"Let's just say, you have a finely tuned sense of injustice," he said.

She looked away, pressing her forehead against the side window. They turned off the main road onto the narrow and deeply rutted orchard road. Just before they reached their shared driveway, Dylan pointed at the ramshackle farm stand.

"Want an after-school job?" he asked.

"Doing what?" she asked.

"It's rough work," he warned.

"Yeah, well, not a problem. The cats have to eat. What is it?"

"How about getting the stand into shape?"

"The apple stand?" she asked.

Dylan nodded. "It's pretty sorry looking. You'd have to clean it out, paint it. I'll fix the shelves."

"And the sign?"

"Yeah. I'll fix the sign. I think it's in the barn."

" 'Chadwick Apple Orchards,' " she whispered. "Isabel and I used to work at the stand when we were little. Granddad used to give us maple sugar and honeycombs and apple tarts."

"I know," Dylan said. "I remember."

"It hasn't been open for so long."

Dylan glanced across the seat at Chloe. Her skin was pale, her eyes were blue with shadows of sleeplessness beneath, her hair straight and dark and unlike anyone else in the Chadwick family. She had torn jeans and an ink star on the back of her hand, and Dylan could almost hear Isabel pleading with him to help her cousin.

"That's why I need your help," he said gruffly, stopping in front of her house.

"Okay, then," she said. "You have it."

"Good."

"Can we sell more than just apples? Like maple sugar and honeycombs and apple tarts?"

Dylan gave her a long don't-get-ahead-of-yourself look.

She laughed. "Just tell me when to start."

"This weekend," he said. "Saturday morning, bright and early."

She nodded, grabbing her book bag and the note he'd left her, running across the yard to her house. He remembered watching the two girls picking dandelions one spring night, gathering handfuls, blowing the silver seeds into the wind, laughing with the sheer joy of being together.

Together.

What did that mean, anyway? Driving away, Dylan wasn't sure he knew anymore.

CHAPTER 6

The Educators' Potluck Dinner was held on the first Friday of every month, in the cafeterias of various schools. Last month it had been at Rogers High School in Newport, the month before at Hope High, in Providence. Tonight it was at Crofton Consolidated, and Sylvie was taking a cake, baked by Jane, that looked exactly like an old and somewhat tattered library edition of *Webster's Second Dictionary.*

Sylvie had given herself a facial, put on her new outfit from Eileen Fisher, applied her new blush and lipstick, added a little teal eye shadow for drama, and was just pulling on her navy spring wool coat, when her mother called her.

"What is it?" Sylvie asked, going to the bedroom door.

"What about me?" her mother asked.

Sylvie froze. "What do you mean?"

"It's first Friday," her mother said. "And I feel so much better today. Can I go with you?"

Jane sat at her bedside, *Great Expectations* open on her knee, looking up with bemusement. "We were reading out loud, but then Mom heard you getting ready and asked me what day it was . . ."

"Mom, you've barely left the house in weeks . . ."

"Isn't that the point, dear?" Margaret asked. "I need to get out."

Sylvie blinked. She thought of John Dufour, wondered whether he would be there. She could almost see him, in his maroon sweater vest, his sensitive brown eyes trained on the parking lot to see whether she would drive in. They got together sometimes to play Scrabble, and she always swooned when their knees touched under the table. They were the shy, middle-aged, academic embodiment of that song, "Working for the Weekend." Sylvie supplied her own lyrics about John wondering whether she'd come out tonight . . .

Torn between desire for romance, for the

chance to walk into the Crofton cafeteria and see John watching the door for her, and her well-entrenched daughterly duty, Sylvie nodded tersely.

"Sure, Mom. If you're feeling up to it."

"She assures me she is." Jane grinned.

"Well, it'll take both of us to get her in and out of the car," Sylvie said, staring at her sister. "So I guess you're coming, too."

Jane sat in the back. Sylvie drove, and their mother occupied the front passenger seat, oohing and aahing as they passed through town, as if she had never seen houses or gardens before.

"Oh, my," Margaret said. "Look at the Jensens' lilac bushes. Aren't they spectacular!" And, "Goodness—what have the Dunlaps done to their house? That's an awful lot of deck for that little ranch." She rolled down the side window, breathing the fragrant air and enjoying the sense of freedom.

Jane smiled.

Her mother seemed happy, Sylvie seemed distracted. She had gotten all dressed up, and at every stop light she'd look in the rearview mirror, adjusting her hair. Jane couldn't wait to see who she was meeting. She relaxed in back, wearing black jeans and her leather jacket, knowing her mother would have been happier to have two daughters in nice blue wool coats, but oh, well . . .

No matter how far inland you went in Rhode Island, and Crofton was almost as inland as you could get, you could smell the sea. Narragansett Bay cut into the state, the most magnificent body of water—in Jane's opinion—on earth. The tang of sea wind and salt marsh filled the air, mixing with the Crofton scents of lilacs and apple blossoms.

Her cake was on the seat beside her. It wasn't bad, considering she didn't have many baking things with her. She ran the Calamity Bakery, just a tiny hole in the wall under the High Line, the abandoned railroad bed, on Tenth Avenue. Through word of mouth, her business had grown, and she baked cakes to celebrate screenings, premieres, Tony and Grammy awards, book parties, art openings.

Her name was well known in Chelsea, TriBeCa, Gramercy Park. Her answering machine was constantly full; it was even now, when her outgoing message said she was visiting her mother and was sorry for all the wonderful celebrations she'd be missing and that everyone should call Chelsea Bakers till she returned.

Arriving at the school, Sylvie pulled up in front. The two girls helped their mother out of the car. She seemed steadier tonight than she had since Jane's arrival. While Sylvie parked, Jane supported her mother as she walked inside.

The cafeteria brought back a flood of high school memories. The cinder-block walls, direct from the cold war, were painted pale yellow; the floor was industrial-strength gray linoleum. The stainless steel serving counter was loaded with casseroles, stews, salads, and sandwiches. Rectangular tables were lined up in three long rows, each surrounded by ten chairs. Many were already full with teachers and administrators, talking and laughing.

But suddenly people caught sight of Jane's mother. The room went almost silent for a moment, and then there was a great swell of excitement—Jane heard it as real joy.

"Margaret!"

"Mrs. Porter!"

"Oh, it's Margaret—look, she's here!"

"Margaret, so good to see you looking so well!"

And she did look well—tall and elegant as always, dressed in a lavender silk dress with lace at the neck, gray hair swept up in a bun, wearing the long gold chain she always wore, dangling with a tiny crystal globe containing a mustard seed. Friends and colleagues surrounded her, kissing her cheek and shaking her hand, and wanting to meet Jane.

"My darling daughter, home from the big city," Margaret said proudly.

"So nice to meet you . . ."

"We've heard so much about you."

Jane nodded, smiling. She wondered: What had they heard? She had never accompanied her mother to one of these before; since leaving Rhode Island at twenty, she had hardly looked back.

She glanced across the room and saw her old English teacher. He had the same craggy face and briar-eyebrows, and he was gazing at her with the same reproach she'd seen in his eyes when she'd told him she was leaving Brown—after all he'd done to help her get in—in order to have the baby. Jane was thirty-five now, and sixteen years had passed since those days, but she felt a wave of shame all the same.

"Hi, Mr. Romney," she said, leaving her mother to a circle of teachers as he walked over.

"My prize student," he said. "Jane Porter."

She blushed, hands deep in the pocket of her jacket.

"How are you?" she asked.

"I'm well, thank you. And you?"

"I'm fine. You look exactly the same."

"Which means I've always looked old. Hmm. Well, tell me, what marvelous things have you done with your life? Written poetry for some experimental literary journal? Or perhaps a play, reaching for the very limits of human emotional experience?" he asked, his voice rising and falling in that old, familiar dramatic way, as if he should have been on the stage instead of before a classroom.

"I dropped out of college," she reminded him, trying not to sound too apologetic.

"Sometimes the most creative people do," he said. "Academia can't contain some of the biggest talents."

She smiled, lowering her gaze.

"Seriously, Jane, how has life been for you?"

"Good, Mr. Romney. I've got my own company in New York City—I'm a baker."

"A . . . baker?" he asked. "That surprises me. You always loved words so much."

"I bake cakes for lots of writers, actors, directors . . ."

"So you surround yourself with literary people."

"Yes," she said.

Just then Sylvie walked in, carrying the cake. No sooner had she entered the room than a portly man—balding, tweed jacket, leather elbow patches—sprinted to the door to help her. Together they bore the cake to the table, just a few feet away from Jane and Mr. Romney.

"I didn't even know you'd be here," Jane said, smiling, following her teacher's gaze to the confectionary replica she'd made of *Webster's Second.* It appeared so realistic, right down to the tattered cover and faded gold letters, that someone might be inspired to try looking up a word. Mr. Romney beamed.

"Well, if you did, you couldn't have made

me happier. You still love words, Jane Porter. I always think I'll open my *New Yorker* one day and see a poem or story by you."

"I don't write anymore," she said.

Mr. Romney looked at her sadly, as if he was seeing the ghost of her talent. He smiled, shaking his head. "I can't believe that," he said. "And I won't. You can't take an old teacher's dreams away that easily. I have to pick up my *New Yorker* every week and still hope, one day, to find you there."

Jane opened her mouth, to joke and tell him not to hold his breath, but she found she couldn't quite speak. She was facing the door, and at that moment she saw Mrs. Virginia Chadwick entering the cafeteria, being pushed in a wheelchair by a younger man. Mrs. Chadwick got a similar reception to Jane's mother—the teachers were thrilled to see her.

"Ah, another beloved teacher," Mr. Romney said. "Just like your mother. Fragile and beloved."

Jane barely heard; she was too busy staring.

The man had a beard and intense green eyes; he looked about ten years older than

Jane. He wore jeans and a black wool sweater and everything about him said he didn't want to stand out, didn't even want to be seen. He hung back, letting Mrs. Chadwick—obviously his mother—be pushed over to the table by her fellow teachers.

He was the man Jane had seen standing in Chloe's orchard.

"Jane," Sylvie said, beaming, grabbing her sister's hand. "I want you to meet my friend, John Dufour . . ."

"Hello, John," Jane said. "It's great to meet you."

Sylvie said, "Hi, Alan," and Jane eased away, leaving Sylvie and John and Mr. Romney to talk. She stood in the corner, her heart pounding hard. Mrs. Chadwick seemed to be scanning the room. Jane had never actually been introduced to her. She hadn't taught at the same school where Margaret had been principal. Their eyes met and locked for a moment; not recognizing her, Mrs. Chadwick kept looking around. Perhaps for her son: he had disappeared.

Jane felt pity for the woman's frail condition, the drooping left side of her face, the way her left arm fell into her lap. But her skin felt singed—her mother was on one side of the room and Mrs. Chadwick on the other: two ailing women, the architects of Jane's life.

She walked outside into the fresh air.

The tall bearded man stood under a yellow light, smoking. Her heart caught. She pictured him standing in the orchard. Knowing there was no way he knew who she was—he was in his forties, a good ten years ahead of her in school; his mother hadn't seen her standing with her mother, couldn't have put it together and figured out her identity—Jane forced a smile, and moved toward him as if homing in on a beacon.

"I know you," he said in a deep voice. "Don't I?"

"I don't think so," she said.

"You look familiar."

"Maybe. It's Rhode Island." She smiled wider at the inside reference to their small state.

He titled his head. "Emmylou," he said.

"Excuse me?"

"You like Emmylou Harris. I saw you driving by my orchard last week. You were playing 'Wrecking Ball,' loud."

"You have a good memory," she said, reddening.

"It's a quiet road. We don't get much traffic."

"So, what are you doing here?" she asked, her heart pounding and her mouth dry. He was either the man who had adopted Chloe or his brother, and she had to know.

"Being a dutiful son. My mother's Ginny Chadwick. She hasn't been feeling up to these things, but tonight she wanted to come. She's been looking forward to it all week."

"So, you're not a teacher?" she asked, not biting on the name, waiting for him to say *I'm an insurance agent.*

"No."

She nodded, waiting, gazing into his eyes. They were deep green, the color of a river, or of apple leaves, and dark and troubled. He wasn't a placid man, that was for sure. She saw him scowl slightly, grind his cigarette under the toe of his boot.

"So, what do you do?" she asked.

"I'm a farmer," he said.

Chloe's uncle. Jane stood still, and she felt a shiver go down her spine. Looking into his eyes was like looking in the mirror. She could see pain and loss there, and when

she took a half step closer, she knew that
what she was feeling was something apart
from Chloe.

"How about you?" he asked. "What do
you do?"

"I'm a baker," she said.

He laughed. "Do you make apple tarts?"

"One of my specialties," she said. "Why?"

"We're reopening the family farm stand,"
he said. "My niece was just saying we
should sell apple tarts again."

"Your niece," Jane breathed, feeling
every cell in her body go liquid.

"Yeah," he said. Squinting, the bright
yellow-orange schoolyard-crime-stopping
light in his eyes, he stuck out his hand. "I'm
Dylan Chadwick."

"Jane Porter," she said, catching her
breath. She watched him for a reaction.
Would he know her name? The adoption
was supposed to be done in strictest confidence, with her name and family identity
known only to his mother. Although handled
by Catholic Charities, Jane knew the details
had been arranged by her mother and his
mother: one child not ready to raise a baby,
another grieving over the inability to conceive, secrecy imperative to all.

"Nice to meet you, Jane."

"You, too."

"What are you doing here, by the way?" he asked, gesturing at the school.

"I'm here with my sister," she said, thinking, *This is my chance, this is my chance.*

She stared up into his eyes. He frowned slightly, as if he recognized his niece in her gaze. She shivered, feeling a physical connection to her daughter.

"Your niece likes apple tarts," she said.

"Yes. Chloe."

"That's a pretty name."

He nodded, not offering up any reasons for why it had been chosen. She wondered whether he even knew. . . .

Jane reached into her pocket. She hoped he couldn't see her hands trembling.

"It's chilly, even for April," Dylan said, mistaking the emotion for shivering.

"Yes, it is. But spring's here," Jane said. "It's just going to keep getting warmer."

He looked unconvinced. Glancing at the door, he asked, "You going back in?"

"In a minute," she said.

Jane wanted him to say Chloe's name again, to talk about her. But of course he wouldn't.

"Nice to meet you," she said.

"You, too."

She shook his hand a second time. It was rough, very callused, the hand of a man who worked in an apple orchard. He held on, for just half a second longer than necessary. Again, she felt a non-Chloe-related shiver go down her back as she stared into his green eyes.

"See you inside?" he asked, and she nodded.

Watching him go back into the school, Jane didn't dare follow. She couldn't chance Virginia, or Dylan, seeing her with her mother and Sylvie. Instead, Jane went to the car.

No one locked doors around here. She climbed in back. It was dark, in this part of the parking lot. She curled up on the seat, pulling her leather jacket around her. It was smooth-grained, very soft, an expensive gift last year from an independent film producer for whom she had baked a cake featuring the movie's title.

The spring air was as chilly as Dylan had said, but she hardly noticed. For so many years, she had felt a hole in her life. She couldn't bear to name it, because there was nothing to be done about it. She had given up her child; there hadn't been an alternative. It had made logical, perfect sense.

And it was so long ago now, over fifteen years, that it sometimes had the distance of a story, something she had read about. But right now, the memories flooded back. She remembered the day she had told her mother: Her hands were sweating, and she was dizzy with morning sickness.

And she remembered her mother's tears and panic. She had cried because Jane would have to take an entire year off from Brown. She could stay at home until she began to show, and then she would have to go away. Margaret contacted the Sisters of Mercy at Salve Regina, and they arranged for Jane to go to the St. Joseph Retreat House in Bristol.

Jane remembered trying to look as small as possible, so she wouldn't have to leave home. She dressed in baggy jeans and oversized shirts. When fall came, she was relieved: she could wear huge sweatshirts. One day, she looked down at her body in the bathtub, and her belly button had popped out. It was a shock. She felt so out of control of everything. She had huddled in the tub, sobbing.

When her mother walked in and found her, she'd put her arm around Jane's naked shoulders and cried too. Jane had felt so embarrassed, but she'd needed her mother's comfort. She'd heard Margaret making the call to Sister Celeste Marie. Sylvie was at Brown by then; Jane was glad she wasn't there to hear it. A car was sent, and Jane went away. Rhode Island is the smallest state in the union, but to Jane, it felt as if she had been transported to Siberia.

There were other unwed mothers there. They were all young, from many parts of the country. It was like a college, where the only curriculum was childbirth. After the babies were born, the women disappeared. Jane turned inward. To pay her way, she worked in the kitchen, making beautiful cakes. The baby growing inside her was her most constant company, and she grew more attached every day.

Her father's actions had made Jane realistic about separation. She had avoided getting close to the other mothers—knowing they would all go their separate ways and never want to relive those months at St. Joseph's. But she couldn't avoid bonding tightly, so tightly, with her baby. Although the nuns told the girls to avoid thinking about naming, or holding, or playing with their children, Jane disobeyed. It was all she ever thought about.

Once she sneaked out.

She took bus fare from a cookie jar in the kitchen and walked out to the main road. When the Providence bus came, she climbed aboard. She took a window seat. The bus roared up the bay, through Barrington and East Providence, into Fox Point, and onto Providence's East Side, and the Brown campus.

It stopped on Thayer Street. Jane pressed her palm against the cold window. She was hungry for tea at Penguin's, a movie at the Avon, poetry at Horace Mann, her carrel at the Rock. She was aching for Jeffrey. And her eyes filled with tears, at the idea of missing Brown, missing her chance to go to college with Sylvie.

"This is where your father goes to school," she whispered to the baby, hand on her protruding belly. "This is where we met, and where you came into being . . ."

As the bus turned onto Angell Street, she caught a glimpse of Jeffrey. He was walking along, all alone, his backpack slung over one shoulder. Jane stared at him. He was lost in thought. She wondered whether he was thinking of her; but she didn't think so.

She and the baby were alone. He had wanted it that way.

When she returned to St. Joseph's, she was met by disapproving nuns. They prohibited her from baking cakes the rest of her time there. They wanted her to learn her lesson: She had made one big mistake, and she had to learn not to make any more.

She had to learn sense. There was such a thing as leaving well enough alone.

But sometimes even the best sense left a person feeling crazy. Jane had done the right thing, and it had left her half out of her mind. Every fifteen-year-old girl she saw made her think of her daughter. She was haunted by the truth—of what she had done, and of the girl she wasn't allowed to know. But she had to know her. Somehow, Jane knew she'd die if she didn't. This trip home to Rhode Island had been a long time coming.

And she had just met Dylan Chadwick

and talked with him about his niece. His niece, Chloe.

And Jane, alone in the dark car, said her name now: "Chloe," she whispered, holding herself. "Chloe."

CHAPTER 7

Maybe it was going to the high school and running into Mr. Romney that sent Jane spinning back through time. Or perhaps it was meeting Chloe's uncle, hearing her name spoken so freely, making her seem so real.

Sometimes Jane wondered whether the whole thing was a dream. Whether she had ever actually been pregnant, had a daughter at all. It had happened so long ago. And that was how she thought of it: as if it had *happened*. As if an event had come to pass, one that Jane had had almost no control over. Her life had been taken over. . . .

But she had had some control. There had been so much love. She couldn't deny that, no matter how convenient it would be to brush it under the rug. She had loved the boy. Chloe's father. She had loved the baby growing inside her. And she had even, mixed in with hate, loved her mother for wanting the best for her.

At night, asleep in her old room, she dreamed of the past. She dreamed of her first love. His name was Jeffrey Hayden. He had curly brown hair and worried eyes. She loved him from the first day she saw him, early September, freshman year at Brown. Both loaded down with books, they bumped into each other on the steps of Horace Mann, on their way in to meet their English professors.

They actually cracked foreheads, and all their books fell in a heap. Jane saw stars. Jeffrey knelt beside her, touching her eyebrow.

"Are you okay?" he asked.

"Yes, are you?"

"No, because you're bleeding . . ."

She laughed. "I'm bleeding, and you're not okay?"

He nodded. He reached into his pocket—he was wearing a plaid short-sleeved shirt and rumpled khakis—for a handkerchief. It was clean and white, immaculately folded. That made Jane think of her sister, Sylvie, who was obsessive about perfectly folded laundry, and the connection was so strong, she was drawn to look deeply into his eyes.

"There," he said, dabbing at her eyebrow.

She felt a rumble of emotion. Her father had left when she was very young. She had had a female pediatrician. Shy and studious, she hadn't had any real boyfriends. She couldn't think of any time in her life that a man had ever been so sweet and caring to her before. She bit her lip.

His touch was gentle. He pressed her cheek with the cool fingers of one hand while wiping away the blood above her eye with the other.

"I think you might need stitches," he said.

"No, I'm sure it's fine . . ." she began, but the sensations in her heart were so strong, she could barely speak.

"I'll worry about you, about you having a scar, if you don't," he said. "I couldn't stand to think I'd caused a scar on your face."

"I don't scar," she said, grinning at him, noticing the flecks of gold in his blue eyes, wondering why he looked so worried. "I'm tough."

"If you say so," he said doubtfully, grinning back. They began to gather their books. Jane took hers; Jeffrey took his. They shook hands and said good-bye.

It wasn't until she went back to her dorm that she realized that she was missing one of her books, *Myths: From Medieval to Post-Modern,* and had one of his, *The History of Literary Criticism.* He had written his name in front: Jeffrey Hayden, Wayland. She wracked her brain for his dorm's location; just across George Street, from where she lived in Little-field.

She carried his book around in her back-pack for a day and a half, till she saw him again, at a table with his friends at the Sharpe Refectory.

When she handed him his book, he reached into his briefcase for hers. They smiled at each other as she saw that he had a big, purple bump on his forehead, just like hers.

He cleared off the seat beside him, and they ate together that day. They began to study together. Both planned to major in English. Jane wanted to write and teach high school. Jeffrey planned to become a professor. From the very beginning, Jane adored his brilliance, but he used to tell her that his mind was only a fraction as huge and sharp as hers. She would be lost in reading, deep into *Beowulf* or *Sir Gawain,* and when she glanced up, she'd catch him staring at her.

"What are you doing?" she asked.

"Studying," he said.

"No, you're watching me."

"Literature's supposed to be the story of the world," he said. "And you're the world."

That was before he'd even kissed her.

Their kisses . . .

These were the things Jane dreamed about, back at home in her old bed, fifteen years later. Jeffrey's kisses.

In her dreams, just as in real life, they had been so tender.

Jane was lying on her back, on the narrow bed in her dorm room. Jeffrey was at the desk. Crazy bright light was coming through the window, as if the sun was setting in the hedge just outside. Jane squinted and shielded her eyes. Music thumped in the corridor.

Suddenly Jeffrey was kneeling on the floor beside the bed. Jane held one hand over her face, to block the angle of the setting sun. It was October. His bruised forehead had long healed. But his eyes were just as worried as they'd been the first day they'd met. She wanted to ask him what he was so worried about. She opened her mouth to ask.

His lips were thin and taut. She stared at them. His fingers touched her cheek; they felt smooth. She remembered their crash—how gently he had caressed her. The memory gave her an involuntary shake—a miniseizure. Then he kissed her.

In her dreams, the kiss was as real as it had been that day. Jeffrey bent down, his face just above hers, kissing her softly, again and again. Just the sweetest, softest brush of his lips, then another, then another. Their arms were at their sides. His mouth was warm on hers. Jane arched, wanting something more.

Her hand touched his arm. His upper arm, his muscle. Her fingers slid up the sleeve of his blue short-sleeved shirt. The twilight made him look tan, although like Jane, he was library-pale. Her eyes opened and closed. She was on fire, and she wanted to be sure she was still alive. His tongue touched hers. It was all over.

They fell in love.

He was from Oceanside, Long Island.

She was from Twin Rivers, Rhode Island.
School was their life. They loved Brown and
each other. They went to football games together, wrapped in each other's jackets as
the Bruins consistently avoided victory.
They thrilled to their classmates shouting,
"Let's go, Bruno—Bruno, let's go!" but were
both too shy to shout themselves.

She had one sister and a mother and had
been abandoned by her father as a young
girl. He had one brother and two sisters,
and his father was a doctor, and his parents
had just celebrated their twenty-fifth wedding anniversary. When Thanksgiving came,
she cried, because they would be apart for
four days.

Christmas break was even harder. They
spent the bare minimums at their homes,
with the families they both adored, in order
to return to Providence the instant the dor-
mitories reopened.

They had sex. It was wonderful. Jane was
Catholic, so there was quite a bit of guilt
and sin to get past. Her mother had drilled
into her the idea that nice girls saved themselves for marriage, and deep down Jane
had absorbed that credo and believed it to
her core. But she loved Jeffrey so much,

and he loved her. It was unthinkable that they would ever be with anyone else, that they *wouldn't* get married.

It was a tautological impossibility.

She was taking Philosophy 101, learning to open her mind in ways she had previously considered impossible—considering that her mind had been youthfully and culturally and religiously and even tribally closed—so she philosophically thought about love, and about sex, and about time, and she decided that time was the problem: Since she and Jeffrey loved each other and always would, what did the sequence actually matter? Sex before or after an actual marriage cere-mony? Connection was the important thing. Connection and love.

Sex was the bridge between their bodies and minds. When Jeffrey held her in his arms, their thin bodies pressing together, they didn't need language. Their skin spoke. It really did. Jane felt his love in his mouth and his arms and his penis. She felt it in her own toes and fingers and breasts.

Being alive took on new meaning. Life ex-ploded. Music had new significance and emotional depth, stories were to be related to their own lives, to each other. Sex was the decoder ring to everything. Jane's mother distrusted men—and sadly, rightly so. Obviously Thomas, Jane's father, was no Jeffrey. For many years, Jane and Sylvie had been soaking up their mother's unhappiness; Jane couldn't wait till her sister met someone like Jeffrey, to prove how wrong their mother had been.

No myth had ever been written that wasn't about Jane and Jeffrey. Pyramus and Thisbe: they had the same kind of love, all but the unhappy ending. Shakespeare had had them in mind when he'd invented Romeo and Juliet—the bliss part, not the tragedy.

There could never be anything tragic about Jane and Jeffrey.

Freshman year, sophomore year. Conscious of their responsibilities to each other, they both practiced birth control. Jane went on the pill. For the first month, until the hormones took effect, Jeffrey used condoms. The pill made her gain a little weight, but Jeffrey loved when her breasts got bigger. She popped out of her old bra, went to Davol Square Lingerie to buy some new ones.

But no matter how sexy Jeffrey found her

new body, Jane never liked the feelings. Her nipples hurt. And she didn't like the fullness that made her old jeans feel too snug and her thighs rub together.

She went back to the doctor and got fitted for a diaphragm. Jeffrey supported her decision, and to be extra safe, went back to using condoms and foam as well. Jane knew the church would condemn her for using birth control, but Jeffrey told her that attitude was patriarchal and, if it made her feel guilty, even cruel—that she was the best person on earth, and she should trust herself, rely on her own goodness and excellent judgment.

Jane loved him for that. To her, birth control was just a tool, a way to help women enjoy their own bodies and lives, to express love to the men they had chosen to spend their lives with.

Sophomore year, she lived with two roommates on Wriston Quad and he shared a suite with three other guys in Morriss-Champlin. They took turns sleeping at each other's dorm; and they began to talk about getting into a coed suite together for junior year. Jane had a part-time job at Sharpe Refectory, and whenever they made pies, she would save a little bit of crust and make tiny fruit or jelly tarts for her beloved.

They began to talk about where they would go to graduate school. Whether they should get married before or after Jane got her master's degree. They knew they couldn't wait until Jeffrey finished his Ph.D.

Jane's recurring dream, the one she had every night after meeting Chloe's uncle, was of the night Chloe was conceived.

It was Campus Dance, the spring of sophomore year. Her dream was as vivid as the night itself had been. The Friday night of graduation and reunion weekend, the campus was transformed into a magical ballroom under the stars, with six hundred glowing paper lanterns.

Seniors and their families, classmates, alumni older than Jane and Jeffrey's grandparents, and Brown faculty gathered together to dance the night away. People wore everything from gowns and tuxedos to Hawaiian shirts and sarongs. Jeffrey wore his father's dinner jacket over one of his habitual plaid shirts; Jane wore a simple black dress she'd had since high school graduation.

They danced to Duke and the Esoterics

on the Main Green, student bands on Lincoln Field, and listened to jazz at Carrie Tower on the Front Green. The night was so romantic, and Jane felt so in love. She was with the man she loved, in the place where they had met, where they belonged.

"I want to take you somewhere," Jeffrey whispered, holding her in his arms as if he couldn't bear to not be touching her constantly.

"Where?"

"Our place," he said. "They're going to change the name after we graduate."

She followed him, having no idea what he meant. They crossed the stately Main Green, transformed from academia to romance by music and lanterns and dancing and laughter. Neoclassical and brick buildings rose around them. Carrie Tower, romantically named for someone's wife—or was it daughter?—looked like an Italian bell tower. The great and massive wrought-iron fence surrounded the green, coming together at the Van Wickle Gates, opened only twice each year: to greet the incoming freshmen and to discharge the graduating seniors.

Running past the Rock—the imposing

and modern John D. Rockefeller Library, where they had done so much studying and kissing at carrels downstairs—they crossed George Street, and there they were. Jeffrey swept his arm into the sky, as if he wanted to give it to Jane, as part of the night's package.

"Here it is," he said. "The Jane and Jeffrey Porter-Hayden English Department."

"That's Horace Mann." She smiled, staring up at the big square brick building.

"Horace who? Wasn't he the valedictorian for the class of 1819? Well, times change. And for all the great oratory and education Horace gave the world, making Brown proud, this building should be known for something more important."

"What?" Jane asked, looking into Jeffrey's gold-flecked blue eyes as he put his hands on both sides of her face and smiled. For the first time, she noticed that he had lost his look of worry. It was totally gone. "What should this place be known for?"

The music from Campus Dance echoed between the buildings. They heard Duke segue from "Moon River" to "Keep on Rocking in the Free World." Jane's heart fluttered in her chest, right up to her throat.

"For us," Jeffrey whispered, pulling her close, dancing with her to the music. "For bringing us together."

"You're right: Horace who?"

They laughed.

He kissed her lips, touched her forehead. She could almost feel the original bruise. She brushed his forehead, and they laughed. He led her up the steps. There were two front doors, an oddity: Before housing the English Department, the building had had the distinction of being the first coed dorm in the Ivy League, and it had separate entrances for men and women.

Jane tried one door, and it swung open. Shocked, they looked at each other. They started to back away, then, laughing quietly, stepped inside. Was a professor working late, or had someone forgotten to lock up?

The hall was dark. Holding hands, they walked along, their footsteps echoing as the strains of Duke drifted in. Shadows came through the tall windows, otherworldly and surreal.

"Geeks," Jeffrey said, kissing her neck.

"Who, us?"

"Everyone else is out dancing under the stars, and we're making out in the English

Department." He tugged on her zipper. She untucked his shirt. Pressing her against the wall, he kissed her hard. Filled with passion, she could barely breathe.

They had never made love in a public place. It was fun, it was funny, it was wildly exciting, it was outrageously adult. No one in their class had ever done this, Jane was sure. No one in her family would be so bold, so daring with love.

Jeffrey led her into a downstairs office. He placed his father's jacket and plaid shirt on the Chinese rug behind the secretary's desk and lowered Jane onto them. Their eyes locked, and she felt the worry showing between her eyes.

"Do you have . . . ?" she began.

"I didn't bring one," he said. "You don't have the . . ."

She giggled. "I don't carry it with me."

He kissed her. His eyes were earnest, but worry-free. "Do you know if it's a safe time?"

"I'm not a math major."

They both laughed, and she tried to calculate, but she had never been sure which were the safe times of the month—some girls said the middle of the cycle was when people got pregnant, but her roommate knew someone who had had sex during her period one month and had missed it the next. So Jane closed her eyes and tried to count back, to remember the dates of her last period, but she wasn't someone who kept track, didn't have a clear mental calendar regarding her body.

"It's just this once," he whispered.

"But . . ." she began.

"I love you, Jane."

"I love you, Jeffrey."

The words rang in the air. Weren't those words what mattered? Didn't they tell a story more profound than any tome that had ever been taught at Brown? Love was the thing. Love was everything. Love was bigger than space. It took up Jane's entire heart, entire being, it took up space, it took Jane everywhere she went.

They made love. He entered her. She closed her eyes, feeling him glide in. The wetness was amazing. He filled her. No two people had ever created such heat. The intensity rushed through her, from the spot just between her legs, straight into her heart. It felt like an arrow, and for the first time in her life, she understood everything about the myth of Cupid.

The arrow struck deeply, and forever.

Jane got pregnant that night.

Jane knew the minute it happened. She held onto the secret, even from Jeffrey. She wanted to be sure. Filled with love, she had expected to be filled with dread. But that expectation and Jane's honest emotions were two really different things.

She fell in love with the baby.

Instantly, totally: as much as—no, more than she was in love with the father. The baby was part of her, and she of it. How was such a feeling possible, and how could she explain it?

She didn't explain it; at least, not at first. After Campus Dance came Pops Concert, and then graduation and the commencement procession, when the Van Wickle gates opened for the second time that academic year. Jeffrey would be going to New York, to a summer job as research assistant to someone at Columbia, and Jane would be working for her mother's cousin at the Twin Rivers Bakery. They would return to Brown in September, along with Jane's sis-

ter Sylvie, who would be starting her freshman year.

Jane had wept to say good-bye. So had
Jeffrey. They had held each other so hard,
never suspecting it would be the last time.
Or almost the last time.

❧

In her dreams in her old room at her
mother's house, Jane cried until her pillow
was soaked. She held her body, as if she
could hold it together, hold everything inside, take everything back, pull all the
pieces of three lives back together.

One night Sylvie, hearing Jane cry, stum-
bled into her room. Cool blue moonlight
came through the almost-bare April trees,
and when Jane opened her eyes, she saw
her sister on her bed in a white nightgown.
Jane's dream had ripped her heart from her
chest, as if the past were a lion that could
eat her alive.

Sylvie held Jane's hand. The wind blew,
and the branches scraped the window.
Jane sobbed, shaking her head.

"Let it be over, Jane," Sylvie whispered.

"But it's not . . ." Jane said.

"It is if you'll let it. Let it all stay in the past."

"It's not possible, Sylvie."

"You're torturing yourself," she said. "It happens every time you come home."

Jane stared at her sister, feeling her breath slow down. She was awake now. The dream was over. Or was it? The dream never really ended.

Jane closed her eyes. If only Sylvie knew what it was like. A scrap of Jane's heart had torn free, was out in the world. Alive and vibrant and living on the edge of an orchard. Liked apple tarts. Named by her mother, named by Jane.

Named Chloe.

CHAPTER 8

Two Saturdays in a row and several after-
school afternoons in between, Chloe
worked on the stand. On the second Saturday, the air was fresh. It smelled of new
grass and wet paint. The apple blossoms
were heavy on the boughs, clusters of hot
pink about to burst into snow white flowers.

Uncle Dylan had let Chloe pick the colors, so she was painting the stand itself
blue, a delicate shade of teal, the color of
eggs laid by Araucana chickens. The
shelves were going to be yellow, as bright
as buttercups.

Chloe wore denim overalls with a blue
T-shirt underneath, and old gym sneakers.
Silver hoop earrings snagged in her dark
hair, which fell in her face. She should have
worn a cap. Not being an expert painter, she

was kind of making a mess. Paint took forever to cover the splintery old wood.
Chloe's hands were both blue, and somehow paint had sprayed finely across her
right cheek.

Her parents were acting very "no comment" about the whole operation. Her father
had grown up on the farm, of which this orchard occupied about forty acres, and he
considered working on the farm stand to be
a big step backward. He had gone to Roger
Williams College and become an actuary
and then a successful insurance agent, just
to get his family's hands out of the soil.

A couple of years ago, for her parents'
twenty-fifth anniversary, Chloe and Mona
had gotten Uncle Dylan to let them have a
barn dance. They had wanted it to be a surprise, but being only thirteen, they had
needed help. Uncle Dylan was too much in
mourning to do much, so Chloe had had to
ask her mother.

She had been so happy. Chloe remembered how her cheeks had turned bright
pink, as if she was a young girl. She had
hugged Chloe so tight. Together they had
made the guest list: Chloe's two grandmothers; her mother's brother and his wife,

who lived in Portland, Maine; her father's
friends from the Rotary; her mother's friends
from the garden club.

Her mother had made beautiful invita-
tions showing the barn, all decorated with
streamers and little white lights. Then, in
real life, they had set out to make the barn
look just like the picture. It was a magical
night—and hardly cost anything! Chloe's
mother made lots of casseroles. They had
plenty of apple cider. One of her dad's Rotary friends was a DJ in his spare time, and
they got him to do the music for free. People danced all night. When Chloe and Mona
got tired, they just climbed up to the hayloft
and fell asleep.

Chloe wished that memories like that
would make her parents like the orchard
more. They were so wonderful in some
ways, but very frustrating in others. They
had a modern vision of the land: Sell it, de-
velop it, say good-bye to it. While Chloe and
Uncle Dylan loved it too much for that.

Right now, Uncle Dylan was working in
the orchard. She could hear him, hauling the
young trees to be planted. Once he drove
by, riding high on his green tractor, the huge
yellow wheels peeking at Chloe like big

eyes. Uncle Dylan waved, and she laughed. He wore sunglasses, and he looked like a spy playing farmer.

He didn't smile back. Uncle Dylan used to be the funniest grown-up Chloe ever knew, in spite of the fact he had a badge and a gun. Both Chloe and Isabel thought he was cooler than any uncle or dad had a right to be. Neither of them would have, in a million years, expected to see him working the land.

Chloe wished she'd worn her watch, but after school yesterday she'd gotten paint on the face, and now it was sitting on her bureau. Mona was supposed to come over. Chloe hoped she'd hurry. The sound of her own paintbrush slapping the wood was driving her truly batty. It was talking to her; was that weird? Not in voices, or anything, but just in a rhythmic little singsong: *I'm bored, are you bored? Will the cats appreciate all you've done to buy them nice food? Araucana chickens eat corn and lay pretty eggs.*

Chloe *really* needed someone to talk to.

And just then, in the strangest twist of fate possible, an old blue car came down the road, slowed as it approached the stand, and stopped.

Chloe craned her neck, to see who it might be. A lady, alone in the front seat. Like Uncle Dylan, she wore sunglasses. She had on a black leather jacket—very cool. And she had dark hair with a long blue scarf tied around it, to keep it out of her face. Chloe really loved the look. The lady stared at Chloe for a few seconds.

Chloe tilted her head. Did she know this person? It seemed as if she did. Chloe wondered: Is she an old teacher, or a friend of my parents? She continued painting, while preparing to smile in recognition the minute the lady told her her name.

The lady got out of the car, carrying a basket.

"Hi," she said.

"Hi," Chloe said back.

"Nice day for a ride in the country," the lady said, walking closer. She was medium height, thin, wearing black jeans and a blue-and-white-striped T-shirt under her black leather jacket. Around her neck was a silver disk hanging from a black cord. She held the basket with two hands; the contents were covered with a flowered cloth napkin.

"Yeah, I guess so." Chloe smiled. "Though,

when you live in the country, it feels like a nice day for a ride in the city."

"Oh, you like the city?" the woman asked, brightening. "I live there!"

"Providence?" Chloe asked.

"New York City," the woman said.

"Oh, wow," Chloe said. She lowered her paintbrush. No one she knew lived in New York. She had loved visiting Isabel there. Aunt Amanda would take them to see the butterflies at the Museum of Natural History, then for hot chocolate at Sarabeth's. And Uncle Dylan would come home from work and take everyone out to dinner at that restaurant high above the city, with views of all the jeweled buildings and bridges, that made it feel as if they were eating in a plane, the one that was gone now . . .

"Do you like New York?" the lady asked.

"I used to go, when I was little," Chloe said. "Is that zoo still there?"

"The one in the Bronx or the one in the park?"

"The park, I think," Chloe said. "The one with that clock on the arch, with the bronze animals that strike the bell."

"The Delacorte clock," the woman said,

beaming. "In Central Park. You've been there . . ."

Chloe nodded.

"That zoo's still there. Actually, they both are. Did you like going?"

"I didn't like seeing those seals in the city," Chloe said, frowning. "Their pool is nice and all, but they belong in the ocean."

"That's a very compassionate attitude," the woman said.

Chloe nodded, starting to paint again. "That's my downfall," she said.

The woman seemed to be holding back a smile. "Really?"

"I care about everything."

Chloe concentrated on covering the next board with blue paint. Her chest heaved with a wave of emotion. She didn't understand it, and she didn't want the woman to see. Maybe it was thinking about Isabel; or maybe it was picturing those seals.

"Certain creatures belong in certain places," Chloe explained after a minute. "It's just the way it is. People always think they can move nature around, but it never works. Seals need the cold ocean, lions need the Serengeti, my cats need this orchard."

The woman cleared her throat. Chloe glanced up. Why was she looking away?

"You okay?" Chloe asked.

"I'm fine," the lady said. "It's just that I feel the same way."

Chloe nodded. Just then, she realized how odd it was to be having this conversation with a total stranger. "Um, we're not open yet," Chloe said, gesturing at the half-painted stand. "I have to give it one more coat, and then we have to figure out what to sell."

The lady smiled. "You're doing a great job."

"Thanks."

"Your uncle said you were helping him. You must be Chloe."

Chloe nodded and smiled.

"I'm Jane."

Chloe felt a slight thrill: How cool to have a grown-up introduce herself by her first name. Who was she? Could she be Uncle Dylan's girlfriend? Chloe had heard her parents speculating on when Uncle Dylan might begin dating again. It had been four years since the tragedy. And Chloe knew, even though it was never talked about, that he and Aunt Amanda had been separated at the time it happened. . . . Just in case, Chloe sized this woman up.

"Do you know Uncle Dylan from New York?" Chloe asked.

"No," Jane said, looking a little confused. "Doesn't he live here?"

"Yeah, but before Isabel . . . Never mind. Yes, he lives here."

Jane let it pass, and Chloe was relieved. She didn't like to talk about what had happened to her cousin.

"I met him the other night, at the Educators' Potluck."

"Oh, right—he drove my grandmother. Are you a teacher?"

"No," Jane said. "I'm a baker." She lifted the basket, and then handed it to Chloe. Chloe hesitated. Her hands were totally covered with blue paint. Jane saw, smiled, and helped out by lifting the napkin.

"Apple tarts!" Chloe exclaimed. She peered inside at the sweetest, prettiest, darlingest apple tarts she'd ever seen. There were four of them, golden brown, each of them decorated differently: an apple, a tree covered in blossoms, a tree with leaves and apples, and a bird's nest. "I love them! Are they for Uncle Dylan?"

"Yes," Jane said. "And you. Since you're doing all the hard work, I think you deserve one."

"I want the bird's nest," Chloe said. She looked up into the woman's clear blue eyes. "See, I love birds. And animals. That's what I'm known for. In fact, it's why Uncle Dylan gave me this job. Because I need money to buy special food for all the orchard cats."

Jane nodded, smiling, and Chloe thought of her saying "compassionate" earlier.

"Thank you," Chloe said. She scanned the orchard, for a sign of Uncle Dylan. Although she heard his tractor, she couldn't see him. Jane followed her gaze.

"It's so beautiful," she said. "With all the trees getting ready to bloom. Look at those blossoms! By tomorrow, the orchard will look like a white cloud. I can actually feel it—"

Chloe's hair tingled, as if there was lightning in the air. Which was ridiculous; the sun was shining brightly. But she knew what Jane meant. "It's like that in the spring," she said. "Something's always about to happen."

"Like what?"

Chloe thought. "Like eggs about to hatch. And the apple blossoms . . ."

Jane nodded. "Anticipation."

"Yeah."

They smiled at each other, and Chloe felt the funny lightning again. It sizzled through her hair, across her forehead, through her body, and out her toes. Just then another car came down the street. Jane jumped—she looked so startled, and she stared intently at the car, as if she expected to know the person getting out. But she relaxed when she saw Mona—obviously someone she didn't know—getting out of her parents' Volvo. Chloe, distracted by Jane's reaction, almost missed taking in the full spectacle of Mona, ready for work.

"Looks like you have a helper," Jane said.

"Oh, my God," Chloe said. Here came Mona, covered from head to toe in a plastic rain poncho, hood pulled over her hair, and safety goggles over her glasses. She was pulling on one pair of rubber gloves, and handing another to Chloe.

"Too late," Chloe said, wiggling blue fingers.

"Darling, paint is hell on your hands," Mona said. Then, smiling at Jane, held out the spare pair and asked, "Want to join the party?"

"I think I'll leave you girls to it," Jane said, backing away.

"No, don't go!" Chloe said, surprising herself. "This is my best friend, Mona. Mona, this is Jane."

"Hey," Mona said.

"Oh, I'd better get home," Jane said. "I need to spell my sister—she's home with our mother, and she needs a break . . ."

"Granny-sitting," Mona said solemnly, giving Chloe a knowing glance through the safety goggles. Chloe winced, hoping Jane wasn't offended by the comment.

"Both our grandmothers had strokes last year," Chloe explained. "We've seen them go through a lot."

"Well, they're lucky to have granddaughters who care so much," Jane said.

Both girls nodded. Chloe heard Uncle Dylan's tractor getting closer. She pointed, but Jane was already climbing into her car. She got behind the wheel and just sat there for a moment, waving at Chloe through the windshield. Chloe waved back. She had the strangest lump in her throat, almost as if she was standing dockside, watching someone getting ready to embark on an ocean journey.

"What's in the basket?" Mona asked, lifting the blue flowered napkin.

Before Chloe could reply, Mona gasped. "Teeny tiny little pies!"

"Apple tarts," Chloe corrected.

"And a business card," Mona said. She lifted it out, between the fingers of her rubber-gloved hand. The glove was quite amusing. It was gaudily adorned with huge fake diamond rings and an emerald bracelet.

Chloe, heedless of her own paint-sticky fingers, took the card. She read it:

Calamity Bakery
512 West 22nd Street
New York, NY 10011
917–555–6402

"Is that hers?" Mona asked.

Chloe stared, nodding. "I think so."

" 'Calamity Jane,' do you think that's what the name means?" Mona asked.

"I'll bet . . ." Chloe said, smiling.

"Cool for an older person," Mona said. "I liked her leather jacket, too."

"What's going on here?" Uncle Dylan

called, roaring over on the tractor. He idled the engine and climbed off. "Break time?"

"Your friend came by," Chloe said, gesturing at the basket and showing him the card. He leaned down to read the print, starting to take the card from her hand, but Chloe didn't let it go.

"Oh, wow," he said, glancing into the basket, still tugging on the card. "I didn't know she was from Calamity . . . best place in New York. And I told her my niece was crazy about apple tarts."

"Crazy for apple tarts," Mona said, doing a spastic little dance. Chloe forgave her; she knew Mona had a significant crush on Uncle Dylan.

"You seem to want her card," he said to Chloe.

"Yeah," she said. "For a souvenir. The first person to stop at the new stand. You know how some places hang the first dollar bill? Well, I'm going to hang the first card."

"Where's a nine-one-seven area code?" Mona asked. "Did she come all the way from freaking Alaska?"

"New York City," Chloe said, feeling proud for some reason.

"Nine-one-seven is for a New York City

cell phone," Uncle Dylan amended. "Or a beeper."

"Huh," Mona said. "A baker on the move. So, do you want me to paint, or what?"

"Here's the brush," Chloe said, reaching for her own private tart, the one with the bird's nest on it. She offered the others to Mona and Uncle Dylan. He reached for the tart with the flowering tree on it, and Mona ignored the question, dipping her brush into the paint. Chloe bit in and closed her eyes. The crust was so flaky and light, and the apples tasted as if they'd just been picked off the tree.

"Whoa, it's good," she heard Uncle Dylan say.

"Yeah. It's good," Chloe said, her eyes still closed. She wondered what Jane was doing in Rhode Island. She wondered when she was going back to New York.

She hoped it wouldn't be soon.

Jane drove to the edge of the orchard, where the country lane met the main road. She knew she should turn left and head for home, but she couldn't. She stared at the white lines on the black tar. Her hands were shaking.

She had just met her daughter.

Chloe had her eyes. She had the same pale, almost-gray, blue eyes as Jane. And she had a raven's wing of dark hair, falling across her finely sculpted cheekbone. Jane looked in the rearview mirror, saw the same straight dark hair, the same facial bones.

She raised her left hand from the steering wheel, smelled the blue paint on her fingers. It was just a tiny bit; she had brushed the top of the stand as she had walked away.

Her hands were small, just like her mother's and sister's. When she was young, she had wished for beautiful hands with long fingers and long nails. Elegant hands for playing the piano, wearing rings, gesturing expressively. She knew that Sylvie had wished the same thing. Before the days of nail salons, the two sisters had made themselves fake nails out of cardboard, just to see what it would look like.

But right now, she loved her hands. They were the same as Chloe's. Jane had seen: the thin wrists, small hands, short fingernails. Chloe had the Porter hands, the same as her mother, aunt, and grandmother.

Jane sat in her car, unsure of what to do next. She knew she had to go home, to stay with her mother while Sylvie went out to dinner with John Dufour. But she didn't want to leave the orchard.

With the car windows open, she smelled flowers and new leaves. It was the scent of the color green, chlorophyll, sharp on the back of her throat. Birds sang in the trees; she watched them fly from branch to branch, blurs of blue and brown.

Questions swirled in her mind, and they all seemed so big, so impossible. What did Jane hope for? Why had she come here today? Why had she come home to Rhode Island with no immediate plans to return to New York, with a sign on her door and a forwarding message on her cell phone?

She couldn't answer; all she knew was that she had a pressure in her heart. Something between heaviness and an ache, as if an old injury had suddenly resurfaced, as if an old scar wanted to remind her it had never quite healed.

Suddenly, after fifteen years of mostly staying away, Jane had known it was time to come home. Right now she didn't seem able to shift into drive, step on the gas, turn on her signal, and drive onto the main road, to arrive on time so that Sylvie could go out. Jane was frozen in place, unable to leave the orchard.

And of all the questions she was asking herself, all the things she had to wonder about, that was the only thing that made perfect sense.

Chloe was here.

CHAPTER 9

On Saturday night, Margaret lay in bed, surrounded by books. They were her friends and companions. She knew them, and they knew her: Dickens, Austen, Christie, Wodehouse, Colwin, Updike, McMurtry, Godden. Their covers comforted her: some old and cracking, others bright and barely opened. She enjoyed reading the more modern books' dust jackets: editorial descriptions, quotes offered by other authors; she took particular interest in the author's photograph.

From the photographs on the back of their books, she had learned that John Cheever loved dogs, that Laurie Colwin had once worn a striped shirt and tilted her head as she'd squinted in the sunlight. These were people Margaret wished she could get to know.

Sighing, she lowered *Family Happiness* to her knees. Colwin's characters came from loving families who weathered each other's weak spots with affection and equanimity.

"Jane," Margaret called. "Jane!"

No reply. Yet Margaret could hear her up in the attic, going through God-knew-what boxes. Fresh from reading some lovely dialogue between *Family Happiness*'s Wendy and her daughter Polly, Margaret wanted to modify but basically reenact the same thing between herself and Jane.

"Jane!" she called louder.

A moment later, her elder daughter walked in, glittering with dust motes. She wore black jeans and a purple T-shirt with a cupcake in the center. That locket she always wore dangled from her neck. Her hands and forearms looked dark with dust. Margaret's lips tightened.

"Dear, what are you doing up there? Sylvie finally has a date and leaves us alone for a night, and you abandon me!"

"*Finally* has a date?" Jane asked, raising her eyebrows.

"Yes. With John Dufour."

"I know who she's with; I just don't think it's very flattering for you to say 'finally.' She's smart and gorgeous, and he's obviously smitten beyond belief."

"Oh, I didn't mean it that way. My God, you misunderstood!" Margaret said. "I mean, she's so dutiful, never wanting to leave me alone, even since you've come home, all they ever do is play Scrabble downstairs . . ."

"You mean she doesn't trust me alone with you?" Jane asked, grinning.

"I don't mean that at *all*! Dear! Please, don't be so contrary," Margaret said, wanting to steer the conversation to something lovely. Surely Laurie Colwin's mothers and daughters would sail through this situation more smoothly.

"I'm sorry," Jane said, perching on the end of the bed, one foot resting on the rocking chair.

"Polly knows how much Wendy loves her," Margaret said, hugging the book.

"Who?"

"The Solo-Millers," Margaret said, as Jane pried the book from her arms. She watched Jane flipping the pages. "I wish we

were more like that. I wish you knew . . .
and I wish you didn't hold so much against
me. Polly doesn't hold things against
Wendy."

"Characters?" Jane asked, looking up.
"In this book?"

Margaret nodded, and to her dismay, she
felt her chin wobbling.

"Mom," Jane said. "We're not characters."

"Neither are they!" Margaret said passionately. "They're real. They love each other. If
Wendy wants Polly to come for Sunday lunch
all the time, it's only because she loves her so
much! So, maybe she made some mistakes
when the children were small, perhaps she
doesn't understand every nuance of her
daughter's personality . . . but Polly forgives
her!"

"Mom . . ."

"What's in that locket?" Margaret asked,
staring at the silver disc around Jane's
neck.

"Nothing," Jane said.

"That's not true," Margaret said. "You
never take it off. You've worn it ever
since . . ." Her voice broke. "Oh, how I regret letting that picture be taken at the hos-

pital. You were so emotional, and you begged me—"

"Stop," Jane said. She sat there, so stiffly. Margaret longed to have Jane reach out, take her hand the way Polly would have taken Wendy's. She longed to have a shimmering moment where her gaze locked with Jane's, where forgiveness could flow between them.

"Do you have her picture in there?" Margaret asked.

Jane didn't reply. She looked down, studying her dusty hands. Margaret saw blue paint smeared on her fingers and wondered where it could have come from.

"Where do you go on your drives?" Margaret asked.

"Mom, I just drive around."

"Sylvie seems nervous about it. That's why I'm asking."

"Mom, let's talk about you instead," Jane said slowly, changing the subject. "How are you feeling?"

"Oh, dear. I'm fine. I really am."

"You've seemed so tired, ever since you went to Crofton."

"Yes, the potluck dinner." Margaret sighed. "Seeing all those people—teachers from my school, other administrators, and the new generation—so many young educators I'd never met before. Saying hello, seeing baby pictures of everyone's children and grand-children. Then, of course, reporting on the state of my health . . . I get so tired of that. You know, when you have good health, you just take it for granted. People say 'How are you,' and you answer 'Fine.' I long for those days. . . ."

"I know you do," Jane said.

Margaret sighed. Her feet and legs hurt. Just one night, over a week ago, on her feet for longer than usual, and she was still in pain. Lately, also, her eyesight had begun to fail. She was finding it harder to read. She dared not tell the girls, though. They would add "deteriorating eyesight" to the minus column, another reason she should be in a home.

"All in all, I have few complaints," she said, trying to smile.

"Mom, we know it's hard for you to get out of bed by yourself," Jane said. "And you don't want to call Sylvie or me late at night . . ."

"Shhh," Margaret said, closing her eyes. She felt herself blushing. Jane was right: She didn't want to disturb her daughters. And last night, not calling for help in getting herself to the bathroom in time, she had had an accident. Nightgown, bedsheets soaked . . .

"We weren't upset," Jane said. "We're just worried about you."

"Do you talk about what to do with me?" Margaret asked.

"I want to," Jane said, her eyes big and steady. "But Sylvie won't."

"You want to get back at me, don't you?" Margaret asked. "For what I did."

Jane shook her head. "Of course not."

"For protecting you, finding a good home for the child."

"The child has a name," Jane said steadily. "Chloe."

Margaret bit her lip. She had never used the name, and she never would. It only made the unbearable even worse. Why did Jane, her lovely, sensitive daughter, do this to herself? She stared at Jane's locket. She wished she could rip it off her neck and throw it out the window. She wished she could throw away all Jane's memories, all those awful feelings. She wished the doctor had never given Jane that time alone with the child, had never let her put the bow in her hair, never let the picture be taken.

"I did it for you . . ." Margaret began.

"Mom, please don't," Jane said. "That was so long ago. The point is to move forward now. To find a way to take better care of you. I'm afraid you'll fall. I'm so afraid that, with your feet in such bad shape, you'll trip and fall and hit your head. Or I'm afraid Sylvie will hurt her back, trying to get you out of bed."

"I'm light," Margaret said. "I don't weigh much . . ." She could eat less; she could lose even more weight. She could take better care of her own feet. She could try that antibiotic salve the doctor had prescribed. She could start using the magnets in her slippers, even in bed.

"What about someone to live in?" Jane asked. "Like a nurse."

Margaret shook her head. She had heard horror stories of friends hiring the wrong person. Silver stolen, phone bills run up, small cruelties such as pinching and shoving. "Why are you talking about this?" she asked.

"Because I don't want to be like my friends," Jane said, "who decide what's going to happen to their parents without discussing it with them. Because that's not my right."

"I'd almost rather have you ship me off, than consult with you about it. It's as if you want to make me an agent of my own demise."

"Demise? Mom," Jane said, smiling.

"Just read Dickens!" Margaret said, grabbing *Oliver Twist* and waving it. "He knew what institutions were like! This is to get me back. Right?"

"You never consulted with me," Jane said quietly. "You just told me where to go and what to do. All those months at St. Joseph's . . ."

"I had your best interests at heart," Margaret said, moaning. "You were a brilliant girl . . . you had your whole future ahead of you . . . I despised your father for his legacy to you! For letting you think you were so unworthy, that you could just be used and discarded! Oh, my love—I was so afraid you'd throw it all away, drop out of Brown . . ."

"And become a baker?" Jane whispered. Just then a phone rang. Jane patted her pocket, pulled out a small silver cell phone, checked the little blue screen, and left the room.

Margaret shuddered, stifling a sob. She put down *Oliver Twist* and picked up *Family Happiness* again. She thought of those wonderful characters, the Solo-Millers, Wendy and Polly. She hung onto them—a mother and daughter with a solid relationship. She felt they were her friends, with her now. And she wished, more than any words in her beloved English language could ever say, that she could have that with Jane.

❧

"Hello?" Jane said, standing in the hallway outside her mother's room. Her heart was racing from the conversation she had just had as she held the cell phone to her ear.

"Jane?"

Jane hesitated, trying to place the voice.

"This is Dylan Chadwick," he said.

"Oh, hi!" she said.

"I got your number from the card you gave my niece. And I wanted to call, to thank you."

"You didn't have to . . ."

"The apple tarts were delicious. And it was really thoughtful of you to drop them off. Just because I'd mentioned that we liked them."

"Well, I haven't been baking much," Jane said, wanting to explain, hoping he hadn't thought it strange. "I was getting rusty."

"Are you still in Rhode Island? Or have you gone back to New York?"

"I'm still here," she said.

"Well, the stand is almost ready," he said. "You could probably see that it's going to be a major summer employment opportunity for my niece and her friend."

"I did see that." Jane smiled.

"The thing is, the apples won't be coming in till September. I've planted some strawberries, which won't be ready till June, tomatoes and corn to sell in July, but right now, it's looking as if I have a freshly painted stand with nothing to sell."

Jane couldn't believe this; Chloe's uncle was about to make a business proposition with her.

"You want me to—" she began.

"Bake apple tarts and pies," he said. "Chloe really loved the ones you made for us. She loved the pictures you made on top, with the crust. She had no idea who you were, of course."

Jane's heart skipped a beat. "What do you mean?"

"The Calamity Bakery."

"Oh," she said, relieved. "You know me from New York . . ."

"I used to live there," he said. "My wife was a designer, and she used to give, and go to, a lot of parties. I remember I was always happy when you did the desserts. Because they were always so good and, I don't know, homey. They weren't fancy, but they were great. And I liked the way you decorated them."

"Really?"

"Yes. Like yesterday: apples and apple trees. Chloe loved it, too."

"I'm so glad," Jane said, thrilled.

"So, will you bake for us? I was thinking, the girls want to work on Saturdays and Sundays. Maybe we could start out with two or three pies for each day. And a bunch of apple tarts."

"Like five?"

"Sure. Five."

"What about the apples?"

Dylan was silent, thinking.

"I mean," Jane said, "everyone will want

to know whether the pies are made out of Chadwick Orchards' apples."

"Really? We don't have any yet. Do you think people will care?"

"No, it'll be okay. In New York, everyone wants to know that the chanterelles came from a certain farm in Stonington, Maine, or that the raspberries were hand-picked by friars in County Wicklow, Ireland . . ."

Dylan laughed. "I remember that from New York. Except for some of the best restaurants in Providence, we're not that picky around here."

"So, you think I can get away with Granny Smiths from the grocery store?"

"I'd say so."

"Okay, then," Jane said. "I'll give it a try."

Chloe's parents were fighting. It was Saturday night. They were in their bedroom, with the door closed. Didn't they know she could hear? If not the actual words, at least the tone of their voices. She knew their fights were usually about one of two things: money or her.

The grounding had finally caught up with her. It had taken a few days of smoldering, but finally her father had told her: Her punishment for getting fired by Ace Fontaine was two weekends of being banned from going out to the movies with her friends.

Chloe wondered what life had been like before her arrival. Had they been happier? She walked through the neat house. Her socks slid on the newly waxed wood floors. She stopped in the living room. The couch and chairs were upholstered in flowered chintz. The butler's table gleamed. The hooked rug had a white background. One of the reasons animals were not allowed inside the house was that fur made a mess. Chloe wasn't allowed to sit on the living room furniture; she was encouraged to use the den, where the chairs had blue cotton slipcovers.

The bookshelf held very few actual books, but lots of decorating and gardening magazines, her mother's collection of milk glass, and some framed pictures. Chloe picked up the one of her parents at their wedding.

Her father's face was wide open, as if he hadn't one care in the world. Her mother's eyes were filled with happiness, her mouth a perfect smile. How content they looked together, and how alike. With their reddish blond hair and brown eyes, they looked almost like siblings. They'd gotten married at twenty-five. By the time they were thirty-seven, they had despaired of ever having a baby. And by the time they were thirty-eight, they were about to adopt Chloe.

She came with a name.

That was part of the deal, a condition of the adoption. Her real mother had held her in her arms, looked into her blue eyes, and given her the name "Chloe." Although her parents would have preferred "Emily," they agreed to abide by her real mother's wishes. That's how much they wanted her.

But did they? Would they have agreed if they'd known how she would change their lives? Into this light-haired, brown-eyed family had come Chloe, the demon seed. Black hair, ice blue eyes, more cat than girl, protester and insurgent.

Chloe walked over to the window, pushed it open. The orchard cats were dancing tonight. She saw them playing in the moonlight, tumbling around in the yard. More new kittens were being born every day. Some of them cried in the distance, as if they had lost their way home and wanted their parents to come and find them.

Upstairs, Chloe heard her father raising his voice. She heard "bills," "money," and "that goddamn orchard." Chloe shivered, from the breeze coming through the open window, but also knowing that her father was talking about Uncle Dylan, wanting him to agree to sell off some of the land.

The phone rang. Chloe ran to get it.

"Hello?" she said.

"It's me," Mona said. "Are you allowed to talk on the phone?"

"Yeah. It's a movie grounding. No movies till next week."

"Oh. That's not *too* bad. What are you doing?"

"Listening to them fight."

"What about?"

"Money," Chloe said. She didn't feel like going into the whole thing, about her father and uncle and Isabel's death and the orchard and how much happier her parents had been before they'd adopted her. But luckily Mona had been her friend for so long, she knew most of the background. She had been there to feel the tension. She knew that Chloe got stomachaches from the fights that never quite exploded.

"You know, it really isn't fair," Mona said.

"What isn't?"

"Well, if you're born into the mayhem, that's one thing. But if you're invited to the mayhem party, that's another."

"What do you mean?"

"It's just that they *adopted* you. If you were their flesh and blood, that would be one thing—you'd have no recourse. But in a way, you're their *guest,* so they've lost the right to the mayhem chip. They *invited* you. You could have gone to how many other families? So shouldn't they be a little more considerate about your emotions? It takes a huge toll on you when they have those closed-door fights."

Chloe's stomach dropped, but Mona was only echoing things Chloe herself often said. She knew that Mona felt the same way about Rhianna. In some ways, adoptive parents and stepparents were quite alike. "Especially when the fights are about me," she agreed. "I've shamed my father with Ace Fontaine at the Rotary."

"Bad girl." Mona chuckled.

"Their real daughter would never have done such a thing."

"Never."

"She would be as perfect as they are.

She would keep her room perfectly clean. She would eat meat with the rest of the family. She would certainly never feed the orchard cats."

"No, no, no."

"And if she did, she wouldn't have to make sure the cat food was nonmeat, nondairy."

"Oh, the cats are vegan?"

"I'm looking into it," Chloe said. "That food is expensive. Guess it depends on how much Uncle Dylan pays us for working at the stand."

"Mmm, Uncle Dylan," Mona said, sounding dreamy.

"Stop," Chloe said. "He's grieving. And he's old."

"He just needs someone to help him learn to love again. I can be that person. He needs me . . ."

"He's forty-eight. He's older than your father."

"But younger than *your* father. How come, if your father is so hot to sell off the orchard, your uncle—his younger brother—gets to have his way and work the land?"

"Because my grandfather wanted the orchard to continue," Chloe said. "So badly, that he put a clause in his will about either of his sons having the right to override the other, if the orchard could keep going."

"Did he love the land more than his sons?"

Chloe held the receiver, listening to the breeze in the branches outside. Moonlight struck the apple blossoms, filling all the tres with white light. The orchard looked magical, as if she could disappear into it and be happy forever. The dirt bikes were absent tonight.

"I don't think so," she said. "I think he thought the land would keep everyone together."

"That's what keeps parents going," Mona said. "The idea that something will keep the family together. Having kids, saving the family land . . ."

"Do you think any of it works?" Chloe asked, hearing the voices upstairs rise.

"Ask our real mothers," Mona said.

Chloe stared out at the gauzy white trees. She nodded and didn't say a word. She didn't need to. In the silence, she could hear Mona's voice catch in a tiny, private sob.

CHAPTER 10

On Sunday morning, Chloe was up and out so early, Sharon Chadwick didn't even have the chance to fix her a good breakfast. Not that Chloe would eat bacon and eggs, the traditional Sunday repast, but Sharon would have cooked her oatmeal or toasted her an English muffin, if given the opportunity.

Instead, she puttered around the kitchen, preparing Eli's. She grated cheddar cheese, chopped a tomato, unwrapped some bacon. Separating the thick slices, she placed them in the nonstick frying pan. She set the long maple table with checked placemats and matching cloth napkins, terra-cotta plates, and brown earthenware mugs.

While the bacon sizzled, she brewed coffee. She heard Eli on the stairs, his tread heavy. Her heart pounded. They had gone to bed angry with each other. The emotions were a fever in her head, making her feel too hot, almost delirious. Her back was stiff, her neck bent over like a staff as she stood over the stove. He silently entered the room, came up behind her, and kissed the back of her neck.

"I'm sorry," he said.

Sharon nodded. Words were trapped inside. She wanted to cry. They had so much; why weren't they better able to make each other happy? They always seemed to be living at the limit of their checkbook; they were bewildered by their teenager; they didn't hold each other the way they had so long ago.

"I'm sorry, too," she said.

He took his seat at the head of the table. She had walked out to the curb earlier, gotten the Sunday paper, placed it on the bench. He reached for it now.

"Where's Chloe?" he asked.

"Working," she said, glancing up with a raised eyebrow.

"That goddamn stand. Am I too old to pound the crap out of my baby brother?"

He shook his head. But Sharon felt relieved. Bonding together against Dylan's plans seemed to strengthen them.

"I know, I know. He thinks he's doing us a favor, giving her a job. But the stand—for the love of God! That eyesore!"

"It's a puzzle, that's for sure," Eli said, "how Dylan can forget how embarrassed he used to be to have an apple stand on the property. He was so cool with the girls, but he'd never want them to come over—"

"I remember," Sharon said. She whisked the eggs, poured them into the pan for an omelet. She had known the Chadwick brothers since high school. Back then, development had just taken hold in the valley, and kids who lived on farms were teased for being backward and holdouts, whose families were stopping the progress of new business.

"I don't want the other kids talking about Chloe the way they used to talk about us," he said.

"I know," Sharon said. Kids had made fun, calling the Chadwick brothers "apple pickers"—but never within their hearing.

"She's so sensitive. Goes to pieces if a

bird falls out of the nest. All this trouble at the grocery store over hurting animals . . ."

Sharon didn't reply. Thoughtfully, she sprinkled the cheese and chopped tomatoes into the eggs. She didn't agree with her husband. Chloe had a huge heart, it was true, but Eli was confusing sensitivity with strength.

"Chloe stands up for herself," Sharon said. "And for others."

"Well, she hasn't spent a summer working at the stand yet," Eli said. "They'll call her 'hayseed' and 'apple picker,' all the other names they used to call me and Dylan."

"Things like that don't bother her," Sharon said.

Eli snorted, shaking his head. "Well, they should. It matters, what people think. She's so busy saving the world, she'll wind up losing in her own life. She's at an age where she has to start thinking about getting ahead. College is coming. . . . But does she care about sports, the yearbook, the school paper? Things that would help her get into good schools? No. Does she care about a decent job she can put on her resume?"

"I know, I know," Sharon said, glancing

at Eli, wanting to steer him off this topic. The day had been off to such a good start. . . .

"Ace Fontaine would have promoted her to cashier—by Memorial Day, he told me. A good job, lots of responsibility, handling cash—that would be her entrée to so many other opportunities. The bank, a law firm, heck—an insurance office! She has to learn to work her way up!"

"Breakfast is almost ready here," Sharon said.

"What's she going to work her way up to from the farm stand? The barn? A stable? She's going backward, not forward . . ."

Sharon folded the omelet in half, slid it on a plate, put it on the table. She forked the bacon—extra-crispy, the way Eli liked it—onto a paper towel, let the grease absorb for a moment. She thought of Chloe's tirade about hogs in their stalls, unable to move or see the sunlight or scratch their hindquarters. Just then she felt an itch behind her leg. She shook it off. Chloe had a way of getting to her, in the deepest ways, when she least expected it.

"Mmm, great breakfast," Eli said, leaning across the table to kiss her.

"Thank you," she said, filling the coffee mugs.

"I'm sorry to get so worked up," he said, shaking his head and digging in.

"You want the best for her."

"She's just, it's just, she's so . . ." he paused, looking up. "So different."

Sharon tried to laugh. "Welcome to life with a fifteen-year-old. All our friends say it's crazy time. And will be, for the next three years—at least. Teenagers are aliens from another planet. They're different by nature."

"I wonder if that's it," he said. "Or whether . . ."

Sharon forked up a piece of omelet, her chest constricting.

"She's so different from us because . . ." he began.

"Don't, Eli. She's ours. We're hers. We're a family."

"Sometimes I look at her, and, so help me, I wonder . . ." He closed his eyes.

"Eli," Sharon said, glancing at the back door, praying Chloe wasn't standing just outside. "She's a teenager. That's all it is. Stop before she hears you."

"I know. I'm sorry," he said. He ate some

bacon, drank some coffee. His eyes looked worried. The situation with Ace had shamed him. Eli was proud of his position in the community. He insured the teachers union and the priests at their parish. He faithfully attended the Rotary, and he couldn't stand the idea of people knowing the trouble Chloe had caused at Ace's store. In spite of that reality, Sharon knew his present unhappiness had much more to do with his brother than Chloe.

Even though Dylan was younger by four years, Eli had always been in his brother's shadow. Dylan was the athletic, popular daredevil in high school; Eli had worked his way through URI—slogging from dawn till dark right here, in the family orchard. Dylan's basketball talent and charming ways had gotten him into Brown University. Shaking the orchard's proverbial pollen off his shoulders, he had gone to the Ivy League and never looked back.

He was a college basketball star, All-Ivy his sophomore year, All-American his junior and senior years. He had rich girlfriends, wealthy mentors, all of whom treated him in ways Eli could only imagine. The family of one girlfriend took him to Europe; another took him sailing to Bermuda. He was recruited for a job in "the government." Big secret, no one was supposed to know, but of course everyone guessed: Was it the CIA, the FBI? Dylan never talked about it. And Eli never got the chance to work it out of him because, guess what? Dylan never came home.

He lived the bachelor's life in Washington, D.C., a brick town house in Georgetown. Sharon remembered visiting. She had been in awe of the tiny back garden, a verdant jewel with ivy and peonies and a brick terrace and garden furniture probably worth more than her bedroom and living room sets combined. It wasn't that he was rich; it was just that he knew how to spend his money. And from what they could see, he worked too hard to find a girlfriend or the time to dote on one. . . .

It was spring. Sharon remembered driving through the city. Dylan had treated them to dinner at Jean-Louis at the Watergate, and now they were all squeezed into his black Porsche 911S, having a tour of the city.

Dylan wore a holster. Sharon, scrunched

in the seat with Eli, could feel Eli staring at the gun, wanting to ask about it.

"Go ahead," Sharon whispered, excited to learn more herself. "He won't mind."

"Dyl, aren't you off duty?" Eli asked.

"Yes," he said.

"So, why the weapon?"

"It's just the job," Dylan said. "I never know."

"When the bad guys are going to come out of the woodwork?" Eli chuckled.

Dylan nodded, not laughing.

"What do you do, anyway," Sharon had asked. She'd known Dylan almost as long as Eli; although he'd never let her—or Eli or his parents, for that matter—get very close, she considered him like a younger brother. "We know you work for the *government* . . ." By then, they all knew he was in the U.S. Marshals Service.

"I protect and serve," he said with a grin.

"What, you think we're going to go back to Rhode Island and divulge your secret missions? Come on, be serious," Eli said.

"I'm on a narcotics detail," he said.

They waited for him to elaborate. Eli held out his hand, said, "Okay, c'mon . . ." When Dylan didn't continue, Sharon felt Eli getting angry. Sitting on his lap, she could literally feel his tension coming through her skin. "I'm your brother—you can't even trust me with some stories?"

"I trust you with everything," Dylan said quietly. "Do you ever think I just don't like to talk about it? Nothing to do with you . . ."

"Screw that," Eli said. He'd had a lot of red wine with dinner, more than he was used to, and Sharon could feel his frustration building.

"Come on," she said, nuzzling his neck. "Come on . . ."

Eli's arms were around her; they were pressed so tightly together. He might have wanted to push her away, but it was impossible. As the car sped through the city, she felt him relax.

Dylan drove them around a corner. He glanced over for their reaction, as if oblivious to the tension in the car. Sharon gasped at the sheer beauty of cherry trees, white and luminous, surrounding the illuminated Jefferson Memorial, their reflections shimmering in the black waters of the Tidal Basin.

"Oh, my God," she said.

"Nice," Eli said. "We come all the way

down from apple country, and you show us fruit trees."

"How's the orchard?" Dylan had asked.

"Falling to wrack and ruin," Eli had said. "Dad's holding on till the bitter end. We could have made five hundred grand from six different developers, but no . . ."

"He should hold on," Dylan had said. The top was down, the fragrant air surrounding them.

"What do you mean?" Eli had asked.

"What the world doesn't need is another housing development, another mall."

"No, and we need another mortgage on our house. You know what the taxes cost on the land?"

"Yes," Dylan said. And Eli went silent, because everyone knew that Dylan had been sending his parents money the last few years, to cover the orchard's expenses. He wasn't rich—just a government employee, however glamorous the family thought his job might be—but he felt passionate about the orchard. And that made him a big hero to their father.

"The land isn't paying for itself," Eli said gruffly. "So tell me—what does the world need, if not another development."

"The world needs more fruit trees—right, Sharon?"

"No comment," she said, trying to laugh. "I know better than to get between the Chadwick boys."

"Look at this," Dylan had said, waving at the cherry trees, a pink-white cloud floating above the water, reflecting the alabaster city. "When I meet the right girl, I'm going to propose to her right here. Or at home, in the orchard."

Eli had finally broken out with a real, true hearty laugh, shaking his head. "Big lawman. You've got a goddamn Porsche, you fly around the country, you know all the best restaurants, and you think *that's* romantic?"

"For one thing, it's a used Porsche, and for another, yeah, I do," Dylan had said.

"Tell him, Shar," Eli had said, nudging her. "You're a woman. Do you want James Bond to propose at a nice candlelit table in a French restaurant, or ankle-deep in the mud with mosquitoes buzzing all around and the smell of rotting apples in the air?"

Sharon had stared at Dylan's face. He was Eli's brother in every way: strong, square-jawed, sensitive deep eyes. But in this one way, they were so different: Eli had never left home, but seemed constantly to want to leave it behind. Dylan had left as fast as he could, but seemed to love the orchard more than anywhere in the world.

"As long as he finds the right girl," Sharon had said, "the 'where' won't matter."

The brothers had laughed—could Dylan hear the bitter edge in his brother's voice? Eli had congratulated her on her diplomacy, and Dylan had driven them past all the beautiful, illuminated monuments toward his home in Georgetown. The whole way there, both Sharon and Eli had their eyes on the clock.

They had been trying to conceive. They were always aware of the time of month, and that night was critical. They made love in the canopied bed in Dylan's guest room; by then, the romance had long gone. By then, sex was a science. Monthly schedules of ovulation, graphs of egg production and sperm counts, fear of failure dooming them before the first embrace. There were some nights they didn't even bother kissing.

When it was over, Sharon lay on her back, legs propped up on the wall, as her fertility specialist had recommended. Eli had turned on his side, fallen asleep—or pretended to. Sharon could still hear Dylan's words, spoken in the car: his dream of proposing to the right girl, while the blossom-scented air had blown through the open car. It had sounded so romantic. Her heart had ached, wondering whether some lives could really be that simple.

Her heart ached now, again, sitting at the breakfast table while Eli read the paper. Dylan had found love; he had proposed to Amanda—not in an orchard, but on the deck of her father's yacht, moored in Newport Harbor. The wedding had been on the lawn of Amanda's family's "cottage": Maison du Soleil, one of the limestone palaces on Bellevue Avenue, with a perfect lawn sloping down to Cliff Walk and a wide view of the sea.

Dylan had been appointed to the U.S. Marshals office in New York City, and they'd moved from Georgetown to the Upper East Side. They had their very own baby, after one short year of marriage, the same year Sharon and Eli—after so many years of trying—had adopted Chloe.

Eli, Sharon, and Chloe; Dylan, Amanda, and Isabel.

The two Chadwick brothers, their families worlds apart in almost all ways. Struggling brother, rich brother. Adopted child, natural child. Small town, big city. Orchard life, Manhattan life.

But death was the great equalizer; nothing brought a man back to the orchard faster than the murder of his wife and child. His father had died years ago, but the issue of selling—or continuing—the orchard surfaced recently, when Virginia became incapacitated.

Sharon closed her eyes. The apple-blossom smell came through the kitchen windows, transporting her back to that night in Georgetown. What if all of them had known then what they knew now?

She thought of Amanda, and what she had done. Would Dylan have ever forgiven her, if she had lived? Sharon knew the question could never be answered. And she opened her eyes, knowing that other questions never could, either. Some couldn't even be asked.

She had stopped Eli just before: "Sometimes I look at her, and, so help me, I wonder . . ." The end of that question would have been: "I wonder what our real child would be like. . . ."

Sharon sometimes wondered the same thing. She just never let the words come out of her mouth. And what did "real child" mean, anyway? Because she loved Chloe more than anything in the world; she had, since that very first day. Chloe was realer than real. Sharon kept eating, even though she had lost her appetite. *Good way to gain more weight,* she told herself. She'd put on fifteen pounds in the last year. Life was stressful.

She heard Dylan's tractor. Also, distant hammering: Chloe repairing the stand. She saw the muscles in Eli's face tighten.

Yes, life was very stressful.

That next week, Dylan set aside several days for planting. Spring had been dry so far, so the soil was packed hard, tough to move. A stiff breeze blew, and low gunmetal gray clouds scudded overhead. White petals drifted off the trees; new leaves were the size of squirrels' ears, a sign that stripers were migrating into the Bay. Dylan's leg, where he'd had the surgery, ached—a sure sign of rain. The steel pins never lied.

On his way to plant, he found some new furrows where dirt bike tires had scraped the earth, scarring some old roots. He bent down, tracing the wood with his hands. The bark was torn off, the wood underneath as raw and white as exposed bone. Dylan shook his head. Kids had always been drawn to the orchard, the paths and trails, the spookiness of all the gnarled trees. He'd have to put up some new fences.

Dylan dug holes two feet deep, twice the diameter of the new trees' root systems. He threw some loose soil back into the hole, loosened the layers of dirt on the sides, to make it easier for the roots to penetrate. With each tree, he took care to untangle the roots, spread them on the loose soil, make sure they weren't crowded or twisted.

As he replaced soil around the roots, he firmed it with his hand, making sure there weren't any air pockets. He checked to make sure the graft union was a good two inches above the soil line. Patting down the earth, he had the sense of burying something he loved. He thought of Isabel. He remembered the day they had lowered her into the ground.

The rain began. The drops were big, and splashed on the dry ground. They fell hard and fast, and within a short time had turned the earth to mud. They pelted the white petals, and they dripped off the branches and new leaves. Dylan kept working. His hands were blistered from the shovel's rough handle, and they began to bleed. The rain turned his blood into water and washed it into the soil.

"Hello!"

He heard the voice and looked up. A blue station wagon was parked in the road, and a woman was coming through the field. It was Jane. She wore a thin white shirt and faded jeans, sneakers on her feet, dark hair in her eyes.

"I've got the pies!" she called, gesturing behind her. "They're in the car!"

Dylan leaned on his shovel. He was almost finished, and didn't want to stop. Something about planting trees made him forget his life for a little while; he got lost in the roots and the soil and the falling rain, and it took him a minute to come back. He stared at Jane, drenched wet as she ran toward him, and thought of an earthbound angel.

"Where should I leave them?" she asked.

"You didn't have to come through the orchard," he said.

"I called you from the road, but you didn't hear," she said.

"Sorry," he said. He had been wearing a flannel shirt, taken it off when he'd started sweating. It was balled up on higher ground, on a rock under an old, established tree, still fairly dry; he shook it out, and tried to cover her head with it. A little shower of dirt rained into her eyes. She tossed her head, laughing. Now she had a streak of mud on her cheek.

"The pies?" she asked, a smile wavering on her lips.

"How about dropping them at my house?" he said. "Turn into that driveway just past the fence—I'll walk over and meet you there."

She nodded, already running for her car.

Jane followed his directions: she followed the split-rail fence, turned onto the dirt driveway. Her hands were shaking. Dylan had tried to cover her head with his shirt. He had actually brushed her cheek with his beard. He had smiled with friendliness, and she couldn't quite smile back. She was delivering pies, but she was on a stealth mission.

He lived in a big, white farmhouse. The word would be "rambling." It had porches and chimneys. The shutters were dark green and peeling. An old wishing well tilted in the front yard. A bright red truck was parked in front of an old weathered silvery red barn. As she watched, Dylan strode out of the orchard, up the front steps, and gestured for her to come inside.

She grabbed the basket of pies and ran, hunched over to shield it from the rain. Dylan had the door open; she flew through. The front hall was dark. They shook their wet heads like shaggy dogs. Dylan led her into the kitchen, but passing through the living room, she noticed cats sleeping on all the chairs.

"Cats love rainy days," she said.

"Well, we've got cats, all right," he said.

"Cozy," she said.

"They make the house smell like one big furball," he said. "But they provide pest control."

"Pest control?"

He nodded. They were in the kitchen, which was a retro fantasy of old cream-colored appliances, enameled table and spindle-legged wooden chairs, and faded gingham curtains. Jane had the clear thought that nothing in this room had changed since 1955.

"The cats eat the rats," he said. "And mice and snakes."

"Good cats," she said.

"We store apples in the barn, and by October, the word gets out, and critters appear from all over. My brother suggested poison, to keep the mice down . . . the family practically broke up over it."

"Why?" Jane asked.

"Chloe," he said, and the name, as much as she had known she would hear it today, sent an electric shiver down her spine.

"What about Chloe?"

"She had a fit. Poison mice?" He shook his head. "She'd rather poison herself. Eli tried telling her there's a special poison that just puts the mice to sleep, a nice gentle shove into dreamland, and she threatened to run away from home if we used it."

"She loves animals," Jane said, holding the new information, precious as a pearl, in her mind.

Dylan nodded. He leaned against the Formica counter, arms folded across his chest. He was tall, and his body was strong and broad, but his face didn't seem like that of a farmer. Jane thought his eyes were too fine. His gaze was too deep. He looked like a man who knew his way around Shakespeare. She thought, uncomfortably, of Jeffrey, then looked down. As she did, a drop of blood fell onto his boot.

"You're bleeding," she said.

"Yep," he said, looking at the palm of his hand. He reached for a paper towel. "Toughen up," he said to his hand.

"What happened?"

"Spent too many years at a desk," he said.

She tilted her head, waiting. He pressed the paper towel harder, wadded it up, threw it away. Almost instantly, another blood drop hit his boot top.

"Give me your hand," she ordered, crossing the kitchen.

"Are you a doctor?"

She nodded gravely. "Yes." She held his hand in hers. His skin was tan and rough. His fingernails were black with dirt. Blisters had formed across the palms of both hands, and the ones on the right were broken and bleeding. She stepped to the deep enameled sink and turned the faucets—heavy chrome with white enamel "hot" and "cold" discs in the middle.

"You have a nice old-fashioned kitchen," she said, still holding his hand as she waited for the water to warm up.

He nodded. "I grew up here."

"Does it remind you of your childhood?"

"It did when I first moved back here. But now it's just where I live. Are you really a doctor?"

"Yes," she said gravely.

"A psychiatrist?" He smiled.

"Oh, because I asked about your childhood? Very perceptive. But no. I'm a brain surgeon." She tested the water with the inside of her right wrist. "This might sting."

"I'm tough."

"Here goes," she said, sliding his hand under the stream of warm water. She watched it wash away blood and dirt. His palm was raw, and she knew the water hurt. "You're being very brave."

"Thank you. I thought you said you were a baker."

"Well, I am," she said. "But I've cut my hand plenty of times, so I do know first aid . . . so that qualifies me to do this. Do you have any antiseptic?"

He opened the door under the sink, and she saw a small plastic kit with a red cross on the front.

She smiled. "I'm not really a doctor."

He smiled back. "Somehow I knew that.

In a former life, I was paid to know when someone was telling the whole truth. I'm cutting you some slack, because I think you just wanted to set my mind at ease."

"You're very perceptive. Hold still," she said, as she dabbed at his palm with a paper towel, opened the case, and took out a tube of ointment. She spread it on, then wrapped his hand in a length of gauze. "There."

"Wow," he said. "Good as new."

She nodded. He motioned toward the kitchen table, pulling out a chair for her. Jane sat down. The enamel table was cream-colored, chipped at the edges, with pink roses in the corners. Dylan's kitchen was like a time capsule. She felt as if she had traveled back to her youth, into the domicile of another time.

"Don't ever redo your kitchen," she said. "People in New York would pay a fortune to have this."

"Ah, New York," he said.

She glanced around, then smiled at him. "Do you miss it?"

He shook his head. "Nope."

"Should we exchange stories about

where we lived and what our favorite restaurants are?"

"And figure out that we bought our newspapers at the same stand?"

"No, I had mine delivered."

"Me, too," he said, grinning.

"So, forget having a newsstand in common. There must be something else."

He nodded, but didn't say anything.

"It's funny," she said. "Growing up here in Rhode Island, I couldn't wait to get away. When I'm in the city, I think of myself as a New Yorker. It's such an intense place to live. It always makes me feel very on edge and alive—but in a good way. Then I come back to Twin Rivers, and I feel I never left . . ."

"How could 'on edge' be good?" he asked, skipping her last statement. The humor had left his eyes; he leaned back against the counter, watching her.

"Well," she said. "I think I know what you're getting at. The not-so-great intense things . . ." She thought. "Like, walking down the street at night, you're always aware of who's around, who's behind you . . . and crossing streets, you know never to trust the red light, because some yellow cab might come careening along and jump the light and you'd be history . . . or a flower pot might fall from someone's terrace twenty stories up and brain you . . . or some cop will be shooting some robber, and there's always that messy off-chance you'll get caught in the cross fire . . ."

Dylan stood, expressionless, listening.

"But there's a wonderful 'on edge,' too," she said. "There's walking down Charles Street on an April morning, and seeing the Callery pear trees in bloom—makes you want to write poetry. And there's opening the paper on Friday morning, seeing that the Eliot Feld Ballet is at the Joyce Theater that night, and calling for tickets. There's waking up hot in the middle of a July night, and missing Narragansett Bay, and going down to Battery Park to feel the harbor breezes and take a ride on the Staten Island ferry."

"Sounds as if you love the city," he said.

"Love, hate. But mostly love." She smiled and shrugged. "It's New York."

He nodded.

Jane glanced around the kitchen. Her heart kicked over, speeding up, as she saw the photo: Chloe and another girl, surrounded by flowers, kneeling with their arms around each other, when they were about five or six. Very slowly, as if by accident, Jane began to migrate over to the wall where it was hanging.

"How did you end up back here?" she asked him.

"I love the land," he said simply.

The quiet answer distracted her, momentarily, from Chloe's picture. "You mean the orchard?"

He nodded. "It's been in my family for a long time. I remember riding on my grandfather's lap on the tractor. He got me started learning about trees, learning one from another by their bark, their leaves . . . My father wanted Eli—that's my brother—"

Jane held still, not reacting to the name of the man who had adopted her daughter.

". . . and me to go to college, have the chance to do something else with our lives. We did . . . but I never gave up the idea of coming back."

"Living in New York, you pined for apple trees?" She smiled.

He nodded. "In a way, yes. I had a great life. I went away to college, lived in D.C., traveled everywhere, wound up living in

New York. Whenever the city would start seeming too big, or squeezing in—"

"Which it always does," Jane said.

"I'd think of being here. It's crazy . . ."

She waited, encouragingly.

"I'd picture myself standing right in the middle," he said. "Trees on either side of me, spreading as far as I could see. All that space and air, and all that green . . ."

"You could breathe again."

He nodded.

"My father and grandfather taught me how to plant," he said. "When I was young, I had my own vegetable garden. Just a few tomato plants on a little square of earth. But I made things grow. That felt good."

Jane turned toward the picture again. Chloe and the other girl were kneeling among flowers. Jane stared at Chloe's beautiful big eyes, filled with love as she gazed at the other girl. "Looks like you have another gardener in the family," Jane said, her heart racing.

Dylan didn't respond.

"How old is Chloe there?" she asked.

"She's five. They both are."

"Who's the other girl?" Jane asked.

"My daughter," Dylan said.

"She's the same age as Chloe?" Jane asked. The question came out so fast, and she felt just the quickest, sharpest prick of awareness: There was so much she didn't know about her daughter. She hadn't even realized she had a cousin.

"Born the same year," Dylan said.

"In 1988," Jane said, the date slipping out before she could stop it. But Dylan didn't seem to notice.

"Yes," he said.

"Chloe was born . . ."

"In February. Our little miracle girl," he said.

Jane clenched her jaw and couldn't look at him. His words packed a punch. How how could he say that, how could they have taken her miracle and made it their own? "Miracle girl?" she made herself ask.

"Yes. All they ever wanted was a child to love. My brother and sister-in-law. Great people, couldn't have kids of their own. It seemed so unfair. But then one day they decided to adopt . . ."

"One day they decided to adopt," Jane said, the words echoing in her head. "Chloe?"

Dylan nodded. "I never think of her that

way. Don't know what made me say it just now . . . guess it's just remembering what a miracle she seemed. Man, she changed everything around here. Brought a lot of joy."

Jane stared at the picture. "I can see why," she said. "Two little girls the same age."

"Chloe was born in February, Isabel in June."

"Four months apart," Jane said. Her heart constricted. She could hardly bear to think of the entire life that had unfolded without her. "They must be close . . ."

"They were."

Jane nodded, awash in her own sadness. But then she looked at Dylan and saw his eyes. They were empty, lost, hopeless. The rich golden green-brown had drained out of them; they were pale, the color of tea, as if he had just become a ghost. Her heart turned over. " 'Were'?" she asked.

"My daughter . . ." he began.

The next words seemed caught in his throat. He opened his mouth to complete the sentence, but he couldn't. She saw him clamp down on the words and the thoughts. He stood there, silent. She didn't know his story, but she knew what he was feeling. His daughter was gone. Jane felt it in her cells. How often had she stood in front of her mirror, trying to see a hint of the woman Chloe would become? Gazing into her own eyes, at her own smile, for a sign of the daughter she didn't know? She was haunted by her own version of "My daughter . . ."

"What happened?" she said. Caught by the pull of Chloe's picture—like the moon held by the earth's gravity—she tried to take a step closer to Dylan, but couldn't move.

"Before," he said, "when you were talking about New York . . ."

She nodded.

"And you talked about the things that can happen . . ."

"The intense things . . ."

Dylan was staring at his bandaged hand; when he looked up, his eyes were on fire. They were no longer empty or lost, but burning with hate.

"Cross fire," he said.

"No."

"Real cross fire," he said. "Just like you said: good guys and bad guys shooting at each other. Isabel and her mother got caught in it. I was an officer, a marshal. I was working on a case, trying to get them away from it. But I didn't—"

Jane, held by the power of the picture, turned to stare at Chloe and Isabel. As much as she saw herself in Chloe, she saw Dylan in Isabel. His daughter was a bright, vibrant, chestnut-haired sprite, caught in Chloe's embrace.

"I'm so sorry," Jane said.

Dylan nodded and shrugged both at the same time. His frown was deep, the lines between his eyes sharply scored. His beard was dark, and his eyes were still pale, the color of stones underwater, washed by the river. He couldn't look at her.

I know what it feels like, she wanted to say, *to lose a daughter.*

She stared back at Chloe's picture. She thought of the years that had passed without her. She thought of the dreams—no, the nightmares—she had had of Chloe being taken from her arms. She thought of the nights she had held her pillow as if it were an infant, crying until the cotton and down were soaking wet.

She looked at Dylan Chadwick and thought of her own heartbreak and knew it wasn't the same at all. Not at all. Glancing down at her own hand, she saw the ghostly patch of blue. The blue paint, from where she had brushed against the apple stand.

That splintery, rickety wooden stand, just painted bright blue, robin's egg blue, by Chloe.

Chloe was alive. She hadn't been cut down by cross fire. She was growing up, living life. The life Jane had given her. Breathing deeply, she found herself able to take one step away from Chloe's picture. Then another. The distance increased—one foot, two feet—until she had crossed the kitchen and found herself standing in front of Dylan Chadwick.

She reached for his hand.

Her hand took hold of his bandaged one. Her heart pounded. She felt his pain pass through their skin. It felt familiar. She understood all the nights he had felt alone in the dark, knowing he had lost his daughter. She understood that very, very well.

Dylan let her hold his hand. She knew he should push her away. He should kick her out of his kitchen, tell her to take her pies and never come back. Because no good could come of her being here—not to his family.

Jane wanted Chloe.

She didn't know how yet, and she didn't know what she was willing to do, but she knew she could never let Chloe go again. She stared up at the man—this stranger— who had become her daughter's uncle and wanted him to see: wanted him to see Chloe in her eyes.

And at the very same time, wanted him never to make the connection.

CHAPTER 12

The room was lovely and quiet. Birds sang in the trees outside the window. An oriole was building a nest in the maple's branches—a soft, silky, gray hanging basket of grass and lichens. Margaret reclined against her pillows, enjoying the serenade. Sylvie sat in the rocking chair across the room, doing embroidery. Jane stood at the window, watching the nest-building.

"Penny for your thoughts," Margaret said, smiling.

"I'm watching the Baltimore oriole."

"Eastern oriole," Sylvie said. "That's what they're calling it now. I wish they wouldn't do that. We spend our whole lives thinking of a bird by one name, and suddenly the scientists decide they should rename the species."

"Virginia Chadwick would approve. She would say that they were an eastern subspecies of the northern oriole," Margaret said. "She was a marvelous science teacher. I'm sure, Sylvie, she would tell you, that precise classification is important enough for you to relearn their identity."

"Identity is key," Jane said, a chill in her voice. "Even for birds."

What was it about that simple declaration that made Margaret's toes curl? And suddenly she realized just what she had done: mentioned Virginia Chadwick in front of Jane.

"I'm sorry, dear," she said, aware that Sylvie had stopped her stitching.

"That's okay, Mom."

"Anyway, what does everyone want for dinner?" Sylvie asked hurriedly.

"I never really knew Mrs. Chadwick," Jane said. "How did you and she become such good friends?"

"Dear, why bring up old business like that?"

"It's not old to me," Jane said softly.

Sylvie resumed her needlework again, with greater concentration. She hunched over her canvas with determination, remi-

niscent of how she used to sit at the dining
table to do her homework.

"We were both alums of Salve Regina—
she was several years ahead of me. We
both became teachers. She taught science
down the hall from where I taught English; in
some senses, she was my mentor. Although
we were in different fields, I admired her
rigor of mind. And, of course, we had the
college connection."

"Catholic," Jane said.

"Yes, dear. A Catholic college. She was—
and is—a fine, fine woman. A very good
friend, very caring and involved . . ."

"And you both had children. You had
girls, and she had boys."

"Yes."

"Do you know her sons?"

"Jane, please . . ."

"Do you know Dylan?"

Margaret frowned. She had expected
Jane to ask about Eli, the one who had
adopted the baby. She felt confused, a bit.

"He drives his mother to the potluck dinners," Sylvie said. "I've met him. Why?"

"What happened to his family?" Jane
asked.

The memories were dim. Margaret

frowned, trying to make them clearer. She remembered Virginia taking a long leave of absence, a month or so. Grieving for her granddaughter and daughter-in-law . . .

"Oh, God, it was horrible," Sylvie said. "They were shot. Dylan was some kind of an agent—FBI, I think—"

"No, he was a U.S. Marshal," Margaret corrected. "The nation's oldest federal law enforcement agency. I remember how proud Virginia was of him. And how devastated . . ."

"What happened?"

The feelings were so overwhelming, Margaret felt dizzy. She reached for the doll Jane had brought her. And she held it to her chest. She remembered holding her own babies. She remembered her old doll, Lolly . . . A sense of comfort spread through her. She couldn't remember the question. When she looked up, she saw both daughters watching her.

Outside the window, the oriole still sang. She saw it dart into the tree, a blur of black and orange. Its nest swung from the branch, a silver basket of eggs. The song was so clear and pure.

"My friend Virginia is a science teacher," Margaret said. "The eastern oriole is a subspecies of the northern oriole. No one calls them 'Baltimore orioles' anymore. . . ."

Sylvie had invited John over to play Scrabble, but now she wondered whether it was a good idea. Her mother seemed very fragile tonight. She had gotten weak, and Sylvie had checked her sugar. Her insulin level was too high, so Sylvie had mixed two spoonfuls of sugar into a glass of orange juice. The entire time, Jane had just sat by the bed with their mother.

Now, downstairs, Sylvie got things in order. She arranged snacks on a tray, set out the ice bucket, checked to make sure she had both soda and beer in the fridge. She checked the lighting in the living room: she didn't want anything too bright. Draping a square rose-colored silk scarf over the lampshade, she heard Jane laughing.

"You have nothing to worry about," Jane said. "You have beautiful skin. You don't have to dim the lights."

"I have little lines under my eyes," Sylvie said, staring at her older sister, who still looked twenty-five. "I should never have sunbathed."

"Ah, you'd trade all those great times at the beach for perfect skin? Don't worry about it. I'm sure he thinks you're beautiful."

Sylvie blushed, glancing over at her sister. Jane was smiling with obvious affection, and it hit Sylvie right in the heart.

"What time is he coming?" Jane asked.

"At eight. Do you want to join us?"

Jane shook her head. "No. I'll stay upstairs, in case Mom needs anything."

"Her levels have been fluctuating lately. She's lost weight, and I think she's getting too much insulin. I'm going to call the doctor tomorrow."

"It's not just her sugar levels, Sylvie."

"But mainly . . ."

"She plays with that doll," Jane said.

"No. She holds it once in a while."

Jane took a breath. Upstairs, their mother was talking to herself. Or to the doll. Sylvie wasn't sure, and it hurt to just stand there staring at her sister trying to pretend it wasn't happening at all. Sylvie didn't want things to change. She didn't want their mother to go anywhere, and she could almost see Jane diplomatically trying to phrase the question.

"Go ahead. I know what you're thinking."

"What?" Jane asked.

"That she's losing it. You can't wait to put her somewhere—"

Jane raised her eyebrows. She just waited, letting Sylvie hear herself saying the words.

Frustrated, Sylvie turned back to the counter and began arranging almonds and dried apricots on a plate.

"Syl, did you see how she got earlier? She was so alert and with-it, and suddenly she started acting like a little girl."

Sylvie nodded, feeling her lips tighten. "Well, she was upset." The words hung in the air, an accusation.

Jane's eyes narrowed. "Because of me?"

"Well, what did you expect? Asking all those questions?"

"They never got answered. Mom drifted off before she could tell me. What do you know about them?"

"Them?"

"Dylan Chadwick and his family?"

Sylvie glanced at the clock. John would be arriving in fifteen minutes. She felt as if she and her sister were dancing around the rim of a very deep well. "Honestly, Jane— what's the point?"

"Just tell me, please?"

Sylvie exhaled. "There was a drug trial, and he was guarding a witness, I think. He felt his family was in danger, and he tried to get them out of New York . . ."

"Was he there?" Jane asked. "Did he see it happen?"

"I don't know," Sylvie said, alarmed by her tone. "I never heard the whole story. Why are you asking about all this?"

"Because I want to know," she said.

"They have nothing to do with us," Sylvie said. "Stop thinking about them."

Jane laughed.

"What's so funny?"

"You," Jane said. "You telling me they have nothing to do with us. They have *everything* to do with me."

"That's in the past," Sylvie said. "You have to let them all be . . . and you have to get on with things, Jane."

"I am," she said. "Getting on with things."

"You're thinking of contacting her, aren't you?"

"She has a name, Sylvie. You were there when I gave it to her."

"Please, Jane!"

"Her name is Chloe."

Sylvie's thoughts raced. She shivered, remembering the moment Jane was referring to. Then she heard her mother, starting to move around upstairs. Jane started for the stairs. Outside, a car turned into the driveway. Sylvie heard the tires on gravel. She glanced out the window and saw John climb out of his car, a box of chocolate under his arm.

"Tell me she's not the reason you came home," Sylvie said, suddenly knowing that seeing about their mother's health wasn't the main story. When Jane didn't reply at first, Sylvie added, "Chloe."

"But she is," Jane said quietly.

And then the doorbell rang, and Jane went upstairs.

⚘

Chloe went into the backyard to feed the cats. The night was dark. The half-moon glowed through the orchard, caught in the branches. It was luminous and magical, and she knew the cats would be dancing by midnight. The only sounds came from the cats, crying with excitement at being fed, and the wind: a swooshing through the new leaves, a clicking of small branches as they tapped against each other.

Suddenly, into the peaceful scene, roared one of the marauders. Chloe heard an engine zinging in the orchard, twice as powerful and much faster than her uncle's tractor. She saw a light careening wildly through the foliage. Dropping the bag of cat food, she tore like a deer into the brush, scaled the fence, and keeping her head down, ran closer to the light.

Her breath tore out of her chest. She crouched on the ground, watching, waiting to bust him. She'd spring out just like a highway trooper, pulling him over. The engine revved. Wheels spun, and she heard dirt spitting out behind. The light sped closer. Her heart raced. The tire hit a root; the bike lurched, tilted, and crashed. The sound of metal hitting rock was jarring, as was the thud of a body landing on the ground. She heard the voice: "Shitfuck."

Shocked, Chloe peered over the tall grass. A boy was standing up, brushing himself off. He was tall and skinny. Moonlight revealed torn jeans and a leather jacket. He had long blond hair held back in a ponytail. By the way he was looking at his wrist, she wondered whether it might be broken.

"This is private property," she said sharply.

"What? Who's there?" he asked, peering in the direction of her voice.

"I suggest you take your sad little bike onto the *public* road and push it home."

"Go fuck yourself," he said, bending over his hand.

"Do you have a broken wrist?" she asked.

He didn't reply. His body was curved over like a question mark, and she thought he was probably in serious pain. Her parents had taught her never to talk to strangers. She was alone in the orchard with a foul-mouthed biker. But just as Chloe couldn't bear to think of hurt animals, she couldn't stand to see an injured human. Creeping out of her nest, she made her way across the rutted ground.

"Let me see," she said, walking closer to him.

"That's okay," he said, still holding his wrist. His dirt bike lay at his feet, the front fender crumpled. A smell of oil was strong, and Chloe saw the black gloss of a spill on the ground.

"That's lovely," she said.

"What?"

"Polluting the land. That oil's going straight into the groundwater. You know what will happen when the wildlife drink from the spring? And then it will seep into the underground tributaries, and drain into the Twin Rivers, and trickle into Narragansett Bay, and striped bass will die."

"All because of me," he said sarcastically.

"At least you're taking the blame," she said. "That's a step in the right direction. And don't even think of suing us. You got hurt on our land, but you're trespassing. Let me see your wrist."

He snorted. "Right."

She looked up at him. He towered over her. He must have been at least six feet tall. His hair was very blond; a whole thatch of it fell into his eyes. Which were green. Bright, shining, beautifully spooky green— just like a cat's. Chloe felt the most amazing tingle rush through her entire body, as if she knew him: as if they had been cats together, in one of their previous nine lives.

"What are you staring at?" he asked.

"Um, you look familiar," she said.

"I go to Twin Rivers High," he said. "You want to see my license?"

"That's not necessary," she said.

"Really? 'Cause you're acting a lot like a cop."

"Excuse me, but this is private property. Didn't you see the 'No Trespassing' signs?"

"Everyone rides here," he said.

"If everyone jumps off the Newport Bridge, does that mean you should follow them?"

He laughed, staring down at her, as if he was amused in spite of himself. "You're, what? In ninth grade?"

"Yes."

"So, how do you wind up sounding like you're sixty-two?"

"If you think that's going to hurt my feelings, I feel sorry for you. Who wouldn't want to be wise? Let me see your hand."

"Forget it," he said, cradling it.

"Come on. I've been taking care of broken paws my whole life. Cats, rabbits . . . how much different can yours be? I probably can't set it, unless you think popsicle sticks and adhesive tape will do the trick. But I can diagnose."

"I'm really going to let some tree-hugging animal-lover old-sounding person take—" he began.

But just then, they heard twigs breaking underfoot, coming from the direction of her uncle's house. "Who's there?" Uncle Dylan called.

The stranger stiffened. He bent to grab his bike. Chloe knew he wanted to make a clean getaway, but he seemed too woozy to be thinking clearly. She felt momentarily torn. Uncle Dylan was her tribe, but she somehow wanted to protect this kid. She just put her finger to her lips and motioned him down. They crouched together.

"Who's that?" he asked.

"The caretaker," Chloe whispered. "Be very still. He's armed."

"Fuck," the kid said.

"Exactly. Shhh."

Uncle Dylan was about fifty yards away. Chloe could hear him walking through the grass. She wondered whether he could smell the oil. But the wind was blowing in the wrong direction. She knew she should call him—he'd been upset about dirt bikers all spring. But the boy was right beside her, and his eyes were so green, and Chloe had never felt this way before. She couldn't stop shivering, and it wasn't even cold.

"You'd *better* hide," her uncle called. "If I catch you, you'll wish you'd never ridden onto my land."

"He means it," Chloe said.

"What's he going to do? Shoot me?"

"That's a possibility. He was a U.S. Marshal."

"Like Tommy Lee Jones?"

Chloe shook her head. "Twice as tough. He makes Tommy Lee Jones look weak. He's an expert at tracking people down . . ."

They heard him coming closer. Chloe ducked her head; the boy did too. Their faces were very close together. She could smell him. He smelled like leather and sweat. The combination made the top of her head sizzle. They had nowhere to look but into each other's eyes. Chloe felt as if she had fallen into a pool of green water.

He smiled. It was so cute, she thought she'd keel over. He had perfect teeth. She smiled back, making sure her lips didn't part. Her bottom teeth were a little crooked, two of them overlapping slightly. She had a small space between her two front teeth. She had to hide it. She forced her gaze upward, back to his eyes.

After a few minutes, her uncle began walking back to the house. She heard his footsteps receding, and then the screen door slammed. The porch light went out. Now the only illumination came from the halfmoon, but the boy's eyes were no less green.

"Thank you," he said.

"That's okay."

"How do you know he's a marshal?"

"He's my uncle."

"So this is your orchard?"

Chloe nodded.

"Cool place."

"You really shouldn't ride here," she said. "It's bad for the ecology."

"You know, you have this really bad habit of sounding like a science teacher."

"My grandmother would be happy to hear you say that," she said. "She happens to be a science teacher, and she instilled certain scientific principles in me, even though it's not genetic."

"See? You're doing it again. Who says 'genetic'?"

"I can't help myself," Chloe said. "I care too much about nature to act dumb around you."

"Why would you act dumb around me?"

She tossed her head. "I thought boys like girls who act dumb."

"Dumb boys, maybe," he said, his eyes shining. She felt a whole new thrill, as if he had just turned her inside out. She liked his voice. It was deep. Yet somehow warm. As if he had decided to like her. Also, it was intelligent.

"I'm Chloe Chadwick," she said.

"Ah. Like Chadwick Orchards."

"I work at the stand," she said.

"I'm Zeke Vaill."

"Hi." She went to shake his hand, forgetting his injury. But it must not have been broken after all, because he shook her hand, then flexed his fingers.

"Getting back to normal," he said.

"That's good," she said.

"My bike's another story," he said. Now that the coast was clear and her uncle had gone back to his house, they left their hiding place and approached his dirt bike. He righted it, tried to push it, realized the front rim was bent.

"Do you live far away?"

"In Twin Rivers," he said—the next town.

"I don't have my license," she said. "Or I'd drive you home."

He just gave her a devilish grin—where the left half of his mouth smiled and the right half stayed impassive—and took a cell phone from his pocket. He dialed a number, waited, then said, "Hey. I crashed. Come get me?" Another wait, then a laugh. "Yeah, wiped out—like you've never done it. The orchard. Ten minutes? I'll be by the far end of the fence. See you."

Chloe's mouth was dry. She wanted to ask him a million questions. She wondered who he could call, just like that, to come get him. And, as if she had asked, he answered.

"My brother," he said. "He'll drive my father's truck, so we can load the bike in back. Sorry about the oil spill."

Chloe nodded, feeling a yearning in her chest stronger than anything she had felt in a long time. She walked beside him as he pushed his bike out to the road. The feeling pulled at her heart. It stretched thin and tight, like an elastic. It reminded her of staring at the sky, looking at those two lone stars.

"Where do you go to school?" he asked. "Crofton?"

She nodded, momentarily unable to speak.

"Do you have brothers or sisters?"

"No," she said.

"You're an only child," he said.

She thought that over. She thought of how much she had loved her cousin. She thought of how nice it must be to have siblings. She wondered whether her birth parents had other children, whether she did have brothers or sisters. Maybe they had a large family, but had been too poor to keep her. Or perhaps they had been young and in love, but unable to marry till they'd finished school, and now they had other kids of their own. Her heart stretched thinner, tighter. She shivered so hard, her whole body shook.

"You're cold," he said.

"No, I'm—" she began.

But he had already taken off his leather jacket, slipped it over her shoulders. She had never worn an animal skin before. The feeling scared her, but it was warm from his body, and when he pulled it closed in front, she closed her eyes and felt all the stars come down from the sky. When she opened her eyes again, she saw him standing there in a torn and faded white T-shirt. He had a tattoo on his left bicep.

"A dolphin," she said, touching it.

"They keep sharks away."

"Sharks?"

"I surf," he said.

"You do?" she asked, picturing all that blond hair with a huge salty wave washing over him.

"Yeah. First Beach. Ever go?"

She shook her head.

"Oh, the ecology," he said, smiling. "Might run over some minnows, right?"

"Something like that," she said, not wanting to explain that her parents weren't beach people. Rhode Island was called "the Ocean State," and practically the only times she went to the beach had been when Isabel was still alive and they'd go stay with her other grandparents at their huge mansion in Newport.

"Well, maybe you'll give it a try some day," he said.

"Maybe."

"If you do," he said, stopping still and looking so deeply into her eyes that she felt his gaze all the way down to her navel. "Remember that dolphins will always protect you from sharks."

She nodded, mouth slightly open. He leaned down, as if he was going to kiss her, and she saw lightning, stars, and thunderbolts, and then she heard her name.

"Chloe!" The voice came from across the orchard.

"That's my mother," she said.

"You'd better go home, before she calls the marshal to come find you," Zeke smiled, standing up straight again.

"Yeah," she said, backing away. Her heart felt tattered. She wanted him to kiss her, wanted him to take her surfing, wanted to meet his brother. Her body felt clamped, as if held between shark jaws. Her mother called again.

"I'd better go . . ."

"Thanks a lot."

"You're welcome."

Her mother's voice was getting closer, and Chloe didn't want her to see Zeke. She felt something close to panic at the idea.

She didn't want her mother to see him, yell at him, threaten to call his parents or the police. So she wriggled out of his jacket and handed it to him, running into the moon-shadowed orchard, without saying good-bye.

CHAPTER 13

Opening day at the stand was a brave and wonderful thing. The stand itself gleamed blue, like a scrap of sky, in the sunlight. The fragrance of just-baked pies rose alluringly from the shelves. Chloe had made banners announcing the grand opening. One depicted a golden-crusted apple pie. One inexplicably featured a dolphin. She and Mona sat on the bench, just as Dylan and Eli used to do, waiting for customers.

Dylan oversaw the operation from the edge of the orchard. He had done his best to clean up spilled oil left behind by one of those idiot bikers, and now he was applying commercial tree wound paint to the roots, battered by heavy tires. He had a pair of lopping shears, and he used them to remove some broken branches, low on the tree, where the biker had crashed through.

He worked carefully, as his grandfather had taught him, making his cuts flush with the collar of the tree, the slight swelling where the branch met the main trunk. He knew that branch stubs took longer to heal than flush cuts, leaving a larger area for disease and rot to enter the tree.

He glanced over at Chloe. She stared expectantly at the road, as if she could will customers to appear. Dylan remembered feeling that way. This was a lonely country road, and till the word got out, customers would be few and far between.

A few minutes later, he heard a car engine. As he watched, Chloe craned her neck. Mona stood up from the bench and walked out to the roadside, as if to wave the traffic down. Dylan turned back to the tree. The roots were scraped bare, split open in places; a great place for fungus to enter. Living things were so vulnerable. *Isabel should be working at the stand with Chloe,* he thought.

The car pulled closer, and as he glanced at the road, it came into sight. He recognized it instantly, and he lowered the shears and watched Jane park on the roadside along the split-rail fence, get out of the driver's seat. He saw Chloe jump up from the bench, he heard Jane's shoes crunch on the gravel. She was thin, athletic-looking, a tomboy in jeans and a black sweater, her hair as dark and glossy as Chloe's.

"You're our first customer!" Mona said.

"Yay," Jane said. "You can frame my dollar!"

"You can't buy anything," Chloe said, laughing. "You baked all the pies!"

"That's okay," Jane said, taking out her wallet, picking up a tart, handing the girls some money. "This is a symbolic gesture, because I believe this is the best apple stand in the whole northeast—"

"The whole northeast," Mona whooped, jabbing Chloe with her elbow. "Wish your mother felt that way!"

Jane didn't say anything, but Dylan could see her eyes widen as she waited to hear more.

"Her parents are in mourning," Mona explained, giggling. "They wanted more for her than a career at the family apple stand . . . they wanted her to be . . ."

"A checkout girl!" Chloe said, breaking into laughter.

Jane smiled, as if she got the joke, but as if she was too polite to laugh at the expense of someone's parents. Dylan liked that. She just stood there diplomatically, waiting for the girls' laughter to subside.

"What's the dolphin for?" Jane asked, pointing at the banner.

Chloe stopped laughing, but a smile came over her face, and the harder she tried to hold it in, the bigger it got. Dylan edged forward; he'd been wanting to know about the dolphin, too.

"Tell her, Chloe," Mona said.

"It's to protect against sharks," Chloe said.

"Sharks? In an orchard?" Jane asked.

"Surfer boy says it works," Mona said.

The girls began to giggle, and it struck them as so funny, Mona let out a shriek. Dylan knew that it was all over now. Chloe and Isabel used to laugh so hard, they'd bend double. Jane just smiled, enjoying the girls' laughter. Seeing her there made him want to go join the party, so he propped the shears against the trunk, and started through the trees.

Jane felt so happy. She loved everything about the moment. Standing there with Chloe and her friend, enjoying the private joke. The sun was warm and bright, making Chloe's black hair gleam like onyx. The dolphin banner rippled in the breeze. The girls looked up at it, collapsing in gales of laughter.

"What's so funny?" Dylan asked, coming through a break in the fence.

"Dolphins in the orchard," Mona squealed. "Cowabunga!"

"Ah, I get it," Dylan said, arching an eyebrow at Jane. "Do you?"

"Totally," she smiled.

"Hi, Jane," he said.

"Hi, Dylan."

"That's right, you two know each other," Chloe said. "Uncle Dyl—Jane's our first customer."

Jane tried to keep her features neutral. Hearing Chloe call her "Jane" came with a slew of intense emotions. She felt something like fever chills running across her skin.

"Something not quite right about the

woman who baked the pies having to buy one back."

"That's what I said," Chloe smiled. "But I am going to frame her dollar. I like that it's from Jane."

Again the name, again a ripple of feeling.

"You've done such a wonderful job with the stand," Jane said, staring into her eyes.

"You think so?" Chloe asked, tilting her head and blushing slightly.

"Yes, I do. Right, Dylan? Isn't it great?"

"Hard for me to be objective," he said. "It's considered the family eyesore."

"He's right," Chloe said. "My parents hate it."

Jane tried not to react to "my parents." Instead, she gazed at the stand, at Chloe's paint job—the bright blue wood, the sunny yellow shelves—and the banners and signs. "I really can't believe you did this all yourself," she said. "It's a work of art."

Chloe laughed. "Really?"

"Really. It's so sweet and pretty, just like candy. If a shop this cute opened in New York, it would be an instant hit. The banners are great."

"An instant hit," Mona said, nodding.

"The banners were a last-minute thing,"

Chloe explained. "I was thinking, how can I get people to stop? The old sign is nice . . ."

Everyone glanced over: Chloe had touched it up, so "Chadwick Orchards" was clearly painted dark blue, with shiny red apples for decoration.

"She has to say that," Dylan explained. "Because her father and I made it when we were her age."

Chloe laughed. "I can't picture that."

"Why not?" Dylan asked.

"Because, no offense, but I don't think of you two as the artistic types . . . especially Dad. Mr. Where's-my-calculator, everyone-needs-more-insurance."

"She's saying we're geeks," Dylan said.

"You're not," Chloe smiled. "But he is."

"Anyway, Jane's right," Dylan said, squinting at the banners. "Yours are much better than the old sign. Let's see, apples and rainbows on one—very good. Dolphins on another . . . Hmm."

The girls laughed.

"It's a great idea," Jane said. "You'll get people to stop, just because they have to find out what the dolphins are all about."

"Zeke and sharks," Mona said mysteriously.

"Mone—" Chloe warned.

A car came down the road; it slowed down when it approached the stand. Everyone—Chloe, Mona, Jane, and Dylan—pretended not to be too interested. The girls bowed their heads, giggling.

"That's right," Chloe said under her breath as if casting a spell. "You know you want a pie; you know you have to have one . . ."

"Come on, come on," Mona said. "Stop right now. Pull over, pull over."

"Calamity Jane pies here," Dylan said. "Only place you can get them outside New York City . . ."

The car came to a complete stop. Jane took an appraising glance. The couple was elderly; they were pointing at the banners. The woman, especially, appeared charmed and delighted. Jane looked at Dylan, who seemed to be staring at her.

"What is it?" she asked.

He started to shake his head, then smiled. "Can't really say too much right now . . ."

She nodded, realizing that he was referring to the girls. The funny thing was, there was a lot she wanted to ask him, too.

"We could have dinner," he said.

"Sure," she said.

"Friday night?" he asked.

Jane nodded. The older couple had gotten out of their car and were walking toward the stand. The man had a cane. The woman had short-cropped gray hair and wore a navy blue dress with white polka dots. Chloe and Mona sat up straighter on the bench. They smiled winningly, and Chloe gestured at the shelf full of Jane's pies.

"Would you care to buy a delicious apple pie or tart?" she asked.

"Well, I think we would," the woman said. "But first, we have to ask—why do you have a flag with a dolphin on it, flying in the middle of an orchard?"

Jane began grinning even before the girls did.

After the old couple drove away, and Uncle Dylan went back to work, and Jane drove away, Chloe was left with the strangest feeling.

Mona was dancing around, holding up the money they'd collected. The sun grew warmer as the day passed, and the two girls took off their shirts; they had bathing suits on underneath. Mona kept pushing her to tell about meeting Zeke, teasing her about needing a tan so she'd look good when he took her surfing, but Chloe just felt tongue-tied.

Something about everyone driving away—the old couple in their car, Uncle Dylan on his tractor, and, for some reason especially, Jane in her station wagon—had left Chloe feeling bereft.

She liked that word: bereft. Well, she didn't actually *like* it, but it seemed to fit.

She had learned it in seventh grade; it had been one of her spelling words, and when she'd looked it up and read the definition ("deprived of the possession or use of something; lacking something needed, wanted, or expected") she had identified completely.

"What's wrong?" Mona asked as she applied suntan lotion to her arms. "You're mighty quiet."

"I'm lacking something needed, wanted, or expected," Chloe said.

"Huh?" Mona asked in an exaggerated attempt to sound dumb.

"I don't know what's wrong. I liked having Jane stop by."

"Yeah, she's nice."

"Why do you think she came back to buy a pie? Considering she baked them . . ."

Mona gave an evil chuckle.

Chloe took the suntan lotion and gestured for Mona to spread it on her back. She gave Mona a questioning look. "What?"

"Two words: Uncle Dylan."

"You think she likes him?"

Mona nodded, swirling the lotion across Chloe's shoulder blades. "A girl knows a rival when she sees one. It deranges me, to see the way he looks at her."

Chloe frowned. This was disturbing information on two levels. One, she wasn't sure how she felt about her uncle looking any special way at another woman. Not that Chloe had liked Aunt Amanda very much— she had found her snobby and cold, if she had to be truthful, and everyone knew about her having the affair with the polo player from Palm Beach, betraying Uncle Dylan and totally breaking Isabel's heart. But Chloe didn't like change, and she didn't know what it might be like if her uncle sud-

denly got all close and romantic with someone.

But the other reason had to do with Jane.
Chloe had had the feeling Jane was coming
to the stand to see her, Chloe. She really
liked the way Jane smiled at her—as if Jane
was looking for and seeing the very best in
Chloe. Not like teachers, always correcting
you, trying to improve you, and not like parents, just waiting for you to do the next
wrong thing, so they could shake their
heads and let you know how disappointed
they were in you. . . .

No, Jane seemed to just like her. She
liked her without wanting anything in return:
didn't want her to do her homework, didn't
want her to start eating meat, didn't want
her to get into a good college, didn't want
her to clean up her room. It was nice. Jane
was obviously too old to be a real friend; it
was a little like befriending a coach, or the
mother of the kids you baby-sat for. Friendship, or whatever you wanted to call it, without any conditions.

It was a rare thing, Chloe thought, glancing at Mona. Even her best friend had expectations. Chloe was supposed to call her
with any news, was supposed to tell her all

her secrets, was supposed to save both Friday and Saturday nights to hang out or go to the movies. It was enough to wear a person out.

Just then, they heard the sound: Chloe's heart began to thump, and she felt her stomach drop as the engine got louder.

"Sounds like a motorcycle," Mona said.

"A dirt bike," Chloe said, adjusting her bathing suit strap.

He came around the bend. His blond hair was streaked with sun; his eyes were warm golden-green. The day was so warm, he'd left his black leather jacket at home; his T-shirt advertised Purgatory Chasm Surf Shop. The dolphin was right there on his bicep. He had a small bandage on his wrist. His dirt bike didn't have a kickstand, so he leaned it against the split-rail fence.

"Good-bye Gilbert Albert," Mona said under her breath, invoking and banishing the boy Chloe had thought she'd loved till now.

"Hey," Zeke said.

"Hi," Chloe said. She couldn't stop smiling. She saw him checking out her bathing suit. It was the faded pink top of an old bikini, but it fit her really well, showing that she actually had breasts. She wore hip-hugger shorts that dropped below her hip bones. She'd managed to get tan, as much as the April-in-Rhode-Island sun would allow, since their only meeting.

"Nice," he said, glancing up at the dolphin banner.

"Got to keep the sharks away," Chloe said.

"Dolphins really do that?" Mona asked. "Chase sharks?"

"Yeah," he said.

"That's so weird," Mona said. "Considering sharks have teeth and are killing machines and dolphins just swim around looking cute."

"They ram the sharks in the belly with their snouts," Zeke said.

"Nice introduction," Mona said, rolling her eyes.

"Oh," Chloe said. "Zeke, this is Mona. Mona, this is Zeke."

"Hi," they both said. But even though Zeke was saying "hi" to Mona, Chloe felt him staring at her. She felt herself glowing and tingling, as if he had just taken hold of her hand.

"Have you ever seen them do it?" Mona

asked, and Chloe knew she meant the dolphins.

"Yes," he said. "Last summer. Surfing, just out past the break at First Beach. Suddenly we saw fins."

"Fins?" Chloe asked.

"Sharks," he said.

"Oh, shit," Mona said.

Just then a car came along, and it slowed down, but it didn't stop. Chloe had to admit she was glad, at that very moment.

"Yeah," Zeke said. "Nothing too big, but still . . ."

"Great whites?" Mona asked, then did the music from *Jaws:* "*Dunh*-duh."

"No. They're rare in Rhode Island. Blue sharks. They're not man-eaters, but they could do some serious damage to a board. Or a leg."

"So what happened?" Mona asked. Chloe was glad she was there to ask the questions; all Chloe could do was gaze into Zeke's green eyes the way he seemed to be staring into hers.

"Dolphin to the rescue. She'd been playing in the surf. We'd seen her; she'd been hanging around all week. But all of a sudden, she burst out of the water, one big leap. Then she sounded—"

"Went down," Mona supplied, as if Chloe hadn't just read *Moby Dick* for the same English class.

". . . and she came up, nose-first into the biggest shark. Flipped him right out of the water. All we could see was his white belly."

"Did she chase him away?" Chloe asked.

Zeke nodded. "Him and all his friends."

"My, you lead a dangerous life," Mona said sternly. "Bike accidents, shark attacks."

"He has dolphins protecting him," Chloe said.

"Yeah," Zeke said. He was standing so close to Chloe, she could smell the orange and coconuts from his tropical sunscreen. She could see the salt crystals on his eyebrows and the blond hair on his arms. The word "bereft" no longer applied. She felt him take her hand. Her fingers interlaced with his, and she knew it was his way of telling her that she was his dolphin.

And suddenly she had the feeling that he was hers.

CHAPTER 14

Where did you say you're going?" Margaret asked, staring at Jane. "She didn't say," Sylvie said. "She's being very mysterious."

"Inscrutable," Jane said, smiling.

Margaret smiled back. Jane looked very pretty tonight. She was dressed in a long black skirt and very sheer teal blue shirt that set off her eyes, made them sparkle like sapphires. Her black hair glistened; she wore it tucked behind her ear with a jeweled hair clip. Sylvie, on the other hand, sat in the rocking chair beside the bed wearing black sweat pants and a faded yellow T-shirt. She bent over her needlework, concentrating fiercely.

"You'll ruin your eyes in that light," Margaret said.

"I can see."

"You girls never took care of your eyes. Don't think I didn't used to know what was going on. I'd kiss you good night, and I'd barely be out the door before you'd have your books and flashlights out."

Jane raised her eyebrows, but Sylvie didn't look up.

"You're mad, aren't you?" Margaret asked.

"No. Why would I be mad?" Sylvie asked.

"Because it's Friday night, and you lost the coin toss. Your sister gets to go out, and you have to stay home with me. Why don't you just put me in a home, let others worry about me?"

Now Sylvie looked up. She looked upset, even panicked. Margaret felt a twinge of guilt, for being manipulative, but she had wanted to get Sylvie's attention. Jane looked frozen, like a deer in the headlights. Margaret felt her chin wobbling. Although she was trying for effect, the emotions were real.

"You should be going out with John tonight," she said. "He's such a nice man, a good teacher . . . and instead you're stuck home with me."

"No, Mom," Sylvie said. "John's coming

over in a little while. I'm going to take a bath and get ready soon. Please don't say I'm stuck with you—"

"But you are. You're throwing the best years of your life away, taking care of me."

"Mom, you took care of us."

"I know," Margaret whispered. She could feel her own heart beating in her chest. Reaching for her doll, she hugged it tight. She wanted the girls to see. It was a subliminal reminder to everyone. Margaret had raised two children alone. She had taught thousands of children; the town had thought enough of her to name her principal. She had always had the welfare of other people foremost in her mind. And right now she was bedridden. She could no longer take care of others—or even herself. She lived in constant fear that her daughters would decide to send her away.

Sylvie saw her tears. She handed her a tissue.

"What's wrong, Mom?" she asked.

"I . . ." Margaret began, her throat closing as tears flowed from her eyes.

She felt the girls waiting. They both looked so worried. Margaret wanted to tell them: I love you. I love my house. This is the home I made for all of us. This is where you both had the chicken pox. It's where I rocked you to sleep when you had bad dreams. It's where I got over your father. It reflects my love of bare wood floors and hooked rugs and the color blue. It holds all the pictures I ever took of you, and as long as I live here or anywhere I'll never stop wishing I'd taken more. It's where I studied for my master's. It's where I learned to inject myself with insulin.

But the thoughts swirled so intensely, like a huge storm in a little inland bay, that they piled up on each other and knocked each other around and churned up the sandy bottom. All the words just flew apart, but Margaret was left with the same emotions as before and no clear way to express them. She held on to her doll, rocking, rocking as the tears flowed harder.

"I," she said. "I, I, I, I . . ."

Downstairs, Sylvie felt drained. Seeing their mother like that upset her so much. Such a sharp, brilliant woman, unable to finish what she was trying to say. Sylvie had a lump in her throat, and she thought Jane did, too.

Jane stood at the foot of the stairs, staring up.

"Is she okay?" Jane asked.

"Yes," Sylvie said. "She just got upset about something."

"She got upset about the idea of us sending her to a home."

"That's what I've been trying to tell you."

"It's not that I want to do it, Sylvie. It's just that I know we have to start to look into it."

"Like she said: She took care of us."

"But we didn't have diabetes and circulation problems and a tendency to fall . . . and we didn't have—"

"Don't say it," Sylvie said.

"Say what?" Jane asked.

"Alzheimer's."

"Don't say it because you're afraid it's true?" Jane asked.

Sylvie shook her head. She felt a wave of panic rising. Every Christmas she held a writing contest in the school library, and then she'd take the students with the winning entries to Marsh Glen Care Center, to read the poems and essays to the residents there. She pictured all the elderly people. Some were so elegant—well-dressed, coiffed, alert, and excited.

But others were strapped into wheel-chairs, their heads nodding, chins resting on their chests, some moaning or snapping their fingers, talking to ghosts or people no one else could see. Seeing them always tore Sylvie's heart out. Who had they been before they got old? She was so afraid her mother was becoming like them.

"Syl," Jane said, grabbing Sylvie and giving her a hug. "We love her no matter what."

Sylvie gulped some air. She felt dizzy, as if she might pass out. Pushing her sister away, she sat down on the stairs. She blinked, looking up into Jane's blue eyes. Her sister looked beautiful, decked out for the night. John was coming over in an hour, to have pizza. The expression in Jane's eyes was pure sisterly love, and Sylvie couldn't bear it.

"You live in New York," Sylvie said. "You're home just to get things straightened out, and then you'll leave again."

"It's not like that," Jane said.

"You have a business to run! I know that. Are you just going to let it fall apart while you stay here indefinitely?"

"This is the first time off I've taken in fifteen years. People won't forget me. And I won't forget how to bake."

"No, of course you won't. The last few days you've been making pies, and I suppose you've found somewhere to sell them in Rhode Island . . ." she trailed off, leaving Jane a chance to supply the place. But she didn't, and Sylvie reddened, knowing why.

"Sylvie . . ."

"Don't think I don't know," Sylvie said. "They're *apple* pies. The whole house smells like apples."

"Come on—"

"Apple peels in the garbage," Sylvie said.

"You checked the *garbage*?" Jane asked, raising her eyebrows.

"I think it's wrong," Sylvie said. "Whatever you're doing."

"I don't think it is," Jane said.

"It has something to do with Chadwick Orchards, doesn't it? You're making apple pies to *bond* with her. She lives in the midst of apple trees, so you're baking your heart out to give her apple pies. If she lived on the beach, I just know you'd be baking with *dulse* . . ."

"You went through the garbage?" Jane repeated, shaking her head as if she

couldn't believe it. Which was funny, coming from Jane. When they were young, she
was a total detective when it came to their
father's whereabouts. She would go
through his drawers and pockets, read his
datebook, rifle his glove compartment.
Sylvie's stomach flipped at the memory.
"That's disgusting," Jane said.

"No," Sylvie said. "What's disgusting is
you bothering the Chadwicks like this. I'll
bet they have no idea of who you are, do
they?"

"They know who I am. I told them my
name."

"Well, you'd better hope they don't mention you to Virginia. She's got an eagle eye
out for her family. You know the conditions
of the adoption! No one was to know your
identity except her—but she *knows,*
Jane . . ." Sylvie trailed off, knowing that Virginia was like their mother, forgetting a little
more every day. She shifted gears. "You
gave that baby up, Jane," she said.

"I know. Mom saw to that."

"Don't you dare blame Mom! You were
too young, you were in college, he refused
to marry you . . ."

Sylvie swallowed. She saw two bright

spots of red on her sister's cheeks and knew she had gone too far.

"I didn't mean that," Sylvie said, wishing she could take it back. She watched Jane look down and away. Sylvie's heart twisted in her chest. She remembered how much Jane had loved the boy. When they were very young, they would look through magazines and find pictures of brides and imagine their own faces there, and they had promised they would ask each other to be maids of honor, but neither of them had ever married.

"That turned out," Jane said quietly, "to be the least important part." She looked up. "That summer, that whole year without him—I wasn't sure I could go on breathing. But I did."

"I know," Sylvie said.

"It was because I loved him," Jane said. "And that's what love does. It takes hold of you so hard . . . takes hold of your breath. Your heart, your pulse, your thoughts, everything."

Sylvie closed her eyes, thinking of John. Did she feel that way for him?

"Everything," Jane repeated. "And it doesn't let you go. You know how I realized I didn't really love Jeffrey, Sylvie?"

She shook her head.

"Because it let me go," Jane said. "Love let me go."

"I'm glad," Sylvie said, thinking that Jane was making love sound pretty terrible, like a trap or a disease.

"But it didn't let me go with Chloe," Jane said steadily. "It's held on this whole time. I can hardly believe ten minutes have passed, never mind fifteen years. I can still feel her—right here—" She raised her arms in front of her, as if tenderly rocking a baby; but her eyes, staring at Sylvie, were ferocious.

"Then you have to let *it* go," Sylvie said, scared by the intensity.

"It doesn't work that way," Jane said. "Love doesn't give you control—it takes control of *you*. Haven't you figured that out?"

Sylvie stood still. She thought of John. Comfortable, kind, nonchallenging John. She felt something building between them, the very first sticks or straws of a nest, something solid and real. He had held her hand—twice. Both times, she had felt a shiver on the back of her neck. The feeling of his knees touching hers under the card table made her shiver. She had bought some lavender bath salts to prepare for tonight, when she hoped he might kiss her . . . But the way Jane was talking . . . no, Sylvie had never felt that way.

"You make it sound mad," Sylvie said. "As if it drives you crazy."

"It does, in a way," Jane said. "When I think about all the years . . . her first steps, her baby teeth, her first day of school, the music she likes . . . when I think about those things . . ." She closed her eyes.

Sylvie wanted to hug Jane and, at the same time, wanted to run away. She remembered a time when she feared for her sister's sanity—and safety. Those days after the baby's birth had been terrible. Jane had slept all the time. If Sylvie passed by her bed at three in the afternoon, there would be a big, long lump completely hidden by covers, and Sylvie would know it was Jane.

And then, almost two weeks after she'd given the baby up, the keening began. Sylvie had started at Brown, but she was homesick and worried and spent a lot of weekends at home. She could still hear the sounds: high-pitched, inhuman, like a loon on the lake at night. Like an animal. Jane had held them inside for so long, all those months at St. Joseph's and the days at the hospital, and now they were forcing themselves out . . . almost as if the cries were alive, the last vestiges of the life that had grown inside her. Sylvie had cried alongside her sister, but in secret—in her own room, holding her own pillow.

"But, Jane—can't you just accept that you did the right thing? For her, for everyone?"

"I feel as if I did the wrong thing," Jane said.

Sylvie watched her eyes. They were so un-calm. They darted around the room, as if nothing there gave her ease or comfort. They couldn't look at Sylvie. Sylvie had a pit in her stomach. Had Jane felt that way this whole time? Back when it had all happened, Sylvie remembered feeling really angry at her: Sylvie had chosen Brown partly so she could be at college with her sister. Then Jane had gotten pregnant and ruined everything. Later, reading Fitzgerald in freshman English, having witnessed Jane's depression, Sylvie worried that her sister would wind up like Zelda—driven crazy by her own heart.

"Please, Jane, you're worrying me. You're driving *me* crazy."

"You?"

"You're my sister," Sylvie said. "I love you. I can't stand seeing you be so destructive—not just to yourself, I'm taking a risk to say this, but to her. Don't you think it's weird, that some older woman would suddenly appear out of the blue, with fresh-baked apple pies? Don't you think she wonders? You'll be lucky if her mother doesn't call the police on you."

"It's not like that," Jane said. "It's not like that at all."

"Only because they haven't figured it out yet. But when they do—"

"Stop, please?"

Sylvie shrugged. It was Friday night. At least Jane was going out with someone, getting her mind off the whole Chloe craziness. Neither she nor Jane was good with dating—their father and Jane's experience had ruined them both for easygoing Friday nights. Sylvie felt like she was seeing a child off for her first date. She critically appraised Jane's appearance: subtle makeup, silver hoop earrings, gorgeous shining hair, sexy blue top. She took a deep breath, smiling at her sister.

"Truce, okay?"

"Okay," Jane said. "We always seem to be saying that."

Sylvie ignored the barb. "Who's the lucky guy?"

Jane didn't reply. She smiled slightly, more inscrutable than ever. Suddenly tires crunched in the driveway. Sylvie started. What if it was John? She wasn't ready. She had to soak in the bath, and give herself a minifacial, and change into something pretty. But then Jane, looking out the window, kissed Sylvie's cheek and said a really fast good-bye, and ran outside to meet her date before Sylvie could say she wanted to meet him.

Sylvie, feeling momentary relief that it was Jane's date, not John, and a thrill that she actually felt so upset about not being ready, almost as if maybe love was taking control in a way Sylvie had never felt before, went over to the window. She stayed behind the sheer white curtain, trying to sneak a peek at who it was.

She saw a truck. It seemed to have a small tree in the bed. Sylvie's mouth turned to cotton. She watched the driver, visible only from behind, open the door for her sister. She saw Jane climb up the step and get inside. The driver slammed the door behind her.

He was tall. He was trim, with broad shoulders. He had brown hair and a beard, and he wore black jeans and a blue oxford cloth shirt. His limp seemed more pronounced than it had the last time Sylvie had seen him: when he'd driven his mother to the potluck dinner.

It was Dylan Chadwick.

CHAPTER 15

Jane climbed into Dylan's fire-engine-red truck, and he slammed the door behind her. She could almost feel Sylvie's eyes on her, staring out from behind the white curtain. The sense of being watched was strong. She could feel her sister's disapproval and blame. Refusing to look at the window, she turned to Dylan with a big smile as he got in. As she did, she felt the first stab of guilt: Their connection was being built on layers of lies about her motives.

"How are you?" she asked, pushing the feelings far down, knowing she'd do anything to get closer to Chloe, knowing too that she genuinely liked Dylan.

"Great," he said. "And you?"

"I'm fine. But I'm *so* ready to go out."

He laughed. "I kind of wondered. I was

halfway to the door, and you practically mowed me down coming out of the house."

"I'm sorry." She smiled. "I was just feeling stir-crazy and housebound. I think I'm too old to sleep in my old room. My mother and sister—"

"I know, I know," he said, shaking his head. "I have my mother and brother . . . our ages may change, but the dynamic stays exactly the same. Whoever you were in the family at fifteen is just who you are now."

Jane was silent. His words rang in her ears. Outside the truck, the land was lush with spring. Lilacs bloomed all along the road. They were white and deep purple and pale purple and lavender and violet; their scent came through the open windows. New leaves covered the trees with sharp, fragile greenery. The early May night was dark and warm.

They headed north, toward Providence. The skyline came into view. Growing up, Jane had known the two tallest buildings as "the Kleenex box and the Superman building." Hospital Trust was tall and square; Fleet, then Industrial National Bank, looked like a rocket ship and had been rumored to be the building featured at the beginning of

TV's *Superman:* the building George Reeve could leap in a single bound. Off to the right was College Hill, with the rosy brick buildings of Brown crowning the rise. Steeples were everywhere, reminding her that Providence was a town founded by the very religious.

"Like coming home," she said.

"Providence?" he asked.

"My other city . . ."

"Mine, too," he said. "Though it can't really compete with New York."

"It doesn't have to," she said softly. "It has magic New York could never begin to understand."

He laughed. They passed the zoo and then the blue cockroach—a huge bug atop a warehouse, advertising an exterminator—and the harbor came into sight on the right. Tankers off-loading oil, container ships discharging cars from Japan. The ferry was in its slip at India Point. Jane's maternal great-grandmother had sailed into that same dock on Christmas Eve, in 1898. Her baby brother had been born on the passage from Ireland, and her parents had let her name him: George. Jane thought of telling Dylan, but didn't trust herself to recount any story involving a baby. She stared at the calm silver water, its surface undisturbed by any breeze.

Dylan merged onto Route 195 and took the Wickenden Street exit. Providence had many cities within its limits: the Italy of Federal Hill, the academic section around Brown, the bohemians sharing Fox Point with the Portuguese, the blue bloods of the East Side, the artists of RISD. Jane glanced over at him.

"What?" he smiled, as if feeling her gaze.

"Just wondering where we're going," she said.

"Don't you trust me to find a good place?" he asked.

She laughed. "No, I do. I'm just curious about where it will be."

Smiling, he drove them up Benefit Street, elegant with gaslights and colonial mansions. The traffic seemed heavier than it should have been. It crept along past the John Brown House. Jane kept her eyes straight ahead. Her alma mater was just up the hill. Chloe had come into being on a street just a few blocks away.

They passed the white-columned neoclassical Atheneum, and the buildings of

RISD, and the majestic brick Rhode Island Supreme Court house, and then Dylan broke free of the cars by turning left and then right into an alley. He came to a chain-link fence, pulled up to a keypad, and punched in a few numbers.

"What's this, a top-secret parking place?" Jane asked, as the fence slid open and admitted them to a small courtyard.

"Got some rare apple stock in the back of my truck," he said. "And I don't want to tempt any wayward horticulturists."

"But how do you even know that combination?"

"Being an ex-agent has its rewards," he said, smiling lethally.

He opened her door and they left the alley, the fence ratcheting along the track, shutting behind them. He offered her a cigarette. She said no. He lit one for himself, and in the gesture Jane observed intensity, passion, and self-loathing. Walking through a maze of alleys, wondering what had brought Dylan into this dark cove, Jane recognized that she was with a man who had secrets of his own.

He led her between two brick buildings, and they emerged on South Main Street.

Several restaurants lined the block. He slid his arm around her briefly, pivoting her through the front door of a very tiny place called Umbria. It smelled of herbs and olive oil. Candles flickered on the tables. The brick walls were bare. Wooden beams were painted pumpkin.

Two women seemed to be doing everything: hostess, waitress, and possibly chef. They wore black Chinese pajamas and cotton slippers. Their jewelry was sculptural; the tattoos on their wrists were mesmerizing, complicated, and beautiful, leading Jane to understand that they came from RISD.

Dylan ordered mineral water; Jane wanted the same. There was no printed menu. One of the women listed the day's offerings. She was warm, but in a completely impersonal way. Jane would have sworn she'd never seen Dylan before, but when she was finished, he said, "Thank you, Oley."

"Oley?" Jane asked.

"Yes. Olympia," he said. "Her partner is Del—Delphine. They met in art school and couldn't ignore the fact they had both been named after places in Greece."

"So, you come here often?"

He shrugged. "I used to come to Providence for this RICO case I was working on, and there was a restaurant in this same space that I liked a lot—Bluepoint. But they closed, and Oley and Del came along, and I was in the habit of stopping in here, so I gave it a try."

"Different from the red-sauce Italian places up on Atwells Avenue," Jane said, dipping a small piece of olive bread into a dish of green-gold oil.

"Very," he said.

"I like it," she said. "I'm glad you asked me to come."

They ate and talked. The conversation was general, about baking pies and planting trees. Oley's tattoo was on her left wrist and Del's on her right.

"Tattoos have come a long way," Jane said, "from when I was young. It used to be that only sailors had them. Now they're practically ubiquitous. Do you have one?"

Dylan shook his head. "No, do you?"

Jane smiled enigmatically, taking her time and savoring a small green olive and trying to be delicate as she removed the pit.

"Would you like wine?" he asked.

"I don't drink," she said. "But feel free."

"I don't drink, either."

"Really?"

He shook his head. "I've had enough. In the big, global, cosmic sense. I liked it too much, for a while . . ."

Jane's heart lurched. She knew what he had to be referring to. Anyone would drink after losing a child. She should know. . . . "I liked it too much, too," she said.

He looked at her, as if knowing there was much more to the story, but they both stayed quiet and ate their salads. She had started out the evening feeling like a thief: with her sister staring reproachfully from behind closed curtains, knowing she was after something that didn't belong to her. But as she ate she relaxed, and when she looked up at Dylan and saw him watching her, she gazed back and felt they were meeting somewhere in the silence.

The door opened and four people walked in. Two couples, different generations. Jane summed it up in her mind, and Dylan said it out loud.

"A Brown kid, out with his girlfriend and her parents."

"What if they're his parents?"

"The girl looks just like her mother," Dylan said. "And the boy is nervous as hell. I remember the syndrome so well—only back in my time, the parents took us to the Harbor Room."

"I remember the Harbor Room," Jane said. "Did you go to Brown?"

Dylan nodded, and Jane put down her fork.

"So did I," she said.

"A few years behind me . . . when did you graduate?"

"I didn't," she said. "I left after sophomore year."

"Oh," he said, waiting for her to continue. She couldn't. Her stomach dropped, and dropped again. Her food was only half eaten. She forced herself to pick up her fork and keep going.

"Well, obviously you didn't need a degree," he said. "You had a calling, to open your bakery . . ."

"It's nice to think of it that way," she said, feeling a jab of dishonesty, knowing she had to hold back the real story.

"How *did* you start baking?" he asked.

The topic seemed neutral, but it wasn't. Jane pretended to be focused on her plate as she spoke. "Some relatives had a bakery in Twin Rivers," she said. "So I grew up liking the whole idea. It seemed magical to me. Mixing ingredients, stirring them together, and poof: a cake. Making bread was the best. Covering the bowl with a damp towel and finding that the dough had risen—took a lot of faith and science to believe in it all."

"And all those good smells . . ."

Jane nodded, closing her eyes. "Yes. They're so wonderful and comforting, even to this day."

"So your work comforts you?"

"It does."

"Is that why you chose it? Did you need to be comforted?"

Jane didn't reply. She pretended he hadn't asked the question. The Brown kids were at the next table, talking about the theater department and the play they were in. "My cousin taught me," Jane said. "Showed me all her secrets of making pie crust, decorating cakes. She was a really generous person—she always wanted to give her customers something beautiful."

"You do that with Chloe."

Jane's eyes opened. Her insides

churned. Talking about Chloe was so necessary to her; but this was a special dinner
with Dylan, and she couldn't bear the lies,
the unspoken lies.

"Yeah," he continued. "The way you
latched on to her working at the stand. And
the way you decorate the pies you make.
She's really proud to sell them."

"I'm glad," she said, her voice stretched
thin.

"She needs this," Dylan said.

"What?"

"This summer, I guess," he said. "A
chance to feel her feet on the ground. She's
a really special kid. Not everyone under-
stands her."

"What about her," Jane asked, unable to
help herself, "is hard to understand?"

Dylan seemed to think about her question. He refilled their glasses. Jane's throat
hurt, and the water did nothing to quench it.

"After the shooting," he said, "I thought I
was alone in the world. With Isabel dead, I
felt as if my heart had left my body. That's
crazy, I know, but—"

"No, it's not," Jane said. "It's not crazy."

He glanced up, maybe wondering how
she would know the feeling. But he went on.

"I came back to Rhode Island. Couldn't stay in New York . . ."

Jane closed her eyes again. She had gone to New York because she couldn't stay in Rhode Island. She was practicing treachery, to get what she wanted. But her feelings were real. She was talking to the man because she had to, because her heart would quit if she didn't.

"I thought I'd be a hermit here. I wanted to hide out, forget about life, quit talking. I thought I'd take care of the orchard. I wouldn't have to see people, wouldn't have to answer the phone. I'd just dig holes and prune trees and think about Isabel."

"And that's what you did?"

"Yeah, but I couldn't hide. Not really. Because, it turned out, someone needed me."

Jane waited.

"Chloe. She felt Isabel's loss almost as much as I did."

"They were close . . ."

"Yes, they were. But it was more than that; like I said, Chloe's special. Different."

"You did say . . ."

"She's only fifteen," Dylan said. "But she's got an ancient heart."

"In what way?" Jane managed to ask.

"You have to see the way she is with animals. Once a bird fell out of its nest, and she ran all the way through the orchard to get me to put it back. She takes care of the cats as if they're her own kids. When Isabel died, she was so worried about me—knowing how I would feel to lose her. I looked into her eyes, and I could see my own pain. You know what I think it comes from?"

"What?"

Dylan opened his mouth, then shut it again. "Never mind," he said. "I'm not a psychologist."

Sitting very still, Jane blinked. She felt transparent. She could imagine Dylan seeing through her skin, seeing her blood rush through her body. She felt he could see her bones, and she wanted him to realize the truth and forgive her for it.

"I wish you'd say," Jane said.

Dylan turned his fork over and over in his hand. His gaze was deep and intense. He stared at the food on his plate as if it couldn't begin to fill him, yet he didn't seem inclined to eat it.

"There's something about you," he said, "that makes me want to talk." He laughed. "I'm not used to that."

"Me, neither," she said. "What is it?"

He seemed to think, staring at her. "I think you know things," he said, "that other people don't. I'm not afraid of shocking you. It's a good feeling."

"So—tell me more about your niece," she said, feeling a slightly queasy lurch of betrayal.

"Shouldn't do that to my brother," Dylan said. "She's his child, not mine."

"But he's a good father, right?" she asked carefully.

"Yes. Very good. A loving man. That's why I ought to just leave it alone." Dylan trailed off. The Brown family at the next table had ordered champagne and were making a toast to the kids' play and to Monday, when they would graduate. Dylan grinned, his face suddenly relaxed and almost happy. "Hey—"

She raised her eyebrows, heart still racing as she waited to hear where he thought Chloe's empathy came from.

But he seemed to have left that topic. He raised his water glass and tapped Jane's. "We might not be able to get you a Brown diploma on Monday, but I know what we can do tonight—"

"Tonight," Jane said, her mind working: Friday night on graduation weekend. She realized what he meant—the traffic on Benefit Street suddenly making sense to her— even as he said the words.

"Campus Dance," Dylan said. "Did you go your freshman or sophomore year? It's pretty cool. I'll take you after dinner. . . ."

CHAPTER 16

Chloe stood in the orchard. She had sneaked out her window, shinnied down the drain pipe, to meet Zeke in the circle of trees. She wore jeans and a filmy white shirt with bees embroidered on the chest. She had stuck an atomizer of *Muguet des bois* cologne into her pocket, and she'd squirted it on once she'd hit the ground, so her parents wouldn't smell it in the house.

Stars were caught in the tree branches. She wished she could keep stars in her pocket, just to give him every time she saw him. The cats kept her company. They swarmed around, meowing their secrets for the world to hear.

She heard his bike, roaring from a long way off. A passionate environmentalist, Chloe would never have thought she'd want to see headlights in the orchard. But as Zeke came bouncing across the bumpy earth, she felt the joy of watching a meteor streak across the sky.

He stopped, both feet on the ground, hands on the handlebars. His hair shined, bleached white in the starlight. His eyes were as green as the cats'. A head gesture told her to climb on behind him. She did, without thinking twice. As if she'd been riding her whole life, she knew what to do: slipped her arms around his waist.

"Hold tighter," he said, and she did. "Watch your left leg," he said. "That you don't burn your calf on the pipe. It's hot. Ready?"

"Yes," she whispered into the back of his neck.

They rumbled through the orchard, low branches clicking into her face. She kept her eyes closed, smelling Zeke's neck. She kissed it secretly—even he didn't know. He rode her around the whole orchard. The feeling of motion was thrilling, but it paled in comparison with the sense of her body pressed against his.

They passed through openings in the rustic fence. The red barn looked ghostly atop the hill. Its cupola had windows on all four sides. Chloe imagined someone watching her, gazing out with love. Isabel, maybe. Or Chloe's real mother. She didn't feel their disapproval, for what she was doing. She felt them being happy for her.

When they came to the stream, he stopped his bike. This was the borderline, where the Chadwick orchard met some neighboring land. Chloe loved it here. This brook was where she had caught her first frog, where she had learned that brown trout spend hot summer days in the deepest holes. Zeke held her hand, helped her across.

She laughed. "Where are we going?" she asked.

"The orchard stops at the brook, right?"

"Right. Why?"

"I want to get you off your family land."

Zeke slid his arms around her. She thought she would faint on the spot. The touch of his hands was light and hot. He slid his hands under her filmy shirt. They held her sides. His fingers were inching their way toward her breasts. He hadn't even kissed her yet, and the top of her head was already on fire.

"Zoe . . ." he whispered.

"Chloe," she corrected him, slightly shocked and scalded.

"I know." He laughed. "I just thought it would be cool if we both had names that began with the same letter."

"Then you can be 'Ceke.' "

Her filmy shirt was working. He didn't laugh at her joke or continue with the banter. He kissed her. This was a kiss to end all kisses. Chloe's knees gave way. Luckily he was big, strong, and holding on tight: He caught her and held her and covered her mouth with his and touched his tongue to hers, igniting her in a way she had never believed humanly possible. She hoped he didn't know it was her first kiss.

"Oh," she said. That was all, and that was enough: It said everything. Oh the sky is falling, oh my God, oh dear, oh wow, oh it's all over. Zeke took her hand. His wrist bandage was gone. His palms and fingertips felt rough. She imagined all the time he spent surfing in the ocean. He led her through the stream. He was wearing motorcycle boots, but she had white sneakers on—now they were dirty, soggy white sneakers.

She didn't care. It seemed fun and romantic. As they climbed the small rise, her ankles itched as if little night bugs were attracted to her wet skin. Tall grass tickled her calves. A pair of deer were grazing off to the left. She tugged Dylan's T-shirt and pointed.

"Aren't they beautiful?" she asked.

He didn't reply, but just hugged her again, more insistently and lovingly than before.

The deer seemed oblivious, although they must have sensed a human presence. Chloe felt an inner shiver and thrill: It was a good sign, like being blessed by the deer. They liked Zeke, or they would have run away. Sometimes when Chloe saw wild deer she thought of her real mother: She would be graceful and beautiful, just like them. She would have big eyes and a patient way. She would blend into nature.

Holding Zeke made Chloe feel like part of nature. The way he held her was the most romantic thing in the world. Both so tenderly—as if he was afraid he'd crush her with his strength, and passionately—as if he wanted to kiss her all night long. His lips were hot and delicious. This spot was invisible from the barn cupola, and Chloe was glad. She didn't want anyone seeing this.

"Chloe," he said, forgetting about the *Z* names.

She couldn't speak because his mouth was on hers. Something big and hard inside his pants was pressing against her leg. She knew what it was. It excited her a little, but scared her a little, too. She imagined what Mona would say. She pushed Mona from her mind, but Mona came back again and made her feel like laughing: this thing was *hard.* What must it be like to be a boy and suddenly, with very little warning, have part of your body turn to rock?

It must feel weird. It must be very inconvenient. Chloe giggled, then felt horribly embarrassed. She hoped Zeke would think she was just clearing her throat. She felt a little nervous: She hoped she wouldn't have to see it. She really wasn't quite ready to see it.

Now Zeke lowered her onto the ground. He patted down the grass, making a nest: Chloe loved that. He understood nature; this was what deer did, when they wanted to lie down together. Chloe stuck her nose into his neck and sniffed, just exactly as if she were an animal. The impulse just came over her!

His hands went up under her sheer shirt.
She arched into the feeling, then caved in
on herself: the sensation was too intense.
Now one hand was unzipping her jeans,
and he was leading her hand to the front of
his pants. His jeans had buttons. Five of
them. The hard thing was pressing against
them. She felt very shy. She didn't really
want it to spring free, but she knew that he
was expecting her to help it do just that. Her
hand seemed frozen. She tried to will her
fingers to work, but they wouldn't. He
guided her and whispered, "Just pull."

What did that mean? She felt a true jolt of
fear. She was afraid of looking stupid. Girls
should know how to do this, shouldn't they?
When a boy said "just pull," girls should
know what to pull. Besides, they should
want to "just pull." What was wrong with
Chloe, that she didn't? Keeping one eye
open, trying to get her fingers to work,
Chloe watched Zeke do it himself: He pulled
the front of his jeans, just gave it one good
yank, and all five buttons popped open.

She almost laughed at herself for being
so dumb, but then she saw what was inside: the thing she had been waiting for and,
okay, kind of dreading. It was her debut

penis. Her first, ever. No brothers, no previous boyfriends to have seen before. She held herself back from saying, "Yikes." It was just there, between them. His hand was inside her jeans, his finger hooking the edge of her panties. It was all so much and weird, she almost jumped up and ran across the brook.

She raised her head just slightly, to look into the big eyes of the mother deer. She was just staring from across the field. Chloe felt her love. Chloe's love flowed back. She had a strange, falling moment of thinking about her own mother, wondering whether her mother had lain down with a boy in the middle of an orchard sixteen years ago.

"Are you okay?" Zeke whispered.

Her eyes filled with tears. She didn't want them to. She wanted to be happy and give him what he wanted. She wanted to feel like doing whatever they had started. But she had a lump in her throat.

"I don't know," she whispered.

"Is it your first time?"

She nodded.

He smiled, brushing the hair back from her eyes. She blinked, and a tear squeezed out of the corner. It ran down her cheek, and he stopped it with his finger.

"We don't have to," he said. "We can stop."

She swallowed, glancing over at the deer. All the other deer had disappeared, but that one, the mother, just stood watch. Chloe felt her telling her it was okay, that she could be brave and ask for what she wanted, that she didn't have to go all the way.

"It's kind of," she began, "the first time we're getting together . . . and I thought . . ."

"We'd just hang out," he said.

She half laughed, half cried. It sounded so normal, but the way he said it made her realize what a boring idea it was. Zeke was a guy who surfed with sharks, rode his dirt bike without a helmet, met dark-haired girls in starlit orchards.

"I thought . . ." she said.

But then he kissed her again, and differently. It was so soft and gentle. He held her as if she was a baby bird, breakable and precious. His hand was tentative. His kiss was warm and slow and it made something inside her rise and grow—the sun, maybe. His kiss made the sun rise inside her. Chloe kissed him.

Her arms were around his neck. Her heart beat against his. She wanted to cry, but she wanted more not to. Their bodies were so close. Their skin slid together. Chloe was starving to be held. She was yearning for touch so much, she thought she might die of it. He was doing something below their waists. Pulling his pants down, inching her panties down. Chloe barely cared.

She just held on tight. His lips brushed hers. Now he brought himself between her legs, easing them apart. It started out sweet and easy, then got, well, rough. He didn't mean to hurt her, but her back chafed on the ground. Dirt and pebbles got into her bottom. He pushed his penis against her.

Should she say it hurt? She bit her lip. Her head hurt from the pressure of not crying out. Was this supposed to be what it felt like?

"Relax," he said into her ear. "Just let it happen . . ."

"No, but," she said, tears hot in her eyes.

"Come on, relax," he said.

In his excitement, he hadn't taken her pants all the way off. They were bunched down at her feet, stuck on her wet sneakers. His pants were around his ankles. His motorcycle boots clunked into her calves. She cried out.

"You've got to let go," he said, his mouth wet against her ear. "Like riding a wave, like surfing a wave . . ."

Now he was inside her—she could hear him groan with relief. He was hard and hot and she was wetter than any wave he had ever surfed, and she felt him surfing her, felt her wave break just as if it were glass. She lay on her back as the wave broke and broke, and her tears were saltier than the sea, and she cried for her mother and the deer and when she looked around for the beautiful dolphins, all she saw was sharks.

When it was over, Zeke gave her another kiss on the lips. Then he rolled over onto his back—not an easy thing, because their legs and pants were sort of tangled together. She reached for a handful of grass, pulling it up out of the ground, and she used it to wipe herself. She did that over and over.

He sat up. She heard him stand, and she looked up and saw him buttoning his jeans. Waiting for him to give her a hand seemed like an exercise in futility, so Chloe just pushed herself up and tugged her panties and jeans up. The sound the zipper made going up seemed violent in the quiet night. Both she and Zeke avoided all eye contact as they finished getting dressed.

"Guess it's late," he said. "I'd better get you home."

Did he think it was a date? Chloe couldn't quite speak.

"You ready?" he asked. He hesitated, then offered her his hand. She was too frozen to take it.

The stars were brighter than ever. They blazed like a trillion bonfires in the sky. Chloe watched Zeke shrug as she failed to hold his hand. She saw him make his way down the hill, and she heard him splash through the brook. Standing still, she heard branches cracking as he made his way up the bank and into the orchard.

"Chloe?" he said.

She didn't reply. She couldn't.

"Bye, then," he said. After a few more seconds, she heard the engine start up.

Bye. Her mouth made the word, but she had no voice.

The stars made her skin glow. She could feel the starlight on her arms and body, all the way through her filmy see-through shirt.

When she turned around, to look at the deer, she saw that it had run away. A cry bumped up from her chest. She had wanted to see the deer's big steady eyes.

Chloe was tired. She wanted to lie down. She walked right past the spot where she and Zeke had been. It wasn't a real nest. She wanted a real nest. She wanted her real mother. When she got to the spot, near the trees, where she had seen the mother deer, she got down on her hands and knees.

She found indentations in the tall grass. The deer had stood right here. Chloe circled around and around. She pressed the grass down, made another nest. Curling up on her side, she felt the warmth surround her. She imagined it was from the deer, or from her mother, or just from the earth. It didn't matter. It was all the same thing.

Then Chloe began to cry, and all the stars disappeared.

⁕

Dylan was true to his word: he took Jane to Campus Dance. They walked up College Hill from the restaurant, toward the sound of the orchestra. Jane hadn't walked around the Brown campus for almost sixteen years—since she had left that spring of sophomore year. When Sylvie had graduated four years later, Jane had been "too busy," at work in New York.

The hill was steep. Every step was an effort, and she knew it had to be even more so for Dylan. She slowed her pace so he could keep up. But the truth was, the closer they got to Brown, the more her heart felt squeezed.

"What happened?" she heard herself ask.

"To my leg?"

"Yes."

"It's nothing," he said.

But she knew it was, so she took the opportunity to stop and catch her breath, while giving him a long expectant look.

"I got shot," he said. "And it did some damage."

He sounded tense, and stopped talking. He resumed climbing Angell Street, and Jane had no real choice but to follow. She had so many questions for him, and she wanted to keep from thinking about her own past, so she caught up and walked alongside him.

"That's terrible," she said.

He didn't reply.

Carrie Tower came into view, the tall brick bell tower that marked the northwest corner of the green. Horace Mann was off to the right. Jane's eyes flicked over, then away. Music drifted across the green. They walked through a space in the wrought-iron fence, and Jane headed for the tower.

"The dance is this way," he said, grabbing her hand.

"I know," she said, her heart racing. It all felt like too much for her. Hundreds of bright paper lanterns illuminated the night sky. They swung in the breeze, lanterns of gold, vermilion, persimmon, and azure. The orchestra played; people danced in the night. It was just like going back in time—sixteen years.

Dylan followed her to the base of the tower. They stood together, looking up. It was almost a hundred feet tall, and Jane knew that it came with a sad, beautiful legend—but she hadn't stayed at Brown long enough to know what it was.

"Do you know the story?" she asked.

Dylan nodded.

"Can you tell me?"

He paused, and she saw him narrow his eyes. He stared up to the clock on top. "It was built by Paul Bajnotti as a memorial to his wife, Carrie. She was the granddaughter of Nicholas Brown."

"Of Brown University," Jane said.

Dylan nodded. He led her to a plaque on the base, and she crouched down to read the inscription. " 'Love is strong as death,' " she read out loud.

Her palms were sweaty, and her head felt light. How could words about death remind her of that night sixteen years ago? She had lain on a floor with a boy she loved, and they had brought Chloe into being. That wonderful girl with the dark hair and cool blue eyes, with the love of animals and enthusiasm for life, had started her journey just across the way.

The music and the lanterns brought everything back, a fast track into Jane's memory bank. Lost in her own thoughts, she almost forgot about Dylan. He just stood there, staring at the inscription.

"It's true," he said. "Love is as strong as death. Stronger."

Jane made the connection: This tower was a memorial to a man's beloved wife. Amanda and Isabel. She looked up into

Dylan's eyes. "What are you thinking?" she asked.

"About those words. And how true they are."

"Your wife . . ."

He hesitated. "We were separated when she died," he said. "I was thinking about my daughter."

"Isabel," Jane said, remembering the picture in Dylan's kitchen.

"You asked me earlier about my leg," he said, gazing down at Jane.

She nodded, waiting.

"I almost lost my leg," he said. "The bullet shattered the femur, and it got infected. I've had twenty-two surgeries, and right now I have more steel than bone in there. But that doesn't matter . . ."

"It does matter," Jane said.

Dylan shook his head. His eyes flicked up the tower again, then back to Jane. "No, it doesn't. Because the day I got shot was the day they died. Amanda and Isabel. I couldn't protect them. After it happened, I couldn't even pick up my daughter. I couldn't carry her—she needed to go to the hospital, but I couldn't even move."

"It wasn't your fault," Jane said, stunned. "I know it wasn't."

Dylan didn't answer. He closed his eyes. Jane's throat ached. She glanced over at the old English Department and felt the presence of Chloe, just as if she was standing right there. She knew that Dylan was sensing Isabel, that his love was stronger than her death. She knew that their daughters were with them.

Without even thinking, she took his hand. The orchestra was playing, and the music was lush and romantic. It filled Jane with emotions she hadn't felt in many, many years. Dylan's hand felt so solid. Paper lanterns illuminated the trees. The shush of the wind sang in the leaves.

He smiled for the first time since dinner. But it was a great smile, brighter than all the lanterns in the trees, and it made Jane smile right back at him. They just stood there, in the shadow of the tower, holding each other's hand. How had they gotten here? Jane and this wounded, reserved man who just happened to be Chloe's uncle. Jane blinked slowly. He linked her with Chloe. They were a secret triangle, the three of them.

"Well," he said, as if the mystery of sudden connection had stunned him as well.

She smiled a little wider.

It happened so easily, almost without them noticing. How could this happen this way, so fast? They each took a small step closer to each other. His arms slid around her. Jane pressed against his chest, and she felt a ripple go through her body, as if she'd just come to life. Her heart beat very quickly. The music was so pretty. She tilted her head back and closed her eyes, and he kissed her.

The paper lanterns turned to stars. They swung wildly in the sky. His beard felt good against her skin. She turned to air. The years flew by and went backward, all at the same time. She was Carrie in the tower, she was Chloe in the orchard. But then, feeling Dylan's hands moving slowly on her own back, tasting his lips on hers, Jane knew that she was solid, real, here.

He whispered, his mouth on her ear: "Dance with me . . ."

She was already in his arms. The music had already taken hold. They moved together. The dance was just like an embrace, only with feet moving. Dylan's limp went away. His leg was perfect, fine, healed. Nothing bad had ever happened. Or, everything that had was swept away by the night, the lanterns, the stars, the tower, the inscription: *Love is strong as death.*

Or, as Dylan had said before they'd started to dance, stronger. . . .

PART TWO

Stars in the Attic

CHAPTER 17

Chloe was tired. It seemed weird that just as summer was about to get rolling, she could barely drag herself out to feed the cats every night. The thing was, it was exhausting to go out in the fresh air. The breeze would move, ruffle her hair, caress her skin, remind her of being touched. The cats would brush up against her—all the mothers and fathers and kittens, meowing and mewing and tickling her skin. Where Chloe had always loved physical contact with the cats before, now it made her want to hurry through the feeding and get back to her room. It reminded her of that night, almost a week ago. Zeke.

Back inside, the house was still. Her parents liked air-conditioning. Chloe used to beg to open the windows. Before, when she was home alone, she used to fly through the house, shutting off air conditioners and throwing open windows. Now she was just as glad to have the mechanical hum, the technological cool. The sound quieted the thoughts in her head.

The phone rang, and it was for her. Chloe had avoided the phone for days. Mona wanted to know when they were working at the stand. Friday, Saturday, and Sunday, Chloe told her. So, why haven't you called and how was the meeting? Mona asked. The big secret romantic in-the-orchard meeting? It was okay, Chloe finally said. But Zeke's kind of a jerk. I don't like him any- more.

Mona seemed surprised by that. Or maybe she was just surprised by the fact Chloe hadn't rushed to call her, and by the cool, quiet way Chloe said the words: as if she didn't really care.

Because Chloe was known for caring. She was the kind of girl who, when she liked a boy (the way she had liked Gilbert Albert for the last ten years) she knew his sched- ule by heart. She saved the straw he drank his Coke with. She wore a Red Sox cap because that was his favorite team. Stuff like that.

So, Mona was probably a little weirded-out by Chloe's nonchalance. Perhaps she mistook it for maturity. Yes, it had been a big year for young Chloe Chadwick; enough to breed maturity, if nothing else. Chloe gave the time line some thought: She had gotten fired from the SaveRite for writing antimeat notes, she had single-handedly brought the family apple stand back from the brink of destruction, she had lost her virginity, and she had very calmly decided she didn't actually like the boy she'd been madly in love with only moments before.

Only that was a lie.

She wasn't very calm at all.

Outside she appeared very serene and mature. Inside, she was hamburger. She felt like a broken watch. She felt smashed and wrecked. She felt like a cow who had been corralled and slaughtered and all ground up.

That was why everything made her so tired. Because all her energy seemed to have left the building. She faked being sick for two days, and then could barely stay awake in school and couldn't wait to get home and take a nap. She barely spoke to

Mona. She yawned when her mother told her to do her homework, when her father wanted to discuss her SATs. Oh, are we boring you? her father had asked at dinner last night.

No, she wanted to cry. I'm not bored. Something happened to me. I'm not sure what it was. Her heart didn't match her head.

Her thoughts were in a jumble. The air conditioner hummed softly, making her feel as if she was sealed up in a refrigerator. Nothing could get in or out. Her house was hermetically sealed. She fell asleep, fully dressed, on her bed right after school.

Her dreams were scary.

In one, she was a star. She twinkled in the sky. People looked up at night to make wishes upon her. Suddenly she was falling. Streaking through the darkness, hurtling through space. She fell to earth. Chloe was a dead star, lying in the sand like a shell, while boys surfed off the shore. A woman was beachcombing. The woman picked her up and carried her home. She put Chloe in tissue paper and packed her into a box. Placing the box in the attic, the woman whispered, "You are my child." Chloe cried in her sleep, knowing that woman was her real mother.

Another dream: Chloe was swimming in a vat of gel. There were fins everywhere. She grabbed for one, thinking it was a dolphin, and it was a shark instead. Then she reached for another, and it was a dolphin, but it had huge teeth and was going to eat her. Crying out, Chloe thought she was going to die. She went under, gulping gel. Fins were everywhere, bumping her between the legs.

When she came up for air, she heard someone calling her name. It was a lady in a boat. Only when the boat got closer, it wasn't a boat at all: it was a pie. The lady leaned over, to pull Chloe out of the fluid. Chloe was crying, squalling like a baby who had just been born. The lady hauled Chloe into the boat, saving her life. Chloe just wept, feeling so happy to be alive and not just a star in the attic.

When she woke up, she had to tell herself it was just a dream. She wished she had someone to haul her out of these gunky feelings. Her mother was downstairs, putting groceries away. Chloe pushed herself up off the bed. She padded down the hallway, down the stairs. She found her mother placing vegetables in the refrigerator.

"Hi, honey," her mother said.

"Mom . . ." Chloe began, standing in the doorway, feeling panicked.

Her mother met her gaze. She seemed to take in Chloe's rumpled clothes and messy hair, and she shook her head.

"Mom . . ." Chloe said again.

"Chloe, you know I'm not thrilled about you working at the stand, but even that's better than you coming home and sleeping all day. Doesn't Uncle Dylan need you today? Because I drove by his house on the way home, and I saw his baking friend's car there."

"Jane," Chloe said softly, realizing that she was the woman in her dream, the woman in the pie.

Her mother nodded and smiled. "I want to meet her. Do you think something's going on? They seem to be spending a lot of time together . . ."

"I don't know," Chloe said, yawning again and rubbing her eyes. She had something to ask her mother, or tell her, but suddenly she was losing her nerve.

"I think it would be wonderful. He's been so shut down since—"

Chloe froze. She didn't want to hear her mother talk about Isabel and Aunt Amanda. Somehow that would be too much. Chloe was sure that talking about them would just crack her open like a walnut and leave her open for the crows to peck to death.

"Well, I just hope she's nice," her mother concluded, packing the lettuce into the drawer. "Because he deserves it."

"She is," Chloe said quietly.

"She certainly knows how to bake apple pies," her mother said.

Chloe nodded. She looked out the window. The backyard was all green, with darker gray green shadows. She thought about walking over to Uncle Dylan's to see him and Jane. She could work an extra day, even though the stand was officially open only on weekends until school got out.

But she decided against it. Things were bothering her, and she needed to deal with them. As much as she would prefer going back upstairs to lie down, there was somewhere she had to go.

"Okay, I'm going," Chloe said, leaving her mother to think she meant she was going to

Uncle Dylan's. "I might stop by Mona's afterward."

"Fine. Why not take some books, so you can do homework together?"

"Great idea," Chloe said, grabbing her knapsack and stuffing books inside. Anything to throw her mother off the track of where she was really going.

"Counting down till the end of school," her mother said, smiling.

"And then the long hot summer," Chloe said, hoping the words didn't sound as ominous as they felt.

❧

Dylan stood at the sink, filling the coffeepot. Jane leaned against the counter. He felt her nearness all through his body, like an electric current. She had come by to drop off pies—the first time he'd seen her since last Friday night—and he'd asked her to stay for coffee.

"You drink yours black, right?" he asked, remembering from dinner.

"Yes, thank you," she said.

He nodded, taking down mugs from the cupboard. Everything seemed so outwardly casual, but every muscle in his body was tense, feeling their kiss. They had talked once on the phone—Jane thanking him for dinner and Dylan placing the pie order. And when he'd opened the door to her today, he'd looked into her eyes and wondered whether she felt the same way he did, whether she'd lost sleep thinking about it, whether she'd mind if he took her in his arms and kissed her again. Again, their quick and sudden ease of connection surprised him; shocked him with happiness.

"I should have brought an extra tart or something," she said. "To have with our coffee."

"We could have one of these," he said, gesturing to the large box she'd brought, "but Chloe made the order, and I know she'll be expecting them all to be there."

Jane smiled. "Then we can't disappoint her. She's doing a good job at the stand?"

"Very. School's out next week, and she'll be working full-time," Dylan said, pleased that Jane seemed so interested in his niece.

"That's great," she said.

Dylan nodded. His chest felt hot. His heart was working hard. It was a big country kitchen, and they were standing a good twelve feet apart, but he could feel energy pouring off her. She wore jeans and a sweatshirt—the pants fit her really well, and the shirt was too big. The shape of her taut body was visible under the fabric, and he just wanted to hold her, and feel her against him.

He hadn't felt this way in so long; it had been years. Not just since Amanda's death—even before. Their relationship had been strained for a long time, and Dylan had shut down. He had thrown himself into his work, and that was easy enough to do. He'd had a work log as big as he wanted it to be: plenty of criminals to catch, witnesses to protect in New York City.

And then the shooting happened, and then he was in the hospital, and when he came out he was still in shock. That's how he had to look at it now: He was going through the motions of life, feeling nothing. Just a man imitating being a man. He blocked out his family, his feelings, his memories. Everything.

Emotions could be overwhelming, and when they were, he did what he'd started doing recently: lit a cigarette. He saw Jane watching him.

"Does it bother you?" he asked.

She shook her head, not very convincingly.

"It does," he said.

"Just," she said, "that it's not good for you."

"I know." He exhaled a long stream of smoke, looking at the picture of Isabel on the refrigerator. He remembered when she was nine, and she'd begged him to quit. "My daughter used to tell me that," he said.

"What did she say?"

"Oh, she'd learned about smoking in school," he said. "I was working long hours that year, and I wasn't home too much. When I was, there was—" He wanted to tell Jane about the tension, wanted to explain that he'd been a good husband, had loved his wife, hadn't been loved in return. But he hated self-pity, and he didn't want to be disloyal to Amanda, even now, so he skipped that part. "Anyway, I was smoking too much. We came to Rhode Island for the summer, and Isabel and Chloe ganged up on me and told me to quit."

"Good for them," Jane said.

Dylan nodded, tried to smile. He couldn't quite tell her that he'd stopped caring about his health, about his own life. Bringing the orchard back to health and life had run parallel with his own feelings of being like a zombie. Who cared if he died? Isabel was the only one who ever really had.

"Did you stay right here, in this house?"

Dylan must have looked confused, because she went on: "That summer? When the girls were nine?"

"Oh," he said. "No. We stayed in Newport. At Amanda's family's house."

"She was from there?"

"Summers. She grew up on Fifth Avenue. But they had a pretty great place on Bellevue Avenue."

"One of the mansions?" Jane asked.

He nodded. Everyone in Rhode Island knew Newport, had spent time there. But most, even those who had lived in the state their entire lives, visited as tourists. They would walk along Cliff Walk, or drive down Bellevue Avenue, or bicycle Ocean Drive; they would have drinks at the Candy Store and the Black Pearl, dinner at The Pier, brunch at the Inn at Castle Hill. They would imagine how it felt to own a yacht, live in a limestone palace, attend a party at Harbor Court.

"What was it like?" Jane asked.

"The house? It was marble and—" Dylan began.

"No," Jane said. "I mean, what was living there like?"

Dylan thought of the black-tie dinners, her father's Hinckley Bermuda 40, her mother's charity ball, their memberships at Bailey's Beach and the Reading Room. "It was tiring," he said.

"Really?" She smiled.

"Yeah. There was always an invitation to something. Isabel and I just wanted to go swimming and play on the beach, but we always had to get dressed up for one party or another."

"Amanda came from a society family?"

"You could put it that way," he said, remembering how he had once said that the family didn't have a Bible—they had the Social Register.

Jane gazed at him, as if trying to figure out how he had fit into such a life. He caught a glimpse of himself in the window glass—beard, frayed old shirt—and had a hard time understanding it himself.

"They were low-key, in their way," he said. "Her father drove a Bentley—he thought a Rolls-Royce was too flashy, because of the hood ornament. And he had his driver wash it himself, in the back courtyard, with the hose, instead of wasting ten bucks at a professional car wash."

Jane laughed. "Sounds like people I bake for, in the city. I'll send my assistant to deliver a big beautiful cake to Park Avenue, and the hostess gives her a dollar tip."

"That's how they stay rich, I was told," Dylan said. "Amanda's parents thought tipping was an affront to free enterprise. They thought if businesspeople paid proper salaries to their employees, then tipping would become obsolete, and the poor employees wouldn't have to rely on the whims of consumers."

"Oh," Jane said, still laughing. "I get it now. They were just doing their part to check whims and further free enterprise. I'll have to tell my next assistant."

"They used to tell Isabel that they were keeping her inheritance safe."

Jane's smile went away.

Dylan hadn't meant to destroy the lighthearted mood, but that's what happened. Isabel was here—she was always here. And the fact that her inheritance was safer than she was, that was just the true and incontrovertible way of the world. Dylan put out his cigarette.

The coffee was ready. Dylan poured it, handed Jane a mug. She took the mug he offered her. Then she took the other one, and placed them both on the counter. His hands were now empty. Jane was staring at him. He felt his heart beating so hard, through his chest, and it felt so outrageous—it made him feel both so alive and as if he might die.

"Tell me about her," Jane said.

"She was amazing," he said.

Amazing: the word shimmered in the air. Jane just closed her eyes; her mouth was open just slightly, as if she could taste the word.

"She was so funny—she loved to laugh. We were always playing jokes on each other. She knew I was a cop, sort of, so she used to make up mysteries for me to solve. She was always leaving me clues . . ."

"Creative," Jane said.

"Very. And so smart. I'd leave her clues, too. I'd come out with really complicated scenarios, and she'd always figure them out."

Jane drifted over to the refrigerator,

where Isabel and Chloe's picture was stuck up with magnets. Dylan took it down and handed it to her, so she could have a closer look. His daughter was so soft, with round cheeks and light curls—so smiling and re- laxed. Beside her, Chloe looked like a dark- haired waif, sharp-edged, with worry behind her smile.

"Beautiful girls," she whispered.

"They look so different," Dylan said. "But they were very close."

"You told me that Chloe and you talked . . ."

"Yes," Dylan said. "When I came back to Rhode Island for the first time after the shooting. Chloe had stopped talking."

Jane lowered the picture to stare at him. Dylan took it from her, looked at it more carefully himself. "She's such a sensitive lit- tle girl. Isabel's death hit her very hard. She knew how it would affect me . . . and she mourned—so deeply for her cousin."

"She was only eleven," Jane said.

"Yes," Dylan said. "But she knows loss. I would never tell my brother and sister-in- law, but Chloe has felt a lot of grief in her young life."

"Well, they must know," Jane said. "I'm

sure they mourned for your daughter as well . . ."

Dylan shook his head. He stared at the picture again, this time focused on his niece and not his daughter. "Chloe's greatest grief is for her mother. Her 'real mother,' as she calls her."

Jane didn't speak. She just stood there, very silently, staring at him.

Dylan put the picture back on the refrigerator. He lined it up, so its edges were straight. When he turned around, he saw that Jane was waiting for him to speak.

"I don't think she'll ever get over it," he said. "Being given up."

Jane nodded. A telephone rang. It wasn't Dylan's—it must have been Jane's cell phone. But she ignored it, and it rang and rang. She was gazing up at him, her expression charged, as if, somehow, she felt as lost as he did. She obviously had a great capacity for caring, and he could see her taking in Chloe's pain like a thunderbolt to her own heart.

"What is it?" he asked her, taking a step closer. As he did, he saw that her eyes were filling with tears.

"I'm just so glad," she said. "That Chloe has you."

"Me? I'm just her uncle," he said. "I always feel I don't do enough for her."

"I'm just glad for her," she said. "That she can talk to you. It's very caring, for you to know those things about her, and to carry them around—someone else might just have set them aside."

"I don't forget," he said, standing right beside her. He wanted to dry her tears. If she'd let him, he'd hold her close for the rest of the night. "It's one of the things I know about myself; I don't forget things," he said, staring into her blue eyes. His own voice caught, and he had to clear his throat.

"Are you okay?" she asked.

He nodded but still couldn't speak.

"No, you're not," she said, touching his cheek, resting her hand on his bearded face. "How could you be?"

"Time's gone by," he said. "I feel as if I should."

" 'Should' is a terrible word," she said. "You don't deserve to do that to yourself."

"Thank you for understanding," he said, barely able to get the words out.

She smiled, and she looked so grateful—

as if he had just handed her a gift—that he loved her for it. He stared at her straight hair, her fresh, freckled skin, the simple silver locket she wore around her neck. He had noticed it at the apple stand, and at dinner the other night. It seemed she never took it off.

Dylan couldn't help remembering another time he couldn't quite speak, in Newport, just before the deaths; he was so unhappy at home, so overwhelmed by thoughts of what he should do, concern over what would become of Isabel if he left the marriage. Amanda hadn't yet announced her decision to separate, but he was having his own ideas about it.

"You know, you remind me of something," he said. "Not because you're anything like her, but because you're so different—"

"Who?"

"My wife," he said. He knew he shouldn't tell the story; he wanted to stay loyal to Amanda's memory. But he had been so alone for so long, and right now he felt such heat and emotion shining out of Jane, that he felt the physical need to unburden himself.

"We were at dinner at her parents' house, and her father asked me to make the toast. I can still see the crowd gathered: tanned, gowned and jeweled, black-tied. I stood, started to raise my glass . . . I was very unhappy. We both were, Amanda and I. As it turned out, she asked me for a divorce later that month. But that night, I was just swamped with feelings of regret . . . longing for something we didn't have . . ."

"But you had to make a big toast and sound the part," Jane said.

Dylan nodded. "So I raised up my glass, and . . . nothing."

"Nothing?"

"No. I started to say something incredibly profound, but no sound came out. I got all choked up. Got emotional," he said. "In front of all those people . . . my in-laws watching with horror, and all their sunburned friends looking as if they wanted to disappear. And Amanda . . ."

Jane's eyes still looked a little sad, but playful and full of affection. Dylan stood still, forcing himself to breathe. He stepped out of the moment, observed it from a distance. He felt so comfortable with this woman. She was giving him a teasing, knowing look, as if she'd known him her whole life.

Strange thing was, he felt that way, too. There was an old-shoe feeling, in the best possible way, about Jane Porter. He felt he wanted to walk around with her forever. What was that about?

He'd been on a sort of fast track in life, which had neglected love. Brown, the Marshal Service, Washington, D.C. Amanda was beautiful, her father was politically connected, she came from Rhode Island: She was his first serious girlfriend, and she became his wife. But staring at Jane, at her sad eyes and hesitant smile, he realized he'd missed something.

He'd missed whatever was going on in his heart right now. His mouth was dry. He wanted to walk over and hold her. On the other hand, he felt shy about trying anything. He loved the way she seemed to care about Chloe. And about Isabel.

Even now, her gaze darted back to the picture. She seemed totally at ease, leaning against the counter.

Could he imagine standing around in a kitchen with Amanda? Nope. There would be drinks on a silver tray, carried out to a terrace. There would be Vivaldi on a stereo. Classical music was key. For some reason, their house always resounded with some orchestra or other.

Dylan liked fiddles and guitars. He liked Steve Earle and the BoDeans. Emmylou. He liked his pickup truck, which he called "the rig." When he dug holes to plant his root stock, he felt a connection with reality. Something about soil made him think of life—how could it not? Roots and dirt and life and love. And Jane. He chuckled.

"What's so funny?" she asked.

"My mind just went through a gyration that made perfect sense to me, but I have the feeling might set you off."

"Yeah? Try me."

"Roots, dirt, and thou," he said.

"You left out apples," she said. Then she stood on tiptoes, tipped her head back, and kissed him. Thunderbolts were all over the place today. He felt them flying out of Jane, right into his body. The charge shook him from head to toe. He held her tighter. He thought he'd die if he ever had to let her go. He was forty-eight years old, but he had never felt this way before.

"Jane," he said, when he felt her lower down from her toes.

"I couldn't help myself," she said, looking up.

"I'm glad," he said. "I'm really glad about that."

She seemed to take half a step back. "What you don't understand," he said, keeping her locked in his arms, "is that I can't let go of you."

She laughed, leaning into him. "Good," she said, "because I don't know what I'd do if you did."

He bent down to kiss her again, and her lips felt so hot and sexy, so flat-out physically exciting, that he almost forget, almost, the wide-open feeling in his heart that told him his feelings were bigger than this kiss, bigger than one moment of passion.

Suddenly her cell phone began ringing again. The tone was muffled but insistent. She ignored it till it stopped ringing, but then it started again. Laughing, she broke away, and reached into her bag.

"Hello?" she said.

Dylan was already thinking about what he'd say to talk her out of wherever she had to go. He was smiling, ready to ask her to come into the orchard with him and then stay for dinner. But the look in her eyes wiped the smile from his face.

"What is it?" he asked.

"That was my sister," she said, just holding the phone as if she had forgotten how to click it shut. "Sylvie's been trying to call me . . . our mother's been taken to the hospital."

CHAPTER 18

Mom fell," Sylvie said when Jane walked off the elevator. "Is she okay?" Jane asked, hugging her sister.

"She broke her hip, and she's in surgery now."

Jane leaned back, trying to read Sylvie's eyes. They were clouded by a kind of despair. She had a hunched-shoulder aspect that made Jane realize that there was more going on than Sylvie was saying.

"What happened?"

"She got out of bed by herself," Sylvie said. "She tried to walk downstairs and lost her footing. When I got to her, she told me she had something she wanted to say to me. Only, she thought I was *you* . . ."

Sylvie couldn't even look Jane in the eyes. "I wasn't there," Sylvie said, all in a rush. Only then did Jane really notice that she was dressed up: blue dress, blue high heels, a lovely curl to her hair. "John asked me to come to school and address his class on ways to best utilize the school library, and little-known facts about the Dewey Decimal System. I had planned to ask you to stay with Mom, but you disappeared before I had the chance. . . ."

"I was delivering pies," Jane said, shivering as she remembered being held by Dylan and what he had said about Chloe grieving for her real mother.

His touch was on her skin. She held herself, to keep it there.

There was confusion. This was a tense situation, yes. Her mother was in the hospital. And Jane was the Mata Hari of Chadwick Orchards. Using Dylan to get close to Chloe, she had somehow missed this possibility: She was falling in love with the man. The way he loved the orchard, the way he loved Chloe, understood her grief. She had felt, for a few moments that afternoon, that she held his heart in her hands.

She incurred a dirty look from Sylvie, but it was nothing to the turmoil in her own being.

"Anyway, it was only going to be for one period. I told Mom what I was planning to do. She thought it was a wonderful idea, and she promised—*promised*—not to get out of bed. I fixed her a little tray, made sure she used the toilet before I left . . . She seemed very content. I left her there, reading Chaucer."

Jane tried to smile. Their mother: She read Chaucer the way some people read thrillers. Hungrily, turning the pages, not to know what happened next—she had read the works a hundred times before—but for the love of the language.

"But somewhere along the way, she got it into her head that she had to talk to you. So she got out of bed, made it to the stairs, and tumbled down." Sylvie looked down at her shoes with remorse. "I don't know how long she'd been lying there when I got home. I stayed a little longer than I'd said . . . John and I went into the teacher's lounge for coffee after class . . . and all my old friends were there, and we were catching up, while . . . Mom just lay on the floor with a broken hip."

"Sylvie, it's not your fault," Jane said.

"I feel like it's both of our faults," Sylvie said.

"Wait a minute—I'm not going to take that on," Jane said.

"I could have sworn you told me you didn't have plans today."

"I said I hadn't *made* plans," Jane said. "But that didn't mean that something wouldn't come up."

"You didn't even tell me you were leaving!"

Jane knew that. She had waited until Sylvie was in the shower, till she could hear the hiss of the hot water, before loading the pies into the station wagon and driving away. She hadn't wanted to hear what Sylvie would say about going to the Chadwicks'.

"You took the car, and I had to call John to come pick me up between periods," Sylvie said reproachfully. "That's bad enough. But our mother was alone, and she *fell*. She lay there for God knows how long in horrible pain. You should have seen her—heard her! She was practically delirious. Grabbing my hand, calling your name . . . saying over and over that she had something to tell you—"

"I'm so sorry," Jane said, closing her eyes against the picture.

"And all because you're living a lie!"

"No, I'm not."

"You were evasive with me about your plans, and you're fooling the Chadwicks. Whatever you're telling them about the pies, or your baking, that's not the real story. It's wrong, Jane."

Jane opened her mouth, to tell Sylvie she didn't understand. But suddenly she knew her sister was right. Her insides seemed to drain out of her, and the stark white hospital lights and the insipid blue walls seemed to close in on her. Dylan's words about Chloe's grief rang in her ears. She felt like a fraud, completely exposed in the bright light.

What was she going to do about it?

"How did she get here?" Jane asked. "Mom, I mean."

"I called nine-one-one. The same ambulance that picked her up before came again. The EMTs remembered her."

"Was she alert?"

Sylvie half laughed, half sobbed. "Alert enough to point out a fly buzzing around in back. And to ask the woman taking her blood pressure what her favorite class in school had been."

"High school principal to the core. What did the woman say?" Jane asked, smiling at the thought.

"Phys Ed," Sylvie said.

"Mom didn't like that answer," Jane said, and she and Sylvie both laughed softly. "Remember, she never really considered gym a class? She used to give us notes to excuse us all the time, so we could stay in the library and read?"

"I do remember," Sylvie said. " 'Please excuse my daughter from gym, as she has a sore toe.' What she wanted to write was, '. . . as she has a superior mind and can't be squandering precious reading time kicking a ball.' "

" '. . . Or baking a cake,' " Jane said.

"Oh, Jane," Sylvie said, her gaze full of sadness.

"I know I disappointed her," Jane said.

"She wanted the best for you," Sylvie said. "She thought that when you gave up the baby, you'd go back to Brown."

"I know she thought that," Jane said. "But I wasn't the same person anymore. She must have forgotten that part—that having a baby changes you forever. Whether you raise her or not."

"You were so young," Sylvie said.

"I was old enough to be a mother."

"Let's not fight, okay?" Sylvie asked. "Not while Mom is lying there, in surgery . . ."

"I don't think we're fighting," Jane said. But her body felt stiff and tense, as if she was an out-of-shape prizefighter. Her family would never understand how she felt. Sylvie couldn't imagine what it felt like, to be twenty years old with huge aching breasts full of milk and no baby to drink it. She would never believe that even now, sixteen years later, once or twice a month, Jane dreamed of giving birth. It had happened in a hospital not very far from here. This surgical floor reminded her of where she had spent her labor and had Chloe.

Just then, a doctor in green scrubs came through the ER doors. He held a clipboard, checked it, and called out, "Sylvie Porter?"

"That's me," Sylvie said.

The doctor walked over. He was about thirty-five, compactly built, with earnest brown eyes and a receding hairline.

"And I'm Jane Porter," Jane said. "We're Margaret's daughters."

"I'm Dr. Becker," he said. "And I did your mother's surgery." He glanced around the room. There were two yellow vinyl seats available in a corner, and he gestured toward them. They all drifted over in that direction, but when they got there, no one sat down.

"How is she?" Jane asked.

"She was in a lot of pain when we brought her in," Sylvie said.

"We've been trying to make some decisions about her care," Jane said, and Sylvie shot her a sharp look.

"The surgery went well," the doctor said, "but there were some complications."

"Complications?" Jane and Sylvie asked at the same time, and Jane's blood turned to ice.

"We found some enlarged lymph nodes," he said. "In her pelvic region."

"Oh," Jane said, shocked not so much by his words, but by the gravity of his tone.

"She has diabetes," Sylvie explained, smiling weakly. "And she develops infection really easily. Isn't that what causes swollen glands? Remember, Jane, we used to always get them when we had sore throats? I can just feel Mom checking my . . . she'd run her fingers along under my chin—"

"These nodes have a different appearance than swollen glands," Dr. Becker said.

"Could it be a *bad* infection?" Sylvie asked.

"I removed several," the doctor said. "To be biopsied."

"Biopsied?" Sylvie asked.

Jane didn't reply. She heard the rush of her own blood in her ears. Now Sylvie sat down in one of the empty yellow chairs. Jane couldn't move. The doctor was talking about slides, freezing tissue, examination by a pathologist, knowing more in a few days. He said the word "lymphoma."

"You're saying that's what she has?" Jane asked as Sylvie let out a moan.

"No," the doctor said. "I'm not saying that at all. I'm just saying that it's a possibility."

Jane looked down at the top of Sylvie's head. It looked so blond and pretty in the harsh hospital light. Sylvie was sitting in the yellow chair, making herself into the smallest shape possible. She was hugging herself, as if she was half frozen to death. Jane sat beside her and took her hand. Glancing up, she thanked Dr. Becker, who went on to explain that the hip fracture had been fairly simple, requiring only one pin. He said that she was in intensive care, and that they could see her soon. He then told them he'd be in touch about the biopsy.

"It can't be, it can't be," Sylvie was saying.

"We don't know anything yet," Jane said.

"I might be correct," Sylvie said, "and she might just have a bad infection—right?"

"Maybe," Jane said.

The two sisters sat silently. Jane closed her eyes. She thought about all the life-changing moments of her time on earth. Was this one of them? Would everything left in life, all the events yet to come, be filtered through the memory of this moment—the exact moment Dr. Becker had said the word "lymphoma" about their mother?

Jane shivered, because she knew all about life-changing moments. She had had, perhaps, more than her share so far. Some were so certain: Bang! Everything transformed in an instant. Several flooded her mind, all at once: when her parents brought

Sylvie home from the hospital, when their father walked out on them.

More recently: the dance at Carrie Tower. And just today, hours earlier: the kiss in Dylan's kitchen. Both had the weight of life-shifting events. Jane felt different, transformed, as the result of dancing with Dylan Chadwick. All the cells in her body felt lighter, and her thoughts seemed inclined in his direction; she found herself touching her cheek, where his beard had rubbed, and she would startle herself in the midst of a daydream of him and the orchard, to realize that she smelled apples where there were none.

But Jane's biggest life-changing moments had to do with Chloe: the night she was conceived, the day Jane got the pregnancy test results, the night Chloe was born.

The elevator door opened, and John Dufour stepped out. He came straight across the shiny tiled floor to Sylvie. Catching sight of him, she stood up and opened her arms. They embraced, and Jane heard her sister softly weeping.

"She might have lymphoma," Sylvie cried. "They're doing tests . . ."

"I'll be right there with you," John said, holding her. "The whole time."

Jane watched. He wore a camel-colored sweater vest over a blue-and-white-checked shirt. He had a bald spot. His potbelly made it hard to hold Sylvie as close as he obviously wanted to. His arms and shoulders strained with tension and passion. The sight of her sister, frail and blond, her eyes squeezed tightly shut as tears ran down her cheeks, embraced so rapturously by her fellow teacher, gave Jane a swooning sense of aloneness.

Her mother was in intensive care, possibly fighting for her life. Her sister was giving every appearance of being in a true and loving relationship with someone who obviously adored her. And Jane, as Sylvie had said, was living a lie.

She was falling in love with someone who had no idea of who she really was and what she really wanted. And the focus of her entire existence was a young girl who grieved for her real mother, who had spent her whole life with adoptive parents who loved her.

"Hi, Jane," John said while Sylvie fished a tissue out of her bag.

"Hi, John. Thanks for coming."

"I want to be here for Sylvie." He smiled. "And you."

Jane smiled back. He was acting like a family member. It felt nice. Jane was happy for Sylvie. She remembered that Dylan had asked her to call him, but there was a sign saying "No cell phones" hanging on the wall.

Leaving her sister and John to keep vigil, Jane decided to go downstairs and find a pay phone.

⚶

Chloe's shoulder ached from the weight of her books in her knapsack, all part of her elaborate ruse. Why hadn't she taken just one? She could have told her mother that she and Mona were doing science home-work, and taken her *Wildlife in the Estuary* paperback, and gotten away with it.

But no. She had to make a big show of packing her book bag, heading out the door, climbing onto her bike. Only, instead of turning left onto Mona's road, Chloe had just kept riding—straight through Crofton, across the old granite bridge that crossed the Williams River, into Twin Rivers.

Chloe wasn't exactly sure what she was doing, but she knew enough to get out of her own town. Her stomach flipped as she coasted down the hill toward the mall. Her pulse was racing so fast, she could hardly stand it. She was in total suspense, as if she were reading a scary book—only the whole story, the happy or unhappy ending, was right with her, in her own body.

She was afraid she might be pregnant.

She hadn't told Mona, hadn't even admitted it to herself. It had only been about a week since she and Zeke had gone to the orchard. Her period wasn't late or anything. But she had the horrible sensation of alien sperm in her body—his unwanted forced-upon-her condomless grossness—and she had to know.

All the pregnancy tests were called things like "Early Detection," "First Thought," and "Right Now." So that must mean they were made for speedy results—a week should be plenty long enough. Chloe realized she could wait for her period—still a few days away—but she didn't think she could last. She had to know *now*.

She knew the mall had a big drugstore, but Chloe was afraid of running into some of her Crofton friends there. So she pedaled past, heading for the old downtown area instead. Twin Rivers was an old mill town with stately old redbrick factories, some turned into condos, but most going to wrack and ruin. Its downtown was pretty thin: just a few old stores that looked tired and sad. A stationers, a law office, a pawn shop.

Chloe rode faster; there had to be a drugstore here somewhere. She cruised up Main Street and down Arch Street. Passing a diner, her stomach growled. She felt hungry. Wasn't that a sign of pregnancy? Eating for two? She pedaled harder.

Around the bend, she saw the big building sitting atop the next rise: Twin Rivers General Hospital. Babies were being born there, probably at this exact moment. Chloe thought of the story of her own birth, or the parts her parents knew about: how they had gone to Women and Infants with the blanket and diaper bag and pink baby clothes they had bought, to bring her home . . .

Knowing that hospitals always had pharmacies, and thinking there was no one she could possibly know there, Chloe rode up the hill. Her calf muscles burned with the effort, and by the time she got there, she was breathless—not just from exertion, but with sheer panic.

She locked her bike to the rack out front. A bunch of orderlies stood by the door, smoking. She thought of Uncle Dylan and felt sad. But almost instantly, her worry returned. She had had sex. And it was sex under a bad sign: with a boy who had tricked her into thinking he liked her.

The lobby was bright, teeming with people. Families sat in clusters, some looking shell-shocked. Bad things happened in hospitals, Chloe thought. It was a mistake to come here. She almost turned right around to leave, but then she saw the pharmacy sign and an arrow. Now or never, she thought.

Hurrying down the hallway, she found the shop. The front was full of magazines, paperback books, and stuffed animals. A display of balloons and flowers was off to the side. Chloe marched past the fun stuff, directly to the shelves of medical-type things. She steeled herself, searching for the tests. Passing a shelf of sanitary products, she almost cried—never had they ever looked so good. Would she ever need Kotex again? She prayed that she would—in a week.

Her hands shaking, she stared. She was such a virgin—or had been, until Zeke—that she'd never even used a tampon yet. Shouldn't pregnancy tests be right here? But they weren't. She searched the shelves, making her way toward the back of the store, to the pharmacy desk.

Oh, shit.

There they were: the little oblong boxes, behind the counter with condoms and yeast-infection ointments. Chloe had had one—a yeast infection—last year, and she remembered that her mother had had to ask the pharmacist for the cure. Oh, God. This was embarrassing. And what if they required ID? What if she had to be eighteen or something, to buy the test?

After she'd gotten busted at family court, for impersonating a twenty-one-year-old, Chloe and Mona had chalked a couple of IDs. She had hers in her wallet; because of her birth year and the difficulty of turning an "8" into anything but a "0," she had made herself born in 1980, which made her twenty-four. She cleared her throat, preparing to sound mature if need be.

"May I help you?" the pharmacist, a young woman, asked.

"Yes," Chloe said. Her mind was scrambled, but she made her voice sound calm. "May I please have a First Thought pregnancy test?" She was ready with her fake ID, and as a fallback, a made-up story, "It's for my older sister, who's out in the car," ready to jump across the counter and grab it off the shelf.

But none of that was necessary. The pharmacist reached for the test, placed it on the counter, rang it up.

"That will be fifteen thirty-seven," she said.

Chloe handed her a twenty—money paid to her by Uncle Dylan, funds that should have gone to feeding the cats. Her palms were so sweaty, she was pretty sure the money would be soaked through. The woman put the test kit in a paper bag and handed Chloe her change. "Have a nice—" she began.

But Chloe didn't wait to hear the rest. Tearing into the hallway, she looked both ways. Where was the ladies' room? Seeing a sign, she ran to the left. Flying around the corner, she saw a bank of telephones, mostly occupied. She came face to face with a man pushing a bucket with a mop sticking out of it. He was just placing a yellow plastic folding sign in the open bathroom door. It said: *Closed for cleaning*.

"No!" Chloe cried out. "I have to go in there."

"Other bathrooms upstairs," he said, gesturing.

"I can't wait!" she wailed.

She was so ready to pee on the stick, she thought she'd have a heart attack. She was too upset to look for other bathrooms—the men's room was right there, next to the ladies', with no yellow sign in the door.

"You can't enter," the janitor said as she slapped her hand on the door handle. "Men inside—"

"No," Chloe wailed.

She was causing such a commotion, all the people on the pay phones turned to look at her. She might just as well have been wearing a sign on her forehead: *I think I'm pregnant and I'm having a nervous breakdown*. Thank God she didn't know any of the people.

Only she did. One of the people was Jane.

Chloe's heart should have sunk, but instead it leapt. She was so glad to see Jane's friendly face, the rescuing dream face of the woman in the floating pie, that Chloe actually ran toward her.

"Chloe, what's wrong?" Jane said, holding a quarter in one hand.

"Finish your call," Chloe said.

"I haven't made it yet," Jane said, her face full of alarm, holding Chloe's hand as she gently steered her away from everyone else's hearing. "What are you doing here?"

"Something happened to me," Chloe gulped, feeling the sob boil up and overtake her. "Something happened to me in the orchard with Zeke . . ."

"Did he hurt you?" Jane asked.

The words ripped the sob right out of her chest, and Chloe felt hot tears on her cheeks. He had hurt her so much . . . She nodded, and there was so much to say, but all she could whisper, in the squeakiest voice humanly possible, was, "I think I might be pregnant."

CHAPTER 19

They were in the car, in the front seat of Jane's station wagon, sitting in the hospital parking lot. Jane knew that Sylvie was expecting her to return upstairs to the ER waiting room, but there was nothing on earth that would keep Jane from Chloe at this moment. She sat in the driver's seat, waiting for Chloe to stop crying.

"Are you okay?" Jane asked, handing her another coffee-stained Dunkin' Donuts napkin.

Chloe nodded her head, blowing her nose. "I think so. I still have to take the test, though. Maybe they've finished cleaning the bathroom by now."

"In just a second," Jane said, wanting to make sure she was really all right. Those words she had used . . . "Chloe, what did you mean when you said something happened to you?"

"Nothing, honestly."

"It didn't sound like nothing; you said something happened in the orchard with Zeke—who is he?"

"Just a big sharky jerk."

"Is he your boyfriend?"

Chloe shook her head fiercely. Her eyes were sharp, her jaw tense. But suddenly she dissolved in tears, and she buried her face in the wadded-up napkins. Jane's heart broke as Chloe sobbed. The pain came from deep inside; she sounded as if she was being destroyed. Jane reached for her hand, wet with tears. Her own insides ached, and she remembered crying like this for Jeffrey.

"I . . . thought . . . he was . . ." Chloe wept.

"What did he do?" Jane asked.

"He . . . called . . . me . . . Zoe!"

"Instead of Chloe?"

Chloe nodded. "He pretended he did it on purpose. Because Zeke begins with a *Z*, he thought my name should, too . . ."

"A conceited way to think."

"But it wasn't even true! I think he just got

my name wrong, and was trying to cover it up!"

"That creep," Jane said. She waited. Was that the worst of it? It was bad—horrible. But Chloe was still crying hard, as if there was more to come. Jane's stomach dropped as Chloe squeezed her hand.

"Did you love him?" Jane asked.

"I think so. I thought so . . ."

"You gave him your heart, Chloe," Jane said, stroking her hand. "You tried to show him how you felt . . ."

"I'm not *like* that, though," Chloe said. "I never do things with boys. I'm the straightest kid around. I used to think I was weird, that there was something wrong with me, because I'd never even gone to second base." She looked up with a tear-streaked face. "Do you know what that is?"

Jane nodded.

"I'm the least likely girl in school to be sitting in a car with a home pregnancy test in my bag."

"That doesn't mean you're wrong or bad, Chloe," Jane said. "You're still the most wonderful girl I know."

Chloe almost laughed. "You hardly know

me. You must not know many wonderful girls."

Jane swallowed, staying calm. Holding Chloe's wet hand with one hand, she felt she was keeping them tethered together. "I have good judgment, when it comes to that."

"You probably wouldn't feel that way if you knew what happened."

"You can tell me, if you want."

Chloe snorted loudly. Jane absently touched her locket. Chloe used another handful of napkins. Into them she said wetly, "Well, I had sex."

"Uh-huh," Jane said, trying not to sound anything but neutral.

"You probably figured that, considering—" Chloe pointed at the bag.

"I did," Jane said. "It's okay, Chloe."

"I was always a good girl," Chloe said.

"You couldn't be anything else," Jane said. "No matter whether you had sex or not."

"The thing is . . . I'm not sure I wanted to," she said.

Jane stared at her. Chloe couldn't look up. Jane's heart smashed against her ribs.

She struggled to stay very calm. "You're not sure you wanted to . . . have sex with him?"

Chloe nodded.

"Did he—did he force you?"

"That's kind of a gray area," Chloe said.

"But you didn't want to?" Jane asked, her pulse gaining velocity.

"It was in the orchard," Chloe said. "Or, rather, that's where we met. It was a beautiful night. It was the night you and my uncle went out. He told me."

Jane bit her lip. When she and Dylan were at Campus Dance.

"There were stars *everywhere*," Chloe said. "They were in the trees."

Jane nodded. "I remember," she said, waiting.

"He held my hand; he walked me through the trees. I loved the smell; it was dark and quiet, and it smelled so green, like brand-new leaves. There were night birds calling; it was romantic."

Jane thought of that Campus Dance so long ago, the night this girl had come into her body. The night had smelled of springtime.

"He led me to the brook. We have this trickling little stream; and he crossed me to the other side . . ." she let out something like a cry. "He must have thought he was doing me a favor—getting me off my family land, before he did what he was going to do . . ."

"What did he do?" Jane asked, trying to make her voice as soft as possible.

"Well, he had me lie down; and then things started." Chloe closed her eyes; she was squeezing them tightly shut.

Jane forced herself to stay silent. A shift must have changed; people were walking out of the hospital. People wearing green scrubs, white uniforms, navy blue uniforms. Cars drove out, other cars drove in. Chloe was oblivious.

"Did you say 'no'?" Jane asked, after long minutes of silence.

Chloe shrugged, tears rolling out of her tightly closed eyes. "I can't remember," she said.

"Is that what you meant?" Jane asked, her body and blood burning.

Chloe nodded.

"Oh, honey . . ."

"I have to take the test," Chloe said. "I have to know. Will you walk me back inside?" She picked that moment to open her eyes, just as a very blond woman walked past the car. Chloe gasped, even as she ducked down. Out of the corner of her eye, the blonde caught the movement, and her mouth opened in an *O* of recognition.

"Drive out, drive out," Chloe commanded.

Jane hesitated, then turned the key.

The blond woman tapped on the window, staring straight at the top of Chloe's head. "Chloe, is that you? It's me—Rhianna! Mona's mom!" She waved at Jane, trying to get her attention.

"Drive," Chloe begged.

Jane shifted into reverse, nearly drove over Rhianna's toe, and peeled out of the parking lot.

"Did she see me?" Chloe asked, inching up to peer over the seat back as Jane sped out of the parking lot.

"She said your name . . ."

"But she might have been mistaken—I might have been some other kid who just looks like me. I might be—your daughter!"

Jane drove, forcing herself to keep her eyes on the white line.

"We both have dark hair," Chloe said. "We both know it's romantic to see stars in the trees. Not everyone knows that. My mother would like to see the orchard cut down, so houses could be built there."

Nodding, Jane didn't say anything. But she registered the words "my mother."

As they drove farther away from the parking lot, Chloe said, "Rhianna's not Mona's real mother. Did you hear how she called herself that? 'Mona's mom.' Well, she's not. And neither is my mom my real mother."

"Oh," Jane said, driving east for no good reason other than that was the direction in which the car was pointed.

"I'm adopted."

"You are?" Jane asked.

Chloe nodded. "But at least my adoptive mother loves me and treats me really well— not like Rhianna and Mona. I'm lucky, in that way."

"In what way?" Jane said.

"That I'm loved. By my adoptive mother. I know one thing." She held up the pregnancy test. "If this is positive, I'm keeping the baby."

Jane glanced across the seat.

"I would never be able to do what my real mother did," Chloe said.

"What did she do?" Jane asked, her mouth dry.

"Gave me up. Had me . . . gave me my name . . . and just gave me away. She was a college girl, and she had to finish her education. College was more important to her than I was."

The car was silent, all except for the sound of the tires turning on the road. Jane couldn't speak. Her skin hurt. Every inch of her body wanted to cry out the truth. But instead she just kept driving. She said, "I'm sure it wasn't as easy as that."

Chloe didn't reply. She had opened the pregnancy test and was reading the directions. After a moment, she raised her head and looked around. They were on a quiet country road, in the middle of nowhere. "Can you stop?" she asked, as if she hadn't heard Jane's words.

"Right here?" Jane asked, shaking. "There's nothing around. Lambton is just a few miles away—I think we'll find a gas station—"

"No—here," Chloe said. "I want to do it in the woods. It will be a good omen."

"Your uncle tells me you love nature,"

Jane said, trying to smile, trying to control herself.

"I do," Chloe said. And the second Jane pulled onto the sandy shoulder of the shady road, Chloe jumped out the door and bounded into the trees. The test directions lay on the seat, a white sheet hastily discarded. Jane's hands were trembling, as she reached out and started to read.

The printed words swam together with her thoughts. She thought of her own mother, coming out of the anesthesia. Sylvie was probably frantic, wanting Jane to be with her to support their mother. And she thought of Chloe's family—her adoptive family—possibly worried, wondering where she was right now. She hoped that Rhianna person hadn't misinterpreted Chloe's ducking down as any kind of threat, a kidnapping . . .

But mainly, Jane thought of Chloe. She imagined what it had been like, being called by the wrong name, then led across the stream. Chloe had wanted to say no, Jane was sure. She was so young, and she had thought she loved him. *Gray area* . . . Jane could relate so well. She read the instructions, her palms damp. The car window was open; she heard an oriole singing in the trees.

After a minute, she heard Chloe's footsteps. The car door opened, then closed.

"I should have taken some napkins," Chloe said, holding the white stick.

"I wish I had some tissue," Jane said.

"That's okay," Chloe said.

Jane drew in a slow breath, shaking her head.

"Pink circle for positive, white circle for negative," Chloe said, staring at the stick.

"How long does it take?" Jane asked, even though she had just read the directions.

"Three minutes," Chloe said. "Then I'll know . . ."

Jane couldn't watch. She could barely sit still. The years disappeared. She remembered sitting in the Planned Parenthood clinic in Providence, having just peed into a cup, waiting for the results. Right now, as then, she was digging her fingernails into her palms so hard, she left half-moon nail marks in her own skin.

She knew what she should wish for. She realized that Chloe was just fifteen, five years younger than Jane had been. She had her whole life ahead of her. She had hopes and dreams and ambitions and plans, to come true. Jane could only wish that a white circle would appear, and she could then drive Chloe home and let her get on with her life.

Maybe this was all a test, in fact—a bigger test than just the white circle/pink circle. Maybe this was a sign to Jane, that Chloe's life was her own, she was a fifteen-year-old girl who already had a family, that Jane should leave her alone and fade away.

"No matter what happens," Chloe said, speaking directly to the stick, "I won't let you be a star in the attic."

"A what?" Jane asked.

"A star in the attic. A dead star—the opposite of live stars in the trees. I had a bad dream the other night. In it I was a fallen star, and my real mother put me up in the attic . . ."

"Why would she do that?" Jane whispered, shocked.

Chloe looked away from the stick, blinking slowly. "Because I wasn't worth anything to her."

"That's not true," Jane said. Then, at Chloe's look of puzzlement, "It couldn't be."

"It doesn't matter," Chloe said. "It was a long time ago."

The words hung between them. Jane's nerves were raw. She wanted to tell Chloe the truth right now. She wanted to explain what it had been like, tell her that she wasn't just some star in an attic—she was an entire galaxy, the whole firmament. Holding her tongue was almost impossible, but she told herself that this wasn't the right time, that Chloe had to get through this next minute and a half.

Then Jane could tell her the truth.

The air would be clear. Being honest with Chloe, she could also tell Dylan. Touching her silver locket, she thought of how good it would feel to no longer carry this burden of secrecy. She wouldn't have to go on lying to these two people she had come to know. And love.

For Jane no longer loved the mere idea of Chloe—the simple fact of a daughter's existence—but she loved the real and actual girl. She loved her direct ways, her sharp blue eyes, her wit, her humor, her loyalty to Mona, her devotion to nature and the orchard, her imagery of stars. Jane stared down at Chloe's hands—the same shape as Jane's and Sylvie's and their mother's—and felt a rush of love that made no sense whatever, yet, at the same time, all the sense in the world.

"Oh," Chloe said suddenly, excitedly, bringing the stick closer to her eyes.

"What?" Jane asked, letting go of her locket.

"It didn't take three whole minutes," Chloe said, and the excitement in her voice drained away, and she sounded strangely crushed.

"What does it say?" Jane asked, reaching over, gently taking hold of Chloe's wrist, pivoting the test so she could see the window:

White circle.

CHAPTER 20

School was out, summer was officially here, and the stand was open for business—minus the dolphin flag. Chloe and Mona sat on stools wearing sun hats and dark glasses. They were pretending to be movie stars in the apple business. Mona had brought an array of Rhianna's nail polish, so they could paint their toenails lots of different colors.

"She *will* kill you," Chloe said, fanning her right foot to dry her puce, orchid, vermilion, white tiger, hyacinth, and flame-colored toes.

"No, these are old colors. She's on to the newest thing. Ever since Dad took her on that business trip to Los Angeles, she only uses Jessica Colours . . . that's 'colors' with a 'u.' These are her castaways."

"What are Jessica Colours?"

"Oh, they come from this really posh nail salon where all the stars go. While she was there, she saw Nancy Reagan. You'd think they were best friends. But enough about that. I'm tired of waiting. WEEKS have gone by, and you HAVE to tell me—was that you she saw at the hospital?"

Chloe squinted, staring at her multicolored toes in the shade-dappled sunlight.

"You've got to tell me! It's driving me crazy," Mona said, knocking over an open bottle of Manic Mauve as she lurched over to hug Chloe. "Are you dying? My mother never told me she was sick, and if you're doing the same thing, I'll never forgive you!"

"Oh, Mone—I'm sorry," Chloe said, hugging her back. She suddenly felt awash with remorse, for making Mona worry. "I'm not sick. I'm fine."

"But it *was* you?" Mona asked, taking off her oversized sunglasses to reveal her normal specs. Her ever-shorter hair was now about a million different lengths. "What were you doing there?"

"I want to tell you," Chloe said, still feeling queasy with shame. "But I also don't want to . . ."

"Whatever it is, I won't tell."

"I know that," Chloe said. "I trust you, Mona. But I don't want you to think anything bad about me. It's about Zeke . . ."

"We don't like him anymore, right?"

"Right. He . . . and I . . . I thought I might be pregnant."

"Oh, Chloe!"

She saw the shock in Mona's eyes, followed immediately by hurt. "I'm not—don't worry. And I would have told you, but I didn't want to talk about it," Chloe said. "I went all the way to Twin Rivers, so I wouldn't see anyone I knew."

"Then who were you with, when Rhianna saw you?"

"Jane," Chloe said.

"The pie lady?"

Chloe nodded. It sounded funny to hear Mona call her that. Jane had started out being just the pie lady—or had she? Chloe had liked her from the start, and now she'd never forget the time they'd had together, sitting in Jane's car while Chloe's heart beat so hard she thought it might rupture, while they were waiting for the white circle.

"What were you doing with her?"

"She was visiting someone at the hospital, where I went to buy the test," Chloe said. "And she saw me."

"Twin Rivers isn't that far away," Mona chided. "Of course you'd see people you knew. You should have told me—we could have hitchhiked to Providence together."

"Well, it worked out. Jane gave me a ride. She's really nice . . ."

"I know, but weren't you afraid she'd tell your uncle?"

Chloe shook her head. She wasn't sure how she knew, but deep down she was positive that she could trust Jane. That whatever was going on between her and Uncle Dylan, she would safeguard Chloe's secret forever.

"Rhianna wanted to call your mother. She was completely wrapped up in doing her maternal duty—you know, joining the SOM: the sisterhood of mothers. Calling your mother to bond over how horrible it is to be raising a teenager. I covered for you, though."

"What did you say?"

"That you were at the hospital for your dialysis."

"Mona!" Chloe said.

"What was I supposed to say? She was

honestly about to pick up the phone and call your mother. And believe me, she would have. She was in a really awful mood, and she *wanted* to get you in trouble. The dermatologist screwed up her Botox."

"Oh, no—what happened?"

"Some leaked into her eyelids. So she looked like Marlon Brando in *The Godfather*—you know, the way he can't seem to keep his eyes open? Luckily, it's not permanent. I can't believe you had sex with Zeke and didn't tell me. Where did you do it, and what was it like?"

Chloe shuddered.

"You still won't tell me?"

Chloe shook her head.

"You mean, I'm the only virgin left in our friendship?"

Trying to smile, Chloe couldn't quite manage.

"Did it hurt?"

Chloe nodded. "A lot," she said.

"Is that why you broke up with him?"

"One of the reasons," Chloe said. She told Mona about the Zoe-Chloe debacle, and the across-the-stream thing, and the fact that she wasn't an entirely willing participant, and Mona gasped, shrieked, and fell silent.

"Rapist," she said after a minute.

"No, it wasn't like that," Chloe said. "I was right there, in it. I just wasn't sure about the timing. I was ready, but not that ready. It was a gray-area moment."

"Why? He deserves to go to the ACI!" Mona exclaimed, and Chloe pictured the Adult Correctional Institute, built of imposing red brick, surrounded by fields of razor wire, lording it over the stretch of I-95 in Cranston.

"No," Chloe said quietly, but she remembered the feeling of sticks scratching her back as she lay on the hard cold ground.

Even as she said the word, she saw Mona jump off her stool, begin rummaging under the pie shelf. A moment later, she pulled out the blue flag. Unfurling it, she exposed the beautiful felt dolphin Chloe had glued on. Now, unscrewing the top from a bottle of purple polish, Mona began to paint the flag.

"What are you doing?" Chloe asked.

"He says dolphins keep sharks away," Mona said, enhancing the fin on the dolphin's back, "but my money is on the shark."

"Yeah," Chloe said, getting into the spirit, opening a bottle of bright red, drawing big sharp teeth. She loved animals and fish—*all* animals and fish—equally. She never cringed from snakes, centipedes, mice, or spiders. At the beach, she loved jellyfish as much as cute minnows. So right now, with the help of her best friend, she was calling on the spirit of the maligned shark to protect her from Zeke and his dolphins . . .

"I still think you should listen to me," Mona said. "And turn him in."

"Mmm," Chloe said. If she did that, then everyone would know. Her parents, Uncle Dylan, lots of people. This way, only Mona and Jane had heard.

"What was she there for, by the way?"

"Who?"

"Jane. Who was she visiting at the hospital that day?"

Chloe had been drawing some magnificently vicious shark teeth, but suddenly she stopped, dripping polish. She didn't know. How selfish could she be? That she could encounter a really good, kind person like

Jane at Twin Rivers Hospital, and not even ask what she was doing there?

"I don't know," Chloe said, staring Mona beseechingly in the eye. "I forgot to ask her."

❧

Other tests had come back negative, as well.

Jane and Sylvie sat at their mother's bedside, surrounded by flowers they had picked from her garden. A bottle of sugar-free sparkling cider was open on her tray table, along with three champagne glasses that Jane had brought from home, to celebrate the fact that her enlarged lymph nodes were, in fact, caused by an infection related to the diabetes.

"I've dodged another bullet," Margaret said.

"You're indestructible," Jane said, pouring the cider.

"But delicate," Sylvie said, smiling.

The three of them raised their glasses and clinked. "Cheers," Jane said. "To Mom's health."

"To all of our health," Margaret amended,

sipping. "This is lovely. If only it were the real thing . . ."

"Real champagne?" Sylvie asked.

"Yes. Your father smuggled Piper-Heidsieck into the hospital for both of your births."

Sylvie lowered her glass. She looked at Jane, who had definitely gone a shade paler.

"What was he thinking?" Jane asked.

Their mother laughed. She looked so much better than she had in weeks: the doctors had tested and adjusted her medicine levels, and the physical therapist had been in to work with her. She was getting electrolytes and vitamins, and her school-principal interest in the entire staff made her a magnet for young nurses and orderlies: They gave her lots of attention.

"You mean, because he broke the hospital rules?" she asked.

"No. I mean because he celebrated our births, then fell off the face of the earth."

"Jane," Sylvie warned.

Margaret's smile faltered. "Oh, dear . . . I wish I knew the answer to that. I've asked myself a million times."

"He must have been happy to have us," Jane said. "At least a little—he bought champagne. So what happened?"

"Dear," their mother said, sipping her cider. "You know as well as anyone alive that sometimes people aren't up to child-raising. The time isn't right, or they find themselves challenged—and they just can't handle it. Your father—"

Sylvie was watching Jane. The expression on her face could only be called "dangerous." She glowered, her eyes growing dark, the storm building inside as she realized her mother was equating her with their father. But then, just raising her eyebrows in an "Okay, Mom" look, she just shook the words' meaning off, as if it no longer mattered. As many times as they had had this conversation about their father, it still never made sense. And never would.

Just then, a team of doctors walked in. Dr. Becker led a group of residents and interns from Brown Medical School as they fanned out around the bed. They smiled at the sight of a family celebration, then went right into a discussion of diabetes and hip fractures and how they impacted each other in Margaret Porter.

Sylvie and Jane walked out into the hall. So much had happened this last week, Sylvie could hardly keep it straight. She had had several meetings with the discharge department, trying to come up with the proper plan for Margaret's release. In the meantime, she had cleaned her mother's room from floor to ceiling, airing all the bedding and dusting all the books.

John had helped. Refusing to let Sylvie do any heavy lifting, he had hoisted the mattress and turned the box spring. He had helped her polish the floor. Along the way, he had started talking about the summer. He loved to kayak and camp, and he asked Sylvie if she'd like to go to Maine with him. He thought she'd find it interesting—he knew a place where moose and bald eagles were often sighted.

Sylvie started to say she couldn't, that she had to stay home with her mother. But she hadn't. Instead, she had said simply, "Maybe."

"What do you think we should do?" she asked Jane now, as they waited in the hall.

"We should just be happy," Jane said, smiling and kissing her. "We should be so glad that Mom's going to be okay."

Sylvie grinned, gazing at her sister. Jane had seemed very buoyant lately. Ever since that day at the hospital, right after Dr. Becker had scared them with the possibility of lymphoma. Jane had disappeared—for hours—without any explanation. And when she'd returned, she had seemed . . .

Happy, lighthearted, on top of the world.

Even now, Jane's eyes danced as she watched Abby Goodheart, the hospital social worker, coming toward them. Large and affable, with a round face and a long graying blond braid, she greeted them with a smile.

"How are you both?" she asked.

"Fine, Abby," Sylvie said.

"Celebrating your mother's good news?"

"Yes," Jane said. "We're so relieved. Thank you."

"You're welcome." Abby's beeper went off; she checked the number, then turned back to Sylvie and Jane. "I thought we might spend a few minutes talking about your mother's discharge plan."

"Discharge? But she has a broken hip," Jane said. "She can barely move . . ."

"And the doctors are just getting her diabetes under control," Sylvie said, feeling a little panicked. She didn't want to admit it, but she was enjoying the freedom of not being her mother's caretaker. Knowing that others were looking after Margaret had given Sylvie several good nights' sleeps.

"The hospital can't keep her here much longer," Abby said. "We'd like to, but with managed care, our hands are tied. I know her doctors want to examine her a little longer, do a complete mental-status work-up. But when that's done, decisions will have to be made."

A few moments of silence passed, and Sylvie could barely look at Jane. She was afraid that her sister would look into her eyes and know that she was wavering. Sylvie had always been the keeper of the flame. While Jane was down in New York, running away from the past and her problems, Sylvie had stayed in Rhode Island, with their mother. But right now, all Sylvie could think about was a cold starry night, a campfire, and John.

"This is hard stuff," Abby said. "I know that. I've seen many families struggle with what's the best solution. . . . You might consider sending your mother to a nursing home on an interim basis. Just so she can get some extra care, some intensive PT, and a chance for everyone to discuss the next step."

"I don't think she'll want to go even temporarily," Sylvie said. "She'll be afraid she'll never get out."

"You'll find that they're not such bad places," Abby said. "I work with several, and I can vouch for them all. They're bright, clean, modern; they have friendly, young staffs, lots of activities."

"Just like school," Jane said, sounding thoughtful and distant.

"As a matter of fact, they are a bit like school. I'd be surprised if your mother didn't like them. She is so sociable, always ready to help others—I'm not sure whether you've noticed, but all the nurses stop in to visit with her. She is such a good listener, and she helps them figure out their own problems."

"She's good at that," Jane said, with just the smallest trace of irony. But when Sylvie glanced over, she saw that Jane was smiling, as if all hard feelings had been forgotten, or forgiven; at least during this crisis.

"I'm going to recommend that you look at Cherry Vale and Marsh Glen," Abby said, writing the names down on a card.

"Our grandmother was in Marsh Glen," Jane said.

"What did you think of it?"

"It was . . . institutional. And she was much older than our mother."

"You'll find that many improvements have been made," Abby said. "As our generation 'matures,' we're demanding better care for our parents."

"Marsh Glen was so far away," Sylvie said. "It took too long to get to."

Abby nodded sympathetically. "You don't have to decide today, but I think we'll need a plan by Monday." She shook both sisters' hands, then hurried off to answer her page.

"Cherry Vale and Marsh Glen," Jane said. "Why is it that all the names of those places sound alike? Scenic, serene, like something you'd find in the Cotswolds."

"I know. Merry old England," Sylvie laughed, relieved that Jane was making a joke.

Jane's eyes glittered as she looked up and down the hall, and she suddenly seemed surprisingly fragile. "We have to decide about Mom," Jane said. "And it's not easy. I hate thinking of her winding up where Grammy went."

"I thought you were all for sending her to a nursing home," Sylvie said.

Jane shook her head. "To Marsh Vale or Cherry Glen? How could I be 'all for' that? I think it makes the most sense, I think it's probably even best for Mom, but it's so hard. We could get a hospital bed for her room at home . . ."

"And a wheelchair, and a little portable toilet in the room," Sylvie said. "But who would lift her? With her broken hip, she needs two people just to get her out of bed."

"We could do it," Jane said. "We're strong."

Was it possible that they were changing roles? Sylvie thought of John, imagining what it would be like to camp under the stars with him. They would share a tent; they would kiss all night. Was it selfish of her to want more of that?

"What about your business?" Sylvie asked. "Aren't you ever going back?"

"I don't think I am, Syl," Jane said. "I've been thinking about it a lot lately. I love it here. I've missed Rhode Island. What if I opened my bakery again, but here—maybe not in Twin Rivers, but Providence?"

"Would you really do that?"

Jane took her hands. When Sylvie looked into her eyes, she could see that something was different: Jane had made up her mind. She was staying. Sylvie had come to know the signs that Jane was leaving: a certain distance, detachment. But right now, Jane seemed so anchored—to Sylvie's hands, to her home, to her family.

"I want to," Jane said. "I was running away from so much before, but now I don't have to do that anymore."

"So you really mean what you said? That the two of us should stay home and take care of Mom?"

Jane shook her head. She hugged Sylvie, kissed her cheek. "No, I don't think we should do that," she said. "But I think we should both live nearby. To visit her as often as we can, to take turns driving her to the library and the Educators' Potluck, and to make sure she's getting everything she needs."

Sylvie held on tight. She was so happy to hear Jane say she was staying in Rhode Island, she could almost, but not quite, overlook the rest of it. Her eyes felt hot with

tears, and the tears were both happy and
sad.

"She'll hate it," Sylvie said.

"We don't know that," Jane said. "Like I
said to Abby, they sound a lot like schools."

"I guess we could check them out . . .
see if they're better than when Grammy
went."

"That's all we'd be doing," Jane said.
"We'll just check them out."

Sylvie nodded. She wiped her eyes and
smiled. She had so much to be happy
about, after all. Her mother had had a good
diagnosis, her sister had come home, and
Sylvie was going to Maine with John Dufour.

If only certain things could change and all
the other things could stay the same, Sylvie
thought. If only their mother could take care
of herself and stay in her own house, everything would be perfect. . . .

Cherry Vale and Marsh Glen were owned by
the same company, Rainbow Healthcare,
and they were similar, if not interchange-
able, in all ways. Built by the same architect,
they were both set on scenic spreads, well
landscaped with fruit trees and tidy flower

beds. The rooms had large windows that opened wide enough for fresh air but not for a resident to fall out. Improvements had been made. Activities were planned with enthusiasm, as if by a cruise director. The decor had been brightened.

"You see that we honor our residents as individuals," said Rosalie Drance, the intake administrator at Cherry Vale, showing Jane and Sylvie that week's schedule. "No matter what their interest, we try to accommodate it. Everything from foreign movies to line dancing."

"Line dancing?" Jane said, glancing around the recreation room, where most of the residents were in wheelchairs.

"We don't let wheelchairs stop us," Rosalie laughed. "We get people moving however we can—if they can dance, great. If they can't, we push them."

"Our mother's not really the line-dancing type," Sylvie said, with quiet dignity. "She was a school principal; she enjoys more quiet pursuits, like reading and writing."

Rosalie smiled. "We never make anyone do anything they don't want to . . . Let me show you our library."

Jane followed along. Rosalie was making

it hard not to see the good in Cherry Vale,
just as her counterpart had done at Marsh
Glen. Sunlight sparkled on the gleaming
floors. Cherry trees waved in the breeze. A
yoga class was taking place in the shade;
about half the participants were in wheel-
chairs. Jane watched them, wondering
whether they were enjoying themselves.
She wondered how often their families visited.

The library was not extensive, but it was
more than perfunctory. There were shelves
of novels, both classic and modern, shelves
of nonfiction, a selection of reference
books.

"You see, we have the *Encyclopedia Bri-
tannica,*" Rosalie said.

"Mom thinks encyclopedias are an infe-
rior way to do research," Sylvie said. "And
as a librarian, I agree."

"We certainly welcome input, and we try
to honor all requests. Are there any specific
volumes you'd like us to get?"

Sylvie folded her arms tightly across her
chest, eyes closed shut, as if making such a
list while trying to hold herself together at
the same time. Both Jane and Rosalie
watched silently.

"Sylvie," Jane said gently, after a minute. "How much research do you honestly think Mom's planning to do?"

"It's just," Sylvie said, breaking down. "This is a nice place, and so was Cherry Vale—"

"This is Cherry Vale," Jane reminded her.

"I mean Marsh Glen, I should know that, it was where Grammy . . . but this is our mother! And she's rigorous and brilliant, and no matter how pleasant it is, it's not home!" Sylvie sobbed.

Jane put her arm around her, nodded to Rosalie, who seemed utterly sympathetic and not even slightly alarmed. "We need to think about it," Jane said.

"I know," Rosalie said. "No matter how many times I show families around, I never forget how hard it is."

The sisters went out to their car, and Sylvie gulped the fresh air as if she'd never breathed it before. "I'm sorry," she sniffled. "I didn't mean to fall apart."

"You did it for both of us," Jane said.

Sylvie wiped her eyes, then looked up. "You feel bad, too?"

Jane nodded. "How could I not?"

"Isn't there some part of you that wants

to control her life—the way she controlled yours?"

"That's a horrible thing to say," Jane said.

But wasn't it true? Just a tiny part? Having spent a little time with Chloe, Jane realized how hungry she was to spend much, much more.

"A star in the attic," Jane said, leaning on the car, staring at a lone woman framed in a third-floor window, staring out at the cherry trees.

"A what?"

"Someone who doesn't matter anymore," Jane said. "Someone you just pack in a box and put in the attic . . ." She kept staring at the woman. Did her family ever visit? Had they forgotten her? Did she feel abandoned by them?

"Is that what Mom will think we're doing?"

Sylvie seemed to think it over, but she couldn't quite answer. They climbed into the car, and Jane started driving. Of the two places, they liked Cherry Vale better; but Jane didn't want to tell Sylvie her reasoning: it was on the far side of Crofton, and their route to visit would have to take them very near Chadwick Orchards. Jane swung down that way now, and Sylvie instantly stiffened.

"Where are we going?" she asked.

Jane didn't reply. Maple tree branches interlocked overhead, making the road dark with green shadows. Deer grazed along the roadside, oblivious to the traffic. The orchard began, hillsides covered with apple trees, and Jane's heart began to beat harder. As they drove closer, Jane saw that Chloe had added some new signs: shaped like apples, painted red, they were spaced about fifty feet apart. In sequence, they read:

An Apple
A day
Keeps the doctor
Away
And so
Do pies
by Calamity Jane!

Jane watched Sylvie lean forward to read the signs.

"Good Lord," Sylvie said.

"Aren't they wonderful?" Jane asked.

"We're about to make the most important

decision of our mother's life, and you're lost in the *past*?" Sylvie asked.

"She's not the past," Jane said.

"Don't do this," Sylvie said, as the stand came into view, and Jane started beeping the horn. Chloe and Mona jumped off their stools, waving madly. Jane's heart swelled with pride, even as Sylvie grasped the car seat—as if she was at the top of the scariest roller coaster she'd ever ridden, about to take the big plunge.

"Too late," Jane said. "They've seen us."

Sylvie sat completely still, staring at Chloe as if blinded by headlights. "She does look just like you," she whispered. "She really does." And for the strangest moment, Jane thought that this wasn't the first time Sylvie had seen her.

"Come meet your niece," Jane said.

Chloe and Mona bounded around the stand, grinning like a welcoming committee.

"Did you see the new signs?" Chloe asked.

"They're great," Jane said. Glancing up, she smiled at the blue banner with the doctored dolphin. "And I love the shark."

"You're the only one who knows the real story—besides Mona, of course."

"Yeah, Zeke's a shark in dolphin's clothing," Mona said.

"I'd like to get my hands on him," Jane said.

They stood close together, a pack of three, smiling at each other. Then, feeling proud and happy, Jane turned around. Sylvie stood on the outskirts, staring at Chloe. Reaching out for her hand, Jane pulled her into the circle.

"Girls, this is my sister, Sylvie," Jane said. "And Sylvie, I'd like you to meet Chloe and Mona."

"Oh, your sister bakes the best pies," Chloe said.

Sylvie stood there stiffly, as if she was acting out a part to which she didn't quite know the lines. She smiled weakly, eyes darting quickly to Jane. "Yes, she does."

"We're both going to be massively overweight by Labor Day," Mona said, gesturing at an empty tart shell on the counter.

"Yes, we can't resist," Chloe said. "Jane, we're eating up all the profits!"

"Don't worry about that," Jane said. "In my next delivery, I'll include two with your names on them."

"She really does that," Sylvie said. "Writes people's names in piecrust."

"Or finds the perfect symbol that only they will understand," Chloe said. "A couple of weeks ago, when we all thought Zeke was okay, she put a dolphin on one pie. But usually she does these beautiful apples, and blossoms . . . then just last week, a bunch of stars."

"I liked that one that showed a house," Mona said. "With a star in the top window."

"A star in the attic?" Sylvie asked.

Chloe gasped. "How did you know about my dream?"

"I told her," Jane said.

They stared into each other's eyes. Jane could see the wheels turning, Chloe registering that Jane cared enough to tell her sister. If only she knew; Jane could hardly contain her emotions right now, introducing her sister and her daughter. Her skin tingled, as if she had a fever. She wanted so badly to tell the truth, to have Chloe know that Sylvie was her aunt.

"It's a beautiful image," Sylvie said. "Very creative. I'll bet your teachers love you."

Chloe snorted. "I wish, but they don't. My biology teacher hates me, because I refused to dissect frogs, and my English teacher thinks I'm demented, because when I did my term paper on Charles Dickens, I did a comparative study on the orphanages of Victorian England compared with the 'animal control' facilities of modern America—they're both barbaric!"

"Yeah, Chloe lives for animal rights, and we both take a special interest in books with orphanages in them," Mona confided.

"Excuse me?" Sylvie asked.

"My mother's dead, and Chloe's real mother abandoned her."

Sylvie was silent. Her hands were clasped in front of her, like a teacher about to address her class. Jane felt as if she had something caught in her throat. She coughed, looking away, wishing she could tell Chloe how she really felt . . . but she didn't have to. Sylvie did it for her.

"I know someone," Sylvie said quietly, "who gave a baby up for adoption. It was the hardest thing she ever did. And although I don't know everything she was thinking, I do know this: She would never have abandoned the baby. Never. If there's one thing I've learned from all my years as a school librarian, it's that most things are not as they seem. Literature exists to show us that very thing."

"Things are not as they seem," Chloe echoed. "So you mean . . ."

"I mean, she might not have given you up willingly."

"She might have been coerced," Chloe said.

Sylvie nodded. "Speaking hypothetically, that seems possible." Jane stood aside. Sylvie's voice was so direct, like a schoolmarm's. Both girls were listening intently. Jane felt tears come into her eyes.

"Adoption is all such a mystery," Mona said. "Who the real parents are, why they did what they did, where they are now. Compared to some stories. Mine, for example. My mother got sick; she died; my father married a witch."

"I like to think she didn't abandon me," Chloe said, gazing straight at Sylvie, as if Mona hadn't even spoken.

"Consider the possibility," Sylvie said in that same bookish voice, "that she would rather die than think that you believe she consigned you to 'the attic.' Although, I congratulate you on a fine literary metaphor. The attic is a place of dust, where people store their discarded things. I just don't happen to believe your real mother would have sent you there."

"Jane, you have a cool sister," Chloe said, speaking to Jane's back. Jane had turned away, to hide the fact that her sister's words and support had completely sliced her heart. "She gets it!"

"Yes, she does," Jane said, when she could turn around again. "She completely does."

CHAPTER 21

Shall we have dinner before or after we visit your mother?" John asked Sylvie as they drove toward the hospital.

She was lost in thought, staring out the window. Her pulse had quickened at the sight of Chloe, and hadn't slowed down yet. She had just met her sister's daughter—her niece! Glancing across the car seat, she wondered what John would think if she told him the whole story.

"Penny for your thoughts," he asked.

"I'm thinking about my sister."

"Jane," he said. "Your own personal black sheep . . ."

Sylvie looked at him. "I've never called her that," she said.

"You didn't have to," John said. "I can just tell. You quit your job, managed your mother's health care up until now; your sister would call now and then, but she never came home . . . You always talked about her, living in New York, as if her life there was edgy, risky, kind of dangerous."

"Did I?" Sylvie asked.

"Yes," he said. "You did. And then I met her, and I saw what you meant."

"What did you see?" Sylvie asked, curious about his impressions.

"Well, I saw her black leather jacket, and a way she has of holding herself back; and I saw a certain suspicion in her eyes, as if she was giving me the once-over and wondering what I wanted from you."

"Jane was hurt once," Sylvie said. "And I don't think she's ever gotten over it. I'm sorry she made you feel she was suspicious of you, of all people . . ."

John reached for her hand. "I liked her for it," he said. "She's looking out for her sister. I admire her for protecting you. I want to do that—"

"I'm strong," Sylvie said, as he turned into the hospital parking lot. Her eyes traveled up the building to the fourth floor, and she found her mother's window. And she felt a lump in her throat as she thought of how strong she had had to be in her life: to withstand her father walking out, and the disappointment of arriving for freshman year at Brown, when she had expected her sister to be there as a junior, and the rumors floating around campus, seeing Jeffrey Hayden with his new girlfriend . . . and sorrow, always, for her mother and then her sister.

She thought of going home for weekends, hearing Jane weep and shriek for Chloe, in the darkness of night; and she remembered Jane moving to New York, because being in Rhode Island was too painful, it was like having the worst sunburn in the world, and she was afraid some reminder of her daughter would bump into her and make it even worse.

"I want my sister to be happy," she whispered, staring up at their mother's window.

"I know you do," John said, squeezing her hand.

"How do you know that?" she asked.

"Because I've fallen in love with you," John said. "And I'm making it my business to know just what it is that makes you happy. Right now, I know we need to get your mother settled. And I'm going to help you do that . . ."

"Oh, John," Sylvie said.

"And then I'm going to take you kayaking on the most beautiful lake in Maine," he said. "And I'm going to spell your name with the stars in the sky . . ."

"Live stars," Sylvie whispered, thinking of Chloe, of her notion of dusty, forgotten stars hidden under the eaves.

"As live as live can be," he said. "And I'm guessing that this means, unless you want to have dinner in the hospital cafeteria, that we're going to eat later."

"That sounds good," she said.

"As long as you're across the table," he said, "it's always good."

And they hugged, long and hard. Jane was coming to the hospital in a little while. Perhaps they could meet with Abby Good-heart and tell their mother about their visit to Cherry Vale. No one had the right to de-cide another's path in life, but Sylvie hoped she and Jane could ease their mother's mind, convince her that this was the best thing, at least as a transition.

It was, wasn't it?

John squeezed her even tighter, giving

her the support she needed. She felt really shaky. Life was changing so fast. Sometimes Sylvie wanted to hold on to the old ways, just because they were so familiar. But then John slid his arm around her waist, starting toward the hospital door— being with him felt so different and wonderful, reminding her that change was sometimes a minor miracle.

As they walked across the asphalt parking lot to see about Margaret, Sylvie thought of how wonderful it was to have such a good friend; and she wished with all her heart that Jane could find the same thing.

🌱

"I hear Chloe met your sister," Dylan said.

"Yes," Jane said. "I brought her by, to see the stand."

Dylan nodded. "Did she approve?"

Jane was silent. They were standing in his kitchen. She had stopped by, to drop off tomorrow's pies, and he had offered her a glass of lemonade. It was tart, just the way she liked it, and the glass was covered with cool, summery condensation that felt good to her hand. She thought about his ques-

tion and knew that her sister had disap-
proved on about ten different levels, but
that in the midst of all that, she had fallen in
love with Chloe.

It was twilight, and the blue sky was fading to lavender. The kitchen windows were
open; the birds were singing their farewells
to daylight. Evening in the countryside was
peaceful, beautiful, far from the yellow-taxi
bustle of Jane's last fifteen years in New
York.

Gazing across the room at Dylan—tall,
bearded, the expression in his green eyes
as open as she'd ever seen, she knew that
she was falling in love with him. And she
knew she couldn't carry the lie any further.
She was supposed to meet up with Sylvie at
the hospital, but that would have to wait.
She took a deep breath and wondered
where to start.

"There's something I have to tell you,"
she said.

"Me, too," he said.

They stood across the room from each
other. Smoke from his cigarette drifted up.
He took a sip of lemonade. Then she
walked over to him; he put his arms around
her waist. They looked into each other's

eyes. Jane saw a strong man. Beyond that she saw depths of vulnerability that gave her the feeling of riding rapids on a river.

He kissed her, and she tasted sharp lemons. The evening was warm, and he wore a T-shirt and she wore a black tank, and their arms were hot as they held each other very close. Jane's heart sped up, because she wanted to kiss him forever.

Their bodies were right for each other. He was very tall, but when she stood on tiptoes, they were almost level. And he slid his arms under hers and pulled her up, so she was standing tiptoed, barefoot on the toes of his boots, and they stayed like that, kissing in the twilight. He had left a radio playing in another room, and the longer they didn't talk, the louder the music became, so that they could hear it clearly, and they couldn't resist starting to dance to it, with her balanced on his boots.

"You're good," he said, pausing the kiss long enough to admire the way they moved together.

"I'm not," she said. "I never dance."

"You're doing it now," he said, his eyes intense and full of humor.

"I seem to be," she said.

They kept dancing, and suddenly Jane knew that it was just a matter of time: they were going to make love. She could feel it in her skin, all the way to her heart, deep, deep inside. He was prolonging it, and the waiting felt delicious. She knew that she was ready to tell him the whole story, and she trusted that everything would work out. The spring air moved across her bare arms, and even though it wasn't at all chilly, it made Jane shiver.

Just then, they heard a knock at the side door.

"Yoo-hoo!" Chloe called.

"Are you decent?" Mona called.

A look of impatience crossed Dylan's brow, and he gave Jane a smile.

"Impeccable timing," she said as they heard the girls running through the house. They burst into the kitchen, stopping at the doorway.

"Don't you believe in turning on the lights?" Mona asked.

"It's more romantic this way," Chloe said, jabbing her with an elbow.

"Hi, girls," Jane said.

"To what do we owe the pleasure?" Dylan asked.

"We want to go out for ice cream," Mona said. "Or fried clams."

"Those are certainly summertime choices," Jane said.

"I know," Chloe said. "But my parents won't take us. They rented a movie, and they made popcorn, and they're trying to tell us that popcorn is as good as ice cream and fried clams. Ice cream for me, clams for Mona."

"Ah, now it's both," Dylan said. "Ice cream and fried clams. Not, hopefully, in that order."

"There's only one place we want to have them," Chloe said. "And only one couple we want to drive us."

"Newport," Mona nodded solemnly. "We want you to take us to Newport."

"In fact," Chloe said, pointing her finger at Dylan. "We're uncle-napping you. And we're taking Jane along for the ride. You really have no choice."

"So let's go nice and peaceful," Mona said. "Out to the car . . ."

Jane glanced at Dylan. Whatever had been building between them was still there, and she saw the amused frustration in his eyes. He gazed at Jane, giving her the chance to get them out of it. Jane hesitated. She knew she was supposed to meet Sylvie at the hospital. She could call Sylvie, try to catch her before she left; she could leave a message. Nothing on earth would stop her from going to Newport with Chloe: a family excursion.

"Well?" Dylan asked.

"I say let's go get some ice cream and fried clams," she said. Making a quick call home, she got the answering machine and left a message. Sylvie would understand.

The ride to Newport was long and cool. No one wanted air-conditioning, so Dylan drove with the windows open. The girls sat in the truck's cramped back seat, singing along with the radio. If they noticed that he and Jane were holding hands, low on the seat, they gave no sign.

Driving across Route 138, he began to remember old trips to Newport. He felt the first tug in his heart—as if he'd been caught by a fishhook, Isabel reeling him in. He went willingly. She was in the truck with them, squeezed into the back seat with her cousin and friend. The sensation was so real, he glanced into the back seat.

"My father used to call this road 'the old washboard route,'" Jane said as they bounced over another pothole.

"Because it's so bumpy," Chloe said. "Wheee!"

They passed through Narragansett, onto the Jamestown Bridge. The bay's west passage was dark silver in the last light. The old, unused bridge arched just south of the new span; Dylan remembered a time, years ago, when a tractor trailer went over the side on an icy Christmas Eve. He had been a young boy at the time, and he recalled feeling grief for the driver's sons.

Across Conanicut Island, then onto the sweeping, graceful Newport Bridge. The city by the sea sparkled down below: white yachts in the harbor, church spires, the cluster of downtown buildings. From the very top, the loom of whale-shaped Block Island was visible on the horizon. Dylan remembered a case he had worked, just a few years ago, in which the criminal had faked his own suicide by leaving a car parked and running here on the bridge's summit. His mind was working overtime, filled with memories, but none as strong as the ones of Isabel.

They found a rare parking spot on Thames Street, and walked into Dylan's favorite hole-in-the-wall clam shack, Commander Paul's. A block off the water, it was small, cramped, and stuffy. The line of people stretched out the door. Waiting in line, they smelled the food, and their mouths began to water. Crushed together, he slid his arm around Jane's waist. She was dressed for summer in jeans and a skinny black top, and he looked at her muscular arms and wanted them to hold him later.

"We're next," Chloe said. "Have your orders ready."

"I've been ready since we came off the bridge," Jane laughed.

"Four clam rolls, four orders of fries, and four Cokes," Dylan said to the college student at the window.

"How did you know that's what we'd all want?" Mona asked.

"Because when you come to Commander Paul's," Dylan said, handing over the money, "that's all there is."

They took the food outside, found spots on the low wall surrounding the entrance, and began to eat. Dylan was conscious of Jane sitting beside him. Her bare arm brushed his; her hip bumped against his side. Chloe gave him her clams—sticking to the buttered rolls and French fries.

"I'm usually a vegetarian," Jane said, "but I can't resist Paul's clams . . ."

"I didn't know that!" Chloe said, eyes gleaming. "We're both animal-friendly! Luckily clams are invertebrates and can't feel anything . . ."

"That's what I was thinking," Jane said.

"You should have told me," Dylan said, gazing at her. "We could have gone some-where that had salads or something."

"Paul's is great," Jane said, bumping shoulders with him. "My first time here in years . . ."

Dylan bit into his clam roll; he knew from experience that it was fried just right, golden brown and tasting of the briny sea, but tonight his senses were on overload and barely noticed. Tonight was all about Jane.

They crossed America's Cup Boulevard and headed for the wharves. The stores were open for summer tourist trade, and the girls ran into the jewelry and sunglass shops while Dylan and Jane crossed the cobblestones on Bowen's Wharf and navigated the throngs of people on Bannister's.

"Summer in Newport," Jane said, breathing the salt air.

"Our first together," Dylan said.

She chuckled. "You're cute," she said.

"Cute is a bunny rabbit," he said. "I'm a retired U.S. Marshal. You think Commander Paul would like to be called 'cute'?"

"I've been eating at his place for ages, but who *was* Commander Paul, anyway?"

"A naval hero," Dylan said. "He served in Vietnam aboard the USS *W.T. Crawford*. He was known for his love of fishing, and he used to tell the guys he'd open a clam shack in Newport, where he'd trained at the war college, after he left the service."

"What happened to him?"

"He rescued a whole crew whose boat had gone down in the South China Sea, just as the sharks were circling their life raft. The crew was literally beating the monsters back with oars, just as Commander Paul steamed in."

"How do you know?"

"He's legend in Newport," Dylan said. "Ironically, his ship was named after William Crawford, head of the Marshals Service in the twenties. So we marshals feel a deep bond with the Commander. He used to come for dinner . . ." Dylan trailed off.

Jane waited. She blinked slowly.

"At my in-laws' house," Dylan said. "Amanda's father had served during World War Two. Even though his great love was yachting, and his second home was the New York Yacht Club, he pined for the days when Newport was a Navy town."

"Sounds like an interesting guy," Jane said.

"For a robber baron," Dylan said, not wanting to add that he had raised a spoiled, snobby daughter. "Isabel loved her grand-parents, but she never bought into the life. Her mother wouldn't have been caught dead in a clam shack. Isabel was hooked, just like me. While the rest of the family would be eating some ritzy catered picnic at Bailey's Beach, she and I would sneak out to Paul's."

"My kind of girl," Jane said, nodding.

"She'd have liked you," Dylan said.

"Well, any girl who has a real apprecia-tion for a clam shack is bound to like apple pies," Jane said.

"That's not why," Dylan said, putting his

arms around her. They were standing in the flow of tourists, ogling the yachts docked at Bannister's Wharf, but he didn't care. He hadn't had a cigarette since leaving the orchard, and he didn't want one. He didn't want to obscure anything about tonight. Any feelings of addiction had suddenly attached themselves to Jane. He had to have her, his body was aching for her, and he knew he couldn't let her go.

"Uncle Dylan!" Chloe called, jostling through the throng of people.

"Yes, Uncle Dylan," Mona echoed. "We need advances!"

"On our salaries," Chloe explained, grinning as she came upon her uncle just about to start kissing Jane. He tried to wipe the frustration off his face.

"Why?" he asked. "I just paid you last Friday."

"I know," Chloe said, smiling wider. "And we're not asking you to give us money— just loan us next week's salary. Because we just found the sweetest, darlingest little things we have to buy."

"They remind us of Jane," Mona said.

Jane smiled and blushed. "Me?"

"Yes, you," Chloe said. Leaning over, she

tickled Jane's locket as if it were a bell. "We found tiny silver lockets just like yours, and we have to buy them."

"Because we're your fan club," Mona confided. "You bake the pies, so we can have summer jobs."

"Without you, we'd be unemployed," Chloe said.

"Hey, what about the honeycombs and maple sugar I give you to sell?" Dylan asked. "What about the apples growing on my trees, even as we speak?"

Both Chloe and Mona laughed. "We can't kid ourselves, Uncle Dylan," Chloe said. "Jane's pies have set a new standard for roadside stands. She's the whole reason people come. Man, the whole state has caught on! So we have to buy lockets just like hers—to commemorate her in our lives."

"We're going to put pictures," Mona began, but broke off laughing.

"Of Jane," Chloe continued.

"No! Of her *pies*," Mona corrected as they both cracked up. "In our lockets."

"What's in yours, Jane?" Chloe said. "I want to see."

Jane was still smiling, but she seemed

awfully quiet. She wasn't joining in the girls' merriment the way Dylan had seen her do before. She reached up, held her locket in her hand as if protecting it. Her face looked very slightly pale as her smile held but wavered. As Dylan watched, his heart jogged slightly: There's a man's picture in there, he thought. Someone she loves in New York.

"A little girl I knew a long time ago," Jane said.

"Let us see," Mona asked.

"Oh, the picture is too tiny to see," Jane said. "And it's not anchored in very securely. It might blow away in the sea breeze."

"Wouldn't want that," Chloe agreed. "Later?"

"Definitely later," Jane said, staring straight into Chloe's eyes. Dylan appreciated the way she smoothed things out with his niece. Her parents were actually pleased at the way her summer was going. Sharon had called the other day, asking to meet Jane. She had told him she and Eli appreciated what he and Jane were doing for Chloe—at first they had objected to the stand, but now they were so relieved her summer was going well. There had been no repeats of her protests at SaveRite. And she hadn't made another run at the adoption office in Family Court.

Aside from all that, Sharon was curious about Jane for another reason. She was the first woman Dylan had really been interested in since his family's deaths. He had been shut down for a long, long time. Sharon was a good sister-in-law; Dylan thought she had probably sensed the trouble between him and Amanda over the years.

"Oh, fuck," Mona said, staring into the crowd. "Excuse my language."

"Oh, double fuck," Chloe said, shrinking against Jane.

"Is that him?" Jane asked, her eyes glacial, sharp, clear blue.

"Uh-huh," Chloe said, and her voice caught, and Dylan saw the glint of tears in her eyes.

"Who?" Dylan asked. Following Chloe and Jane's sight lines, he spotted a young man standing at the Black Pearl hot dog stand. He had long, blond hair, stringy with salt. He wanted people to think it was lightened by the sun, but Dylan had observed enough jerks to know the sun came out of a bottle. He wore shorts and a surf shop T-shirt. On his arm, he saw the tattoo of a dolphin. Dylan made the connection instantly: Chloe's banner.

"What should I say to him?" Chloe asked Jane.

"You don't have to say anything to him," she replied.

"But I have to walk right past him," Chloe said. "To get off the wharf . . ."

"What did he do?" Dylan asked.

"You don't want to know," Chloe mumbled.

"Tell your uncle," Mona urged. "So he can deck the creep!"

Dylan's fatherly blood was pumping hard. He didn't know what the guy had done, but he disliked him on sight. He had dead, lifeless green eyes—scanning the crowd like a predator, the way a shark would look at a school of bait. Dylan could easily picture him on the wrong side of an investigation: drugs, paper, fraud, whatever might get him a little more of whatever he wanted. Sex, drugs, money, women.

Glancing at Chloe, Dylan ruled out the middle two. He steamed, thinking it must have been the first and last: using his niece.

Jane had her arm around Chloe's shoulders, and Dylan noticed the upset in both of their eyes.

"He surfs in Newport," Chloe explained. "That must be what he's doing here. Look how blond and tan he is."

Dylan wanted to tell her he was a fake, but he held himself back. He also wanted to walk across the wharf and shove the hot dog down his throat, but he held himself back from that, too.

"He's the one," Mona said, touching Dylan's wrist, "who rode his dirt bike through the orchard. He tore up the roots!"

"He's the one?" Dylan echoed. Now, as if the guy could feel the energy emitting from their group, he looked their way. Chloe was blocked from his sight by Jane, but the guy caught Dylan staring at him. Over the years, Dylan had mastered the cop's stare: eyes deader and harder than any shark. He actually saw the blond guy flinch.

"Don't say anything to him," Chloe begged.

"You should arrest him," Mona said. "Honestly, Uncle Dylan—he's really bad. He really did something awful . . ."

"Mona," Jane warned. "Let Chloe decide what she wants to do, okay?"

"I just hate him," Mona said hotly. "For being such a jerk to my friend."

"Chloe," Dylan said. "Do you want me to talk to him?"

Chloe shook her head. When they looked again, the surfer had abandoned his spot—one of the top trolling sites in New England, Bannister's Wharf on a warm summer night—and was walking quickly away. Dylan had him in his sights and watched him with a pitiless gaze.

"What's his name?" he asked.

"Zeke," Mona said as Jane and Chloe stood silently aside.

Dylan wanted to go after him for the trees and their roots, for his niece and whatever he had done to hurt her. But he knew by Jane's tenderness, by the way she was enfolding Chloe as if she were a baby bird and Jane had wings, that that would just make things worse for Chloe right now.

Dylan loved Chloe, and he wanted to protect her the way he would have his own daughter.

The jewelry store was just down the wharf. Holding Jane's hand, he led the kids through the door. He pointed to the locket around Jane's neck, and he asked the sales clerk for two just like it. His heart was very full as he saw the happiness in Chloe and Mona's eyes. Even fuller, as he saw the satisfaction in Jane's. His eyes darted to her locket; he couldn't help himself, wondering whether she really had the picture of a little girl inside, or whether it was of some lover she hadn't yet let go of.

Dylan considered it his job to chase away any bad guys from his niece; he considered it his duty to get Jane to let go of any and all old lovers. He hoped to accomplish that tonight.

When the girls asked him to take the price of the sterling silver lockets off their next paychecks, he just laughed and shook his head.

"They're a present," he said. Isabel would have wanted it that way, he knew.

CHAPTER 22

Before leaving Newport, Chloe wanted to take a ride past Isabel's grandparents' old house. So they bought ice-cream cones at Newport Creamery, then headed back down the hill. Out Thames Street, around the corner and down the stretch past the Ida Lewis Yacht Clubs and Harbor Court—the music of clanking halyards and boats at their moorings coming through the open windows—past Hammersmith Farm . . .

"The summer White House," piped up Chloe from the back seat. "When John F. Kennedy was president."

"That's right," Jane said. "When I first got my license, I'd drive down to Newport with my sister, and we'd always try to see into the yard—looking for Jacqueline Kennedy Onassis. We'd always wish we'd see her walking along the road, on visits home to see her mom."

"What would you have done?"

"Offered her a ride," Jane said.

"My mother was always proud of the fact the first Catholic president got married right here in Rhode Island," Dylan said.

Chloe snorted. "Grandma is weird."

Everyone chuckled. Dylan drove them onto Ocean Drive—the long, magical expanse of open road, with rocky coves and hidden bays and the entire Atlantic Ocean on the right. The smell of salt and rockweed and a damp mist blew in; they might have been on a ship at sea. Dylan pointed into the darkness, where black waves broke into white spume.

"Breton Tower used to be out there," he said. "And until not so many years ago, the America's Cup races were held here in Newport."

"Curse Dennis," Jane said of Dennis Connor, the skipper who had lost the cup. "For a while, that was the state motto."

"Rhianna always talks about the sailors she used to screw—I mean, date," Mona said. "Australian sailors who used to drink champagne out of their topsiders. Vile, if you ask me."

"Better than surfers," Chloe murmured.

Jane half turned, to look at her. She had been traumatized by the sight of Zeke. Jane had been so glad to be there with her. She thought of all the years she had missed—all the threats and dangers Chloe had faced along the way, without Jane to protect her. She had survived, nicely. Her adoptive parents had done a fine job. But the reality of Chloe's survival and safety did nothing to address the longing Jane felt inside, to hold her little baby of a teenaged girl, and protect her from the rest of life's trials.

"You okay?" Jane asked.

Chloe nodded, licking her ice-cream cone. The moment of closeness hadn't ended; it shimmered between them. Chloe had taken the small locket out of its box, put it around her neck. Jane saw it glinting in the starlight coming through the truck window, and it made her feel as if she were in a small sailboat, sliding down the back side of an ocean wave.

Rounding the last curve on the drive, Chloe pointed.

"There's Bailey's Beach," she said.

"Snobville," Mona said.

"Isabel's grandparents belonged. Its real name is 'the Spouting Rock Beach Association.' There's a spouting rock somewhere. Isabel and I used to look for it. We thought it would be like a little beached whale, spouting away."

"Rhianna would sell her soul to be invited in there," Mona said. "And she would certainly class the place up, that's for sure."

Chloe kept her head turned, watching until the beach club disappeared from sight. They drove past Rough Point, Doris Duke's great stone house, and several other gated estates, and finally they stopped in front of an enormous wall. Well-trimmed bushes and vines clung to the stones. An iron gate was partially opened, revealing a floodlit courtyard and magnificent limestone chateau, reminiscent of the Loire Valley.

"There it is," Chloe said, breathless. "Maison du Soleil."

"House of the Sun," Mona said, leaning forward to stare.

"Are they still there?" Chloe asked.

"Your aunt's family? Yes," Dylan said.

"Do you visit them?"

"No," he said.

"But you were their son-in-law," Chloe said.

"I was," he agreed, and Jane wondered whether Chloe picked up the subtle emphasis on the past tense. The sea breeze was less extreme here, blocked by the house and the trees and the wall. But Jane knew that the Cliff Walk ran along the other, seaward side of the property; years ago, she, Sylvie, and their mother had walked it many times. Until this minute, she hadn't been sure which of the mansions belonged to Amanda's family; but now that she knew, she remembered looking through the hedge, seeing women in white dresses sitting on a wide terrace. Had one of them been Dylan's wife as a young girl?

"Can we go in?" Chloe asked.

"Yeah," Mona said. "So I can tell Rhianna I partied with the elite?"

The car was so quiet; the only sound came from traffic rushing by on Bellevue Avenue. Jane sensed Chloe and Dylan connected by unspoken words that had to do with love and memories of Isabel. Jane closed her eyes, thinking of the picture on

Dylan's refrigerator—those two smiling girls, their daughters.

"I don't think so," Dylan said after a long moment. "We might remind them of things they'd rather not think about."

"Of what happened to Isabel and Aunt Amanda?"

Dylan nodded, just staring through the gate. Although it was wide open, Jane knew that to Dylan it felt locked and barred. Years in New York without this young girl in the back seat had taught her that feeling very well. She reached across the seat and touched his thigh.

His hand closed over hers. Jane felt the presence of their daughters in the truck. For, although Isabel was four years gone, her spirit tonight was as alive as Chloe and Mona's. Jane breathed and took the girl into her heart. She glanced back, to look at Chloe. To her amazement, Chloe was staring at the back of her head, as if willing Jane to turn around.

Jane's heart skipped a beat. She wanted this night, this moment to go on forever. The lie she was living with Dylan and Chloe suddenly seemed enormous, a weight she could carry no longer. If Mona weren't with them, she would tell the truth right this minute. As it was, she had to hold it inside a little longer.

And she did.

🌱

Mona was spending the night at Chloe's, so they dropped the girls off in her driveway. Tired and happy, they gathered their things and waved good-bye before walking inside. A woman leaned out the back door, waving.

"Sharon," Dylan said, hitting the horn lightly and waving. "My brother's wife."

"Chloe's . . ." Jane tried to say, but couldn't get the word out: *mother*. The woman looked pleasant, gentle, suburban. What did that even mean, Jane wondered? That she wasn't wearing a skinny black tank top?

"Tell me about that jerk Zeke," Dylan said as he drove the quarter mile to his house.

Jane shivered, coming almost face-to-face with the woman who had raised her daughter. She tried to concentrate on Dylan's question, but she was too shaken up.

"Keeping her confidence?" he asked. "I guess that's right. Let her tell me or her parents herself, when she's ready."

"Do you remember, at the start of this evening," Jane asked as he parked the truck in front of his red barn, her heart racing so hard she was sure it was going to burst, "when I said I had something to tell you?"

"Yes," he said. "And I told you I had something to tell you, too."

"I have to talk to you," she said, gazing across the truck seat.

He nodded, then let himself out of the cab. He came around the front and opened Jane's door, never taking his eyes off her. He put his arms around her, pulled her close, and touched his forehead to hers. The orchard was alive around them. Crickets sang and an owl called in the distance.

"Will you believe me," he said, "if I tell you that I want to hear it all, every word, but that I have to kiss you first?"

She frowned, smiled, felt her heart bump. If only she could just get the words out. "I believe you," she said. "Because I feel the same way."

And then he kissed her. And all her plans and intentions to do the right thing and tell him were put on hold.

They went upstairs. It wasn't awkward or forward, because they'd been aiming toward it all night, maybe even since the first day they'd met. Jane tried to shut her mind down and stop the words in her head—because her body was winning out. Heat and chills coursed all through her body. She had to tell him, she knew she had to tell him. And then the harder she tried, the more her mind worked. She wondered how many times he had climbed these stairs with Amanda. Maybe it was all a way of stalling—because she was terrified to tell him the truth.

Everything registered: the old sepia-toned photographs on the wall, the newer framed photos on the bureau. She searched the new ones, found that they were all of Isabel and Chloe, Eli and Sharon—there were none of Amanda. She looked around the room—comfortable and old-fashioned, very masculine.

"Dylan?" she said, trying to form the words.

"Yes?"

"That thing I have to tell you? It's important."

He nodded. And he kissed her again.

A big brass bed, heavy maple furniture, a pair of muddy boots leaning on their side, a pile of shirts on a chair. A bay window overlooked the orchard; gazing out, Jane could see that the house was built on a slight hill, and the fruit trees sloped away, into a gentle valley. A stream ran through the land; she could hear the rush of water, see the black and silver flash, reflecting the stars.

Dylan came up behind her, encircling her with his arms from behind. They felt so solid, and she leaned back into his chest. She rocked there for a minute, feeling the tension of their bodies pressing together. She tried to get him to bend, but he wouldn't; they both laughed softly.

"Dylan?"

"Forget it," he murmured. "Whatever it is. Forget—"

Turning around, she kissed him on the lips. He tasted of salt spray and, faintly, of tobacco. She gripped his biceps with her fingers. He reached up and slid the thin straps of her black top down. The motion felt erotic and left her weak in the knees. Standing by the open window, they undressed each other.

Jane wanted his hands on every inch of

her skin. She leaned into the calluses on his hands. She thought of how hard he worked in the orchard, driving his broken heart into a place he could stand. She did the same in her kitchen. Her own hands were scarred and burned from trying to bake away her longing for Chloe.

He leaned over, kissed her locket—and she gasped, because he didn't even know what was in it, but he knew it had to be precious to her. He kissed her breasts. She hadn't been touched this way in so long, she felt her heart being sliced open. Undoing the buttons on his jeans, she pushed them down. He wasn't wearing underwear.

She smiled, but they didn't speak about it. They walked to the bed. Holding hands, it felt so right and comfortable, they might have been walking to beds together their whole adult lives. But at the same time she felt she was drowning in passion, and she wasn't sure she could swim safely to shore.

"I haven't," she said as he supported her waist and lowered her onto the bed, "done anything like this in a very long time . . ."

"Neither have I."

They were side by side, heads on the same pillow. Jane blinked slowly. She wanted to see everything and read all his thoughts in his eyes. He kissed her again, pulling her against him, and the thick hair on his chest tickled her nipples and made her feel unspeakably sexy, and she couldn't help smiling through the kiss.

"Wow," she said.

"Me, too," he said, running his hand down the curve of her side, touching her legs. She quivered, doing the same to him. Her fingers found his scar, and she hiked up on her elbow to first look at and then kiss it.

It felt hard and jagged, raised like a piece of rope. And on either side, all the way down to his knee, were the rungs of a ladder, the teeth of a zipper: the stitches that had held his tissue and bone together.

"This is where they shot you," she said, feeling the chill of death.

"Yes."

"Thank God you're still here," she said.

"In a lot of ways," he said, stroking her face, "I was already dead when it happened. I had stopped believing in love a long time before. And I'm not sure I started believing in it again till this spring."

"You believe in it now?" Jane asked, kissing his neck.

"Yeah," he said.

And then he seemed to set about making her believe in it, too. He caressed every spot on her body. She felt his lips, hot on her skin. All those years in big, bad, New York City, and she was experiencing these things for the first time in the countryside of her youth. She arched into his touch, shimmering under his fingertips, her entire body wanting more.

He touched her between her legs, and she felt as hot and wet as a garden, and she reached down and felt him harder than she could imagine. Their eyes locked, she couldn't even dream of looking away, and he entered her.

She bit her lip. Tears filled her eyes, because she felt locked into him, inseparable physically. Their hearts were touching. She reached up, her fingers trembling, and touched his cheek.

"Jane, you don't know . . ." he began. "I've never felt this way . . ."

"I know," she said, feeling him so deeply inside her. "Neither have I . . ."

Their bodies were alive and wide awake, on fire for each other. Jane closed her eyes, reached back to grab the brass bars of his bed. A cool breeze came in the window, cooling her skin, making her arch her back just to stay close to him.

She couldn't stand to have the amazing, wonderful feelings keep building inside her—a whole lifetime of love held in, held back—and neither could he, because they both held on and let go at the same time, as the stars danced in the trees and blazed just outside the window, where white curtains lifted softly, softly, in the evening breeze.

Stunned and depleted, yet so full, Jane lay back on the pillow. She saw pinpricks of light behind her eyelids. Were they stars or something else? Dylan was right there, right beside her. He touched her face. His lips were moving, he was whispering, and she heard him say:

"I told you I had something to tell you . . . I'm falling in love with you, Jane. That's what I wanted to say . . . wanted to tell you."

Jane grasped his hand, kissed his fingers. Her mind swam, but with bliss and emotion, not coherent thought. The truth of Chloe pulled at her gut, like an undertow trying to pull a swimmer into the deepest part of the sea. Her body was spent, but her soul was just starting up.

She must have slept.

Dreams spun through her mind. She saw the orchard, stars in the trees, and an open window in Chloe's attic, more stars lying on shelves inside . . . and the stars came to life . . . and they were girls, dancing . . . Chloe and Isabel . . . and Jane saw them all together, a family at a table, Jane and Dylan and Chloe and Isabel . . . and she felt his kisses on her lips and his touch on her collarbone . . . and she dreamed of the look in his eyes, that she had seen when he didn't think she'd noticed, in the truck earlier, when the girls had asked about her locket . . . the expression revealing his concern that she wore someone else, another man's picture, always close to her heart . . . but it's not a man, she wanted to tell him now . . . it's not a man at all: It's what I have to tell you . . . it's my daughter . . . it's . . .

"Chloe!" he said.

And Jane woke up, lying in Dylan Chadwick's bed, to find him by her side, the chain still around her neck as he held her locket, open, in his hand, looking at the nearly sixteen-year-old picture inside.

CHAPTER 23

Dylan," Jane said, pulling away, clutching the open locket in her hand.

"What are you doing with Chloe's baby picture?" he asked in a gravelly voice.

Jane couldn't speak. She was half asleep, hazy from making love. He had let her borrow a T-shirt, and it smelled like them, like their bodies. Oh, God, why had she let him talk her into waiting? He'd been propped up on his elbow, and now he sat upright, staring down at her. His eyes flashed green in the darkness; an owl screamed in the orchard, going in for a kill.

She pulled the sheet around her body, pushing herself up, and reached out for his hand. He leaned back and refused to take hers.

"I have the same picture," he said. "Or

one very similar." He got off the bed, walked to his bureau. There, from the gallery of framed photos, he came over to the bed with a picture of Chloe—as a baby, just days old. With the bow in her hair: the little yellow bow the nurse had given her, setting her apart from all the other babies.

Jane let out a small exclamation of emotion, just to see. The picture was five by seven, much larger than the one she had in her locket. Chloe's little fists were bunched up at her chin; she had apple cheeks and a thatch of dark hair. Her eyes were squeezed tightly shut, as if she was trying to hold on to her dream. And the yellow bow looked like a butterfly. The same bow, both pictures.

"Chloe," Jane said.

"She's in your locket, Jane," Dylan said. "Her hair, the bow—it's unmistakably her. What are you doing with her picture?"

"She's my daughter," Jane said.

The words were out. The window was open, and the breeze swirled in, tossing the white curtains. The breeze took Jane's words, spun them around. They rang in her ears. They made Dylan take a step backward, made his face redden.

"She's your *daughter*?"

"I had her when I was twenty," Jane said. "When I was at Brown . . . she's the reason I dropped out."

Dylan didn't say anything. He stood very still, in the middle of the room, staring at Jane. Was he seeing his niece's blue eyes, dark hair? The dimples of her smile? The worry line between her eyebrows? Her fine cheekbones? Or was he seeing a person who had broken his trust? Jane shook, not knowing.

"I loved her," Jane said. "I held her. In this picture," she tapped the locket, "I was holding her. The nurse gave me that bow, and I made her take a picture of Chloe, and I promised her I'd never take the locket off. I never have."

"But what—?" Dylan began to ask, trailing off as if the question was too huge to ask.

"My mother convinced me it was for the best," Jane said. "That I was too young. That I had to complete my education. That it would be better for the baby to have a real family—a mother and a father."

"My brother and Sharon . . ."

Jane nodded, hugging her knees. "My

mother knows your mother. She knew about how your brother was trying to start a family . . . It seemed a perfect fit."

"It was. It is," Dylan said, his eyes harsh.

"I wanted to keep her," Jane whispered. Her heart was crushed. She could feel the future closing in on her. She could see it in Dylan's eyes: He hated her for what she had done. Probably not for giving up her daughter, but for coming back for her. For intruding when she wasn't wanted.

"You did the right thing," Dylan said. "Giving her a better life."

Jane couldn't speak. She happened not to believe that that was true. She thought of the bond between her and Chloe, and she grieved for the fifteen years they'd been deprived of each other.

"I'd better go," Jane said. She had felt so happy, just a few minutes ago, so comfortable lying in Dylan's arms, but right now she felt naked and exposed, and she pulled the sheet around her as she went to get dressed.

Dylan stood very still—a statue in the blue starlit darkness, bearded and scarred, unable to move or speak. He stared out the open window, not at Jane. He made no move to stop her. It was as if she had already left the room. Her heart was racing, in her throat, as she tried to come up with the words to make everything right, to take everything back. But she realized, pulling on her shirt, that she couldn't: The past was the past, and this was the price she had to pay for what she had done.

"Tell me one thing," Dylan said as she stood watching him, wanting to find a way to say good-bye.

"Yes, of course."

"Her name," he said. "You made that part of the adoption agreement—that she keep the name Chloe. Why was it so important?"

Jane closed her eyes, remembering her last moments with the infant. She had held Chloe to her breast, making her a promise. It was a secret, between mother and child, deep and so simple.

"I can't tell you that," she whispered.

He nodded, eyes hard. She watched him writing her off.

"I know you think I shouldn't have come back into her life," Jane began. "But—"

Dylan shook his head and let out a howl: "Is that what you think?"

"Yes," she said.

"You're wrong, Jane," he said, the statue

coming to roaring life. He tore around the room, discharging violent energy. She felt him wanting to smash his fist through the wall, and she drew in a sharp breath. "I know you had to do that. She would probably even want you to—she's curious about her real mother. It's the *way* you did it. It's the way you fucking lied to me. You let me fall in love with you . . ."

"Dylan," she said, taking a step toward him. He stopped her with a ferocious stare.

"You let me trust you, but you had this secret the whole time. Not a little secret, either. Something that could rip my family apart."

"I know. I'm sorry . . ." He was talking, telling her what he felt, and she thought— just for a second—that there was a chance. They still had time to make it right. She could explain, he could forgive. He could try to understand. She could tell him how she'd been carrying this burden all this time, her entire adult life: this awful, heavy, terrible burden of love.

"No," he said, hand up.

"Oh, Dylan," she said, wanting to explain what that much love, an entire lifetime of love for a baby girl, too secret to be revealed or offered, could do to a person. It had turned Jane into a hermit. A baker, just like a baker in a fairy tale or a fable, toiling over a mixing bowl, throwing in magical ingredients along with the flour and sugar: love, prayers, hugs, wishes . . . all for baby Chloe. And toddler Chloe. And little girl Chloe. And now, teenager Chloe . . .

"You were right before," he said coldly. "You'd better go."

"I never knew what I was missing," she said, her voice tight. "Until now . . ."

"Well, at least you have that," he said. "At least you've had a little time with your daughter."

"I was talking about you, too," she said, letting out a sob.

"Funny," he said. "I thought the same thing."

And then the owl screeched again, just outside the window, and rose with squirming prey in its talons; the great, winged shadow obliterated the stars, darkened the window. Jane shuddered. Dylan was silent, letting her know there was nothing more to say.

Walking out of the house of the man she loved, Jane tried to maintain her dignity and a little composure. She succeeded, except for the tears pouring down her cheeks. The screen door closed softly behind her. When she got to her car, she looked up at his bedroom window. He stood there watching her, framed in the sash, massive as a giant, as the person who'd just put an end to her dreams.

Only that was wrong: Dylan wasn't the one.

Jane had done that to herself.

Chloe and Mona showed up for work the next day. The sun was bright, but there was still morning dew all over the stand. Chloe wiped it down, unlocked the little cupboard, took out the flags, banners, and signs. Working in early silence—although Chloe was a morning person, Mona wasn't—they set up for the day.

Feeling kind of queasy, Chloe wished she had a cold soda. Her system was unused to anything but vegetables, and she worried that maybe some clam juice might have gotten on her roll. Who was she to discern between big furry cows and slippery little mollusks? Mammals, bivalves, creatures were creatures, and maybe she was being punished for patronizing a clam shack.

Uncle Dylan delivered the pies on his tractor, but he had a really grumpy look on his face. Deeply scored lines on either side of his mouth, and furrows of worry in his forehead struck Chloe with the thought that he looked the way he used to, in the days after Isabel's death but before Jane had come along. She mulled that over, wanting to ask him what was wrong, but feeling too crummy.

"Boy, what's wrong with the Chadwick family today?" Mona asked. "You're in a snit and you're uncle's in a huff."

"I'm not in a snit," Chloe said. "I just feel clam-sick."

"What?"

"It's payback for the little mud critters. They're letting me know I shouldn't have eaten that roll they were in."

"They're dead. They're fried," Mona said, twirling her hair. "They don't have voices. And you didn't even eat any—at most you ate a roll that *brushed* a clam."

Chloe gave her a look.

"Well, at least I don't waste a beautiful sunny morning worried about being haunted by the spirits of dead fried clams. So, what's *his* problem?"

"Uncle Dylan's? I don't know," Chloe said, watching his tractor disappear into the orchard. "I was wondering the same thing."

"You think he's getting any from Jane?"

"What is wrong with you, Mona?" Chloe laughed. "You're being really disgusting today."

"What's disgusting about sex? Unless it's with someone creepy named Zeke? Hey! I have a great idea! Let's get shark tattoos. I'm going to wrap mine in a ribbon that says 'virgin slut.' "

Chloe raised her head, bemused by the idea. "Yeah!" she said. "I can see my parents definitely being on board for that!"

"I'm serious. Just to counteract dolphin-boy's body art. We'll chomp him."

Chloe laughed. She had always wanted a tattoo, although she had thought of using the image of a sheep or cow, to foster love of farm animals. On the other hand, the shark was a maligned fish, and it could probably use some support.

"Guaranteed to chase Zeke away," Mona said, temptingly.

"I don't think he's coming back," Chloe said, holding her stomach.

"Unless," Mona said, raising a cautionary eyebrow, "what you have isn't clam-poisoning at all, but morning sickness."

"Mona!" Chloe exclaimed, making a cross with her two index fingers.

"Think about it . . ."

"No—I don't want to."

"Chloe . . ."

Chloe closed her eyes, counted the days. What if she had taken the test too soon? When was her period due, anyway? She figured it out: six days ago.

"No . . ." she said out loud.

Mona looked worried, as if she had just told a joke that turned out to be real and true. "Don't tell me you're late," she said.

"Six days," Chloe said, her eyes wide.

"I was only kidding, though—"

"But what if this *is* morning sickness?"

"It can't be. You only did it once. You're practically a virgin, still."

"There's no 'practically' about it."

"I was only kidding when I said 'virgin sluts' before," Mona said. "I was trying to be funny. I'm trying to shed my inner dork."

"Don't worry," Chloe said fondly, but with

a ton of panic building. "You're the least slutty person I know. I'm the second least."

"What are you going to do?"

"I have to take another test," Chloe said. "But I have the same problems as before— I don't want anyone in town to see me buying it."

"You could always call Jane," Mona suggested. "And have her buy it for you. Or even get her to take you . . ."

Chloe nodded. Her stomach turned. That was what she would do.

"I'll do that; I'll call Jane, and I'll take the test again . . ."

⁂

Dylan rode his tractor through the field. His hands gripped the steering wheel tightly, as if he didn't quite trust himself not to slide off, under the tires. His mind was spinning, and his heart was nowhere to be found. He'd caught the look in Chloe's eyes: *What's wrong with him?*

A good question. A really good question.

He wouldn't be feeling so let down, that was for sure, if he hadn't let himself get up so high. He knew all that crap about armor—that's what addiction was all about.

Anyone who smoked or drank too much, anyone who ate too many cookies, anyone who sat glued to the TV was piling on the armor to avoid feeling pain.

Any pop psychologist could tell you. Just to prove the point, Dylan lit up. The first time in over twenty-four hours. He had armor, all right. It was a giant shell, heavy as hell, impermeable. He was a tank, he could barrel through life. As a marshal, he had carried a gun. Several of them, as a matter of fact.

He could go to the range, hit the bull's-eye. Once a drugged-out spurned husband had tried to run through Dylan with a machete, to get at his ex-wife, the witness Dylan was protecting, and Dylan shot him dead. Not to stop him, not to wound him, but cold dead—right in the body mass. It took armor to kill a man that way, and, paradoxically, the act of killing caused the existing armor to thicken.

Having a beautiful wife not love you enabled and quickened the growth of armor. Having her cheat on you with a rich polo player didn't exactly encourage you to open your heart, let your vulnerable side show through. Telling you she wanted to leave you—or, more accurately, wanted you to move out of the apartment you'd shared to-gether, to which you'd brought your baby daughter home from the hospital—was like Miracle-Gro for armor.

And having her die in your arms, with that same then-eleven-year-old baby daughter, could easily have been the sealant, the con-crete, the iron seal on all that armor you'd already grown.

And then, along came Jane . . .

Dylan thought about it now. He drove through the rows of apple trees, spreading fertilizer. He had tested the soil to determine the need for lime, potassium, and magne-sium. Since most of his stock was under renovation pruning, he was holding off on the nitrogen. Keeping track of chemicals seemed almost impossible, so he parked in the shade of a half-dead tree and shut off the tractor.

He limped over to lean his back up against the trunk. It felt good and solid to have his spine meet the bark. He had learned, years ago, that he could count on trees. They responded in predictable ways to the right kind of care. You wouldn't catch an apple tree causing a person to thicken their armor.

Jane.

Dylan tried to breathe.

Voices carried in the orchard. He heard Chloe and Mona talking to someone who had stopped by to buy a pie. The words were unintelligible, but the tones of their voices soothed him.

Chloe didn't know. Neither did Eli or Sharon. Dylan was the sole holder of the big secret. Jane was Chloe's mother. The woman he had just decided it was okay to love was Chloe's natural mother. She had kissed him, embraced him, opened his heart. No armor there. Nothing between them. He had told her more about Isabel, his feelings for what had happened, than he had anyone on earth.

His job had sent him to a shrink. All expenses paid by the United States. In fact, a leave of absence and his presence required on the couch, one day a week. Okay, the shrink didn't have a couch. She had a nice cozy office with two chairs facing each other and a view out her window of the church across the street.

Dylan had sat in that chair for six weeks straight. He had stared at the church, trying to think of things to say. At one session, he felt such rage at God, he asked the doctor to pull the blinds. She thought he had the sun in his eyes.

When they were finished—when he had satisfied the Service's requirement that he get psychological help—the doctor had smiled at him sadly. She was pretty and wise. He liked her, and he had believed that if he could talk to anyone, it would be her. She had said:

"Do you know, you've only said her name twice?"

"What?" he had asked.

"In all the times you've come here, in all of our six sessions, you have only said Isabel's name twice."

"Isabel," he said.

"Three times. Why did you just do that?"

"Because I like the sound of it," he said, squinting at the light reflecting off the rose window across the street. But he knew that was a lie. He'd said her name again just to prove he could.

With Jane, he hadn't had to prove anything.

He had wanted to tell her everything, and more. And he had wanted to hear her whole story, whatever it was, right back. He would

have listened, he told himself. He wouldn't
have judged her; he would have helped her
find a way—to do what?

That's where he had to stop himself. Because nothing about this story could have a
happy ending. If Jane got close to Chloe, Eli
and Sharon would be hurt. If Dylan protected his brother's family, Jane would be
left out. He stared at a bee, buzzing from
one meadow flower to another. The sound
was loud in his ears.

She shouldn't have lied to him, shouldn't
have kept her real purpose such a secret.
She had ingratiated herself to him and
Chloe; had any of her feelings or motives
been true?

The bee circled a funnel up through the
air, up to the tree branches. He watched it
trace figure eights in the blue sky. Its wings
were a black blur. It was doing its work, pol-
linating the trees. Without the bee, the orchard would die. Just like without love,
people died. Dylan had felt himself draining
away, before Jane. He scowled, watching
the bee, thinking about how some things in
life were impossible. In fact, he thought,
most things.

This orchard, for instance.

It was one big crazy, uphill climb. One huge cosmic impossibility.

Dylan sat under the tree, watching the bee, thinking about it. All apple varieties were unable to pollinate themselves or flowers of the same apple variety. To achieve high-quality fruit, it was necessary to cross-pollinate by planting different varieties of apple trees together. Bloom dates had to overlap, so that both trees would bloom at the same time.

And how was a human being—a goddamn retired lawman, at that—supposed to coordinate bloom dates? Other factors had to be considered. Some apple varieties, such as Jonagold, Stayman, Winesap, and Mutsu, produced sterile pollen, and could never be used as pollenizers. Yet pollen from other varieties could be used to pollinate those pollen-sterile trees.

Really, the honey bee did all the work.

Dylan sat on the warm ground, staring at that bee. He thought of Jane, carrying Chloe's picture in her locket for over fifteen years. He thought of Chloe, doctoring her ID in order to trick the clerk at Family Court into giving up her adoption records.

Two people after the same thing: connection.

In some ways, the whole thing seemed so right. Then why did it feel, to Dylan sitting under the half-dead apple tree, so wrong?

CHAPTER 24

Jane drove away from Dylan's in a daze, and she started to go home, but instead she pointed her car toward town, the hospital. She wanted her mother. It was a sudden, instant, primal desire. She parked close to the entrance, walked up the sidewalk, pushed the elevator button, all in a state of numbness.

When she got to the room, she found her mother sitting up in bed, the TV tuned to a game show. Jane stood in the doorway. Her heart caught, for about a hundred different reasons. Right at the top of the list, in that exact moment, was the sight of her brilliant, scholarly mother watching some tanned and blond game show host awarding microwave ovens to the winners on his show.

"Hi, Mom," Jane said.

"Oh, honey," her mother said, fumbling for the remote, turning down the sound. "You caught me."

"Caught you?"

Her mother blushed. "I was so bored, I've resorted to something I swore I'd never do—watching TV during the daytime. But the medication makes me so sleepy, I can't really concentrate on reading. I start a book, and I get drowsy halfway through the first page!"

"That must be hard," Jane said, pulling the chair over. "I know how you love to read."

"Books have saved my life," her mother said, with complete seriousness. "During all the hard times . . ."

"I know what you mean," Jane said, thinking of how often she'd gotten lost in wonderful books over the years, made friends with the characters and authors, felt herself elevated, even temporarily, from the difficulties of her own life.

Her mother gestured at the TV screen. "Game shows, programs like that, are . . . well, they're like cotton candy. They taste sweet and easy, and the more you eat, the more you think you want. But they leave you feeling a little . . . depleted."

Jane listened, closing her eyes. Dylan's words and the look in his eyes resonated, echoing through her whole body. She had to hug herself, to keep herself from shaking.

"Books do the opposite," her mother said. "No matter how entertaining, or thrilling or romantic, they nourish a person. They're like a full-course meal for the heart and soul . . ." Her voice broke, and she buried her head in her hands.

"What is it, Mom?" Jane asked, leaning forward.

"I miss my books!" her mother cried.

"Oh, Mom . . . you'll have them soon enough. The social worker told me and Sylvie they want to discharge you soon."

"To . . . a . . ." her mother gulped, "nursing home!"

Jane held her mother's hand. Being part of a family was such a mystical thing: you could walk in, thinking you had the most terrible problem on earth, and someone you loved would come at you with something even worse. How had her mother heard about this? Jane and Sylvie had planned to talk to her together.

"Who talked to you about that?" Jane asked.

"Sylvie," her mother said, sniffing. "Last night."

Jane nodded, feeling guilty. She hadn't realized that Sylvie might have had an agenda. Or perhaps Abby had seen her there and grabbed the moment.

Jane had dropped the pies off at Dylan's, and then Chloe and Mona had begged for the ride to Newport; if only Jane had kept her plans with Sylvie. She could have supported her sister and mother, and Dylan wouldn't have looked in her locket. Her body trembled from head to toe: an earthquake of emotion.

"Is that where you think I belong?" her mother asked now, as if she hadn't asked the same question several times in the past weeks.

"You've been falling," Jane said, as if she hadn't said the same thing several times before.

"And forgetting," her mother said, covering her eyes. "That's the worst part; I was lying before, honey, when I said the medication makes me forget what I'm reading. It's not that at all—it just happens. It's just my mind . . . I was so smart!"

"Oh, Mom, you still are!"

Her mother shook her head, sobbing softly. "I can barely follow the game show. I forget what is happening. My books, my books . . ."

Jane closed her eyes, feeling her mother's thin hand. She thought of the blood running through her mother's veins, a river of time and love, passing it to Jane and Sylvie, passing it to Chloe. She thought of her mother's love of books, of stories, a river of words carrying symbols and meaning, tying them all together. Books and mothers and children, beloved to Margaret, beloved to Jane.

"Oh, Sylvie, oh, Jane," her mother said, getting her daughters confused, lifting their clasped hands to her lips. She kissed Jane's hands. Then, fingers interlocked, she used the back of Jane's hand to wipe her own eyes. "You look so sad . . . I'm sorry for telling you my problems."

Jane tried to smile, but she couldn't. She felt grief for her mother's forgetfulness and inability to read. The sorrow, the reality, of not being able to hold on to the things you loved washed through her.

"What is it, honey?" her mother asked, looking deeply into her eyes. "What's wrong?"

"I want my baby," Jane whispered.

Her mother didn't speak, and she didn't let go of Jane's hand. She just sat still, in her hospital bed, gazing at her daughter. Her skin was very soft, remarkably unlined; a lifetime of loving books had kept her in the shade, out of the sun.

Words were impossible. Jane couldn't explain what was going on inside her heart just then. A physical need to see her mother, to be with her blood, had pulled her straight from Dylan's room to the hospital; the same pull existed in the opposite direction. It had nothing to do with reasoning or logic; the signal came from the heart.

Her mother was silent. But Jane could read in her eyes that she understood. Margaret Porter, school principal, finally understood. That fact was amazing. It was as if, losing certain connections in her brain, she found the link in her heart.

"I wanted what was best for you," her mother said, finally.

Jane tried to nod.

"Your father had left us," she said. "I was

bitter. He had left me with the responsibility of raising two sensitive, brilliant young girls. When that boy did what he did—"

"Got me pregnant," Jane said.

Her mother flinched, but she nodded. "I hated him. I despised him for robbing you of a chance at life. I let my own feelings for your father leak into my decision making. I saw the pregnancy as something that was *done* to you—I forgot all about the fact that there was someone else involved."

Jane squeezed her eyes tight, the pain suddenly acute.

"Chloe," her mother said.

Jane stared. Her mother had never used her daughter's name before. She could hardly believe it—her mother had refused to personalize the baby, make her part of the family enough to acknowledge that Jane had given her a name.

"I did you both a disservice," her mother whispered.

"What do you mean?"

"I was so focused on scholarship—on your chances to excel in English, to become a professor; I knew, from raising you and Sylvie alone, how hard it was. Yet, oh,

God . . . I wouldn't trade one minute of it. I know that now . . ."

Jane heard sorrowful regret in her mother's voice, and she leaned over the bed rail to hold her mother tight. "I had worked for my master's," her mother said. "Trying to compete with younger students, without any families to take care of. I looked at you, so young, setting the world on fire— setting the Ivy League on fire! And I felt it was my motherly duty to step in. But what I've deprived you of!"

"It wasn't your fault, Mom. I've blamed you, it's true. But I know, deep down, I was afraid of being a mother. I didn't know till after I gave her up what it would do to me."

"What did it do to you?" her mother asked, head hidden in Jane's shoulder, as if afraid of hearing the answer.

"It turned me inside out," Jane said, still hearing baby Chloe's cries as they took her from her mother's arms and carried her away.

They held each other for a long time. Abby Goodheart poked her head into the room, but when she saw them hugging, she went away. Jane had longed to hear her mother say these things for so long. She thought of Dylan, the look in his eyes last night.

"I know you've seen her," Margaret said. "You haven't told me, but I've guessed that's where you go."

"She's wonderful," Jane said.

"I expected nothing less of your daughter."

"I wish . . ." Jane began.

Margaret tilted her head, waiting.

Jane looked out the window. Heat rose from cars parked in the hospital lot. "Her uncle knows who I am. He figured it out last night. It's over now."

"What's over?" Margaret asked her daughter.

"My chance to be in Chloe's life."

"Why do you say that?"

"Because he caught me in a lie; I entered their world under false pretenses. He sees me as a bad person, and he'll tell her that."

Margaret began to smile. Her soft cheeks drew back, and the smile widened.

"What are you smiling for?" Jane asked.

"Because, my darling, if nothing else, you should learn from my colossal stupidity."

"Learn what?" Jane asked.

"That family members, no matter how

well-meaning, don't know what they're talking about."

"But he's her uncle—he has her best interests at heart."

"As did I. For you . . ."

Jane's heart began to quicken. She saw
Dylan looming over her, staring at Chloe's
picture in her locket. Then thrusting his own
photo of Chloe into Jane's hands. People
dueling with love: that was the image that
filled her mind.

"I love her," Jane said.

"Then that is what must guide you," her
mother said.

"He loves her, too."

"Love isn't mutually exclusive. . . . Let it
guide you."

Jane nodded, standing up. As she did,
the cell phone that she had put on vibrate
buzzed against her hip. She took it out, read
an unfamiliar Rhode Island number, decided
to check it when she got outside. "It always
has; I just wasn't sure where to go before."

"But you do now?"

"I do," Jane said.

Her mother kissed her. Sylvie entered the
room; the sisters exchanged a look. Sylvie's
was full of reproach.

"You were supposed to be here last night," she said.

"I know. I'm so sorry; I didn't realize you were meeting with Abby."

"We didn't have it scheduled—she happened to be free, and she passed by the room. John and I were here, so she pulled up a chair . . . and we started talking." She cast a glance at their mother, who was leaning back on her pillows, eyes closed, smiling slightly, as if remembering what she and Jane had said at the end. The TV was on, a picture without sound. Their mother had fallen asleep. Probably not very deeply—it was just a catnap, one of many she took in a day. But her eyes remained closed, and her head had dropped down so that her chin was resting on her chest. "How is she today?" Sylvie asked.

"She's sad about her books," Jane said.

Sylvie glanced over at the bed. Their mother's skin was pale, but she had two bright spots of color on her cheeks.

"She doesn't look sad," Sylvie said.

"We talked about Chloe," Jane said.

Sylvie's eyes widened.

"She called her by name," Jane said. "It was the first time . . ."

At that, Sylvie shook her head.

"She said her name often, to me," Sylvie said. "Mom wasn't denying Chloe's existence—she just couldn't stand seeing you in pain. She thought if we didn't mention her, you wouldn't miss her so badly."

"But how could I not?" Jane asked. "How would that be possible?"

Sylvie nodded. She looked happier, fuller, somehow. Jane knew that she had fallen in love with John, and that love had changed her. It had warmed her, filled her, made her whole. Jane had started feeling that way with Dylan. She forced herself past thinking of him. She had to concentrate on Chloe now; on making things right with Chloe. "At least you got to see her, to meet her," Jane said.

"Oh, Janey," Sylvie said, hugging her really hard. "Do you think we never saw her before? Mom used to visit her school every year. On some pretext—the principal seeing how they did it in other schools. And after the first few times, she always took me with her."

"What did Mom think? To see her?" Jane whispered, staring at their mother.

"She thought the same thing I did, that she's beautiful. That's she's got your spirit."

"Thank you for telling me," Jane said.

"Were you with them last night?" Sylvie asked.

Jane stared at her hands—Chloe's hands. She thought of the drive through Newport, the feeling of salt wind coming through the cab of Dylan's truck. She thought of the hurt, furious look in his eyes. Her gaze flickered up to meet Sylvie's. When they were young, before Chloe's birth, they had been so close. And then Jane had become a mother.

A ghost mother.

With as much love as any live mother in the world, but no baby to give it to. And Jane had changed. The heart had gone out of her. Nothing was ever the same. So now, wanting to confide in Sylvie about what had happened last night, Jane had to hold back hot tears.

"What is it, Jane?" Sylvie asked, stepping forward.

Jane bit her lip. Love did such strange

things. It gave people a reason to live. It caused heartache and betrayals. It brought families together and drove them apart—sometimes at the same time. Right now, it was causing Jane to keep her own counsel until she had the chance to set things straight with Chloe.

"Can I tell you later?" Jane asked. "I want to talk to you, but not right now . . ."

"Sure," Sylvie said, looking worried.

Just then, their mother woke up.

"Hello, girls," she said, covering her mouth as she yawned. "Where have you been all day? I've been so lonely, waiting for you to arrive!"

"Mom—I was here," Jane said, feeling panicked to think her mother might have forgotten what they'd talked about, wanting to ask her about the times she had secretly visited Chloe's school. "Remember? We spoke about Chloe . . ."

"Sssh," her mother said, blinking the sleep from her eyes, raising a finger to her lips. "Sssh . . . don't mention her name. Jane might hear, and it would make her so sad . . . so very sad . . ."

"We'll talk later," Sylvie said, leaning over to hug Jane.

Jane nodded. That was just as well. She kissed her sister. She was done with words for the moment. She had to go outside and think of what she was going to say to her daughter.

🌹

And as things turned out, she didn't have long to wait. When she checked her messages, to see who had called, she heard Chloe's voice asking to call her back on Mona's cell phone. She did, right away.

"Hello?"

"Hi, Mona? It's Jane—"

"Oh! Hi! Chloe's right here!"

Jane held on, listening to Chloe finish up a pie transaction at the stand. After half a minute, Chloe came on the line.

"Hi, Jane?" she asked.

"Yes, Chloe, I'm here," Jane said, trying to breathe, hoping Dylan hadn't talked to her yet.

"Jane—can you come pick me up? At the stand? I need to get another egnancy-pay est-tay," Chloe said as Mona shrieked in the background, "You goon! I'm the only one here, and I already know all about it!"

Jane stood on the hospital sidewalk, ear

pressed to the phone. And of course she answered, "I'll be right there." When she hung up, she stood there for just another few seconds, feeling pierced by Chloe's voice, and her request, and the fact that she'd been the one Chloe had called, and every single thing.

CHAPTER 25

Chloe waited by the side of the road. Mona was going to hold down the fort till she got back. It was just before noon, and the day was hot. Steam was rising from the pavement. A dunk in the stream would feel good. Chloe raised her eyes, looked through the apple trees, past the barn. She wished she were a little child who could just abandon her cares and enjoy the summer day.

"What time is she coming?" Mona asked.

"Any minute," Chloe said as she resumed watching the road. Her stomach dipped.

"Think good thoughts," Mona instructed. "Tell your body it cannot be pregnant. It will listen to you."

"Sex is a bad thing," Chloe said grittily.

"You think?"

Chloe nodded. She wondered whether she looked as pale as she felt. A thin line of sweat had formed above her top lip. Once she and her parents had taken the Block Island ferry in a gale, and the boat had pitched and rolled. Chloe got massively seasick. She felt almost that bad right now.

"You are going to be okay," Mona said.

"I hope so."

Mona giggled, pushing her hands against her mouth, as if to stop herself from laughing.

"What is it?" Chloe asked.

"Oh, God, I can't stop myself," Mona said, looking around. "We have a soundtrack to the moment. Chirp-chirp, buzz-buzz."

"The birds and the bees," Chloe said, laughing in spite of the fact she felt like throwing up.

Birds twittered in the trees: cardinals, jays, finches, sparrows. Swallows swooped out of the barn, snatching bugs from the sky. Honeybees hummed in the apple tree branches and meadow flowers.

"I have a sick mind," Mona said. "I shouldn't be making jokes at a time like this."

"You can't help yourself," Chloe said, glad they had laughed.

"Besides, it wasn't really a joke. It was a witticism. And I have another one," Mona said. "I'm sitting here, watching you stand by the roadside, and I can't stop thinking about that cross-stitch picture you have in your front hall."

Chloe pictured it. Her mother had made it when she'd first married her father and come to live in the orchard. It showed their little white house, the fence, all the apple trees, and the red barn on the crest of the hill. Her mother had stitched words across the top, like a banner.

Mona quoted them now: " 'Let me live in the house by the side of the road and be a friend to man.' "

"That's me," Chloe said. "A friend to man."

"I didn't mean it that way," Mona said.

"I did," Chloe said, feeling sick.

"I just meant, you look so nice, standing there on the side of the road, waiting for Jane. Maybe we can get your mother to edit her cross-stitch. A friend to *woman*."

Chloe nodded. She thought of her mother making that sampler. She had been a young woman back then. What must it have been like to move out here to the orchard? Her grandfather had been alive then; her mother had helped her father take care of him, the whole time wishing for a baby. When she had sat in her rocking chair, stitching that tableau, had she been dreaming of her very own child?

The thought made Chloe blink. How was it that pregnancy was the most normal thing in the whole world—for every single person on this earth, there had been a pregnancy; billions and billions of them—yet it had eluded her mother? Envisioning her mother stitching that sampler made Chloe feel very sad.

Just then, Uncle Dylan drove up on his tractor.

"What are you doing, standing in the road?" he called.

"Waiting for someone," she called back, over the motor's rumble.

Uncle Dylan cut the engine. "I want to talk to you," he said.

"Um," Chloe began nervously. She definitely didn't want to tip her uncle off that anything was wrong. But until she went with Jane to get another First Thought test, she wasn't going to be able to listen to one thing he had to say.

"You could talk to me," Mona said flirtatiously, and Chloe wanted to kiss her.

Uncle Dylan didn't even smile. He looked as if he had turned into the same old cranky man o' the orchard he always used to be P.J. —Pre-Jane.

"What's wrong, Uncle Dylan?" Mona asked. "You look upset."

"Nothing's wrong," he said. "Chloe, take a walk with me. Mona can look after the stand for a few minutes . . ."

Just then, Jane's car pulled up. Chloe glanced at her uncle, expecting him to melt like a Popsicle. Instead, to her surprise, he looked even stonier. The lines in his face deepened. His eyes looked like thunderclouds.

"What are you doing?" he asked Jane as Chloe opened the car door.

"We won't be long," Jane said as Chloe slid in, and Chloe felt grateful to her for protecting her secret.

"Don't," he said, hands on the car door.

Jane didn't say another word. She stared at him, giving him several long, slow blinks. Chloe loved her for that. In cat language, that was a message of love. It was a sign of nonaggression, a signal that the blinking cat meant peace and friendliness to the other. If Uncle Dylan received the signal, he gave no indication. He had a storm in his eyes.

"Jane, stop," he said.

But Jane just drove away.

Chloe turned, to ask her what that was all about, and she saw that Jane now had a similar weather pattern on her face: clouds, lightning, rain. Her eyes glittered as she glanced across the seat at Chloe.

"Are you okay?" she asked.

Chloe started to nod, then shook her head. "No. I feel sick."

"You're afraid it's morning sickness?"

"Yes. It might be bad karma, but . . ."

"What about your period?"

"It's late," Chloe said. Forgetting about Uncle Dylan, she now could think only of the mess she was in. "A week late. What if I took that last test too soon?"

"It's possible," Jane said softly. But the storm had cleared from her eyes, and she gave Chloe a warm smile.

They drove along, and as they did, Chloe's anxiety mounted. She touched her stomach. What if there was a baby growing in there? She swallowed, feeling strange. The idea of driving fifteen minutes, back to Twin Rivers Hospital, seemed like too much. She turned to Jane.

"Let's just get the test in Crofton," she said. "If you buy it, no one will suspect."

"Okay," Jane said, sensing Chloe's panic. She pulled into the mall, parked near the Food Court entrance. They walked in together. There was a Good Health Pharmacy just past the Orange Blossom Bridal Shop, so Chloe waited outside while Jane went in. She was standing in the main corridor of malldom, watching all the summer shoppers rushing in and out, so they could get to the beach, when she heard her name:

"Chloe?"

She wheeled around. Her mother was walking over, holding a bag from Langtry's— Chloe's favorite store.

"Mom!" Chloe exclaimed.

"Honey, why aren't you at work?"

"Oh," Chloe said, feeling herself turn hot and red. She bit her lip. She was going to have to lie. There was no way—absolutely no other way—out of this. "Um, I came on an errand, with a friend . . ."

Just then, her mother noticed where they

were standing: in front of the pharmacy, but across from Rhode Island Pets, Inc. Her mother's face fell, as if she had just learned that Chloe had flunked out of school. She turned as pale as Chloe was red.

"Chloe," she said. "You're not planning . . . an action, are you?"

"A what?"

"The pet store. I wasn't born yesterday, Miss Chloe Chadwick. What are you protesting in there?"

"Mom, nothing—I swear!" Chloe glanced at the pet store window. A bright macaw was chained to a perch. Several cute puppies romped in newspaper-lined cages. Chloe's eyes filled with tears at the sight. What kind of girl was she? So wrapped up in her own problems, she hadn't even noticed the animals?

"What is it this time? Puppy mills? Parrots being stolen from the Amazon?"

"That's not a parrot," Chloe corrected, following her mother's line of sight to the store window. "That's a macaw."

"Chloe—I don't care if it's a bald eagle," her mother said, grabbing her wrist and giving her a beseeching look. The expression in her mother's eyes was so worried and full of love, Chloe had to look twice. "Honey, your father had to convince Ace Fontaine not to press charges, down at the grocery store. If you do something here at the mall, you could get *arrested*. I know you love animals—you have the biggest heart of any girl I've ever known. But please, please, Chloe, don't—"

She was stopped by the sheer weight of Chloe throwing herself against her body in a full-press hug. Chloe could barely talk. Here she was, on a secret slut mission, and her poor mother was worried sick about her animal activism.

"I promise, Mom. I promise," Chloe said. She was inches away from breaking down and crying, confessing everything. Her mother held her for a moment more. Chloe loved the smell of her hair—it was like lavender, and it smelled like Chloe's childhood. She loved the slightly padded feeling of her body. She wasn't all vain muscle, like Rhianna, who basically lived on a StairMaster.

Chloe's mother power-walked the country roads around the orchard. She danced to old videos on VH–1 when she thought no one was watching. Chloe had once caught her dancing to "Into the Groove" as if she was Madonna herself. Chloe had joined in, and they had whirled around the room together. Her mother liked to move, but she didn't do it with one eye in the mirror.

"Well, as long as you promise, I believe you," her mother said, pushing back. "Where's Mona?"

"At the stand."

"Then who are you here with?"

Just then, Jane came out of the pharmacy. She held up the white bag, like the Stature of Liberty's torch, but dropped her arm at the sight of Chloe's mother. Chloe was about two seconds from throwing up on the mall's shiny floor.

"Hello," Jane said, approaching.

"Hi," Chloe's mother said, smiling in a confused way.

"Mom, this is Jane. Who bakes the pies? Jane, this is my mom."

"Sharon Chadwick," her mother said, shaking hands. "I've heard so much about you. And your pies are delicious."

"Thank you," Jane said. Her eyes looked wide, startled. She stood very still, holding the bag. Chloe noticed how different she looked from her mother—any local mother, actually: She wore a black tank top that said "Om" in silver on the front. On the back, it said "Shanti Yoga, Perry Street." Her dark hair looked cute and young. It slanted across her right eye. Her army pants were worn low, revealing the waistband of her Calvin Klein underwear, and a tiny tattoo of the letter "C" on her hip. Oddly, they were the same clothes she had worn to Newport. And so were her shoes: black, clunky, slightly dangerous looking.

Chloe's mother, meanwhile, wore a long sundress from her favorite catalogue—sweepy and cool, bright yellow with sunflowers splashed all over it, and a straw hat. She wore comfy sandals. Her earrings dangled with beads and symbols of the sun. Her fingernails were rimmed, ever so slightly, with dirt from the garden. She had a warm and hopeful New-Age-y vibe that reassured everyone who encountered her.

"Chloe just came on an errand with me," Jane said, although Chloe's mother hadn't asked.

"That's my girl," her mother said, squeezing her shoulders. "Always helpful."

Chloe tried to smile or speak, but she couldn't. She felt herself shrinking. Lying to her mother felt awful. It always did, but never more than now. Because today, the stakes were so high: This lie had to do with other lies. With sneaking out, with having sex under the stars, with maybe being pregnant.

Chloe swallowed hard. She looked at Jane. In that moment, seeing the two women side by side, Chloe didn't like Jane very much. She had just lied to her mother. Although Chloe knew she had done it to help, it still felt bad.

"Okay, I have to get back to the orchard," Chloe said.

"Want to ride with me?" her mother asked. "I just stopped by to buy us some flip-flops, and I'm heading home."

Chloe shook her head. The word "flip-flops" was like a knife to the heart. Such a sweet summery word, in the midst of such lies and betrayal. She felt very ashamed. Glancing at Jane, she saw her open her mouth—perhaps to lie again. Chloe spoke quickly, to prevent that from happening.

"Jane can drive me," she said. "We have the pies . . ."

"Of course," Chloe's mother said, smiling. "Well, it was nice meeting you. My husband and I would like to have you and Dylan over for dinner sometime soon."

"Thank you," Jane said. But she barely smiled—as if she wasn't at all interested.

Chloe's skin contracted. Watching her mother walk away, she felt like running after her. Jane represented the world of grown-ups, independence, the big city. Chloe's mother represented the world of childhood, safety, the countryside. Chloe's throat caught. Jane looked at her, eyes full of concern.

"Should we find a bathroom?" she asked.

Chloe nodded—but she couldn't make it. She threw up on her own feet and Jane's, right in the middle of the mall.

*

Jane hustled her out to the car. Chloe was embarrassed, crying. Jane knew she had hated lying to her adoptive mother; it was an awful moment. She wished she could call it back, smooth it over. But how? Chloe was in a crisis—one that Jane remembered all too well. Sharon Chadwick would be involved soon enough. . . . It had been so hard for Jane to face her. The two women had stared deeply into each other's eyes, and Jane was sure Sharon was about to make the connection and see the truth.

How could she not? Those eyes were the same as Chloe's. And Jane's love for the girl they both considered their daughter was written all over her face.

She drove slowly out of the parking lot. Chloe didn't want to stop at a gas station or restaurant. She wanted to return to the exact spot they had gone before—the shady road, where she had peed on the stick in the woods. So Jane headed east, in that direction, in turmoil. They passed the driveway to Cherry Vale. They passed a sign that said PROVIDENCE—10 MILES.

Beginnings, endings. Providence, the place where Chloe was conceived; Cherry Vale, the place where Jane's mother was going to live till she died. She felt the station wagon was a missile hurtling through time. She pictured Dylan—the intensity in his eyes as he'd approached the car, tried to stop Chloe from going with Jane. For a second, seeing Sharon Chadwick with Chloe in the mall, Jane had thought Dylan had sent her after them.

As they drove along, silence echoed in the car, both Jane and Chloe lost in thought.

The moment had an aura of dishonesty. Perhaps it was the lie told to Sharon Chadwick that painted it in such stark relief: Jane had seen Chloe's recoil when Jane had said they were on an errand for her. So, now Chloe knew how easy it was for her to tell a lie.

And not just tell one—live one.

"Oh, Chloe," Jane said out loud.

Chloe glanced across the seat—Jane could feel her gaze. This was a very different ride from the last one. Then, Jane had had the feeling Chloe considered her a saving angel. Right now, she felt that they were both drowning in falsehood.

Jane pulled over to the side of the road, her heart beating in her throat. Dylan knew the truth; it was only a matter of time before he told. She looked into the rearview mirror, saw her own light blue eyes. She gulped, then looked over at Chloe—at the same light blue eyes.

"Why are we stopping?" Chloe asked.

Jane struggled to breathe. "Look at me," she said.

"What?" Chloe asked, confused.

"Can't you see?" Jane asked, her voice thin.

"See what?"

"Who I am."

"You're Jane . . . you bake our pies." She tried to laugh, but she knew too much—she knew there was nothing funny now. "You're the pie lady."

Jane closed her eyes, digging her fingernails into her palms. She wanted to stop, yet she couldn't. It had to come out.

"I'm something else, too," Jane said softly. The summer air was hot and close. The car windows were open, and in some neighborhood behind the trees, an ice-cream truck was cruising through; the bell tinkled insistently.

Chloe stared, holding the white bag. Her gaze was sharp, intense; a vertical line crinkled between her dark, finely shaped eyebrows. Jane could almost feel her laser stare as parts of the jigsaw puzzle shifted together, making a clear picture out of jumbled images.

"You're . . ." Chloe began, fingers flying to her lips.

"I'm your mother," Jane said.

"My . . ."

"I'm your mother," Jane said again, as if it were too important not to say twice.

Chloe stared, as if Jane were speaking a foreign language. Her eyes widened. She took in the color and shape of Jane's eyes, the outline of her mouth, the sharpness of her cheekbones.

"I've dreamed of you," Chloe whispered.

"Oh, Chloe . . . I've dreamed of you," Jane said, her voice catching.

"Why?" Chloe asked. "Why did you leave me?"

"I was young," Jane tried to explain. "I wasn't much older than you are."

"That doesn't matter," Chloe said, touching her own belly. "I would never, never leave my baby. Why did you leave me?" she asked in a moan.

Jane closed her eyes. "I did it for you. I thought it was best. But I've never, ever, for one minute, stopped thinking I made the biggest mistake in the world . . ."

"My parents love me," Chloe said.

"I know."

"You put me in the attic," Chloe said. "I was something you didn't even want. You hid me away . . ."

Chloe began to cry. She dropped the white bag. She brought her knees up to her face, buried her head in her arms, and shook with silent sobs. During the last fifteen years, Jane had rehearsed this moment so many times. She had sometimes imagined it in a golden haze of wisdom and forgiveness. Other times she had seen them talking earnestly, amazed by their similarities, working out a way to share moments in their lives. Nothing had prepared her for the guttural, animal sounds coming from her daughter's mouth. Nor for the reaction—as if they were still connected by the umbilical cord—of pain deep in her own body.

"Chloe?" she asked, weeping.

But Chloe was past hearing. The day had been too traumatic. The lie, the truth, the fear—embodied by the white paper bag holding a pregnancy test—of history repeating itself. She just sat on the seat, curled in an upright fetal position, sobbing her heart out.

One thing Jane knew was that the Chadwicks loved Chloe. Chloe had called them her parents—and they had been, for her entire life. Jane knew where Chloe belonged right now. Turning the car around, she drove back the way they had come. Past Cherry Vale, past the mall.

The orchard appeared, green and magical. Small apples had begun to grow on the branches. They were green, waiting to ripen. The ones in the direct sun were glossy and bright, filled with green light. She followed the split-rail fence, driving past the apple stand without stopping. Mona waved. Jane waved back, but Chloe didn't even see.

Jane put on the blinker, turning into 114 Barn Swallow Way. She stopped the car behind the family minivan. Dylan was standing there, his tractor idling off to the side. Sharon Chadwick had just gotten home; she stood in her driveway, bags dropped at her feet, flip-flops scattered on the asphalt. They both looked up; Dylan's eyes were hard and accusing. Sharon's were pools of shock and hurt.

As the two Chadwick adults approached the car, Jane saw disapproval and a protective drive in Dylan's dark green eyes—he wanted to get Chloe out of the car right now. He wore jeans and a blue shirt, and his hands were tan with beautiful long fingers, and Jane remembered staring at them with love last night, but right now she realized he thought she was his family's enemy. And perhaps she was . . . Sharon was right behind him, her lips set and hard.

Chloe barely seemed to notice where she was. Her uncle called her name. She ignored him. Very slowly, she looked over at Jane as if coming out of deep sleep. Jane was shocked at the pain in her face, and she realized that Chloe's reaction wasn't from just one season of lying: it was from her whole life of feeling abandoned.

"I didn't mean to hurt you, Chloe," she whispered, in shock at the anguish in Chloe's blue eyes.

"My name," Chloe said huskily.

"Yes?"

Angry faces pressed against the window; Dylan tried the door handle. Jane had automatically pressed the power lock button, so he couldn't open the door.

"They—my parents—wanted to name me Emily. But they couldn't . . . because of what you said. . . ."

Jane closed her eyes, remembering the condition she had put on the adoption: that the baby keep the name she gave her.

"I'm sorry," Jane said. "Did you wish you were named Emily?"

Chloe shook her head, and the motion unlocked the tears in her eyes. They spilled down her face into her mouth. "I'm Chloe," she said. "That's my name . . ."

Jane couldn't speak. Chloe unlocked the door, and Dylan pulled it open. He reached for Chloe's hand, pulling her out of the car. He was behaving as if he'd just rescued a young girl from her kidnapper. Sharon wrapped Chloe in her arms, and Jane could hear them sobbing.

Their eyes met for one moment: hers and Dylan's. His look seemed to say that she didn't deserve the tears she was crying. She saw the betrayal in his gaze, but it was nothing compared to what she had just seen in Chloe's. She couldn't speak; she couldn't even blink. Putting her car in reverse, she backed out of the driveway.

It wasn't until she had sped past the stand, past the weathered fence that marked the edge of the orchard, past the old red barn on the gentle rise amid the apple trees, that Jane noticed two things that Chloe had left behind: the white bag containing the pregnancy test, and a splotch of blood on the car seat.

Chloe had gotten her period.

A smile flickered across Jane's lips. Just a small one as she realized it must have been bad karma after all. And then the smile disappeared.

PART THREE

Light of the Silvery Moon

CHAPTER 26

Time went by so slowly. Margaret wondered why they even had clocks here at Cherry Vale. When she looked, it was nine A.M. She looked again, and it was nine-ten. On the other hand, the days flew by. Monday blurred into Tuesday, which transformed into next week. The longest day of the year came and went. So did the Fourth of July, with a cookout and sing-along.

They had a calendar. A very large square of paper, with the month's dates ready to be crossed off. Beside it was a piece of cardboard with informative squares of manila paper, replaced daily, to aid the residents in marking the passage of time. It said:

Hello! Today is:
Sunday, July 30.

The weather is: SUNNY (picture
of smiling-faced sun)
The temperature is: 85°
The next holiday is: Labor Day.

Sitting in her wheelchair outside the
nurses' station, Margaret stared at the sign.
She was in a row of seven other residents,
waiting to be wheeled into lunch. The man
to her left was dozing, snoring loudly. A
thick, rather unattractive spindle of drool
ran down his chin. He was bald, wore gold
specs, and had a copy of the *Wall Street
Journal* open on his lap.

To her other side, another gentleman was
scratching a scaly patch on the back of his
hand. He scratched so hard, Margaret was
afraid he would draw blood. She held her
tongue, thinking of how often she had
stopped children in the hallways, telling
them as gently as possible to stop scratching their mosquito bites or poison ivy. The
man had full white hair and thick horn-
rimmed glasses, and she was quite sure he
knew enough to stop scratching his own
skin.

Margaret's eyes pooled with tears. Her
feet ached, and her shoes had magnets in

them. Her broken hip was healing; she spent so much time doing physical therapy, she hadn't had time for other activities, or to get to know anyone. The smell of urine, from some of her incontinent floor-mates, was profoundly discouraging. The nurses were rushing around, smiling, saying "Hello, Jack," "Hello, Sam," "Hello, Dorothy," in very loud voices, as if everyone was deaf.

They didn't say hello to Margaret, however. At least, not by name. She had been here for thirty days. The weekday nurses knew her, but this was Sunday, and the weekend ones weren't completely familiar with her yet—it was the middle of summer, and vacations had wreaked havoc with the shifts. Margaret understood trying to staff a large institution, and she tried to make allowances. The nurses smiled and nodded, but no one said, "Hi, Margaret"—loud voice or no.

She sniffled, pulled a tissue from her sleeve, dabbed at her eyes. Then she put a positive look back on her face. She had always said to her daughters, as well as to her legions of students, that keeping an upbeat outlook was quite attractive and would always breed success in the world at large.

Margaret knew, if nothing else, that she had to keep an upbeat outlook.

Staring at the smiling-faced sun, she tried to smile back, but instead shook her head. She must have sighed. Because the itchy man turned to her and said, "They think we're twelve."

"Excuse me?" Margaret asked.

"The staff. Making a sign like that. What do they think? We checked our brains at the door?"

Margaret chuckled, in spite of herself. "I know what you mean. I taught school for forty-five years, and that's exactly the kind of sign you'd expect to see in a first-grade classroom. So twelve's too old."

"You're right," the man said. "They think we're five. So. You're a schoolteacher?"

"High school principal," she said.

"Pleased to meet you," he said. "I was a probate judge. That's how we introduce ourselves around here—by what we used to do. So no one will think we're just white-haired lumps who sleep all day. They'll know we were once something else. My name is Ralph Bingham."

"Hello, I'm Margaret Porter."

"Pleasure to meet you. I've seen you

pass by my door, but until this morning I was flat on my back the last two weeks. Having some problems with glaucoma. So . . . do you come here often?"

She smiled at the joke, but at the same time, she felt a surge of emotion—a tidal wave sending tears back into her eyes. "Unfortunately," she said.

"Oh, it's not that bad," he said. "How could a place called Cherry Vale be all bad?"

She attempted a smile, but got caught on a sob. "My daughters found it for me," she said. "I have two lovely daughters."

"And I have three," Ralph said. "As well as a son."

"Isn't that nice?" Margaret asked.

"I'm not sure," Ralph grumbled. "It's Sunday, and they said they were coming to take me out. If they do, it's nice. If they don't, I still have time to rewrite the will. How about you? Will your daughters come see you today?"

"Sylvie will," Margaret said, falling silent. "My other daughter, Jane, went back to New York."

"New York? The Big Apple?" Ralph asked.

"Yes. She was here for most of the spring, getting me settled. But, she has a business to run . . . a very fine bauble."

"A what?"

"A very fine bathtub," Margaret said. She knew it was happening, knew she had lost track of the word . . . she frowned, trying to get it back. "Bakery," she finished. "Jane runs a very fine bakery."

"Ah," Ralph said.

"She . . ." Margaret trailed off. She had seen Jane crying. That last day there, when she decided to return to New York, she came to visit Margaret. Margaret thanked her for everything she'd done, and encouraged her to see her daughter—but Jane said the timing was wrong, and that she was going back to New York.

There'd been nothing Margaret could do to stop her.

"New York isn't too far away," Ralph said. "She can come visit you."

"I hope so," Margaret said sadly, knowing that Rhode Island had a force field that kept Jane away.

Ralph kept scratching his hand. Margaret looked at his face. He was missing some back teeth, and he had some scaly patches on his cheek. His nice white hair could use a washing—he had a bit of a dandruff problem, and the flakes were all over his dark plaid shirt. But she could see that he had been a handsome, imposing man. She could see intelligence and compassion behind his cataracts. And she was glad he had told her he'd been a judge. He smiled at her, as if he knew she was sad about Jane.

"Let me introduce you to my friend," he said, leaning across her to tug on the snoring man's arm. "Bill—hey, Bill! Wake him up, will you, Maggie?"

Margaret looked for a dribble-free patch of arm to tap, feeling the strangest thrill at his use of a nickname. She touched his shoulder. "Excuse me," she said politely. "Bill, is it? Bill, Ralph wants you to wake up . . ."

"Rhuhhngh?" Bill asked, shaking himself awake. "Closing bell?"

"Nah—this isn't the Stock Exchange," Ralph said. "It's Cherry Vale, Billy. Wake up—meet Maggie!"

"Margaret," she corrected, in spite of how nice the nickname made her feel.

"That's formal," Ralph said.

"Well, I'm a rather formal person," she said.

"High school principal," Ralph said, nodding, leaning over so Bill could hear.

"Eh?" Bill asked.

"Margaret was a high school principal!" Ralph shouted.

"I thought you said her name was MAGGIE," Bill shouted back.

"Either is fine," Margaret said, trying to maintain dignity as the two old men leaned closer, their heads just about meeting at her chest.

"Bill was a stockbroker," Ralph said.

"Had a seat on the floor of the New York Stock Exchange," Bill said proudly.

"That's marvelous," Margaret said.

"Got stocks and bonds?" Bill asked in an embarrassingly loud voice.

"Not too many," she said. "On an educator's salary, you know . . ."

"What about your husband? He invest?" Bill inquired at the top of his voice.

"Why don't you just ask her to show you her bankbook and be done with it?" Ralph reproached. "For God's sake, man. Pay him no heed, Meg."

"Meg?" she asked.

"Or Peggy. Peggy's a nice name for a girl."

"My name," she said chillingly, feeling as if she had somehow wandered into an Ionesco play, "is Margaret."

"He's a big pain in the ass," Bill said, touching Margaret's hand. "He can't stand if you don't have a nickname. He's been calling me Billy since I got here, and it's the damnedest thing—I haven't been called Billy since my mother passed."

"Does he have a nickname?" Margaret asked.

"No," Ralph said. "And that's the problem. Can't do much with Ralph. I always wanted to be Chip or Skip or Terry or something, but nothing ever stuck. Darn, if I had a name like Margaret or Bill, I'd just run with it . . ."

Margaret couldn't help herself: she looked at Ralph and suddenly saw the fifth-grader he used to be. Bookish, short, perhaps overweight. Those glasses, while distinguished on a jurist, would have been unfortunate on a little boy. She smiled at him. At the same moment, Bill began to babble, temporarily unable to make sense of the language, and he began to cry. Margaret reached into her sleeve, and as she had done with more children than she could count, wiped Bill's eyes.

"There," she said.

"Gurk yon," he said.

"You're welcome," Margaret said, understanding what he meant. Over the years, she had helped many immigrant children assimilate. She had instituted a program for the hearing-impaired. Even when she couldn't speak someone's language, she could translate with her heart. Right now, staring at Bill, lost in his inability to thank her, she felt sorrow for her own losses and gratitude for what she still had. On top of her list were her two daughters.

"You're a good girl, Maggie," Ralph said.

"Thank you," Margaret whispered, thinking of how shockingly fleet life was.

"Don't mention it," Ralph said. "We're going to get along fine, I can tell. Can't you, Billy? Doesn't she add a lot?"

Bill nodded. Then, as Bill's language skills kicked back in, he said, "She certainly does. She's a rose between two thorns."

And then the aides came, to push them all into the dining room for lunch.

CHAPTER 27

Camping was sheer heaven.

John had a wonderful orange tent with a blue flap made of thin fabric so high-tech it could keep out the heat of a desert and the frost of Maine. While Rhode Island suffered through an August heat wave, Maine enjoyed an autumnal chill—bright sunny days followed by cold, clear nights.

Sylvie and John sat just away from the campfire, staring up at the sky. They were wrapped in a sleeping bag, holding each other as they listened to the logs crackle and watched for shooting stars. The fire threw heat, but they had moved away just far enough to escape the light and see the stars.

They had delayed their trip, to get her mother settled into the home. John had been wonderful about it—in fact, the delay had been his idea. After getting to know Sylvie, he realized that she couldn't be happy unless she was sure her family was in order. Her mother was in good hands at Cherry Vale. Jane, on the other hand . . .

Thinking of Jane made Sylvie's shoulders hunch forward. Protecting her own heart, she wished she could protect Jane's. She didn't know all the details of what had happened, but she knew that Dylan Chadwick had turned against Jane. And Jane had gotten the message from Chloe that she didn't want her in her life. Jane had heard it loud and clear, and she had returned to New York. Sylvie had driven her to the train. The sight of Jane climbing aboard, body stiff and jaw set, eyes focused somewhere far away, had crushed Sylvie's heart.

"I'm glad we changed our dates," John said, his mouth against her ear.

"Our . . ." she began, still thinking of her sister.

"Our date for this trip," John said. "Think of all the wonderful things we've seen this week that might not have been here in July."

Last night they had witnessed the northern lights. Today they had hiked up Mount

Katahdin and seen a bear and her cub. And tonight, in each other's arms, they were watching the Perseid meteor shower.

"Thank you for seeing it that way," Sylvie said.

"What other way is there to see it?" he asked.

Sylvie squeezed his arms, wrapped around her from behind. She felt grateful that John was someone who cared about her mother, and who could roll with the ups and downs of life without taking them too personally.

"This is so beautiful," Sylvie said, gazing up. "I never dreamed . . ."

"Never dreamed what?" John asked, kissing the back of her neck.

"That anything could be so lovely. With all the books in the library, all the accounts I've read of sleeping under the stars, hiking up a mountain trail, the words pale in comparison to this."

"I've been camping and hiking my whole life," John said. "And all those trips pale in comparison to *this*."

Sylvie smiled and shivered; John felt it, and he held her tighter. How could this be? Sylvie had never been an outdoors person;

she hadn't enjoyed sports of any kind. Her summers had been spent—blissfully—reading. She was beginning to understand that their mother, so hurt by loving their father, had turned away from the world and into books, and she had taken her daughters with her. Sylvie certainly didn't begrudge her that—she revered her mother, for fostering a love of literature and learning. But being with John, feeling the cold air, sharing a sleeping bag, hearing loons cry on the black lake—those were experiences worth having.

Only one thing kept her from feeling complete happiness.

Jane.

How could Sylvie feel really happy, knowing that her sister was hurting? She stared up at the sky. John held her. For the first time in her life, Sylvie had fallen in love. She had kept herself walled off, protected from trying to love someone who might abandon her. Her teenage years had been spent studying, trying to get into Brown. And her Brown years had required so much effort to stay at the top of her class. Jane's tragic tale was right there: a graphic illustration of what love could do.

So Sylvie had hidden her heart. She had

lived at home, flourished as a librarian, commuted to school with her mother, and let love pass her by.

And then John had come along. If not for him, she might never have known what an open heart could feel like. From the loftiness of academia, she had looked down on her sister. Deep down, she had blamed Jane for what she had allowed to happen to her. Jane, she thought, had brought her problems on herself. And Sylvie had blamed her for not being able to straighten them out enough for her to feel comfortable, to return home regularly. Because Sylvie had missed her.

"Can I tell you something?" she said to John now.

"Anything," John said.

"It's about my sister," Sylvie said. "I've been unfair to her."

"In what way?"

"All those years, when she was living in New York, and she never wanted to come home . . . I was so angry with her. I thought she had made a mess of her life. She had given in to a moment of weakness—with her boyfriend at Brown—and she had ruined her life."

John was silent, listening.

"I felt very superior to her," Sylvie said, her throat tight. "For many years."

"But you don't now?"

Sylvie shook her head and stifled a sob. "No," she said.

"What changed?" John asked.

"You," Sylvie whispered. "Until you, I never knew what love was like. I never knew how total it was."

"It's total for me, too," John said, squeezing her tenderly.

Just then, a loon called from the lake. The sound was crazy, passionate, out of control. Sylvie closed her eyes for a moment. The call reminded her of Jane's keening those days after she had given Chloe up. Sylvie had felt helpless; there'd been nothing she could do.

"I wish I could help her now," she said.

"Just be there for her," John said. "That's all you can do."

"How did you get to be so wise about love?" Sylvie asked, half turning to look at him. The sight of his wide brown eyes, high forehead, gentle expression, soothed her heart, and she smiled.

"My parents showed me, for starters," he said. "And then I met you."

"I wish I could have met your parents," Sylvie said; John had told her they had died within six months of each other, five years earlier.

"They'd have loved you."

"Thank you. My mother loves you," Sylvie said. "My father, on the other hand . . ."

"Your father doesn't deserve the name," John said, holding her tighter. "How he could have walked out on your family, I can't understand."

"No," Sylvie said.

"Children need to know their parents love them," John said. "No matter what."

Sylvie stared up at the sky, her heart aching. She knew that he was right. Sylvie—and Jane—were living proof of two girls who'd missed out on their father's love. But then she thought of Jane and her daughter. Chloe's lifetime had passed without Jane in it. Yet no one had ever loved anyone more than Jane loved Chloe.

"You're thinking of your sister," John said; he knew, because Sylvie had confided the whole story.

She nodded, unable to speak.

"Let's wish on a star for her," John said.

"A shooting star?" Sylvie asked.

"Yes. The next one we see will be for Jane—that everything works out for her and Chloe."

"Jane and Chloe," Sylvie whispered, staring at the sky.

A long time passed. After a whole night of seeing two, three, shooting stars a minute, suddenly the sky was still. Stars burned, the Milky Way traced the deepest part of the heavens, but there were no shooting stars.

Sylvie thought of Jane. She saw her as a young girl, but still Sylvie's older sister, with braids and an intense look in her eyes. She thought of her as a teenager, hitchhiking to Hartford, with Sylvie in tow, to find their father. She heard her crying like a loon, missing her baby. And she saw her as she had been this spring—blooming like a flower, in touch with Chloe, falling in love with Dylan.

"Jane," she said.

Just then, a meteor streaked through the sky. It was a fireball, a silver disk, Jane's locket, leaving a trail of fire behind. Sylvie jumped out of John's arms to stand and watch. She swore it was headed straight for the lake as it seemed to split the night.

Things happen, Sylvie thought. *Miracles come out of nowhere. . . .*

"Don't give up hope," she whispered, fingernails digging into her palms. She was talking to her sister, but she was also talking to herself: Love and meteors come out of the blackness and change the whole world, just when you least expect it.

The meteor disappeared. It left the sky scarred with a white-blue stripe; as she watched, it faded to silver, and then to black, so that after a moment, Sylvie wondered whether she had ever actually seen it at all. But then John walked over, took her in his arms, and kissed her.

And his kiss made the meteor live on.

⚬

"Did you see that?" Eli Chadwick asked, three states away, on his back porch in Rhode Island.

"I did," Sharon said, sitting on the step beside him. "A regular fireball."

"Chloe!" Eli called. "Come out and look at the shooting stars!"

No answer.

Sharon looked up at Chloe's bedroom windows. The lights were on, the window open. Some of the orchard cats had climbed up the drainpipe and were sitting on Chloe's windowsill. One of them yowled, as if for the sheer joy of a summer night.

"What's she doing in there?" Eli asked.

"I don't know," Sharon said, gazing up.

"She asked me for all my old magazines," Eli said. "When I passed by, she was cutting them up."

"Making a collage," Sharon said. "She and Mona were doing that before. I thought they had finished."

In the silence, now that she knew what to listen for, she heard the "snip-snip" of scissors cutting paper.

"She's a complicated one," Eli said. "She begged to work at Dylan's stand, and now she seems to want no part of it. Now that the pie source has dried up, and he's buying from some wholesaler, she's completely lost interest."

"We know why she doesn't want to work at the stand anymore," Sharon said. "And it has nothing to do with wholesale pies."

"That woman," Eli said. "I'd have her arrested, if I could."

Sharon set her jaw. She shook her head,

looking up at Chloe's light. "That would do no good."

"She had no right coming here," Eli said. "Under false pretenses, trying to worm her way into Chloe's life. And Dylan's!"

"Dylan can take care of himself," Sharon said. "He looked happy this summer—for the first time in years. Since he lost Isabel."

"Don't tell me you're letting her off the hook!"

Sharon didn't reply right away. Her mind was racing with memories, many more troubling than what had happened this summer. She remembered the year Isabel died, when Chloe had stopped talking. She remembered trying to rock her daughter, trying to hold and comfort her, and how inconsolable Chloe had been. Only Dylan had been able to get through to her, and Sharon had known—understood at a level too deep for words—that Chloe was connecting with him over loss.

The loss of her natural mother.

Adoption was a strange, wonderful, painful, joyful thing. Chloe had come into Sharon and Eli's life, turned it into a garden. She was a gift from above. They had prayed for children, and been given Chloe. Over the years, they had

known the delights and frustrations of parenthood. When things went well, they congratulated themselves as parents. When they
encountered difficulties, they wondered—
Sharon was ashamed to think this even now—
whether things would be different with their
own child. Whether Chloe's intensity, passion,
fierceness were results of her genes.

They wanted to mold her into a Chadwick, and they had done the best they
could, raising her, but deep inside, she carried the genetic makeup of her real mother
and father. And because she was so intensely emotional, she felt things more
strongly than Sharon and Eli; and she carried within her a true, visceral, cellular love
for the woman who had brought her into the
world.

"I think I reacted badly," Sharon said,
staring up at Chloe's light.

"What do you mean?"

"When Dylan told me the truth of who
Jane Porter was . . . and she drove into the
driveway with Chloe . . ."

"How could you possibly react any other
way?" Eli asked. "She had practically kidnapped our daughter."

"No, she didn't," Sharon said softly. She

closed her eyes. Although she had never given birth, she knew what it was to love a child with every bit of her heart. She had had Chloe all this time; every day of every year, Jane had missed her. And, although it hurt Sharon desperately to think it, Chloe had missed Jane.

"Stop this," Eli said.

"Remember when Chloe put on my high heels and a fake wedding ring and went to Family Court to try to see her birth records?"

"Don't remind me."

"That was a very brave thing to do," Sharon said.

"Sharon," Eli said, taking her hand. "It was a foolish thing to do. She was just a teenager looking for trouble. Look at what happened this summer. Was Chloe happy to actually *meet* her birth mother? No, she was not. She was traumatized. She cried and wouldn't talk for three days straight. She's just beginning, only now, to really come out of it."

"She was shocked, that's all," Sharon said.

"Shocked by the lies," Eli said.

"What was Jane supposed to do?"

Sharon asked. "Waltz in here and announce who she was? Do you think we would have accepted her?"

"She was supposed to stay away," Eli said. "Instead of coming here and stirring up trouble. She was supposed to put Chloe's welfare above her selfish need to be a mother—and what kind of mother, anyway? She didn't want her baby—she made that choice almost sixteen years ago. She signed the papers!"

Sharon held Eli's hand and watched his face get redder and redder. She loved him for it. He was working his way into a fit, all because he was being the Papa Bear. He was protecting his family. She wondered whether he remembered that he had been against the adoption. He had thought that if God hadn't seen fit to bless them with children, maybe they should just let it be. . . .

But she had the feeling that he had forgotten. How could they even imagine a life without Chloe? She was part of everything they did. The orchard cats surrounded them, meowing from the fence posts, from the bushes, from deep in the orchard. Those orchard cats were alive because of Chloe. Sharon gazed up at Eli, knowing that he had a very unsentimental, farm boy's approach to unwanted animals.

Chloe was in their mornings, noons, and nights. She was in every plan they made, every dream they had, every star they wished on. It was all for her. She had been born to Jane Porter, but she had become their daughter. For that, Sharon felt eternally grateful to Jane.

And her heart tugged now, as she stared up at Chloe's window, thinking of what had happened in this very driveway. Sharon had been angry—angrier than she ever had been in her life. Dylan had really gotten her stirred up. She would never forget Dylan's hurt eyes, thin voice, as he told Sharon the truth of what he'd found out about Jane.

But now, looking back, Sharon knew why he was so upset. Not just because a woman would want to meet the child to whom she had given birth; not even because she had done so under false pretenses.

Rather, because Dylan felt betrayed. After all those years with Amanda, trying to love a woman who didn't love him back, and then losing her—and Isabel—to the violence of his own job, Dylan had finally fallen in real love. With Jane.

Real love . . .

Sharon thought about that now. She had it—she had never for one moment doubted that—for Eli Chadwick. He was her sweetheart, best friend, and partner. He was her mate.

And Sharon had real love for Chloe. Biology didn't matter one bit; Sharon knew that she would be there for Chloe, would love her until the end of time, would happily die herself to protect her child from any threat that could ever come her way. Because of that real love, Sharon was glad that this summer wasn't over yet, that there was still time.

Because she also loved her brother-in-law. He was her family, every bit as much as her husband and daughter. Dylan needed her, whether he wanted to think so or not. He had become the old man of the orchard again—withdrawn, taciturn, armored. And so, right now, as the meteor shower of August streaked the orchard skies, Sharon stood and brushed the dirt from the back of her dress.

"Want to take a walk with me?" she asked Eli.

"Where're you going?"

"I thought I'd take a stroll through the orchard," she said.

Eli shook his head. "No, thanks," he said. "I'm still waiting for Dylan to come to his senses and sell those overgrown acres. We're sitting on a family gold mine, and he just wants to get old pruning trees that ought to be bulldozed to the ground. Make nice new houses for young families . . ."

"Okay, dear," Sharon said, kissing the top of his head. "You wait here, and I'll be back soon."

"If you see that brother of mine, try to talk some sense into him, will you?"

"That's what I'll try to do," she said. "If I see him."

CHAPTER 28

Dylan sat at his kitchen table, a circle of light coming down from the old lamp hanging above. He held a knife in one hand, an apple in the other. It was a ruddy Empire, the first of the season. He sliced off a piece and ate it. Then, using the tip of the knife, he dug out the five seeds.

They lay on the oak table. Dylan thought of John Chapman, who had walked the country in rags, carrying apple seeds in his deerskin bag. Johnny Appleseed. He slept in trees with possums. He wore a tin pan on his head instead of a hat. People thought he was crazy, but they loved him for what he left behind.

Dylan pushed the seeds around the table, thinking about things left behind. His orchard was a paean to his family, to his father's legacy. When they were young, kids used to make fun of Dylan and Eli—their name, "Chadwick," was very like "Chapman." Dylan Appleseed, Eli Appleseed . . . They endured it all. Dylan cared a lot less than Eli; all those years in the cities, Washington and New York, Dylan had just been waiting to get back here, to the orchard, to the place his father had left behind.

Through the blue smoke of his cigarette, he looked at Isabel's picture on the refrigerator. She seemed so excited, so alive, as if she could spring to life and give him a hug right now. She had been here for so short a time, yet Dylan felt her with him every second of every day.

These apple seeds contained all the mysteries of apple trees past and future: they were hard, black, inanimate. But Dylan could go out and plant them tonight, and within the blink of an eye, they could turn into trees. They would bear apples of their own.

It was mystical and romantic, the way life sustained itself. Apple trees, human beings. Apple seeds made apple trees. People had kids; the line went on. Or they didn't have kids, or the kids died, and the line stopped.

And did any of those origins matter? Sitting at his table, Dylan wasn't sure.

He heard footsteps on the path outside. Without moving from the table, he listened as someone came onto the porch. He narrowed his eyes. Who could it be? He'd left the porch light off for a reason.

"Dylan?" came the voice through the screen door.

It was Sharon. She stood outside, hands cupped around her eyes to see better. Dylan hesitated. He wanted to tell her to go away, but he couldn't.

"Come in," he said.

She walked through the kitchen. She looked good with her summer tan. Her long dress was black, and it made him think of Jane. Jane always wore black. He raised his gaze to look into her eyes.

"What brings you over here?" he asked.

"You," she said firmly.

The world tipped a little. He felt his stomach drop, but he kept his eyes hard and steady. He didn't want this. Whatever she had in mind, Dylan didn't want to hear. So he turned on his sister-in-law—a woman he adored—his fiercest perp stare. He narrowed his eyes and let her have it.

"Don't," he said.

"Don't tell me 'don't,' Dylan Chadwick," she said. "You got us into this mess. I want you to get us out of it."

"What mess?" he asked, irate.

"This summer. Giving Chloe a job at the stand."

"She still has the job," he said. "It's August, she's losing interest, she's a kid—that's natural."

"She hates the pies you're selling," Sharon said.

Dylan hardened his stare, as if she was the worst drug dealer in the state. "The pies are fine."

"They're commercially produced," Sharon said. "They're like cardboard."

Dylan took a long drag and stared menacingly through the smoke. She reached out her hand.

"What?" he asked.

"Give me that," she said.

Dylan leaned back in his chair. He remembered when they were young, before he'd gotten married, how he and Sharon would smoke together. Eli had never approved. So she'd follow Dylan out behind the barn after dinner, sneak a cigarette while practicing smoke rings and getting him to tell her old stories about her husband's childhood, then come back inside. He handed her the cigarette now.

Sharon took in a long lungful of smoke, blew out three perfect, concentric smoke rings, and smiled. "I can still do it," she said.

"Yeah, you've still got—" Dylan started to say as she ground the cigarette out in the ashtray. "Hey!"

"Enough of this," she said.

"Of what?"

"Self-destruction, isolation, misery—for starters! What kind of example are you, smoking up a storm in front of your niece."

"My niece is nowhere to be seen right now," he said.

"Well, then, think of Isabel," Sharon said.

"Go to hell," Dylan said before he could stop himself. His chest bubbled over with hurt and rage. But then, because he loved his sister-in-law and would never want to hurt her, he reached for her hand. "I'm sorry."

Her eyes were unperturbed. He hadn't upset her at all.

"I can take it," she said softly.

"I can't," he said.

"I know that, Dylan," she said.

He couldn't reply. Everywhere he looked, he saw things left behind. Isabel's picture, Chloe's picture, his mother's baking bowls, his father's cane, the crummy commercially produced pies . . . they reminded him in reverse of Jane.

"Something happened this summer," Sharon said quietly.

Dylan stared at the table, at the five apple seeds.

"I didn't always like it," she said. "It hurt like hell at certain times. But I'm very glad for it now."

"Glad?"

Sharon nodded. "Oh, yes," she said.

"How can you possibly say that? Chloe was upset. As upset as I've seen her since Isabel died."

"Is that all bad?" Sharon asked.

Dylan shook his head; she was blowing his mind. "Yeah, I'd say so. Wouldn't you?"

"No," Sharon said firmly. "It proves she has deep feelings. It's a sign that she's alive. We've started down this road many times before; remember Family Court? And remember her research through adoption registries? Eli and I wouldn't give our okay—we thought she was too young."

"She is, obviously. Look how she handled it, when confronted with—"

"Her mother. Go ahead, Dylan. You can say the words. You had no problem saying them that day in my driveway—and I love you for it. I love how protective you are of us. So, sweetheart—"

She had to stop herself, and Dylan stared up and watched the tears glitter in her eyes. Now it was his turn to be on the receiving end of a cop's hard stare. His sister-in-law was taking it to a new level—narrowed eyes, thinned lips.

"Sweetheart," she said steadily. "Now the tables are turning. It's my turn to protect you from yourself." She took his cigarettes off the table and tossed them into the garbage.

"I'll only get them out when you leave," he said.

"Very mature," she said.

"And I'll buy more."

"Congratulations—you have a wallet. But the bigger question, Dylan, is: Do you have a heart?"

"Sharon, stop."

"Answer me. You owe me that."

"*Owe?*"

"You've cared about us all these years. Now sit back and take it, while I do the same for you. Do you have a heart?"

Dylan didn't reply. His pulse was racing. His eyes lit upon the cardboard pies, and something deep in his rib cage ached as if being ripped out.

"I'll answer for you," Sharon said, leaning forward. "You do. It's the biggest heart around. It led you into your job, where you made it your business to protect a lot of people you didn't even know. It made you a great husband—"

Dylan shook his head violently, and Sharon grabbed his hand.

"Yes, Dylan. A great husband. Just because she couldn't accept it didn't mean you weren't offering. And you were a great, stellar, wonderful, top-of-the-line father. You were, you were. Even she couldn't deny that—all she had to do was watch you with Isabel."

"Sharon."

She went on, as if she hadn't heard. "You're the best brother in the world. The best—to Eli, to me. We love how you are to Chloe. She couldn't have a better uncle . . . no matter what . . ."

Dylan wanted to say thank you, but he couldn't speak.

"So I know all about your heart," Sharon said. "You don't even have to say a word. But you do have to listen. You do, Dylan. I need you to hear ... I need to give you something, to give you back everything you've given to us. Over the years, being a great brother and uncle. I need to tell you this: Go to New York."

"What?"

"New York, Dylan."

"What are you talking about?"

"You were so happy for a while," Sharon whispered. Dylan closed his eyes. He heard nightbirds calling in the apple trees. A fresh breeze was bringing September weather, and the air was fragrant with apples. Way in the distance, he heard the whine of dirt bikes.

"The spring, early this summer ... when she was here."

"She?"

"You know who I mean," Sharon said, and of course Dylan did know. He had never been able to get by acting cool to Sharon; she saw right through him.

"Jane," he said.

"I want you to go see her," Sharon said.

"How can you say that?" Dylan asked. "After all the trouble she made? She was one big lie—and we all fell for it."

"We all lie, Dylan," Sharon said. "Some lies are bigger than others. I used to lie to Eli, going out behind the barn to smoke with you. I'd tell him I wanted to get a breath of fresh air."

"That's different," Dylan said. "And you know it."

"Yes, it is. Lies are always different, and I suppose they're never really very good. But some come from better places than others. Amanda's came from selfishness. From wanting to go behind your back."

"Enough about that!"

"Exactly," she said. "Enough! Amanda's dead. You can't go filtering everyone else through what she did. Jane is different. She lied because of love."

"This from you?" Dylan asked. "She comes back to Rhode Island to take your daughter away, and you're defending her?"

Sharon shook her head. "She wasn't trying to take Chloe away. She was just trying to know her a little. Because she loves her so much."

Dylan got chills when she said that, up and down his spine.

"And I think you know how that feels," Sharon said. "About Jane. I think she was just what you needed."

"What if she was?" he asked. "That's over now."

"It seems to me that 'over' is a very funny thing," Sharon said. "It seems to have rules of its own."

"What do you mean? I thought you'd want no part of her. I figured you, of all people, would hate what she did this summer."

"Dylan—I, of all people, understand," Sharon said. "I'm a mother."

Dylan's heart pounded in his ears. He thought of the last time he had held Jane. He thought of the look in her eyes, as she pulled into the driveway with Chloe, when she saw him talking to Sharon. His heart twisted now, because of the betrayal: not what she had done to him, but what he had done to her. Sharon was right: Jane had gone back to New York. Dylan knew, because he had gotten a postcard from her. Just a picture postcard of Greenwich Village with the words "I'm so sorry" written on the back.

The dirt bikes got louder. There was no porch light on, so the riders probably thought Dylan was in for the night. Anger built in his chest. He thought of his land being invaded, and he thought of everything he had lost. What Sharon didn't know was that everything was too late. Some damage was too great to undo. He went to the closet by the back door, took his shotgun down.

"What are you doing?" Sharon asked, grabbing his arm.

"They're trespassing," he said, coldly. Holding a gun was second nature. Driving bad guys away was a hundred times easier than talking with Sharon about his heart. He actually felt glad for the chance to face conflict head-on.

"Don't do anything stupid," Sharon warned.

"Right," he said, taken by an overwhelming feeling that none of it much mattered anymore, anyway.

⁕

Chloe was deep into her collage. Her father had given her a stack of old magazines. She had assembled scissors, Bainbridge board, and double-sided tape. Then she'd cut out a pile of pictures and snippets of words and was putting them all together in a big dream sequence of a picture.

One thing Chloe knew about herself: When her feelings were too big, words deserted her. They fled her brain, leaving her in mute confusion. Emotions threatened mutiny from within, and she was sure she'd be the youngest girl to die of a heart attack with no preexisting condition to blame.

With the windows open, she let the cool orchard breeze ruffle her scraps of paper. Cats had sneaked through the open window and reclined in the most inconvenient places: sprawled across the magazines, playing with the tape dispenser, rubbing against Chloe's leg. Usually Chloe would stop everything, drop to her knees, and become a cat herself. But right now, she was on a mission to finish her collage.

The phone rang. And rang, and rang.

"Hello!" Chloe shouted to her parents. "Would somebody GET that?"

When nobody did, she figured they were still out on the back step, so she lurched for the receiver and said hello. It was, of course, Mona.

"Mother of God," Chloe said. "I am in the middle of something here."

"Yes, well, isn't that nice for you? I, on the other hand, am bored shitless. Rhianna and Dad have gone out to dinner to plan where they're going for dinner next week—for Black Saturday."

Chloe chuckled. "Their anniversary?"

"*Bien sûr.* They're having the big party on Sunday, but they have to go somewhere romantic the night before—so he can give her the jewelry he bought her."

"So she can wear it to the party."

"They're so vile," Mona said. "So what are you in the middle of?"

Chloe hesitated. Her language problems extended even to telling Mona about what was going on. She hadn't told her about the collage—the fact of making it or the actual content. She gazed at it now: Images of importance only to Chloe and, possibly, one other person, adorned the heavy board.

An apple tree. A pie. A mother holding her infant. An ad for "First Look" pregnancy tests. A dolphin and a shark. The word "Calamity."

"Oh, not much," Chloe said.

"Equivocate. See if I care."

"I'm flowin' again," Chloe reported, changing the subject.

"Yay—so you're doubly not pregnant," Mona said.

"Right. Second period since the scare."

"Good to know you're on track."

"I can't believe how sick I felt," Chloe said. Through the window came a familiar, terrible sound. At first she thought it was chain saws, but then she realized: dirt bikes.

"Maybe you should tell Jane."

"No," Chloe said.

"It would be the polite thing to do."

Chloe stared at her collage again, lost in thought and drowning in unspoken words. The sound of the dirt bikes got louder. She poked her head out the window. Her parents were no longer sitting on the step. They must have come inside. A ripple went all through her body and she knew she had to do it: confront Zeke.

"Hear that?" Chloe asked, holding the phone to the window.

"Evil exists," Mona sad.

"In our orchard."

"Call Uncle Dylan to drive it away."

"Why send a man to do a woman's job?" Chloe asked, sticking her scissors in the waistband of her shorts. "This is *my* mission."

"Be careful," Mona said, sounding alarmed.

"I will," Chloe said, hanging up. She thought of her word problem. She had stopped speaking after Isabel's death. Then she had started talking again, and had kept it up till this summer. Although it hadn't been as severe or extreme—the average person wouldn't notice—Chloe had become internally tongue-tied.

She knew it had to with Jane, and with Zeke. She had things she had to say to each of them, words trapped inside her chest. They were live things, eating her from within. She had to find ways to let them out.

The collage was one way.

Scissors in her belt were another.

Chloe scrambled out onto the roof, slid down the drainpipe. The cats left behind in her room meowed and cried. I'll be back, she thought, saluting them. Meteors streaked through the sky, lighting her way. She climbed over the rail fence and ran barefoot into the trees.

The engines roared and whined. Chloe had insider knowledge of where Zeke liked to ride. She remembered his circuitous route over the hills and around the barn, back to the stream. Crouched low, to keep from running into apple tree branches, Chloe sped through the orchard.

She saw the lights. They bounced like illuminated balloons, like silvery moons. Hiding in the bushes, her heart was in her throat. They came closer, and she heard sticks and branches breaking under their tires. She thought of that time she had waited for Zeke, when she had been so excited. The memory almost brought tears to her eyes, for the innocent girl she had been back then.

Just as the bikes cleared the crest of the hill, she yanked the scissors from her waistband and jumped out. She stood right in the middle of the path, seeing the lights bear down on her.

"What the fuck?" the first driver yelled, swerving to avoid her. He went off the trail, into the narrow strip of grass between the rows of trees, managing to right himself just before crashing. The second driver, Zeke, stopped right in Chloe's face.

"Hey," Zeke said. His eyes were blank, but he smiled.

"Hey," she said back. "What do you know? It's Zoe."

"Huh." He laughed.

"Zeke, man," the other driver said. "Come on . . ."

But Chloe was blocking the way. They weren't getting around her. She stood very still, scissors out in front of her. "You're not going anywhere," she said.

"Hate to tell you, Chloe," Zeke said. "But you can't stop us. You can't really stop us at all, you know?"

"I know you think that," she whispered.

The other guy laughed. "This the one?"

"This is Chloe," Zeke said, and that was enough of a signal for his friend. He laughed, wheeled closer to see her.

"She's cute," he said. "I'd do her."

The night was dark. A canopy of branches arched overhead, blocking any light from the stars. Chloe wasn't afraid. She barely even looked at the other one; her gaze, her derision, was all for Zeke.

"I despise you," she said.

"You didn't act that way in June," he said.

"Tell yourself that," she said.

"I don't have to tell myself anything," he said, sounding impatient and showing the first signs of anger. "I know it when I see it. You came on to me."

"You're pathetic," she said. "That you actually believe that."

"I believe what I see," Zeke said.

"We saw you in Newport," Chloe said, remembering standing on Bannister's Wharf with Jane and the others, seeing him eat that hot dog. "And you ran away."

"Who needed to meet your parents?" he asked. "The girls I date don't generally spend their weekend nights hanging out with Mom and Dad."

Chloe felt a strange sensation, hearing someone call Jane her mom and having it be true. But she refused to be diverted, and just stared him down.

"You're a coward," she said. "And I want you to know I know that."

"Her body's saying 'go' right now," the friend said. Chloe walked over to him. She looked him straight in the eyes. Then she raised her scissors over her head. She thought of the pictures of babies and mothers and apples she had just cut out of her father's magazines. She thought of herself and Jane and the pain girls had to go through because of heartless boys. And she stabbed his front tire.

"Fucking bitch!" the friend exclaimed, jumping off his bike as the air hissed out of his tire.

"You just bought yourself a tire, Chloe," Zeke said laconically. She stared him right in the eyes, then stabbed his front tire.

"Two," she said. "And you're still a coward."

"Cunt!" Zeke exploded. The cords on his neck stood out as he vaulted off his bike and lunged at Chloe. She had the scissors in her hand, but in the half-second she had to process the moment, she knew she couldn't use them. Tires were one thing, but she was constitutionally incapable of harming any creature—even a clam, even Zeke.

Still, she was fast, and she knew the orchard better than anyone, so she ducked and ran. She flew up the hill, from where the bikes had come. She dodged through the apple trees, hearing the boys crashing behind her. They were gaining on her, but she had superhuman speed.

Chloe had spoken. She had told Zeke what she had to say, and she had reclaimed the orchard from those bad memories. Her collage was her poem, her song, and when it was done, all that was left would be for her to sing it. Courage gave her wings. She flew through the trees. She came to a wide meadow—and there, on the other side, was the barn.

The beautiful old red barn, with the cupola on top. Chloe had to get to it, and then she would be safe. There was no place to hide in the meadow, but if she managed to get across, she would make it to the barn. She could lock the door behind her, and they'd never get in. Uncle Dylan's house was just over the next rise, and she'd go up into the cupola and yell so loud, he'd hear her.

The cupola. Gazing at it, hearing the boys gaining, an old memory shot through Chloe's mind. She had thought it had eyes. She had thought the cupola was home to angels, owls, protective spirits.

Chloe had thought it was home to her real mother.

The memory made her gasp with a sob. Kicking into higher speed, she took off into the tall grass of the wide meadow. The grasses tickled her legs, all the way up to her waist. She ran as fast as she could, arms

working to give her more speed. Thirty
yards, twenty yards. She wanted to glance
back, but she didn't dare.

She just ran on blind faith. Chloe felt
someone was protecting, watching over
her. She had learned this summer that
things weren't always what they seemed,
that the obvious sometimes hid unimagin-
able mysteries. The sky was alive with meteors, crashing through the darkness,
leaving trails of fire.

"Help," she called as she ran.

Pound, pound, pound: her feet, their feet.

They were gaining on her. She felt someone pluck the back of her shirt; tearing
away, she poured on more speed.

"Help!" she called again, breathless.

How could she get into the barn without
them catching her? And what if the doors
were locked? Could she scramble up to the
open hayloft? She was used to climbing the
drainpipe into her room. . . .

It came up fast. The red barn had been
just a shadow in the starlight, but now it was
there, smack in front of her. She flew against
the door, rattled the rusty old iron handle,
moaned as she found it locked.

"Think you can run away?" Zeke asked.

"Bitch," his friend said.

Chloe faced them both, back up against the wall. Zeke's hair looked dirty and long; how had she ever seen beauty in his cruel face? His friend leered—he had a shaved head and barbed wire tattooed around his neck. Chloe shuddered, but she kept her eyes steady and vowed not to let them see she was afraid.

"You can't—" Zeke said, walking over, tangling his hand in her hair. Chloe could smell his beer breath. His friend stood beside him, panting. "—run away. You never could."

Just then they heard a gun being cocked: *che-che.*

"She doesn't have to run away," Uncle Dylan said, pointing a shotgun right at Zeke's head. "She's home."

"Fuck," the friend said, backing away.

"I'd like to shoot you," Uncle Dylan said to the friend, though still aiming at Zeke. "So keep talking. You—" he prodded Zeke in the head with the gun, "let Chloe go."

Zeke released her hair, and Chloe stepped away and went to stand beside her uncle.

"See how it feels to be humiliated?"

Uncle Dylan asked, still aiming the gun. "You like that?"

"No," Zeke said in a high voice.

"No one does," Uncle Dylan said, his voice very reasonable, belying the fact he was holding his Winchester firearm with every muscle in his body cocked and ready.

"Uncle Dylan," Chloe said, nervously. She'd never seen his eyes look this way before.

"Can we go?" the friend asked. "Please let us go?"

Chloe's uncle didn't move or speak. He just held that gun so tight, she could feel him wanting to pull the trigger. It was scaring her, and she knew the fear came not just from the boys and the gun and the feeling of danger, but from the knowledge—and Chloe had it herself—that this was how far a broken heart could push a person.

It had pushed Chloe into the orchard with nothing but a pair of scissors to defend herself. And it had pushed Uncle Dylan all the way from Isabel to Jane to this moment with the shotgun and a crazy desire to shoot.

"Uncle Dyl," she whispered.

"Take your wallets out of your pockets," he said. "Slowly."

"Are you going to shoot us?" Zeke asked. Overhead a few thin clouds had drifted into the sky, and the meteors flashed behind them.

"You have ID in those wallets?" her uncle asked.

"Yeah," Zeke said.

"You?" Uncle Dylan asked the friend.

"Yes—my license."

"Throw 'em on the ground. You're never gonna ride on my land again," Uncle Dylan said with cold intensity. "And you're never, never going to mess with my niece again."

"She told me you're a marshal," Zeke said. "Way back . . . I shoulda listened. I'm sorry!"

"He's shooting us dead," the friend wailed.

"Please, Uncle Dylan," Chloe begged, because she believed the friend was right. "Isabel, Isabel . . ."

His eyes flickered. That was all: just a touch of light, then nothing.

"Say you're sorry to Chloe," her uncle said.

"I'm sorry," the boys said at once.

"Now run!" Uncle Dylan said, and he shot into the air.

The boys took off across the field, twice as fast as they'd run before. Chloe watched them go, and then she watched her uncle pick up their wallets. She tried to smile at him, but his face seemed broken. He couldn't smile, he couldn't frown. "I need these," he said. "Because those two are going down hard. I'm calling the cops as soon as we get inside. You okay?"

Chloe tried to nod. "Are you?"

He tried to nod.

Chloe hugged him. "Thank you," she said.

He didn't reply, and he couldn't let go. "They wanted to hurt you, Chloe," he said. "Do you know what I'd have done if they did? I can't bear to lose you, too . . ."

"I know," she said, her chest aching hard.

"I don't know what you think you were doing, running around in the orchard this late at night—"

"I was standing up for myself," she said defiantly. "I was taking care of what's important."

"It doesn't always work that way," he said harshly. "I was standing up for Isabel and Amanda, taking care of what was important—and look what good I did."

"You were with them," Chloe whispered. "You were trying. You got to hold Isabel's hand, while she died. Imagine how it would have been for her if you weren't there . . . you were with her, Uncle Dylan."

"But what good does that do?" he asked, and through the hard lines in his face, through the anger in his eyes, she saw sharp, shining tears. "When the bad thing happened anyway?"

Chloe closed her eyes. She saw Jane's face. She saw her black hair and blue eyes, her wonderful wide smile, the way she'd always seemed to know the exact right things to say. She saw the way Jane had come into their lives with pies, the way she had held the hand of Chloe's brokenhearted uncle and made him smile again, the way she had gone with Chloe to get the pregnancy tests, just sitting there so quietly, without any judgment, waiting with her . . .

It had to do with knowing that Jane had stayed away for Chloe's whole life. She had loved her enough to give her a name, and she had come to the orchard this summer, but she had forced herself to stay away for all that middle time. And even though she was away, she had worn Chloe's picture in her locket—every day, every night.

Although miles away, Jane had been right there with Chloe, every step of the way. Her parents and Uncle Dylan had loved her day in and day out, had raised her with more love than any child Chloe knew, but Jane had loved her, too. . . .

"There's something I don't understand yet," Chloe said. "But it has to do with being there."

"Being there?"

"Like you with Isabel."

Uncle Dylan just listened. "You were with her—at the beginning of her life, and at the end. You're with her now, right?"

"I think she's with me . . . yes."

"Same thing," Chloe said. "People do their best."

"And sometimes it's not good enough."

"See," Chloe said. "I think it is. I think it is good enough. . . . Look at Jane."

"Come on now," her uncle said, checking the action on his gun, resting it on his shoulder, starting to walk away. "Enough of this. Let's get you home."

"I want to see her," Chloe said, feet planted on the ground. She thought of her

collage. She hoped this wouldn't hurt her
mother and father; somehow, she didn't
think that it would upset her mother.

In fact, lately, she had started getting the
idea that her mother thought she should call
Jane. Chloe had gone down to breakfast
the other day and found a copy of the *New
York Times* open on the table—her mother
subscribed, for the food and house and garden sections on Wednesday and Thurs-
day—to a very small article titled "Calamity
Jane Rides Back Into Town."

There was a photo of Jane in a white
baker's hat, standing outside her bakery on
a tree-lined street. Chloe had stared for a
long time. Jane wasn't smiling in the picture. She was trying, but she just couldn't
seem to make it real. The article said she'd
be baking a lot of apple tarts for fall. Chloe's
mother had left it there without a word.

"You're not going to see her," her uncle
said.

"I say I am."

"That's a bad idea, Chloe."

"She's not your mother."

"I'm aware of that. She didn't raise you—
my brother and Sharon did. They love you."

Chloe stifled something that was half

sob, half laugh. Could her uncle really be so dense? She looked around. The meadow was alive with tall, beautiful grasses, crickets, and foxes. Deer grazed the far edges. An owl lived in the hayloft and feasted on mice. Apple trees were everywhere, laden with fruit. The moon was starting to rise in the east, illuminating the orchard. The cats danced.

"What's so funny?" Uncle Dylan asked.

"Just check it out," Chloe said, holding out her hand, taking it all in.

"Chloe, what are you talking about?"

"Remember the barn dance? We had it for Mom and Dad's anniversary?"

"Yeah, I remember. What about it?"

"We need another one, Uncle Dylan. And fast. Before you fade away."

"I'm not fading away. I'm taking you home, and then I'm calling the cops to report those two—"

"You said Mom and Dad love me," Chloe said, grabbing her uncle's rough hand.

"They do."

"I know they do," she said. "They've given me so much love, I have that much left over . . ."

"Chloe," he said.

"For you, for Isabel, for Mona, for the cats . . . for my real mother."

He didn't speak. He stood so still, holding his gun, frozen like a statue in the light of the rising moon.

"Jane," he said, after a moment.

"Admit it, Uncle Dylan—you love her, too."

Once again, he turned into a statue. The moon rose higher, making his eyes glow darkly. Chloe could see him thinking about Jane.

"I miss her pies," he said.

"The ones we're selling at the stand," Chloe said, "are garbage."

"I know."

"She's bakin' in New York," Chloe said. "I saw an article in the paper. Mom left it for me to see. I'm going to go find her. I'm heading into New York, and I'm going to find Jane."

Uncle Dylan stared at Chloe, trying to give her his really-tough-guy look. He had the eyebrows right, and the jaw. But his sneer was off—it was looking remarkably like a smile.

"I can't let you do that," he said.

"You can't stop me."

"Then I'm going to have to drive you. I can't let you go in alone," he said. "If your parents agree, that is."

"They will."

He laughed, shaking his head. "Knowing you, Ms. Chadwick, I think you're right."

"We'll bring back pies," Chloe said, linking arms with her uncle as they began to make their way through the orchard behind the barn, down the rise to her house. "And we'll bring Jane an invitation."

"To what?" he asked.

"To the barn dance. Don't worry—Mona and I will plan it."

"That's what I'm afraid of," he said, limping.

Chloe looked up at the moon. It was a bright silver disk, its edges blurred by the last of summer's heat. She reached out, as if she could hold it in her hand. At that moment, she believed that she could. She would carry it in her pocket, give it to Jane as if it were a silver apple.

"I just hope we can arrange one of those for the barn dance," she said, gazing up at the magical sky. "All we need is a silvery moon."

Her uncle laughed. He didn't say anything, but he laughed. And when they got to Chloe's yard, her parents were standing out in the driveway, waiting for the police to arrive. They had heard the gunshot and called them. At the sight of Chloe, her mother let out a cry. She opened her arms, and Chloe ran into them.

CHAPTER 29

The order was for a wedding cake, but as Jane mixed the batter, she found herself holding back. She stirred and measured, measured and stirred. She made sure that all the ingredients were present, and in the right proportions. The cake would be delicious and beautiful, unaffected by her emotional restraint.

But she reflected, big mixing bowl in one hand and oversized wooden spoon in the other, that things had changed. She felt very flat these days, like a one-dimensional baker. Before, whenever she had a wedding cake—or a birthday cake, or opening night cupcakes, or a Thanksgiving pie, or bat mitzvah cookies—to make, she would enter into the spirit of the occasion and add an ingredient uncalled for in the recipe.

She would call forth all the love she had—often by thinking of Chloe, wherever she was, whatever she was doing—and put it right into the cake. You'd never find this instruction in any cookbook, but Jane believed it was her secret weapon as a baker. It was what made her cakes so sought-after. As the *New York Times* had said, "Cakes from Calamity Jane are baked with the skill of a professional and the heart of your mom."

But right now, Jane was coasting a little. No secret ingredient this week. She hoped her clients wouldn't notice, but she was phoning her work in—treating her kitchen as a lab, following the measurements to a *T,* afraid of slipping up and adding too much or too little to the mix.

That seemed to be the problem in other areas of her life, too. Too much or too little, all at the wrong times. She poured the batter into three round pans, then had to start over—she had forgotten to butter and flour the cooking surfaces.

Once she got the cake into the oven, she was ready for a break. She wore a baseball cap backward, to keep the hair out of her eyes, but she used the back of her hand to brush some stray strands away from her face. She poured herself a glass of juice and sat down at the table. The commercial oven kept her kitchen hot, and Jane was glad. Because she felt so cold.

Her assistant was on the road, delivering baked goods around the city. This was a new person, someone Jane was breaking in after advertising for help in the *Village Voice.* So far, so good. Her last assistant had left, of course, when Jane took her prolonged leave—although Jane had liked her, she understood that that was just a price she had to pay for her spring in Rhode Island.

Spring and part of the summer . . .

She had a calendar on the wall, a panoramic reminder of her home state with photos of Newport and Providence; she took it down, laid it on the table, and did something kind of crazy: she counted the days.

Sixteen days in March, thirty in April, thirty-one in May, fourteen in June. She added them up: Ninety-one days altogether.

The Ninety-one days of Chloe . . .

Jane put her hand on the calendar, as if she could take those days right in through her skin, her pores, into her blood and bones, hold them forever. But time didn't work that way. Time was all about the present. It was where you were and what you were doing, in any given moment, that gave life its meaning. It was August now, and weeks had passed since that sacred time in the orchard. . . .

Right now, Jane forced herself to breathe. Every breath hurt, a little, because it was taking her farther from her time with Chloe. At first, the fact of being apart from her hurt almost as much as the days right after her birth. All Jane had been able to see was the shock and hurt in Chloe's eyes, mixed with the fear that she might be pregnant, and the confusion of being a young teenager and having someone she'd thought was a friend tell her she was instead her mother.

Jane had handled it badly. There were probably a hundred ways she could have done it better. What if she had been honest right off the bat? Driven up to Chloe at the stand and said, "Hi. I know this is going to sound strange, but I'm your mother." Or, if she had shaken Dylan's hand that first night at the Educators' Potluck and said, "You

don't know me, but I'm your niece's real
mother, and I need your help . . ."

Oh, Dylan . . .

She couldn't even begin to think about
him yet. The sight of his cold, cop's eyes, regarding her as if she were the criminal to end
all criminals, was like an icicle to her heart.
She had dreamed of him—possibly every
night since they had lain together and made
love and overwhelmed each other with
wholeness. That was the word she couldn't
get out of her mind: wholeness. Because
with Dylan, she had felt she had a chance of
feeling whole, instead of like just a halfway
woman.

Love made a person whole. Jane knew
that now. Not the helpless longing kind of
love she'd felt most of her life—not that. Not
the aching yearning, the middle-of-the-
night-feeling-of-falling-off-the-edge-of-the-
world variety of love. Not the wondering
kind of love: *Where's Daddy, when's he
coming home?* And not the chasing-after-
someone, doesn't-he-love-me brand of love
that she'd had, after all, with her father, and
with Chloe's father.

Jeffrey Hayden.

After returning to New York—leaving her

mother to Sylvie and John, slipping out on that responsibility because it was, after all, just one agony too many for one baker— Jane had gone on-line to the Brown University Web site. She had looked up Jeffrey's name—something she hadn't done in a couple of years.

He had started his career, she knew, as a teaching assistant at Brown. And then he had become a full-fledged instructor in the English Department. All this was pre-Internet, and she had learned it from the Class Notes section of the Brown alumni magazine, each sighting of his name causing a slight case of the cold sweats.

Then, with the Web site, she had kept track for a while. He had gone to Harvard. He had become a professor. He was on the academic fast track, publishing in journals, *The New Yorker, Harper's,* and the *Atlantic.* He wrote a series of books, including one that broke out of the university bookstores and hit national best-seller lists: *The Literature of the Heart.* It was, according to the review, a hybrid of the postmodern and the romantic, analyzing the way literature takes the writer more deeply into his own heart by the unflinching examination of his own losses.

Jane had been unable to read the book. And for several years, she'd stopped looking Jeffrey up on the Internet. Till this summer.

One day in late July, when New York was deep into an air-conditioning-overload-induced brownout, covered with sweat and trying to stay cool by rubbing her face with melting ice cubes, Jane logged on to the Brown Web site, found Jeffrey's pertinent information.

His office was at Harvard. He lived, according to the listing, on Trapelo Road, in Belmont. Jane called his office number, although it was after hours. Her heart pounding, she listened to his voice—same inflections, same gentle humor behind the words. Okay, she was ready. She called his home.

A child answered.

"Is your daddy there?" Jane asked.

"Daddy!" the child called.

And then Jeffrey came on. "Hello?"

Jane bit her lip as the ice cube slipped from her fingers. "Hi, Jeffrey," she said. "It's Jane." She left out her last name.

It didn't matter. He knew.

"Jane," he said. Was that a gasp? It was followed by silence. Then, "How are you?"

"I saw her," Jane said. "I met her and spent time with her."

More silence. Long silence.

"Where?" he asked, finally.

"In Rhode Island. She lives there. At the edge of an orchard in Crofton. She's beautiful, Jeffrey. And smart, and funny . . . so unusual and eccentric and lovely . . . passionate . . . the brightest—"

"Jane," he said, stopping her.

"I—" she began. Why had she called? She'd known when she'd first dialed. Her heart cracked like a walnut shell, and tears streamed down her face. She was mad, and she knew it. She licked the tears from the corners of her lips. The man at the other end of the line was Chloe's father. They had made her together.

"I'm married now," he said. "I have three children."

"I know," she said, containing herself. "I saw in the alumni magazine."

"Some things need to remain in the past," he said.

As if it were a tomb—with walls and a

lead lining. Things can get in, but they can't get out. Jane held the phone, shaking. It was so hot, she was filmed with sweat, and she was wearing nothing but her underwear. It was as if naked was the only way she could talk to him. Naked and insane with love—not for him, but for their daughter.

"Don't you think about her?" Jane whispered.

"I try not to," he said.

"Then don't you dream about her?"

Another long silence. "I do," he whispered. "Of you, too. That's why I wrote the book." His voice stopped, and the sound of someone young asking him a question filled the distance. Jane gulped, waiting for him to say something more, but he didn't. He just hung up the phone.

She had gone, that very night, to the Barnes and Noble on Sixth Avenue and Twenty-second Street, to get the book. And she'd bought it and carried it home. And she'd tried to read it, looking for clues: Somehow Chloe was responsible for this big, weighty, well-reviewed book. Opening the back cover, she stared at Jeffrey's photo. She wasn't really looking at him, she realized, but was searching for signs of Chloe: the shape of his eyebrows, a tendency for his smile to lift more on the left . . .

And Chloe was there.

She had always been his daughter, so much a part of him. From the minute Jane had realized she was pregnant, she had thought of them as a family. Lightning had struck, fusing them together. How could they ever be apart?

With his book in her hand, she remembered the day she told him. She had taken a train to New York City, met him at Penn Station. He was waiting for her under the sign board, with all the train times. Seeing him, she began to run. She dropped her bag and put her arms around him; he had felt her shaking.

"You made it, this is so great," he said. "The Long Island Railroad is downstairs, and we have about forty minutes before our train—my parents are really glad you're coming, and they want us to have dinner there tonight, but tomorrow there's a concert at Jones Beach and—"

"Oh, Jeffrey—"

Her face pressed into his chest, she

formed the words before she said them out loud. They sounded so strange in her imagination: *I'm pregnant.*

College girls didn't say those words. Intelligent English majors didn't say them. Girls from good Catholic families didn't say them. Girls who had just traveled from Rhode Island to New York to meet their college boyfriends shouldn't say them, first off. . . . Her face turned red. While her heart beat faster, faster, and her knees felt weak, a whole story went through Jane's head: the words would shock Jeffrey, almost certainly, but his love and his goodness would help him to help her through whatever happened next.

"What's wrong?" she heard him asking . . . she was so rarely at a loss for words. They were English majors, in love with language and literature, and they loved to talk and argue and discuss and expound, and they'd been apart for the last three weeks. But right now, she was a shy girl with her face in his lapel and an inability to form words.

"I . . ." she began. But then something changed the words in her head, and she said, "We . . ."

"We?"

"We're going to have a baby," she said.

She had expected many things. Shock, silence—anything but what came next. He laughed. "Good one, Jay," he said.

"We are," she said, drawing back, so he could see that she was serious.

They locked eyes. He was smiling, surprisingly, because they weren't really jokey people, they didn't tease each other a lot. But as he realized that she wasn't kidding, his gaze met hers in steadiness and gravity.

"Jane," he said, as if her name somehow reassured him. Then, "Are you sure?"

"I'm sure. I went to Planned Parenthood . . ."

He held her, rocked her. His lips brushed hers. The relief of telling him was so great, and he was holding her so tightly, she had the sudden, sure sense that everything was going to be fine. She was going to get through this: *They* were. They all were . . .

"I feel as if it's . . . she's . . . a girl," Jane said. "I know it's crazy, how can I know, but I just feel—"

"Don't do that to yourself," he said, still rocking her.

"Do what?"

"Girl, boy . . . Don't think like that, Jane. Don't get attached."

Jane laughed, looked up into his eyes. "But I'm more than attached. I'm her home! She's—or he's—in my body!"

"Stop," he said. And his eyes were harder than his voice.

"Stop . . ."

"We have to figure out what to do."

"To do?"

"Jane! You know what I'm saying. Look. I'm going to call my parents and tell them we're getting a later train. I'll say . . . I don't know—I'll say your train is late, and we can't make the connection. I don't want to have us all sitting around the table making small talk while you and I—"

She tried to breathe. *While you and I plan the future. While you and I hold each other. While . . .*

"While you and I try to make some kind of sense about what the hell we're going to do. There was a senior on my floor who got his girlfriend pregnant—"

Jane opened her eyes wider.

"Planned Parenthood—good going, there. I think that's where they went. Or, rather, she did. He wouldn't go with her. I'm not letting you go alone, though."

"Go where alone?"

"For an abortion."

Jane blinked slowly. She believed every woman had that right. But she touched her belly. She said hello. The baby said hello back, right there in Penn Station. She shook her head.

"No abortion," she said.

"Jane—"

"Jeffrey."

"We have two years left at Brown! We have grad school, dissertations . . ."

"I know."

"Tell me you're not thinking we're going to keep the baby!"

"That's what I'm thinking."

"I love you, Jane. I know we're going to get married some day. But we can't do this."

"We can't? Or you can't?"

"Shhh. Jane."

"I'm not having an abortion. I think, I want, I want to keep the baby. Or maybe I can give her, or him, up for adoption. If we find the right family. I'm a realist! I know we're young! I understand these things, Jeffrey," she said, and her voice was rising because other travelers were looking at her. "I understand! I'm emotional! We conceived her at Campus Dance, we love each other, she came from us . . ."

"Shhh, Jane . . ."

"I know, I'm sorry. So I'll miss next semester. I'll live at home. I'll do home study! We can get an apartment! Off campus . . ."

He shook his head, and his lips got tight, and that's when she knew: This was over. He wasn't discussing this. He might listen and he might talk, but Jeffrey didn't want the same thing she did. Jane knew, and in that moment, her heart died a little.

"I'd be distracted," he said. "Brown is the Ivy League. We can't just coast through, having a baby one week—"

"I can," she said.

"No," he said. "I don't think so. If you have the baby, you can say good-bye to junior year. You'll miss the whole year."

"So what?"

"It's our education," he said.

"But this is our life," she said.

Those words, "our life," shimmered and rose in the air between them, seeming to fill all of Penn Station. All of the travelers and commuters, the people meeting trains, the redcaps, the ticket agents, the parents holding tight to their small children, the college kids on their way home or to visit friends, the younger children on their way to summer camp . . . all of them were living their lives. Incredible, diverse, specific lives: theirs alone.

Jeffrey frowned, and his eyes looked angry. They filled with instant, hot tears, and Jane got to see him as he might have been as a young boy, disappointed with something.

That was when Jane knew: "Our life" meant something very different to Jeffrey than it did to her.

"Oh," was all she could say.

"You're too smart for this," he said.

"Apparently I wasn't," she said, trying to smile. "It happened."

"No. I mean, for this. For whatever happens next. For what you decide . . ."

You, she heard. Not *we* . . .

"What do you mean?"

DANCE WITH ME 567

"You're not some hick."

Jane closed her eyes. What did he think hicks looked like? Did he think they couldn't go to places like Brown? She knew his family was well-off. They lived in a nice suburb. His father was a radiologist. His mother volunteered at the hospital. Jane had been looking forward to seeing them, but feeling slightly nervous. She knew her family was from a different social league.

"This isn't a movie," he said.

"No kidding," she said.

"You're acting as if this is romantic," he said. "But start thinking literature, Jane, not cheap paperback."

Jane exclaimed—not a word, but just an awful sound. Her mother had taught her and Sylvie to love all books and stories, and she felt shocked and freshly offended. Her head was spinning. This was *their* story: not a movie, not Thackeray or Fielding, not *any* writer's. He was the one thinking of it in those terms, not Jane. She thought of literature classes, she thought *beginning-middle-end,* and she suddenly realized that, for Jeffrey, this was the end.

"This can't happen to us, because it will wreck our lives," he said.

"You are not," she said slowly, "who I thought you were."

"Jane . . ." He took a step toward her, but didn't touch her.

Tears filled her eyes. "I feel sorry for you, Jeffrey. I wish you could feel what I'm feel-ing—her—him—inside me. To know that she came from love . . . you'd never be able to say what you're saying."

"I'm not allowed to want a future?" he asked. "Not just for me, Jane—for you, too!"

"Our future is *forever*," she said, tears rolling down her face now. "And it has a baby in it. Whether she lives with us or not, she is going to be here. We made her."

"I'm not in it," he said, holding up his hands. "I can't believe you're saying these things. I'm telling you right now, Jane—I'm not in it. I don't want this."

"Then I don't want you," she said.

Their eyes met in a hot stare. Her body flooded with emotion, with love. And then it all turned cold, like a winter river, like the runoff of all the snows from the top of the northern mountains. She felt like ice, and she hated Jeffrey for abandoning the baby they had created by their love.

And at that moment, Jane stepped away. She stared at him. Her eyes were clear and dry. She took another step backward. Then another. He got smaller. She didn't kiss him, and she didn't wave good-bye.

He was making his choice, and she was making hers. Jane used the second half of her round-trip ticket to return to Rhode Island that night. She slept on the train the whole way. Being pregnant made her very tired.

She wanted to cry. Jeffrey was her father, all over again. She had loved him, and he had let her down. She knew there was a chance he might change his mind, but she didn't think so. Somehow, on that train trip, it began not to matter. She had her baby. Ever since the beginning, she had thought it was a girl.

That night, she was sure. She rocked herself and the baby and the train rocked them both. In a dream, Chloe had told her things that only a mother and daughter could know. . . . Jane had spent that whole train ride with her baby.

Jane thought of Jeffrey saying "education." She felt sorry for him, and for most of that train ride she tried to hate him. Because she also thought of her mother. A woman who revered education more than almost everything, but not just for its own sake: for what it could teach a person.

What it could teach a person about herself, about the world.

About love.

Jeffrey had a lot to learn about love, and no university in the world, not even Brown, could teach it to him.

Jane stuck the book on the top shelf and left it there.

August progressed. The days grew cooler, then hot again. Jane found herself typing other names into Google: her father, for example. Thomas J. Porter.

She spent one whole night reading the entries, looking for likely candidates. His last known stop had been Glastonbury, Connecticut, but he was long gone from there. He could be anywhere. She remembered how she and Sylvie had loved to sing along to the Allman Brothers' "Ramblin' Man."

They had sung it with anger and derision. What kind of loins had they sprung from, anyway? A man who would desert his family?

Perhaps that was the worst part of this long, hot summer, Jane thought as the wedding cake baked; knowing that Chloe felt the same way about her. Seeing that shock and almost visceral aversion in Chloe's eyes gave Jane a message: *This is the kind of person you are, this is what she thinks of you.*

It was really too much, in a whole host of ways, to bear. So Jane baked wedding cakes for other people. She sweetened the celebrations of other families' lives. In a couple of cases, when her assistant was delivering to other places, Jane went to the venues herself, to drop off her wares, and she'd see the party firsthand.

She always cried at weddings. Birthday parties and bat mitzvahs, too. Any kind of ceremony or celebration. They were always so filled with hope and good wishes; they represented the lengths to which people would go to gather together.

Sometimes the families came from Europe, Asia, Ohio, New Jersey, to be there. Aunts and uncles, husbands and wives, grandparents, nieces, nephews, cousins, second cousins, second-cousins-once-removed, brothers, sisters, mothers—all together in the hall, posing for pictures, telling old stories, creating new memories, eating Jane's cake . . .

They'd laugh at Jane for crying. But in a nice way, a fond way.

"Oh, my God! You don't even know us, and you're crying at my daughter's graduation party!"

"I wish her all the best," Jane said, eyes streaming. "You're so blessed to all be together . . ."

"Oh, we know it. Thank you."

Luckily, fall was fast approaching. If there was one thing Jane had learned from the last time she'd been separated from Chloe, fifteen years ago, it was that time did heal all wounds. Well, not completely. But after a fashion. Time put a big Band-Aid on them. So that life could go on.

While recovering, Jane knew that she would have to participate in her own healing. She would have to avoid apples, for example. She would have to prohibit herself from shopping the fruit aisle, picking out the reddest Empires, the most golden Delicious. Cinnamon would have to be expunged from her cabinet. And there could be no piecrust formed in the shapes of apples, barns, fruit trees of any sort. Getting through September without baking an apple pie would be hard—but critical.

And she'd have to stay off the Internet. She had to avoid temptation to type names into Google. Chloe's, for example. Or Dylan's. As she had done just last night.

Dylan Chadwick: nine thousand hits.

Most of them had to do with Dylan Thomas or Rufus Chadwick, the composer. But a few were for Jane's Dylan. She still thought of him that way in her weaker moments, i.e., most of the time.

She read articles about his service in the U.S. Marshals. He sounded heroic and brave. He had brought down drug lords and gambling czars. He had protected sequestered juries in Manhattan and Brooklyn. He had tracked a kidnapper across the country, apprehended him in Wyoming. Because a lot of his work was very secret, most of it didn't make it to the Internet.

But the story of Amanda and Isabel did.

Jane read the *New York Times* account. The headline read: "Mother, Daughter Killed in Midtown Shooting." And it went on to describe the scene. Unmarked town car stopped on Seventh Avenue in front of Penn Station, Dylan Chadwick escorting his wife and daughter into the station, gunfire exchanged—Amanda Chadwick, 33, and Isabel Chadwick, 11, dead on arrival at St. Vincent's Hospital; Dylan Chadwick in critical condition.

It went on to say that Chadwick, a marshal in the Southern District of New York, had been working a drug detail, a far-ranging case involving heroin, jury tampering, and execution-style murder. It was an organized-crime case, and Chadwick had been trying to get his family out of town.

Reading the article, Jane found herself back in Dylan's kitchen. She could hear the apple tree boughs rustling in the wind outside, she could see Isabel's picture on his refrigerator. Two eleven-year-old cousins, heads together, smiling for the camera.

Jane could see the way the corners of the photo curled, after years of humidity. And she curled a little herself, inside, thinking of how awful it was that Isabel's picture lasted so much longer than she had. She knew Dylan felt the same way.

And thinking of Dylan, she had to close her eyes.

Sitting there at her table, eyes closed as the sweet fragrance of a wedding cake baking filled her senses, she almost didn't hear the bell tinkle. It was very faint, almost as if a ghost had opened the door to her bakery, slipped in off the Chelsea streets.

Go away, she thought.

She didn't want to bake anything else. Not just today—ever. She wasn't sure her heart could take another celebration. Maybe if she sat very still and didn't make a sound, whoever had slipped in would just as quietly slip out. The smell of the baking cake was a dead giveaway, she realized. She knew that whoever was out there would assume, correctly, that cakes didn't bake themselves.

The thing was, she wanted to hold on to that memory of Dylan a little longer. Dylan in his kitchen, bearded and a little ragged in his work clothes, his heavy boots, his rough hands, his blue eyes. Jane swore she could look into those eyes forever. She was haunted by his eyes.

The bell tinkled again.

Good, she thought. *They've gone.*

But then, some instinct hit her like a brick. It literally knocked the breath out of her. She jumped up, cracking her shin on the chair as she tried to get around it. The pain shot to her knee, but she didn't even notice. She flew out of the kitchen into the tiny front office—nothing but a desk and two chairs, for people to place their orders.

No one was there. She looked at her window—plate glass, with "Calamity Bakery" spelled out in front, the letters reading backward from inside. Beyond the letters, she saw the street. Her quiet Chelsea street, lined with Callery pear trees, now heavy with green leaves and the dust of late August in the city. Cars parked on both sides of the street. A red truck parked there.

Red truck.

Oh, it touched her heart. Four wheels, a red cab, an open bed with something green inside. A truck just like Dylan's, transporting greenery. She leaned closer, forehead touching the window glass, to see the license plate.

A Rhode Island plate. White with blue numbers, a sailboat heeling into the wind, the words *Ocean State.* She was so focused on the numbers and letters and picture of the boat, she almost didn't see the people.

She saw their feet: white sneakers, mud-encrusted boots.

And their legs: jeans. They were both wearing jeans.

And their faces: not quite smiling, but not quite not smiling. Looking anxious, a little hopeful, like two people who had just driven two states to see an old friend and weren't sure of the reception they would get. They stared at Jane through the plate-glass window, and she stared at them.

Then she opened the front door. Heat from the sidewalk rose to meet her. She nearly swooned from the rush of heat and ghosts and love and fear. Her heart was in her throat, making words impossible.

Chloe took over. She stepped forward.

"I missed you," she said.

Jane stared into her eyes, drinking her in, unable to move. Dylan was just over her shoulder, and he nodded, as if to give Jane permission to do what she most wanted—no, what she had to do. So, because she still couldn't speak and because words had never been able to say it anyway, she just leaned forward with her arms open and brought her daughter to her heart.

EPILOGUE

It's the Harvest Moon."

"No, that's in October. It's something else. What's the full moon in September?"

"The Back-to-School Moon?"

"Bite your tongue," Chloe said, making an anti-vampire cross with her fingers. "Curse Labor Day for summer's end."

"You're really poetic, you know that?" Mona asked. "You should really consider getting a job writing fortunes for fortune cookies."

"Maybe it's the Fortune-Cookie Moon," Chloe said, as they sat in the barn's cupola, watching the amazing, enormous, full moon rise, orange-pink as it cleared the treetops, spreading its light on the orchard just like one of Jane's special icings.

"Yeah," Mona said. "So, tell me, O Wise One: What would our fortunes say?"

Chloe considered. There she was, sitting with her best friend in the cupola of Uncle Dylan's barn while guests assembled below. The barn dance was Chloe's brainstorm, and it had actually come to fruition. Jane was actually down there now, with Uncle Dylan—talking to Chloe's parents. Jane's sister and soon-to-be brother-in-law were down there, too. Even Jane's mother was invited—the nursing home was supposed to drop her off in a van. The whole family would be here. Freakily, Chloe's parents thought it was a great idea.

"Let me guess," Mona said. "They would say, 'beware of sharks in dolphins' clothing.' "

Chloe chuckled. Mona had that right. Leaning toward the cupola window, Chloe looked down at the ground, where Uncle Dylan had apprehended the marauders. He had followed up on his promise to call the police, and both Zeke and Brad, his friend, had been arrested.

"Wonder if Zeke'll get any prison tattoos?" Mona mused. "He'll need that dolphin to protect him . . ."

Chloe nodded. She shivered, thinking of how close a call she had had. But now the music began—a guitar, a bass, and a fiddle—and it was too pretty to make her think about ugly things. The notes drifted up, through the rafters and the hay.

"I used to think angels lived up here," Chloe said. "In the cupola."

"Is that your fortune?" Mona giggled.

Chloe's eyes widened. Because, in a way, it was . . . She had been loved and watched over by angels. Isabel; the orchard cats; the deer; her real mother, Jane.

"Maybe it is," she said. " 'You have angels in the cupola.' "

"So, what's mine?" Mona asked.

" 'Best friends are the best,' " Chloe said.

"No, I want something profound," Mona said. Chloe gave her a long, somewhat exasperated look, as if she felt beleaguered by Mona's insatiable demands on her heart and intellect. The truth, of course, was that Chloe loved her like a sister, and she wanted to hug her. But, then, tonight she wanted to hug everyone.

"How about this," Chloe said. " 'In the absence of sisters, we find sisters. In the absence of mothers, we find mothers. In the absence of family, you are my family.' "

"That's my fortune?" Mona asked, as the moon rose higher and the band really began to play.

"Yeah," Chloe said.

"I like it," Mona said simply. Then, taking the hug burden right off Chloe's shoulders, she threw herself right into her best-friend-sister-family with the biggest hug the cramped little cupola would allow.

⁂

The barn dance was gearing up. Sylvie and John danced the first dance, "Kentucky Waltz." Sylvie had worn a full turquoise skirt and white peasant shirt. The shirt had bright embroidery, and she had worn it in high school. She'd had to dig it out of a trunk in the attic for the occasion. Her mother would cluck with disapproval—she had always thought the shirt was too gauzy for public wear—if she ever actually got here. Perhaps Sylvie and John should have picked her up themselves. . . .

Sylvie must have been trembling, because John held her tighter. "You okay?" he asked over the music.

"I'm nervous," she said. "I'm afraid something awful will happen."

"Like what?"

"Like Chloe's mother—adoptive mother— will go up to Jane and have it out with her."

"But my understanding is that she invited Jane," John said, wheeling Sylvie around the floor. "Isn't that what you told me?"

"Yes, but doesn't that seem very strange to you? Very big of her—almost too big of her?"

"It's wonderful of her," John said. "Shows that she has Chloe's best interests at heart."

Sylvie fell silent as they danced. As a school librarian and the daughter of a high school principal, she knew that very often the best interests of children were very, very low on the totem pole of life. What she was experiencing right now, it seemed to her, was a true ideal of family.

"It's unbelievable, I must say; lovely, but almost unreal," Sylvie said, forehead wrinkled in a little frown. John kissed her right between the eyes, and she leaned back, surprised. "What?" she asked.

"My goal as your fiancé," he said, "is to get you to trust the world a little more."

Sylvie's frown deepened. "Don't I trust the world?"

John just chuckled, cheek against the top of her head.

"Don't I?" she asked.

"Let me tell you how much you trust the world," John said. "Right now, you're thinking that you and I should have driven your mother. Am I right?"

Sylvie smiled.

"Sylvie?" he asked, squeezing her a little tighter. "Am I?"

"Well, yes," she said.

He laughed, waltzing her around the floor. Sylvie caught a glimpse of Jane standing with Dylan, his brother, and his brother's wife. Jane looked so sweet and vulnerable, her heart on her sleeve, that Sylvie thought her own heart would break again—as it had, for her big sister, so many times. But Jane was home again, and that was what counted. . . .

"By the time we are married," John was saying, "I'm going to have you feeling so secure, you'll never worry again. That's my promise."

"Oh, John," she whispered, looking at her arm slung around his neck, at the beautiful

diamond ring he'd slid on her finger that
starry night in Maine. "That's impossible."

"It's not," he said firmly, kissing her.
"You'll see. I promise. And I never break my
promises."

She kissed him back, but with one eye
wide open, trained on the barn door, for a
sign that the van from Cherry Vale had arrived.

⚘

Sharon held Eli's hand. He had had severe
misgivings about this night, but she had
made sure to load up the guest list with the
entire Rotary Club, and he was too busy
saying hi to everyone to give in to his
doubts.

"Great party," Ace Fontaine said, walking
over with his wife, Dubonnet.

"Thanks, Ace," Eli said.

"Didn't realize you owned an orchard."

"It's my brother's, actually," Eli said.
"Dylan took it off my hands when our father
died."

"It's his, too," Dylan said. "No matter
what he says, this orchard belongs to the
Chadwick family, and he's—"

"The Chadwick family," Eli said, grinning at

his brother, but casting a little side glance at Jane. Sharon squeezed his hand, keeping him in line.

"Well, great apples," Ace said, casting an appraising grocer's gaze on the food table: Chloe and Mona had done their artful magic, arranging baskets of apples, platters of cheese and grapes, and Jane's pies and tarts on a long red-checked cloth. "Maybe I should order some for the localproduce section."

"Sure," Dylan said. "Just tell Eli what you want."

"Hey, that'd be great," Eli said, shaking Ace's hand. "We'll make it happen."

"Sure thing," Ace said, leading Dubonnet onto the dance floor.

That left Sharon, Eli, Jane, and Dylan alone again. The two brothers stood side by side, trying to out-tough each other in the look department.

"I'm so glad you could be here," Sharon said, smiling at Jane.

"Thank you for having me. Us," Jane said, looking very pretty and terribly nervous. Sharon noticed that she and Dylan hadn't danced yet. In fact, there seemed to be quite a bit of distance between them.

"I hope your mother can make it . . ."

"Thank you. The home said they'd drive her; she should be here at any time."

"She's in Cherry Vale?" Eli asked, and Sharon could have kissed him—actually making conversation.

"Yes," Jane said. "She seems happy there. My sister and I are so relieved."

"It's never easy," Sharon said. "We had to put my mother in Marsh Glen, just before she died. . . ."

"Did she adjust well?" Jane asked.

"Well, she had Alzheimer's . . . so I'm not sure."

Jane nodded. "My mother is in the early stages. She's aware of where she is and what's happening, which in some ways makes it worse."

Sharon smiled sympathetically. It was so much easier for her and Jane to talk about the previous generation than the future one. But Dylan seemed to think that it was time to change all that.

"Chloe did a great job making this party happen," he said. "Right, Eli?"

"She's a good kid," Eli said.

"Oh, she is," Sharon said, gazing into Jane's eyes. "She's so bright, sweet . . ."

LUANNE RICE

"Mind of her own, that one," Eli said.

"I can tell," Jane said softly. "You've done such a wonderful job of raising her. Th—" She stopped herself from thanking them, and Sharon was glad she did. Why should Jane thank them for doing what they were born to do? To raise and love their daughter? The privilege of being a parent was sacred and eternal, and Sharon had come to believe it was just as deep as the actual act of giving birth.

"I see so much of you in her," Sharon said.

Jane nodded. "Thank you so much for saying that. For giving me that . . ."

"Yes, she has your eyes," Eli said gruffly. "Didn't get those baby blues from me or Sharon, that's for sure. Not just the color, but the . . . beauty. She's got heartbreak eyes."

"Well, some people in the family have them," Sharon said, smiling at Dylan.

"Don't remind him," Eli said. "He'll start batting them at you."

And everyone laughed, because the statement was so cranky, funny, and inane. Sharon was so proud of Eli for rising above his own insecurities tonight. She smiled at Jane a little wider.

"Chloe has always wanted to know about you," she said.

"A kid's curiosity," Eli said, to mitigate the statement.

"I'm sorry for intruding the way I did," Jane said, "last spring . . ."

"The situation was a hard one," Sharon said. "None of us knew what to do."

"How to handle it," Eli said.

"You did just fine," Dylan said. "Look at you, all of you—together tonight, for Chloe."

"Where do we go from here," Eli said, "is the question."

Dylan nodded gravely. The two men frowned, appearing to ponder. Sharon smiled at Jane, and Jane smiled back. They knew that there was nothing to ponder. There was no answer to Eli's question. They would just go along. They would see.

Sharon, who had spent years praying that she be given a child, praying and wait-ing as the months went by, a seemingly endless parade of babyless days, knew that life was nothing *but* a question. Answers were temporary; the question was constant. Women knew that better than men, she thought. Maybe it had to do with the way the moon took hold of their bodies, pulling them like the tides. . . . In that way women learned that life was a mystery, and that something bigger than they were was in charge. Jane might have been thinking the exact same thing: Her smile grew, as did Sharon's.

"We'll see," Sharon said.

"Yes," Jane said. "We'll just see . . ."

The band slid into "Newport Blues," so Sharon grabbed her husband's hand. After so many years of standing beside dance floors together, words weren't even necessary. She raised her eyebrows, and he nodded.

"I hope your mother comes soon," Sharon said.

"Will Virginia be here?" Jane asked, inquiring about Eli and Dylan's mother.

"No," Sharon said. "We thought it would be a little much for her, to see all of you and realize what's going on. She's pretty frail these days. She's from the generation that thinks everything should be kept a secret."

"My mother, too," Jane said.

Sharon swallowed. She knew those two

older women were largely responsible for
her and Eli being able to adopt Chloe. And
as grateful as that made Sharon for them,
she knew it had to make Jane equally am-
bivalent. But tonight was a night for joining
together, not blaming or pushing apart, so
she was relieved to see Jane smile.

"I want to meet your mother," Sharon
said.

"She wants to meet you," Jane said.
"And—" Again she bit her tongue before finishing her thought.

"Chloe," Eli said, completing it for her, reminding Sharon of why she loved him so
much. "She must want to meet her granddaughter."

"Yes," Jane said. "Yes, she does."

And full of love for her own life and gratitude for the grace of the moment, Sharon
embraced her husband and let him swirl her
into the dance.

＊

Jane and Dylan were left standing alone.
She wore a white dress with a silver buckle,
and he wore a black shirt with a string tie.
She felt shy with him, and had ever since

that day on the street in New York. They had talked, little by little, about what had happened. He had forgiven her—or at least decided to forgive her; it took a lot for him to say how he had thought they were so close, and how he'd felt so betrayed. And Jane knew. She tried to tell him how her need to see Chloe had been so strong, as imperative as a tidal wave, that she had had to obey it. They were gaining in understanding, but their old closeness had yet to come back.

So now, when he slipped his fingers through hers, her whole body turned liquid, and she thought her legs might give out.

"Come on," he said, pulling her.

"What? Where?"

"Just come on."

The band played, slow and sweet, and Dylan led her out of the crowd to a ladder attached to the barn wall. It stretched up to a square hole in the ceiling. He pointed, indicating that she should climb. And she did—hand over hand, up the rungs, to the hayloft. Once up there, he gestured that she should sit down in the hay. She hesitated. So he put his arms around her and pulled her down.

"We need to talk," he said, lying right beside her in the hay.

"Yes," she said, sort of surprised that he would want to do it prone, their faces six inches apart.

"I've asked you why, and you've told me," he said.

"As best I can," Jane said calmly, gazing into his blue eyes. She had missed those eyes . . .

"I'm tired of the answers," he said.

"I know. I'm tired of giving them."

"Jane," he said.

"Dylan," she whispered. They touched each other's cheeks so tenderly. Her fingers brushed his beard. She thought of those stories on the Internet, her memory of Isabel's picture in his kitchen, and she realized that she had stayed connected to him through their shared grief. "I wish," she began.

"Tell me what you wish," he said.

"I wish we could begin again. I wish I could have been wise enough to handle everything better. I wish . . ."

"You handled it fine," he said. "I was wrong."

"No," she said.

"I was. You just wanted to—know Chloe."

She kept her hand against his face, waiting.

"You wanted to know your daughter. And she's so great, so worth knowing! She's right here, living in the orchard, keeping us all in line. And you know what, Jane?"

"What, Dylan?"

"I think I was jealous. Am jealous, in a way."

"But of what?"

"That you can know your daughter," he whispered. "And I can't know mine."

Jane's heart smashed open. She heard the fiddle playing downstairs, and it coaxed tears from Dylan's eyes, and Jane could only kiss them away. She tasted his salt tears and thought of the Narragansett Bay tides and the wash of the great Atlantic on the cliffs outside Maison du Soleil.

"You can know her," Jane whispered. "You already know her . . ."

Dylan didn't speak.

"I knew Chloe," Jane said. "Even before I met her last spring. I knew her; she was of me, Dylan. Just as Isabel is of you . . . and with you. I know she's always with you. Forever."

He put his arms around her and held her close. She felt his strong chest and shoulders enveloping her as if he wanted to make her a part of him, too, and him a part of her. Their lips met, and they kissed, and it was so slow and warm and eternal that with her eyes closed, Jane honestly wasn't sure where their separate bodies began and ended.

"I like that word," he said.

"Which one?"

"Forever," he said. "I like it a lot."

"It's a good word," she agreed.

The music spun downstairs, a sweet reel. Dylan opened his mouth to say something, then just smiled and kissed Jane again. They lay in the hay, hearts beating madly against each other, as the dance went on beneath them and the moon rose higher in the sky outside. Suddenly they heard a thud. And then another.

"Someone's throwing apples at us," Dylan said.

"Let me guess," Jane said, looking up, grinning as her eyes locked with Chloe's, beside Mona, leaning down from the cupola.

Margaret was dressed and ready. She wore her best fall coat—a lovely brown cashmere coat she had bought at Gladdings, just before her retirement. Not knowing what life on a principal's pension would be, she had treated herself. And what a good investment it had turned out to be: Ten years later, and it was still as beautiful as the day she'd purchased it.

The van traveled along the dark country roads, cloaked in darkness. Margaret had asked the driver to open the window a little, and the scent of autumn, rich with the decay of fallen leaves, filled the van. Margaret was strapped in, restrained in a sense, but when she smelled those leaves and the autumn air of her beloved Rhode Island, she felt young and free.

"I'm going to a dance," she said out loud.

"That's right, Margaret," the driver called back.

"My daughters will be there."

"I know. That's wonderful."

"I'm going to meet my granddaughter."

"You must be very excited."

"Oh, I am. Her name is Clove."

"Clove is an unusual name."

"Not Clove. Rosie."

"That's pretty."

"No, wait. It's not Rosie. It's . . . something else . . ."

Margaret closed her eyes. The van was bumpy. The others were asleep. They slept all the time. People in the home got so tired. Perhaps it was all that life they had already lived. So much life! With so many memories, each chock-full of joy and sorrow. That was one of the lessons Margaret had learned. . . .

Perhaps more important than math, history, science, or even—yes, even English, were the lessons of the heart. Margaret the principal could scarcely believe she was having such heretical thoughts. But her life on this earth had taught her this: that love, in the end, was all that mattered. Friends, families, suitors, husbands: Goodness abounded in all of them.

If only she had imparted that teaching to her darlings, her daughters. She feared that she had been too strict with them. Too held-back in ways of love, too restrained. So hurt by their father, she had taught them that all men were to be mistrusted.

Looking to her left, looking to her right,

she felt a strange mix of sadness and joy, to realize that she was learning a different lesson now.

"Ralph," she said, tapping his right arm gently. Then, turning to the other side, tugging Bill's sleeve. "Billy—wake up. We're almost there."

"Arrch," Ralph said. "We there yet?"

"Not quite, but almost," Margaret said.

"You rouse Billy?" Ralph asked.

"I'm trying," Margaret said. "He's having quite a nap."

"It's a sad day," Ralph said, "when two grown men can't stay awake the fifteen miles it takes to escort their lady to a dance."

"Am I your lady?" Margaret smiled.

"Yes," Ralph said, squeezing her hand. "But don't tell Billy. Get him up, now. We want him pulled together by the time we walk in. And I say 'walk in' with a grain of salt. My lady . . ."

She couldn't stop smiling. Leaning over, she jostled Bill's arm. "Dear," she said very loudly. "We are ALMOST THERE."

"Trunngh," Billy said, babbling as a bit of spit slid onto his lovely blue tweed jacket.

Margaret had her tissue ready; he started to cry. "Freniiii. Laxiday. Grennwill!"

"I know, Billy," she soothed, wiping his eyes. "I know."

"Come to, man," Ralph commanded. "We'll be fighting over who gets to dance with Margaret first, and I want a fair battle. Get yourself into fighting trim here."

"Fine," Bill said. "Very good. We almost there?"

"We are, in fact," Margaret said, as the van was suddenly filled with an almost magical scent of apples. Spicy, sharp, sweet . . . it was as if, driving through the split-rail fence that delineated the boundary of Chadwick Orchards, they had just entered the Garden of Eden.

"I get first dance," Ralph said, kissing her left cheek.

"No, I do," Billy said, kissing her right one.

Margaret closed her eyes, but the moon was so full and bright she could see pictures and faces and scenes from her life. She thought of how much she had loved to dance with the girls' father. Thomas had been such a wonderful dancer. He had given her many happy times on the dance floor. He had given her two beautiful daughters.

Daughters, Margaret thought. *Tonight I shall officially meet Jane's daughter.*

The driver parked the van. Music filled the air. Margaret adjusted Bill's hearing aid so he could hear it. Ralph squeezed her arm. Margaret smelled the apples. The driver slid open the van door. He was a nice young man—his name was Ernest. Margaret smiled at him.

"Ready, Margaret?" he asked.

She nodded. And then she remembered.

"Chloe," she said. "My granddaughter's name is Chloe."

They all saw the van's arrival from the cupola: Chloe, Mona, Dylan, and Jane. It drove up the winding hill through the apple trees, with slow grace, as if it held visiting dignitaries. Jane sensed Chloe's excitement mingled with nervousness.

"What if she doesn't like me?" Chloe asked.

"She'll love you," Jane said.

"She might be mad at me."

"How could she be?"

"For almost ruining your life," Chloe said.

Jane swallowed hard. The others were standing right there in the small space, but she had eyes only for Chloe. The girl looked up at her, eyes blue and clear as a hillside stream. They held impenetrable mysteries and questions and every answer Jane had ever dreamed of.

"You could never do that," Jane said.

"I think I could," Chloe said. "And did . . . see, I know."

Jane stared.

"You know I know, because you were there. It wasn't for long—certainly not nine whole months—but for a little while in June, I thought, I thought . . ."

Dylan took a deep breath. Had he heard this before? Jane didn't know, but she knew it was so courageous of Chloe to say.

"Thought I was pregnant," Chloe said.

"But you weren't," Jane reminded her.

Chloe nodded. "But in those days, when I was afraid I was . . . I felt like you did. I didn't realize it at the time. All I knew was that I was so scared, so worried. I pictured my parents finding out, my life changing forever. School would be over; everyone would see me getting bigger . . . they'd all know."

"Oh, Chloe," Jane said, closing her eyes, involuntarily touching her own stomach, remembering what it had been like to be so young and be so visibly pregnant, to be sent away to live at St. Joseph's.

"And all I could think was, my life was ruined . . . like yours."

Jane's eyes flew open. "But my life wasn't! Not at all! I had you—"

"And had to give me up," Chloe said. "When I thought I was pregnant, I thought about what I would do. And the hardest part, the thing I couldn't stand, was imagining handing my baby away . . . It would be like having all the bad stuff, all the life-ruining bad stuff, and then giving up the best part. The baby."

"You were the best part," Jane said, eyes shining, in awe of her daughter's empathy.

"But you had to let me go," Chloe said.

Jane nodded. "But I held you. I held you for such a short time, but . . ." She stopped, swallowed. "It was enough. In a way, it was enough."

"How?" Chloe asked. "Could it have

been? It wasn't enough for me . . ." She grabbed Jane's hand.

"She's here now," Dylan said, stepping forward as if he knew they were both about to start crying so hard they might never stop.

"You found each other again," Mona said.

"We had radar for each other," Chloe said, smiling. "Yeah, that's what it was."

"Radar," Jane said. "Okay, I can see that."

"Can I ask you one thing?" Chloe asked. "Before we all go downstairs to the party?"

"The hootenanny," Mona corrected.

Chloe nodded. "Right," she said.

"Sure," Jane said. "Ask me anything."

"Why'd you name me Chloe?" She asked the question and lost a shade of color. Even her lips were pale, as if she thought the secret to her existence might be hanging on Jane's answer. Jane saw her actually take Mona's arm, as if she needed the physical support.

"Do we need a drum roll?" Mona asked.

Dylan laughed, but even his eyes were full of anticipation.

Jane smiled, blushing slightly. She thought back. She had never said these things out loud. The story of Chloe's name had always been so private, just between her and . . . Chloe. . . .

The idea, as she faced her teenaged daughter now, made her laugh out loud.

"What's so funny?" Chloe asked.

"It's funny," she said, "because you told me."

"Told you my *name*?"

Jane nodded. She felt time spinning, making her almost dizzy, as she went back to that train ride home from seeing Jeffrey at Pennsylvania Station. She had been so tired, and she had slept. And she had dreamed . . . and she had dreamed of Chloe.

"I was on a train," she said. "And I was very tired . . . slept the whole way . . ." She decided to leave out her feelings about Jeffrey. She would have to think about what to say about him, if anything. "And the train was rushing all along the shoreline, that stretch of the Connecticut coast, where you can see a lot of water. Harbors and beaches, Long Island Sound . . ."

"Okay," Chloe said, raising one eyebrow skeptically. "Who were you with?"

"I was alone, but I was with you," Jane said.

Chloe just listened.

"We were together," Jane said. "It's hard to explain now, but that's how I felt. That it was you and me, on the train. I had just found out about you. And I had no idea of whether you were a boy or a girl. But I did have an idea—as a matter of fact, I knew for sure."

"That I was a girl?"

Jane nodded. "And I had this dream." She closed her eyes for just two seconds, and the whole dream came back, just as if she was still having it. Which, in a way, she was, she realized as she looked into the eyes of her daughter.

"And the dream was of you. You were beautiful. You were tiny, but not quite an infant. Maybe three or four. With dark, dark hair, and bright blue eyes. And you spoke in complete sentences—just like an adult."

"She did," Dylan filled in. "That's what actually happened."

Jane nodded, not at all surprised. "I said to you, 'What are we going to do?' And you said, 'I want to go to the beach.' And I said, 'But what will happen if I look away, and I can't see you?' And you said, 'You'll call for me.' I had to say, because I didn't know, 'What will I call? What is your name?' "

"And I said, 'Chloe,' " Chloe said quietly.

Jane nodded.

They stared at each other for a long time. Jane didn't dare speak for a long moment. Because the girl in her dream had just become this girl in real life, and she suddenly realized, with a swift shock, that the dream had been true all along.

Downstairs, the music was so pretty. The guitar went off on a twangy riff, and then the fiddle came in to lift the song right up to the stars. Jane thought of them all, standing on this platform in the sky. She couldn't take her eyes off Chloe.

"The story of your name," Mona said, sighing.

"It's even better than I thought," Chloe said.

Jane nodded. It was better now, because she had had the chance to tell it. The music downstairs changed, and Jane heard applause.

"That's for the old people," Chloe explained.

"It is?" Jane asked.

"It's a barn dance tradition," Dylan said. "We clap for our elders."

"Because they're so wise," Chloe said.

Jane and Dylan exchanged a skeptical look. The girls gathered the remaining apples in their skirts, bunched them on their hips like drawstring bags, and climbed down the stairs. Jane stood in the cupola, gazing down at the glossy top of her daughter's raven-dark head. It made her feel like a melting ice cube.

Dylan touched her hand. "Look," he said, pointing out the window.

A cluster of deer were grazing in the startling, brilliant, silvery moonlight. Their coats were rich and brown. The fawns were dappled, almost invisible in the tall wheaten grass. A lone owl cruised among the trees. Red apples were heavy on the boughs.

"It's the most beautiful thing I've ever seen," Jane said.

"It is," Dylan agreed.

The band struck up a waltz. It was a long way down, and Dylan's limp made him move slowly. Jane thought of her mother, waiting. She thought of Chloe emerging from the hayloft, being led across the floor to be introduced—perhaps by Sylvie and

John, perhaps by Sharon and Eli. Maybe by all four. Chloe had a lot of family.

Jane wanted to witness the moment. But the waltz was playing, and as she had learned that hot day in New York, life was in the moment, and love was in the moment, wherever you happened to be. So she held out her arms.

Dance with me? her eyes seemed to say.

Dylan knew what she meant. So there in the cupola, with the fiddle playing far below, they stepped into each other's arms and let the music take them wherever it wanted.

ABOUT THE AUTHOR

LUANNE RICE is the author of *Dance With Me*, *The Perfect Summer*, *The Secret Hour*, *True Blue*, *Summer Light*, *Safe Harbor*, *Firefly Beach*, *Dream Country*, *Follow the Stars Home*—a Hallmark Hall of Fame feature—*Cloud Nine*, *Home Fires*, *Secrets of Paris*, *Stone Heart*, *Angels All Over Town*, *Crazy In Love* (made into a TNT Network feature film), and *Blue Moon* (made into a CBS television film). She lives in New York City and Old Lyme, Connecticut.